DIANA PALMER

The prolific author of more than one hundred books, Diana Palmer got her start as a newspaper reporter. A multi-*New York Times* and *USA TODAY* bestselling author and voted one of the top ten romance writers in America, she has a gift for telling the most sensual tales with charm and humor. Diana lives with her family in Cornelia, Georgia.

BARBARA DUNLOP

writes romantic stories while curled up in a log cabin in Canada's far north, where bears outnumber people and it snows six months of the year. Fortunately she has a brawny husband and two teenage children to haul firewood and clear the driveway while she sips cocoa and muses about her upcoming chapters. Barbara loves to hear from readers. You can contact her through her website, barbaradunlop.com.

New York Times Bestselling Author

DIANA PALMER

HEARTBREAKER

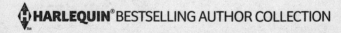

HARLEQUIN® BESTSELLING AUTHOR COLLECTION

ISBN-13: 978-0-373-01024-0

Heartbreaker
Copyright © 2015 by Harlequin Books S.A.

The publisher acknowledges the copyright holders
of the individual works as follows:

Heartbreaker
Copyright © 2006 by Diana Palmer

In Bed with the Wrangler
Copyright © 2010 by Barbara Dunlop

Recycling programs
for this product may
not exist in your area.

This edition published by arrangement with Harlequin Books S.A.

For questions and comments about the quality of this book,
please contact us at CustomerService@Harlequin.com.

⊕ HARLEQUIN®
TM www.Harlequin.com

Printed in U.S.A.

CONTENTS

HEARTBREAKER   7
Diana Palmer

IN BED WITH THE WRANGLER   203
Barbara Dunlop

HEARTBREAKER

Diana Palmer

To Tara Gavin and Melissa Jeglinski, with love

One

It had been a grueling semester. Tellie Maddox had her history degree, but she was feeling betrayed. He hadn't shown up for her graduation exercises. Marge had, along with Dawn and Brandi, her two daughters. None of them were related to Tellie, who was orphaned many years ago, but they were as close to her as sisters. They'd cared enough to be here for her special day. J.B. hadn't. It was one more heartbreak in a whole series of them in Tellie's life that J.B. was responsible for.

She looked around her dorm room sadly, remembering how happy she'd been here for four years, sharing with Sandy Melton, a fellow history major. Sandy had already gone, off to England to continue her studies in medieval history. Tellie pushed back her short, wavy dark hair and sighed. Her pale green eyes searched for the last of her textbooks. She should take them to the campus bookstore, she supposed, and resell them. She was going to need every penny she could get to make it through the summer. When the fall semester began, in August, she was going to have to pay tuition again as she worked on her master's degree. She wanted to teach at college level. No chance of that, with just a bachelor's degree, unless she taught adult education as an adjunct member of staff.

Once she'd thought that one day J.B. might fall in love with her and want to marry her. Those hopeless dreams grew dimmer every day.

J. B. Hammock was Marge's brother. He'd rescued Tellie from a boy in the foster home where she'd been staying since her mother's death. Her mother had been the estranged wife of J.B.'s top horse wrangler, who'd later moved out of state and vanished. Tellie had gone to a foster home, despite Marge's objections, because J.B. said that a widow with two children to raise didn't need the complication of a teenager.

All that had changed with the attempted assault by another foster child in care with the same family. J.B. heard about it from a policeman who was one of his best friends. He swore out a warrant himself and had Tellie give a statement about what had happened. The boy, only thirteen at the time, was arrested and subsequently sent to juvenile hall. Tellie had slugged the boy when he tried to remove her blouse and sat on him until the family heard her yelling. Even at such a young age, Tellie was fearless. It had helped that the boy was half her size and half-drunk.

J.B. had jerked Tellie right out of the foster home the night the boy was arrested. He'd taken her straight to Marge for sanctuary. Marge had loved her almost at once. Most people did love Tellie. She was honest and sweet and generous with her time, and she wasn't afraid of hard work. Even at the age of fourteen, she'd taken charge of the kitchen and Dawn and Brandi. The sisters were nine and ten at the time respectively. They'd loved having an older girl in the house. Marge's job as a Realtor kept her on the road at all sorts of odd hours. But she could depend on Tellie to keep the girls in school clothes and help with their homework. She was a born babysitter.

Tellie had doted on J.B. He was very rich, and very temperamental. He owned hundreds of acres of prime ranch land near Jacobsville, where he raised purebred Santa Gertrudis cattle and entertained the rich and famous at his hundred-year-old rancho. He had a fabulous French chef in residence, along with a housekeeper named Nell who could singe the feathers off a duck with her temper at ten paces. Nell ran the house, and J.B., to an extent. He knew famous politicians, and movie stars, and foreign royalty from his days as a rodeo champion. He had impeccable manners, a legacy from his Spanish grandmother, and wealth from his British grandfather, who had been a peer of the realm. J.B.'s roots were European, despite his very American cattle operation.

But he did intimidate people. Locally he was known more for chasing Ralph Barrows off his place on foot, wielding a replica fantasy sword from the Lord of the Rings movie trilogy. Barrows had gotten drunk and shot J.B.'s favorite German shepherd for growling at him and barking when he tried to sneak into the bunkhouse in the small hours of the morning during roundup. Drinking wasn't allowed on the ranch. And nobody hurt an animal there. J.B. couldn't get to the key to his gun cabinet fast enough, so he grabbed the sword from its wall display and struck out for the bunkhouse the minute his foreman told him what was going on. The dog recovered, although it limped badly. Barrows hadn't been seen since.

J.B. wasn't really a social animal, despite the grand parties he threw at the ranch. He kept to himself, except for the numerous gorgeous women he squired around in his private jet. He had a nasty temper and the arrogance of position and wealth. Tellie was closer to him than almost anyone, even Marge, because she'd taken charge of him when she was fourteen and he went on a legendary drunk after his father died. It was Tellie who'd made Marge drive her to J.B.'s place when Nell called in a panic and said that J.B. was wrecking the den and the computers. It was Tellie who'd set him down, calmed him and made cinnamon coffee for him to help sober him up.

J.B. tolerated her interventions over the years. He was like her property, her private male. Nobody dared to say that, of course, not even Tellie. But she was possessive of him and, as she grew older, she became jealous of the women who passed through his life in such numbers. She tried not to let it show. Invariably, though, it did.

When she was eighteen, one of his girlfriends had made an unkind remark to Tellie, who'd flared back at her that J.B. wouldn't keep *her* around for much longer if she was going to be rude to his family! After the girl left, J.B. had it out with Tellie, his green eyes flaming like emeralds, his thick black hair almost standing up straight on his head with bad temper. Tellie didn't own him, he reminded her, and if she didn't stop trying to possess him, she'd be out on her ear. She wasn't even part of his family, he'd added cruelly. She had no right whatsoever to make any claims on his life.

She'd shot back that his girlfriends were all alike—

long-legged, big-breasted, pretty girls with the brains of bats! He'd looked at her small breasts and remarked that she certainly wouldn't fit that description.

She'd slapped him. It was involuntary and she was immediately sorry. But before she could take it back, he'd jerked her against his tall, lean body and kissed her in a way that still made her knees weak four years later. It had been meant, she was sure, as a punishment. But her mouth had opened weakly under his in a silent protest, and the tiny movement had kindled a shudder in the muscular body so close to hers.

He'd backed her up against the sofa and crushed her down on it, under the length of him. The kiss had grown hard, insistent, passionate. His big, lean hand had found her breast under her blouse, and she'd panicked. The sensations he caused made her push at him and fight to get free.

She jerked her mind back to the present. J.B. had torn himself away from her, in an even worse temper than before. His eyes had blazed down at her, as if she'd done something unforgivable. Furious, he'd told her to get out of his life and stay out. She was due to leave for college the same week, and he hadn't even said goodbye. He'd ignored her from that day onward.

Holidays had come and gone. Slowly tensions had lessened between them, but J.B. had made sure that they were never alone again. He'd given her presents for her birthday and Christmas, but they were always impersonal ones, like computer hardware or software, or biography and history books that he knew she liked. She'd given him ties. In fact, she'd given him the same exact tie for every birthday and every Christmas present. She'd found a closeout special and bought two boxes of identical ties. She was set for life, she reasoned, for presents for J.B. Marge had remarked on the odd and monotonous present, but J.B. himself said nothing at all. Well, he said thank-you every time he opened a present from Tellie, but he said nothing more. Presumably he'd given the ties away. He never wore one. Tellie hadn't expected that he would. They were incredibly ugly. Yellow, with a putrid green dragon with red eyes. She still had enough left for ten more years…

"Are you ready, Tellie?" Marge called from the door.

She was like her brother, tall and dark-haired, but her eyes were brown where J.B.'s were green. Marge had a sweet nature, and she wasn't violent. She had a live-wire personality. Everybody loved her. She was long widowed and had never looked at another man. Love, she often told Tellie, for some people was undying, even if one lost the partner. She would never find anyone else as wonderful as her late husband. She had no interest in trying.

"I just have a couple more blouses to pack," Tellie said with a smile.

Dawn and Brandi wandered around her dorm room curiously.

"You'll do this one day, yourselves," Tellie assured them.

"Not me," Dawn, the youngest, at sixteen, replied with a grin. "I'm going to be a cattle baron like Uncle J.B. when I get through agricultural college."

"I'm going to be an attorney," Brandi, who would be a senior in the fall at seventeen, said with a smile. "I want to help poor people."

"She can already bargain me into anything," Marge said with an amused wink at Tellie.

"Me, too," Tellie had to admit. "She's still got my favorite jacket, and I never even got to wear it once."

"It looks much better on me," Brandi assured her. "Red just isn't your color."

A lot she knew, Tellie thought, because every time she thought about J.B., she saw red.

Marge watched Tellie pack her suitcase with a somber expression. "He really did have an emergency at the ranch," she told Tellie gently. "The big barn caught fire. They had fire departments from all over Jacobs County out there putting it out."

"I'm sure he would have come, if he'd been able," Tellie replied politely. She didn't believe it. J.B. hadn't shown any interest in her at all in recent years. He'd avoided her whenever possible. Perhaps the ties had driven him nuts and he'd torched the barn himself, thinking of it as a giant yellow dragon tie. The thought amused her, and she laughed.

"What are you laughing about?" Marge teased.

"I was thinking maybe J.B.'s gone off his rocker and started seeing yellow dragon ties everywhere…"

Marge chuckled. "It wouldn't surprise me. Those ties are just awful, Tellie, really!"

"I think they suit him," Tellie said with irrepressible humor. "I'm sure that he's going to wear one eventually."

Marge started to speak and apparently thought better of it. "Well, I wouldn't hold my breath waiting," she said instead.

"Who's the flavor of the month?" Tellie wondered aloud.

Marge lifted an eyebrow. She knew what Tellie meant, all too well. She despaired of her brother ever getting serious about a woman again. "He's dating one of the Kingstons's cousins, from Fort Worth. She was a runner-up for Miss Texas."

Tellie wasn't surprised. J.B. had a passion for beautiful blondes. Over the years, he'd escorted his share of movie starlets. Tellie, with her ordinary face and figure, was hardly on a par to compete with such beauties.

"They're just display models," Marge whispered wickedly, so that her daughters didn't hear her.

Tellie burst out laughing. "Oh, Marge, what would I do without you?"

Marge shrugged. "It's us against the men of the world," she pointed out. "Even my brother qualifies as the enemy from time to time." She paused. "Don't they give you a recording of the graduation exercises?"

"Yes, along with my diploma," Tellie agreed. "Why?"

"I say we get the boys to rope J.B. to his easy chair in the den and make him watch the recording for twenty-four straight hours," she suggested. "Revenge is sweet!"

"He'd just go to sleep during the commencement speech," Tellie sighed. "And I wouldn't blame him. I almost did myself."

"Shame on you! The speaker was a famous politician!"

"Famously boring," Brandi remarked with a wicked grin.

"Notice how furiously everybody applauded when he stopped speaking," Dawn agreed.

"You two have been hanging out with me for too long," Tellie observed. "You're picking up all my bad habits."

They both hugged her. "We love you, bad habits and all," they said. "Congratulations on your degree!"

"You did very well indeed," Marge echoed. "Magna cum laude, no less! I'm proud of you."

"Honor graduates don't have social lives, Mother," Brandi pointed out. "No wonder she made such good grades. She spent every weekend in the dorm, studying!"

"Not every weekend," Tellie muttered. "There was that archaeology field trip…"

"With the geek squad." Dawn yawned.

"They weren't all geeks," she reminded them. "Anyway, I like digging up old things."

"Then you should have gotten your degree in archaeology instead of history," Brandi said.

She chuckled. "I'll be digging up old documents instead of old relics," she said. "It will be a cleaner job, at least."

"When do you start your master's degree work?" Marge asked.

"Fall semester," she replied, smiling. "I thought I'd take the summer off and spend a little time with you guys. I've already lined up a job working for the Ballenger brothers at their feedlot while Calhoun and Abby take a cruise to Greece with the boys. I guess all those summers following J.B. and his veterinarian around the ranch finally paid off. At least I know enough about feeding out cattle to handle the paperwork!"

"Lucky Calhoun and Abby. Wow," Dawn said on a sigh. "I'd love to get a three-month vacation!"

"Wouldn't we all," Tellie agreed wistfully. "In my case, a job is a vacation from all the studying! Biology was so hard!"

"We don't get to dissect things anymore at our school," Brandi said. "Everybody's afraid of blood these days."

"With good reason, I'm sorry to say," Marge mused.

"We don't get to do dissections, either," Tellie told her with a smile. "We had a rat on a dissecting board and we all got to use it for identification purposes. It was so nice that we had an air-conditioned lab!"

The girls made faces.

"Speaking of labs," Marge interrupted, "who wants a nice hamburger?"

"Nobody dissects cows, Mom," Brandi informed her.

"We can dissect the hamburger," Tellie suggested, "and identify the part of the cow it came from."

"It came from a steer, not a cow," Marge said wryly. "You could use a refresher course in Ranching 101, Tellie."

They all knew who'd be teaching it at home, and that was a sore spot. Tellie's smile faded. "I expect I'll get all the information I need working from Justin at the feedlot."

"They've got some handsome new cowboys working for them," Marge said with sparkling eyes. "One's an ex–Green Beret who grew up on a ranch in West Texas."

Tellie shrugged one shoulder. "I'm not sure I want to meet any men. I've still got three years of study to get my master's degree so that I can start teaching history in college."

"You can teach now, can't you?" Dawn asked.

"I can teach adult education," Tellie replied. "But I have to have at least a master's degree to teach at the college level, and a PhD is preferred."

"Why don't you want to teach little kids?" Brandi asked curiously.

Tellie grinned. "Because you two hooligans destroyed all my illusions about sweet little kids," she replied, and ducked when Brandi threw a pillow at her.

"We were such sweet little kids," Dawn said belligerently. "You better say we were, or else, Tellie!"

"Or else what?" she replied.

Dawn wiggled her eyebrows. "Or else I'll burn the potatoes. It's my night to cook supper at home."

"Don't pay any attention to her, dear," Marge said. "She always burns the potatoes."

"Oh, Mom!" the teenager wailed.

Tellie just laughed. But her heart wasn't in the wordplay. She was miserable because J.B. had missed her graduation, and nothing was going to make up for that.

Marge's house was on the outskirts of Jacobsville, about six miles from the big ranch that had been in her and J.B.'s family for three generations. It was a friendly little house with a bay window out front and a small front porch with a white swing. All around it were the flowers that Marge planted obsessively. It was May, and everything was blooming. Every color in the rainbow graced the small yard, including a small rose garden with an arch that was Marge's pride and joy. These were antique roses, not hybrids, and they had scents that were like perfume.

"I'd forgotten all over again how beautiful it was," Tellie said on a sigh.

"Howard loved it, too," Marge said, her dark eyes soft with memories for an instant as she looked around the lush, clipped lawn that led to the stepping stone walkway that led to the front porch.

"I never met him," Tellie said. "But he must have been a lovely person."

"He was," Marge agreed, her eyes sad as she recalled her husband.

"Look, it's Uncle J.B.!" Dawn cried, pointing to the narrow paved road that led up to the dirt driveway of Marge's house.

Tellie felt every muscle in her body contract. She turned around as the sporty red Jaguar slid to a halt, throwing up clouds of yellow dust. The door opened and J.B. climbed out.

He was tall and lean, with jet-black hair and dark green eyes. His cheekbones were high, his mouth thin. He had big ears and big feet. But he was so masculine that women were drawn to him like magnets. He had a sensuality in his walk that made Tellie's heart skip.

"Where the hell have you been?" he growled as he joined them. "I looked everywhere for you until I finally gave up and drove back home!"

"What do you mean, where were we?" Marge exclaimed. "We were at Tellie's graduation. Not that you could be bothered to show up…!"

"I was across the stadium from you," J.B. said harshly. "I didn't see you until it was over. By the time I got through the crowd and out of the parking lot, you'd left the dorm and headed down here."

"You came to my graduation?" Tellie asked, in a husky, soft tone.

He turned, glaring at her. His eyes were large, framed by thick black lashes, deep set and biting. "We had a fire at the barn. I was late. Do you think I'd miss something so important as your college graduation?" he added angrily, although his eyes evaded hers.

Her heart lifted, against her will. He didn't want her. She was like a second sister to him. But any contact with him made her tingle with delight. She couldn't help the radiance that lit up her plain face and made it pretty.

He glanced around him irritably and caught Tellie's hand, sending a thrill all the way to her heart. "Come here," he said, drawing her to the car with him.

He put her in the passenger side, closed the door and went around to get in beside her. He reached into the console between the bucket seats and pulled out a gold-wrapped box. He handed it to her.

She took it, her eyes surprised. "For me?"

"For no one else," he drawled, smiling faintly. "Go on. Look."

She tore open the wrapping. It was a jeweler's box, but far too big to be a ring. She opened the box and stared at it blankly.

He frowned. "What's the matter? Don't you like it?"

"It" was a Mickey Mouse watch with a big face and a gaudy red band. She knew what it meant, too. It meant that his secretary, Miss Jarrett, who hated being delegated to buy presents for him, had finally lost her cool. She thought J.B. was buying jewelry for one of his women, and Miss Jarrett was showing him that he'd better get his own gifts from now on.

It hurt Tellie, who knew that J.B. shopped for Marge and the girls himself. He never delegated that chore to underlings. But, then, Tellie wasn't family.

"It's…very nice," she stammered, aware that the silence had gone on a little too long for politeness.

She took the watch out of the box and he saw it for the first time.

Blistering range language burst from his chiseled lips before he could stop himself. Then his high cheekbones went dusky because he couldn't very well admit to Tellie that he hadn't bothered to go himself to get her a present. He'd kill Jarrett, though, he promised himself.

"It's the latest thing," he said with deliberate nonchalance.

"I love it. Really." She put it on her wrist. She did love it, because he'd given it to her. She'd have loved a dead rat in a box if it had come from J.B., because she had no pride.

He pursed his lips, the humor of the situation finally getting through to him. His green eyes twinkled. "You'll be the only graduate on your block to wear one," he pointed out.

She laughed. It changed her face, made her radiant. "Thanks, J.B.," she said.

He tugged her as close as the console would allow, and his eyes shifted to her soft, parted lips. "You can do better than that," he murmured wickedly, and bent.

She lifted her face, closed her eyes, savored the warm, tender pressure of his hard mouth on her soft one.

He stiffened. "No, you don't," he whispered roughly when she kept her lips firmly closed. He caught her cheek in one big, lean hand and pressed, gently, just enough to open her mouth. He bent and caught it, hard, pressing her head back against the padded seat with the force of it.

Tellie went under in a daze, loving the warm, hard insistence of his mouth in the silence of the little car. She sighed and a husky little moan escaped her taut throat.

He lifted his head. Dark green eyes probed her own, narrow and hot and full of frustrated desire.

"And here we are again," he said roughly.

She swallowed. "J.B..."

He put his thumb against her soft lips to stop the words. "I told you, there's no future in this, Tellie," he said, his voice hard and cold. "I don't want any woman on a permanent basis. Ever. I'm a bachelor, and I mean to stay that way. Understand?"

"But I didn't say anything," she protested.

"The hell you didn't," he bit off. He put her back in her seat and opened his car door.

She went with him back to Marge and the girls, showing off her new watch. "Look, isn't it neat?" she asked.

"I want one, too!" Brandi exclaimed.

"You don't graduate until next year, darling," Marge reminded her daughter.

"Well, I want one then," she repeated stubbornly.

"I'll keep that in mind," J.B. promised. He smiled, but it wasn't in his eyes. "Congratulations again, tidbit," he told Tellie. "I've got to go. I have a hot date tonight."

He was looking straight at Tellie as he said it. She only smiled.

"Thanks for the watch," she told him.

He shrugged. "It does suit you," he remarked enigmatically. "See you, girls."

He got into the sports car and roared away.

"I'd really love one of those," Brandi remarked on a sigh as she watched it leave.

Marge lifted Tellie's wrist and glared at the watch. "That was just mean," she said under her breath.

Tellie smiled sadly. "He sent Jarrett after it. He always has her buy presents for everybody except you and the girls. She obviously thought it was for one of his platinum blondes, and she got this out of spite."

"Yes, I figured that out all by myself," Marge replied, glowering. "But it's you who got hurt, not J.B."

"It's Jarrett who'll get hurt when he goes back to work," Tellie said on a sigh. "Poor old lady."

"She'll have him for breakfast," Marge said. "And she should."

"He does like sharp older women, doesn't he?" Tellie remarked on the way into the house. "He's got Nell at the house, taking care of things there, and she could scorch leather in a temper."

"Nell's a fixture," Marge said, smiling. "I don't know what J.B. and I would have done without her when we were kids. There was just Dad and us. Mom died when we were very young. Dad was never affectionate."

"Is that why J.B.'s such a rounder?" Tellie wondered.

As usual, Marge clammed up. "We don't ever talk about that," she said. "It isn't a pretty story, and J.B. hates even the memory."

"Nobody ever told me," Tellie persisted.

Marge gave her a gentle smile. "Nobody ever will, pet, unless it's J.B. himself."

"I know when that will be." Tellie sighed. "When they're wearing overcoats in hell."

"Exactly," Marge agreed warmly.

That night, they were watching a movie on television when the phone rang. Marge answered it. She came back in a few minutes, wincing.

"It's Jarrett," she told Tellie. "She wants to talk to you."

"How bad was it?" Tellie asked.

Marge made a face.

Tellie picked up the phone. "Hello?"

"Tellie? It's Nan Jarrett. I just want to apologize…"

"It's not your fault, Miss Jarrett," Tellie said at once. "It really is a cute watch. I love it."

"But it was your college graduation present," the older woman wailed. "I thought it was for one of those idiot blonde floozies he carts around, and it made me mad that he didn't even care enough about them to buy a present himself." She realized what she'd just said and cleared her throat. "Not that I think he didn't care enough about *you*, of course…!"

"Obviously he doesn't," Tellie said through her teeth.

"Well, you wouldn't be so sure of that if you'd been here when he got back into the office just before quitting time," came the terse reply. "I have never heard such language in my life, even from him!"

"He was just mad that he got caught," Tellie said.

"He said it was one of the most special days of your life and I screwed it up," Miss Jarrett said miserably.

"He'd already done that by not showing up for my graduation," Tellie said, about to mention that none of them had seen him in the stands and thought he hadn't shown up.

"Oh, you know about that?" came the unexpected reply. "He told us all to remember he'd been fighting a fire in case it came up. He had a meeting with an out-of-town cattle buyer and his daughter. He forgot all about the commencement exercises."

Tellie's heart broke in two. "Yes," she said, fighting tears, "well, nobody's going to say anything. None of us, certainly."

"Certainly. He gets away with murder."

"I wish I could," Tellie said under her breath. "Thanks for calling, Miss Jarrett. It was nice of you."

"I just wanted you to know how bad I felt," the older woman said with genuine regret. "I wouldn't have hurt your feelings for the world."

"I know that."

"Well, happy graduation, anyway."

"Thanks."

Tellie hung up. She went back into the living room smiling. She was never going to tell them the truth about her graduation. But she knew that she'd never forget.

Two

Tellie had learned to hide her deepest feelings over the years, so Marge and the girls didn't notice any change in her. There was one. She was tired of waiting for J.B. to wake up and notice that she was around. She'd finally realized that she meant nothing to him. Well, maybe she was a sort of adopted relative for whom he had an occasional fondness. But his recent behavior had finally drowned her fondest hopes of anything serious. She was going to convince her stupid heart to stop aching for him, if it killed her.

Five days later, on a Monday, she walked into Calhoun and Justin Ballenger's office at their feedlot, ready for work.

Justin, Calhoun's elder brother, gave her a warm welcome. He was tall, whipcord lean, with gray-sprinkled black hair and dark eyes. He and his wife, Shelby—who was a direct descendant of the founder of Jacobsville, old John Jacobs—had three sons. They'd been married for a long time, like Calhoun and Abby. J. D. Langley's wife, Fay, had been working for the Ballengers as Calhoun's secretary, but a rough pregnancy had forced her to give it up temporarily. That was why Tellie was in such demand.

"You'll manage," Justin's secretary, Ellie, assured her with a smile. "We're not so rushed now as we are in the early spring and autumn. It's just nice and routine. I'll introduce you to the men later on. For now, let me show you what you'll be doing."

"Sorry you have to give up your own vacation for this," Justin said apologetically.

"Listen, I can't afford a vacation yet," she assured him with a grin. "I'm a lowly college student. I have to pay my tuition for three more years. I'm the one who's grateful for the job."

Justin shrugged. "You know as much about cattle as Abby and Shelby do," he said, which was high praise, since both were actively involved in the feedlot operation and the local cattlemen's association. "You're welcome here."

"Thanks," she said, and meant it.

"Thank you," he replied, and left them to it.

The work wasn't that difficult. Most of it dealt with spreadsheets, various programs that kept a daily tally on the number of cattle from each client and the feeding regimen they followed. It was involved and required a lot of concentration, and the phones seemed to ring constantly. It wasn't all clients asking about cattle. Many of the calls were from prospective customers. Others were from buyers who had contracted to take possession of certain lots of cattle when they were fed out. There were also calls from various organizations to which the Ballenger brothers belonged, and even a few from state and federal legislators. A number of them came from overseas, where the brothers had investments. Tellie found it all fascinating.

It took her a few days to get into the routine of things, and to get to know the men who worked at the feedlot. She could identify them all by face, if not by name.

One of them was hard to miss. He was the ex–Green Beret, a big, tall man from El Paso named Grange. If he had a first name, Tellie didn't hear anyone use it. He had straight black hair and dark brown eyes, an olive complexion and a deep, sexy voice. He liked Tellie on sight and made no secret of it. It amused Justin, because Grange hadn't shown any interest in anything in the weeks he'd been working on the place. It was the first spark of life the man had displayed.

He told Tellie, who looked surprised.

"He seems like a friendly man," she stammered.

He lifted a dark eyebrow. "The first day he worked here, one of the boys short-sheeted his bed. He turned on the lights, looked around the room, dumped one of the other men out of a bunk bed and threw him headfirst into the yard."

"Was it the right man?" Tellie asked, wide-eyed.

"It was. Nobody knew how he figured it out, and he never said. But the boys walk wide around him. Especially since he threw that big knife he carries at a sidewinder that crawled too close to the bunkhouse. Cag Hart has a reputation for that sort of accuracy with a Bowie, but he used to be the only one. Grange is a mystery."

She was intrigued. "What did he do, before he came here?"

"Nobody knows. Nobody asks, either," he added with a grin.

"Was he stationed overseas, in the army?"

"Nobody knows that, either. The 411 is that he was in the Green Berets, but he's never said he was. Puzzling guy. But he's a hard worker. And he's honest." He pursed his lips and his dark eyes twinkled. "And he never takes a drink. Ever."

She whistled. "Well!"

"Anyway, you'd better not agree to any dates with him until J.B. checks him out," Justin said. "I don't want J.B. on the wrong side of me." He grinned. "We feed out a lot of cattle for him," he added, making it clear that he wasn't afraid of J.B.

"J.B. doesn't tell me who I can date," she said, hurting as she remembered how little she meant to Marge's big brother.

"Just the same, I don't know anything about Grange, and I'm sort of responsible for you while you're here, even though you're legally an adult," Justin said quietly. "Get the picture?"

She grimaced. "I do. Okay, I'll make sure I don't let him bulldoze me into anything."

"That's the spirit," he said with a grin. "I'm not saying he's a bad man, mind you. I just don't know a lot about him. He's always on time, does his job and a bit more, and gets along fairly well with other people. But he mostly keeps to himself when he's not working. He's not a sociable sort."

"I feel somewhat that way, myself," she sighed.

"Join the club. Things going okay for you otherwise? The job's not too much?"

"The job's great," she said, smiling. "I'm really enjoying this."

"Good. We're glad to have you here. Anything you need, let me know."

"Sure thing. Thanks!"

She told Marge and the girls about Grange. They were amused.

"He obviously has good taste," Marge mused, "if he likes you."

Tellie chuckled as she rinsed dishes and put them in the dishwasher. "It's not mutual," she replied. "He's a little scary, in a way."

"What do you mean? Does he seem violent or something?" Brandi wanted to know.

Tellie paused with a dish in her hand and frowned. "I don't know. I'm not afraid of him, really. It's just that he has that sort of effect on people. Kind of like Cash Grier," she added.

"He's calmed down a bit since Tippy Moore came to stay with him after her kidnapping," Marge said. "Rumor is that he may marry her."

"She's really pretty, even with those cuts on her face," Dawn remarked from the kitchen table, where she was arranging cloth for a quilt she meant to make. "They say somebody real mean is after her, and that's why she's here. Mrs. Jewell stays at the house at night. A stickler for convention, is our police chief."

"Good for him," Marge said. "A few people need to be conventional, or society is going to fall."

Brandi looked at her sister and rolled her eyes. "Here we go again with the lecture."

"Uncle J.B. isn't conventional," Dawn reminded her mother. "He had that football team cheerleader staying at his house for almost a month. And his new girlfriend was a runner-up Miss Texas, and she spends weekends with him..."

Tellie's hands were shaking. Dawn grimaced and looked at her mother helplessly.

Dawn got up and hugged Tellie from behind. "I'm sorry, Tellie," she said with obvious remorse.

Tellie patted the hands around her waist. "Just because I'm a hopeless case, doesn't mean you have to walk on eggshells around me," she assured the younger woman. "We all know that J.B. isn't ever going to get married. And even if he did, it would be some beautiful, sophisticated—"

"You hush," Marge broke in. "You're pretty. Besides, it's what's inside that counts. Beauty doesn't last. Character does."

"Her stock phrase," Brandi said with a grin. "But she's right, Tellie. I think you're beautiful."

"Thanks, guys," Tellie murmured.

She went back to her task, and the conversation became general.

The next day Grange came right up to Tellie's desk and stood staring down at her, wordlessly, until she was forced to look up at him.

"They say that you live with J. B. Hammock's sister, Marge," he said.

She was totally confounded by the question. She stared at him blankly. "Excuse me?"

He shrugged, looking uncomfortable. "I didn't come to Jacobsville by accident," he said, glancing around as Justin came out of his office and gave him a faint glower. "Have lunch with me," he added. "It's not a pass. I just want to talk to you."

If it was a line, it was a good one. "Okay," she said.

"I'll pick you up at noon." He tipped his wide-brimmed hat, nodded toward Justin and went back out to the feedlot.

Justin went straight to Tellie. "Trouble?" he asked.

"Well, no," she said. "He wants to talk to me about Marge, apparently."

His eyebrows arched. "That's a new one."

"He was serious. He wants me to have lunch with him." She grinned. "He can't do much to me over a hamburger in town."

"Good point. Okay, but watch your step. Like I said," he added, "he's an unknown quantity."

"I'll do that," she promised.

Barbara's Café in town was the local hot spot for lunch. Just about everybody ate there when they wanted something home cooked. There were other places, such as the Chinese and Mexican restaurants, and the pizza place. But Barbara's had a sort of Texas atmosphere that appealed even to tourists.

Today it was crowded. Grange got them a table and ordered steak and potatoes for himself, leaving Tellie to get what she wanted. They'd already agreed they were going Dutch. So he must have meant it, about it not being a date.

"My people were all dead, and Marge and J.B. took me in," Tellie said when they'd given their orders to the waitress. She didn't add why. "I've known the Hammocks since I was a child, but I was fourteen when I went to live with Marge and her girls. She was widowed by then."

"Are you and J.B. close?" he queried, placing his hat in an empty chair.

"No," she said flatly. She didn't elaborate. She started to get the feeling that it was not Marge he wanted information on.

His dark eyes narrowed as he studied her. "What do you know about his past?" he asked.

Her heart jumped. "You mean, generally?"

"I mean," he added with flaming eyes, "do you know anything about the woman he tried to marry when he was twenty-one?"

She felt suddenly cold, and didn't know why. "What woman?" she asked, her voice sounded hoarse and choked.

He looked around them to make sure they weren't being overheard. He lifted his coffee cup and held it in his big, lean hands. "His father threatened to cut him off without a cent if he went through with the wedding. He was determined to do it. He withdrew his savings from the bank—he was of legal age, so he could—and he picked her up at her house and they took off to Louisiana. He was going to marry her there. He thought nobody could find them. But his father did."

This was fascinating stuff. Nobody had said anything to her about it, certainly not J.B. "Did they get married?"

His face tautened. "His father waited until J.B. went out to see about the marriage license. He went in and talked to the woman. He told her that if she married J.B., he'd turn in her brother, who was fourteen and had gotten mixed up with a gang that dealt in distribution of crack cocaine. There had been a death involved in a drug deal gone bad. The boy hadn't participated, but he could be implicated as an accessory. J.B.'s father had a private detective document everything. He told the woman her brother would go to prison for twenty years."

She grimaced. "Did J.B. know?"

"I don't know," he said uncomfortably. "I came here to find out."

"But what did she do?"

"What could she do?" he asked curtly. "She loved her brother. He was the only family she had. She loved Hammock. She really loved him."

"But she loved her brother more?"

He nodded. His whole face clenched. "She didn't tell Hammock what his father had done. She did tell her father."

"Did he do anything?"

"He couldn't. They were poor. There was nothing he could do. Well, he did get her brother to leave the gang when she killed herself. It was all that saved him from prison."

She was hanging on his every word. "What about the woman?"

"She was already clinically depressed," he said in an odd monotone, toying with his fork, not looking at her. He seemed to be far away, in time. "She knew that she could never be with Hammock, that his father would make sure of it. She couldn't see any future without him." His fingers tightened on the fork. "She found the pistol her brother had hidden in his room. She shot herself. She died instantly."

The iced tea went all over the tablecloth. Tellie quickly

righted the glass and grabbed at napkins to mop up the flow. Barbara, seeing the accident, came forward with a tea cloth.

"There, there, we all spill things," she told Tellie with a smile. "Right as rain," she added when she'd mopped the oilcloth-covered table. "I'll bring you a new glass. Unsweetened?"

Tellie nodded, still reeling from what Grange had told her. "Yes. Thanks."

"No problem," Barbara said, smiling at them both as she left.

"You really didn't know, did you?" Grange asked quietly. "I'm sorry. I don't want to hurt you. It's not your fault."

She swallowed, hard. It all made sense. Why J.B. never got serious about a woman. Why he refused to think of marriage. He'd had that death on his conscience all his life, when it wasn't even his fault, not really. It was his father's.

"His father must have been a horror," she said unsteadily.

Grange stared at her. "Have been?" he queried.

She nodded. "He died in a nursing home the year I moved in with Marge," she said. "He'd had a stroke and he never fully recovered from it. It left him in a vegetative state. J.B. paid to keep him in the facility."

"And the old man's wife?"

"She died long before I lived with Marge. I don't know how."

He looked odd. "I see."

"How do you know all this?" she wondered.

"Her brother is a friend of mine," he told her. "He was curious about the old man. I needed a job, and this one at the feedlot came available. I like Texas. It was close enough that I could find out about old man Hammock for him."

"Well, now you know," she said, trying not to let the trauma show in her face.

He frowned. His hard face went even harder. He stared down into his coffee cup. "I didn't realize it would have such an impact on you."

"J.B. is like an older brother to me," she told him, lying through her teeth. "But nobody ever told me why he plays the field like he does, why he won't consider ever getting married. I thought he just liked being a bachelor. I guess he blames himself for what happened, don't you think?" she added, surprising an odd look on Grange's face. "Even though it was his father who did the real damage, J.B. surely realized that if he'd never gotten mixed up with the poor woman, she'd still be alive."

He winced. "You don't pull your punches, do you?"

"It's the truth, isn't it?" she added thoughtfully.

"So he doesn't want to get married," he said after a minute.

She nodded. "He has lots of girlfriends. The new one was a runner-up in the Miss Texas pageant."

He didn't even seem to be listening. He finished his steak and sat back to sip cold coffee.

Barbara came around with Tellie's new glass of tea and the coffeepot. She warmed Grange's in his cup.

"Thanks," he said absently.

She grinned at him. "No problem. You're new here, aren't you?"

"I am," he confessed. "I work for Justin and Calhoun, at the feedlot."

"Lucky you," she said. "They're good people."

He nodded.

She glanced at Tellie. "How's Marge?"

There was something in the question that made Tellie stare at her. "She's fine. Why?"

Barbara grimaced. "It's nothing, really."

"Tell me," Tellie persisted. It was her day for learning things about people she thought she knew.

"Well, she had a dizzy spell the last time she ate lunch here. She fell into one of the tables." She sighed. "I wondered if she ever had a checkup. Just to make sure. I never knew Marge to have dizzy spells."

"Me, either," Tellie said, frowning. "But I'll find out," she promised.

"Don't tell her I told you," Barbara said firmly. "She can light fires when she's mad, just like J.B."

"I'll ask her gently, I promise," Tellie said, smiling. "She won't get mad."

"If you do, you'll eat burned hamburgers forever," Barbara told her.

"That's just mean," she told the older woman, who grinned and went back to the kitchen.

"Well, it's your day for revelations, apparently," Grange observed.

"I don't think I know anybody anymore," she agreed.

"Listen, don't tell Hammock's sister about any of this," he said suddenly. "I'm not here to cause trouble. I just wanted to find out what became of the old man." His eyes darkened. "I suppose J.B. knew what his father did?"

"I have no way of knowing," she said uneasily.

He put cream into his hot coffee. He drew in a long breath. "I'm sorry if I shattered any illusions."

He had. He'd just put the final nail in the coffin of

her dreams. But that wasn't his fault. Tellie always felt that people came into your life for a reason. She forced a smile. "I don't have illusions about J.B.," she told him. "I've seen all his bad character traits firsthand."

He searched her green eyes. "One of the boys said you're in college."

She nodded. "I start master's work in the fall."

"What's your subject?"

"History. My field is Native American studies. I hope to teach at the college level when I finally get my master's degree."

"Why not teach grammar school or middle or high school?" he wondered.

"Because little kids walk all over me," she said flatly. "Marge's girls had me on my ear the first six months I lived with them, because I couldn't say no. I'd make a lousy elementary school teacher."

He smiled faintly. "I'll bet the girls loved you."

She nodded, smiling back. "They're very special."

He finished his coffee. "We'll have to do this again sometime," he began, just as the café door opened and J.B. walked in.

J.B.'s eyes slithered over the patrons until he spotted Tellie. He walked to the table where Tellie and Grange were sitting and stared down at Grange with pure venom. His eyes were blistering hot.

"What are you doing here in Jacobsville?" he asked Grange.

The other man studied him coolly. "Working. Tellie and I are having lunch together."

"That doesn't answer the question," J.B. replied, and he'd never sounded more menacing.

Grange sipped coffee with maddening calm. "So the

old man did finally tell you what happened, did he?" he asked with a sudden, piercing glance. "He told you what he said to my sister?"

J.B.'s big fists clenched at his side. He aged in seconds. "Not while he was alive. He left a letter with his will."

"At least you had time to get used to the idea, didn't you?" Grange asked icily. "I found out three weeks ago!" He forced his deep voice back into calmer channels and took a deep breath. "Care to guess how I felt when my father finally told *me*, on his deathbed?"

J.B. seemed to calm down himself. "You didn't know?" he asked.

"No," Grange said harshly. "No, I didn't know! If I had...!"

J.B. seemed suddenly aware of Tellie's rapt interest and he seemed to go pale under his tan. He saw her new knowledge of him in her paleness, in her suddenly averted face. He looked at Grange. "You told her, didn't you?" he demanded.

The other man stood up. He and J.B. were the same height, although Grange seemed huskier, more muscular. J.B. had a range rider's lean physique.

"Secrets are dangerous, Hammock," Grange said, and he didn't back down an inch. "There were things I wanted to know that I'd never have heard from you."

"Such as?" J.B. asked in a curt tone.

Grange looked at him openly, aware that other diners were watching them. His shoulders moved in a curious jerk. "I came here with another whole idea in mind, but your young friend here shot me in the foot. I didn't realize that you were as much a victim as I was. I thought you put your father up to it," he added tautly.

Tellie didn't know what he meant.

J.B. did. "Things would have ended differently if I'd known," he said in a harsh tone.

"If I'd known, too." Grange studied him. "Hell of a shame that we can't go back and do things right, isn't it?"

J.B. nodded.

"I like working at the feedlot, but it's only for a few months," he said. "If it helps, I'm no gossip. I only wanted the truth. Now I've got it." He turned to Tellie. "I shouldn't have involved you. But I enjoyed lunch," he added quietly, and he smiled. It changed his dark eyes, made them deep and hypnotic.

"Me, too," she said, flushing a little. He really was good-looking.

Grange shrugged. "Maybe we can do it again."

She did smile then. "I'd like that."

He nodded at J.B. and left them to go to the counter and pay for his meal. J.B. sat down in the chair Grange had vacated and looked at Tellie with mingled anger and concern.

"Don't worry, J.B., he didn't spill any state secrets," she lied as she sipped tea. "He only said your father had done something to foil a romance years ago, and he wanted to know how to get in touch with the elder Mr. Hammock. He said he wanted to know for a friend of his." She hoped he believed her. She'd die if he realized she knew the whole terrible secret in his past. She felt sick to her stomach, imagining how he must feel.

He didn't answer her. He glanced at Grange as the younger man left the café, and then caught Barbara's eye and ordered coffee and apple pie.

Tellie was trying not to react at the surprise of having coffee with J.B., who'd never shared a table in a restaurant with her before. Her heart was beating double-time at just the nearness of him. She had to force herself not to stare at him with overt and visible delight.

Barbara brought coffee. He grinned at her and she grinned back. "Dating in shifts these days, huh, Tellie?" she teased.

Tellie didn't answer. She managed a faint smile, embarrassed.

J.B. sipped his coffee. He never added cream or sugar. Her eyes went to his lean, darkly tanned hands. There was a gold cat's-eye ring on his left ring finger, thick and masculine, and a thin expensive watch above it on his wrist. He was wearing a lightweight gray suit with a cream Stetson. He looked expensive and arrogant and seductive.

"I don't like the idea of your going out with that man," J.B. told her curtly.

"It wasn't a date, J.B., it was just lunch," she said.

"It was an interrogation," he corrected. "What else did he want to know?"

She knew she'd never get away with lying. "He wanted to know about your father," she said.

"What about him?"

"If he was still alive. I told him he wasn't. That was all."

"What did he say?"

"Not much," she returned. She searched his green eyes. They were troubled and stormy. "Just that a friend had asked him to find out about your father, over some romance of yours that went bad years ago. He didn't say anything specific," she added without looking at him. He usually could tell when she was lying.

His face tautened as he looked at her. "I never meant

anyone to know about what happened except Marge and me," he said tightly.

"Yes, I know, J.B.," she replied, her voice weary and resigned. "You don't share things with outsiders."

He frowned. "You're not an outsider. You're family."

That, somehow, made things even worse. She met his eyes evenly. "You sent Jarrett out to get my graduation present. You'd never do that to Marge or the girls. And you lied about being at the graduation exercises. You were in the office with some businessman and his daughter. I gather that she was a real looker and you couldn't tear yourself away," she added with more bitterness than she realized.

His eyes almost glowed with anger. "Who told you that?"

"I took classes in ESP in college," she drawled facetiously, and with a bite in her voice. "What does it matter how I know? You lied to me!"

His indrawn breath was audible. "Damn it, Tellie!"

"Why can't you be honest with me?" she demanded. "I'm not a kid anymore. You don't have to protect me from the truth."

"You don't know the truth," he said curtly.

"Sure I do. I'm a liability you assumed because I had no family and you felt sorry for me," she replied.

"I felt sorry for you," he conceded. "But I've always included you in family activities, haven't I?"

"Oh, yes," she agreed. "I get to have Christmas and summer vacation and all the other holidays with Marge and the girls, I even get to go on overseas trips with them. I've never doubted that I was part of Marge's family," she said meaningfully.

He frowned. "Marge is part of my family."

"You're not part of mine, J.B.," she replied. Her heart was breaking. "I'm in the same class as your big-boobed blondes, disposable and unimportant. We don't even rate a handpicked present. You just send out the secretary to buy it, and to lie for you when you avoid events you'd rather not be forced to attend."

He glared at her. "You've got the whole thing upside down." He cursed under his breath. "Damn Grange! If he hadn't barged in...!"

Something was fishy here. "You know him!"

His lips made a thin line. "I know him," he admitted reluctantly. "I went to see him at the feedlot when I realized who he was. But I barely had time to say anything to him before Justin showed up. I didn't go back."

"Who is he, J.B.?" she asked, but she was sure that she already knew the answer.

"He's her brother," he said finally. "He's the brother of the woman my father kept me from marrying."

Three

The look in J.B.'s eyes was painful to Tellie, who loved him with all her heart, despite the knowledge that he was never going to be able to love her back. She could almost feel the pain that rippled through him with the words. The woman, the only woman, he'd ever loved had killed herself, because of him. It was a pain he could never escape. And now the woman's brother had shown up in his own town.

"Why is he here, do you think?" she asked.

J.B. sipped coffee. "Revenge, perhaps," he said tautly, "at first."

"Revenge for what?" she asked, because she knew the answer, but she didn't want him to realize how much Grange had told her.

He glanced at her appraisingly. "It's a story that doesn't concern you, Tellie," he said quietly. "It's ancient history."

She finished her own coffee. "Whatever you say, J.B.," she replied. "I have to get back to work."

She stood up. So did he. "How are you going to get back to the feedlot?" he asked abruptly. "Didn't you ride in with Grange?"

She shook her head. "It was Dutch treat."

"Are you coming to the barbecue Saturday?" he added.

It was the end of roundup, one that he gave for the ranch hands. Marge and the girls, and Tellie, were always invited. It was a comfortable routine.

Tellie had never felt less like a routine. "No, I don't think so," she said abruptly, and was pleased to see his eyelids flicker. "I have other plans."

"What other plans?" he demanded, as if he had the right to know every step she took.

She smiled carelessly. "That's not your business, J.B. See you."

She went to the counter and paid Barbara. When she left, J.B. was sitting there, brooding, his face like steel.

It wasn't until that night Tellie finally had time to digest what she'd learned. She waited until the girls went to bed and then cornered Marge at the kitchen table where she was piecing a quilt.

"Do you know a family named Grange?" she asked Marge.

The older woman blinked, surprised. "Grange? Why?"

That wasn't an innocent look Marge was giving her. Tellie folded her hands on the table. "There's a man named Grange who came to work at the feedlot," she said. "He's tall and dark eyed and dark haired. J.B. was going to marry his sister a long time ago…"

"Him! Here! Dear God!" Marge exclaimed. She put her hands to her mouth. "No!"

"It's all right, Marge," she said at once. "He came looking for your father, not J.B."

Marge's eyes were wide, frightened. "You know?" she asked huskily.

She sighed heavily. "Yes. Grange told me everything. J.B. doesn't know that," she added quickly. "I said that Grange only mentioned that there was a romance gone bad in the past."

Marge drew her hands over her mouth. "It was much worse than that, Tellie. It was a nightmare," she said heavily. "I've never seen J.B. like that. He went crazy after she died. For three months, he went away and nobody even knew where he was. We couldn't find him. Dad cried…" She took a steadying breath. "I never understood what happened, why she did it. J.B. thought it was because they'd had an argument about her giving up her house to live with us. They parted in anger, and he didn't know what had happened until her best friend called him and gave him the news. He blamed himself. He lived with the guilt, but it ate him alive. Dad was so kind to him afterward," she added. "They'd had problems, like some fathers and sons do. They were both strong willed and domineering." She sighed. "But Dad went out of his way after that to win J.B.'s affection. I think he finally succeeded, before he had the stroke." She looked up. "Did Grange have any idea why she did such a desperate thing?"

Now things were getting sticky. Tellie hesitated. She didn't want to destroy Marge's illusions about her father.

And obviously, J.B. hadn't told his sister about his father's interference that had caused the tragedy.

Marge realized that. She smiled sadly. "Tellie, my father never cared one way or the other about me. I was a girl, so I was a disappointment to him. You don't need to spare my feelings. I would like to know what Grange told you."

Tellie took a deep breath. "All right. He said that J.B.'s father came to see the girl and told her that if she married J.B., he had enough evidence to put her fourteen-year-old brother in prison for the rest of his life. The boy was involved in drugs and part of a gang."

She gasped. "So that was it! Did he tell J.B.?"

"Yes," she said. "He did. Apparently Grange only just found out himself. His father only told him when he was dying. I'm sure he was trying to spare Grange. He'll go through his own pain, realizing that he provided your father with the reason to threaten his sister."

"So many secrets," Marge said, her voice thready. "Pain and more pain. It will bring it all back, too. J.B. will relive it."

That was painful. But it wasn't all Grange's fault. "Grange just wanted to know the truth." Tellie defended the stranger. "He thought J.B. put his father up to talking to the woman."

"My brother doesn't have any problem telling people unpleasant things," she replied musingly. "He does his own dirty work."

"He does," Tellie agreed.

She frowned at the younger woman's expression. "What are you not telling me?"

She shrugged. "Jarrett let something slip."

"J.B.'s secretary? Did she? What?" she asked with a lazy smile.

"J.B. wasn't at the graduation exercises, Marge," Tellie said sadly. "He was in a meeting with a businessman and his attractive daughter. He made Jarrett cover up for him. She was really upset about what he said to her. She was more upset when she found out that the present he wanted her to buy was for me, for my graduation."

"Wait a minute," Marge replied, frowning. "He lied about being at the stadium? He actually did that?"

Tellie grimaced. "Yes."

"I'll strangle him!" the older woman said forcefully.

"To what end, Marge?" Tellie asked. She felt old, tired, worn-out. "Can you make him love me? Because that isn't ever going to happen. I thought he was just a carefree playboy who liked variety in his women. But it's not that at all, is it?" She sat back in her chair, her face drawn and sad. "He blames himself because the woman he loved died. He won't risk feeling that way about another woman, setting himself up for another loss. He thinks he doesn't deserve to be happy because she killed herself."

"And all along, it was our father who did the dirty work." Marge's eyes were thoughtful. "I noticed that he seemed haunted sometimes, absolutely haunted. And I'd ask him if anything was wrong. He'd just say that people had to pay for their sins, and he hoped his punishment wouldn't be as bad as he deserved. I didn't know what he was talking about, until today. I suppose he was afraid to tell the truth, because he knew he'd lose J.B. forever."

"You couldn't have blamed him. Whatever he thought of the woman, it was J.B.'s life, and his decision. The old man couldn't live his life for him."

"You didn't know him, honey. He was just like J.B. There's the wrong way, and there's J.B.'s way. That was Dad, too."

"I see."

Marge reached across the table and held her hand. "I'm sorry you had to find it out like this. I told J.B. we should tell you, but he said—" She stopped suddenly. "Anyway, he wouldn't hear of it."

Tellie knew what Marge had avoided saying, that it was none of Tellie's business because she wasn't family. She smiled. "Don't pull your punches. I'm getting tougher by the day since I graduated."

"J.B.'s helped, hasn't he?" she said with a scowl.

"He can't change the way he feels," she said wearily. "If he was going to fall head over heels in love with me, it wouldn't have taken him seven years, Marge. Even now, I'm just a stray that he took in. Well, that *you* took in," she corrected. "J.B. decided that both of you would take care of me, but you'd do the daily work." She laughed. "And it's just like him."

"It is," Marge had to admit. She squeezed Tellie's hand and then let go. "Maybe it isn't a bad thing that you know the truth. It helps explain the way he is, and why there was never much hope for you in the first place."

"Perhaps you're right," Tellie agreed. "But you mustn't ever let J.B. know. Promise me."

"I'll never tell him what you know, Tellie," Marge agreed. She hesitated. "What is Grange like?"

"Mysterious," she replied. "Dangerous. Nobody knows much about him. They say he was in Special Forces."

"Not in the Mafia?" Marge replied dryly, and she wasn't totally kidding.

"He said that his sister's death took him right out of drug use and gang participation, although he told me at first that it was a friend and not himself," she replied. "The tragedy saved him, in fact. He felt guilty, I'm sure, when he realized that she died partially because J.B.'s father threatened to put him in prison. The awful thing is that he didn't know that until three weeks ago. I expect he's hurting as much as J.B. did when he read the letter his father left him."

"That was another bad month, when J.B. got that letter attached to Dad's will," Marge said. "He got extremely drunk." She frowned. "That was the year before you graduated from high school, in fact. You came over and took a gun away from him," she added, shocked at the memory. "I yelled at you, and you wouldn't listen. You went right into his den, poured the bottle of whiskey down the sink with him yelling curses at you, and then you took away the pistol and popped the bullets out on the floor. I screamed..."

"You thought he'd hit me," she agreed, smiling. "But I knew better. J.B. would never hit a woman, not even if he was stinking drunk. Which he was, of course."

"You led him off to bed and stayed with him all night. The next morning he carried you into the living room where I was, and laid you out on the sofa under an afghan. He looked very funny. When I asked him why, he said it was the first time in his life that he'd ever had a woman take care of him. Our mother wasn't domestic," she added quietly. "She was never very nurturing. She was a research chemist and her life was her work. Housekeepers raised J.B. and me. It was almost a relief for Dad, and us, when she died. I did admire her," she added. "She did a socially beneficial job. A dangerous one, too. She was working with a terrible virus strain, looking for a cure. One day in the lab, she stuck a needle, accidentally, into her hand through her rubber glove and died. I was sorry, and I went to the funeral. J.B wouldn't go and neither would Dad. They said she deserted all of us for her job."

"That sounds like him," Tellie agreed.

"J.B. never stopped fussing about the way you took care of him," she recalled on a laugh. "But then he'd lose his temper when you weren't around to do it. He was furious when you spent your summer vacations with those friends at Yellowstone National Park."

"I had a good time. I miss Melody. She and I were wonderful friends, but her parents moved overseas and she had to go with them."

"I don't think I have one friend left in Jacobsville, from my school days," Marge recalled.

"What about Barbara?"

"Oh. Yes. Barbara." She chuckled. "She and that café. When we were girls, it was what she wanted most of all, to own a restaurant."

"It's a good one." Tellie hesitated. "Now, don't get angry, but she's worried about you," she added.

"Me? Why?"

"She said you had a dizzy spell."

Marge frowned. "Yes, I did. I remember. I've had two or three lately. Odd, isn't it? But then, I'm prone to migraine headaches," she added carelessly. "You get all sorts of side effects from them. In fact, I see fireworks and go blind in one eye just before I get one. The doctor calls them vascular headaches."

Tellie frowned. "Why? Does blood pressure cause them?"

Marge laughed. "Not in my case, honey. I have the lowest blood pressure in two counties. No, migraine runs in my family. My mother had them, and so did her mother."

"I'll bet J.B. doesn't have them," Tellie mused.

"That's a fact," came the laughing reply. "No, he doesn't get headaches, but he certainly gives them."

"Amen."

Marge went back to her piecing. "Maybe it's just as well that you know all about J.B. now, Tellie," she said after a minute. "Maybe it will save you any further heartache."

"Yes," the younger woman agreed sadly. "Maybe so."

Grange didn't ask her out again, but he did stop by her desk from time to time, just to see how she was. It was as if he knew how badly he'd hurt her with the information about J.B.'s past, and wanted to make amends.

"Listen," she said one day when he gave her a worried look, "I'm not stupid. I knew there was something in J.B.'s past that, well, that caused him to be the way he is. He never cared about me, except as a sort of adopted relative." She smiled. "I've got three years of college to go, you know. No place for a love life."

He studied her quietly. "Don't end up like him," he said suddenly. "Or like me. I don't think I've got it in me to trust another human being."

Her eyes were sympathetic. He was blaming himself for his sister's death. She knew it. "You'll grow old and bitter, all alone," she said.

"I'm already old and bitter," he said, and he didn't smile.

"No gray hairs," she observed.

"They're all on the inside," he shot back.

She grinned. Her whole face lit up.

He gave her an odd look and something in his expression softened, just a little.

"If you really want to look old, you should dye your hair," she pointed out.

He chuckled. "My father still had black hair when he died. He was sixty."

"Good genes," she said.

He shrugged. "Beats me. He never knew who his father was."

"Your mother?"

His face hardened. "I don't talk about her."

"Sorry."

"I didn't mean to growl," he said hesitantly. "I'm not used to women."

"Imagine a man ever admitting that!" she exclaimed with mock surprise.

He cocked an eyebrow. "You're sassy."

"Yes, I am. Nice of you to notice. Now would you mind leaving? Justin's going to come back any minute. He won't like having you flirt with me on his time."

"I don't flirt," he shot back.

"Well, excuse me!"

He shifted. "Maybe I flirt a little. It isn't intentional."

"God forbid! Who'd want to marry you?" she asked curiously.

He scowled. "Look here, I'm not a bad person."

"Well, I wouldn't want to marry you," she persisted.

"Who asked you?" he asked curtly.

"Not you, for sure," she returned. "And don't bother," she added when he started to speak. "I'm such a rare catch that I have men salivating in the yard, wherever I go."

His dark eyes started to twinkle. "Why?"

"Because I can make French pastry," she told him. "With real whipped cream and custard fillings."

He pursed his lips. "Well!"

"See? I'm quite a catch. Too bad you're not in the running."

He frowned. "Even if I were interested, what would I do with a wife?"

"You don't know?" She gave him such an expression of shock and horror that he burst out laughing.

She grinned at him. "See there? You're improving all the time. I'm a good influence, I am!"

"You're a pain in the neck," he returned. "But not bad company." He shrugged. "Like movies?"

"What sort?"

"Science fiction?"

She chuckled. "You bet."

"I'll check and see what's playing at the theater Saturday, if you're game."

Saturday was the barbecue at J.B.'s that she was determined not to attend. Here was her excuse to miss it. She liked Grange. Besides, no way was she going to sit home and eat her heart out over J.B., especially when she'd already told him that she had other plans. "I'm game."

"Your adopted family won't like it," he said slowly.

"Marge won't mind," she said, certain that it was true. "And I don't care what J.B. thinks."

He nodded. "Okay. It's a date. We'll work out the details Friday."

"Fine. Now please go away," she added, glancing at

the door, where Justin was just coming inside the building. "Or we may both be out looking for work on Monday!"

He grinned and left her before Justin got the door closed.

Marge was less enthusiastic than Tellie had expected. In fact, she seemed disturbed.

"Does the phrase, 'rubbing salt on an open wound,' ring any chimes?" Marge asked her somberly.

"But Grange didn't do anything," she protested. "He was as much a victim as J.B. was."

Marge hesitated, uneasy. "I understand that. But he's connected with it. J.B. will see it as a personal attack on him, by both of you."

"That's absurd!"

"It isn't, if you remember the way my brother is."

For the first time since Grange had asked her out, Tellie wasn't sure she was doing the right thing. She didn't want to hurt J.B., even if he'd given her reason. On the other hand, it was a test of control, his over hers. If she gave in now, she'd be giving in forever. Marge was her friend, but J.B. was Marge's brother. It was a tangled situation.

Marge put an arm around her. "Don't worry yourself to death, honey," she said gently. "If you really want to go out with him, go ahead. I'm just saying that J.B. is going to take it personally. But you can't let him run your life."

Tellie hugged her back. "Thanks, Marge."

"Why don't you want to go to the barbecue?" the older woman asked.

Tellie grimaced. "Miss runner-up beauty queen will be there, won't she?"

Marge pursed her lips. "So that's it."

"Don't you dare tell him," came the terse reply.

"Never." Marge sighed. "I didn't even think about that. No wonder you're so anxious to stay away."

"She's really gorgeous, isn't she?"

Marge looked old and wise. "She's just like all the other ones before her, Tellie, tall and blonde and stacked. Not much in the way of intelligence. You know," she added thoughtfully, "I don't think J.B. really likes intelligent women much."

"Maybe he feels threatened by us."

"Don't you believe it," Marge scoffed. "He's got a business degree from Yale, you know."

"I'd forgotten."

"No, I think it has to do with our mother," she continued. "She was always running down our father, making him feel like an idiot. She was forever going to conventions with one of her research partners. Later, they had a serious affair. That was just before she died."

"J.B. didn't have a great respect for women, I guess."

"Not in his younger days. Then he got engaged, and tragedy followed." She seemed far away. "I lost my first love to another woman, and then my husband died of an embolism after surgery." She shook her head. "J.B. and I have poor track records with happily-ever-after."

Tellie felt sad for both of them. "I suppose it would make you gun-shy, when it came to love."

"Love?" Marge laughed. "J.B. doesn't believe in it anymore." She gave Tellie a sad, gentle appraisal. "But you should. Maybe Grange will be the best thing that ever happened to you. It wouldn't hurt to show J.B. that you're not dying of a broken heart, either."

"He won't notice," Tellie said with conviction. "He used to complain that I was always underfoot."

"Not recently."

"I've been away at college for four years more or less," she reminded the older woman. That reminded her of graduation, which he hadn't attended. It still stung.

"And going away for three more." Marge smiled. "Live your life, Tellie. You don't have to answer to anybody. Be happy."

"That's easier said than done," Tellie pointed out. She smiled at Marge. "Okay. If you don't mind me dating Grange, J.B. can think what he likes. I don't care."

Which wasn't the truth, exactly.

Grange was good company when he relaxed and forgot that Tellie was a friend of J.B.'s.

The movie was unforgettable, a film about a misfit crew aboard a space-going freighter who were protecting a girl from some nasty authorities. It was funny and sweet and full of action.

They came out of the theater smiling.

"It's been a good year for science-fiction movies," he remarked.

"It has," Tellie agreed, "but that was the best I've seen so far. I missed the series when it was on television. I guess I'll have to buy the DVD set."

He gave her an amused look. "You're nice to take around," he said on the way to his big gray truck. "If I weren't a confirmed bachelor, you'd be at the top of my list of prospects."

"Why, what a nice thing to say!" she exclaimed. "Do you mind if I quote you frequently?"

He gave her a quick look and relaxed a little when she laughed. "Quote me?" he asked quizzically.

Her shoulders rose and fell. "It's just that nobody ever said I was marriageable before, you see," she told him. "I figure with an endorsement like that, the sky's the limit. I mean, I won't be in college forever. A woman has to think about the future."

Grange stared at her in the light from the parking lot. "I don't think I've ever been around anyone like you. Most women these days are too aggressive for my taste."

Her eyebrows arched. "Like doormats, do we?" she teased.

He shook his head. "It's not that. I like a woman with spirit. But I don't like being seen as a party favor."

"Now you know how women feel," she pointed out.

"I never treated a woman that way," he returned.

"A lot of men have."

"I suppose so," he conceded. He gave her a smile. "I enjoyed tonight."

"Me, too."

"We'll do it again sometime."

She smiled back. "Suits me."

Grange dropped her off at Marge's house, but he didn't try to kiss her good-night. He was a gentleman in the best sense of the word. Tellie liked him. But her heart still ached for J.B.

Tellie assumed that Marge and the girls were in bed, because the lights were all off inside. She locked the door behind her and started toward the staircase when a light snapped on in the living room.

She whirled, surprised, and looked right into J. B. Hammock's seething green eyes.

Four

"What...are you doing here?" she blurted out, flushing at the way he was looking at her. "Has something happened to Marge or the girls?" she added at once, uneasy.

"No. They're fine."

She moved into the room, putting her purse and coat on a chair, her slender body in jeans with pink embroidered roses and a pink tank top that matched. Her pale eyes searched his dark green ones curiously. She ran a nervous hand through her wavy dark hair and grimaced. He looked like an approaching storm.

"Then why are you here?" she asked when the silence became oppressive.

His eyes slid over her body in the tight jeans and tank top and narrowed with reluctant appreciation. He was also in jeans, but his were without decoration. A chambray shirt covered his broad, muscular chest and long arms. It was unfastened at the throat. He usually dressed casually for barbecues, and this one didn't seem to be an exception.

"You went to a movie with Grange," he said.

"Yes."

His face tautened. "I don't like you going out with him."

Her thin dark eyebrows arched. "I'm almost twenty-two, J.B."

"Jacobsville is full of eligible bachelors."

"Yes, I know. Grange is one of them."

"Damn it, Tellie!"

She drew in a steadying breath. It was hard not to give in to J.B. She'd spent most of her adolescence doing exactly that. But this was a test of her newfound independence. She couldn't let him walk all over her. Despite his reasons for not wanting her around Grange, she couldn't let him dictate her future. Particularly since he wasn't going to be part of it.

"I'm not marrying him, J.B.," she said quietly. "He's just someone to go out with."

His lean jaw tautened. "He's part of a painful episode in my past," he said flatly. "It's disloyal of you to take his side against me. I'm not pushing the point, but I gave you a home when you needed one."

Her eyes narrowed. "*You* gave me a home? No, J.B., *you* didn't give me a home. You decided that *Marge* would give me a home," she said emphatically.

"Same thing," he bit off.

"It isn't," she replied. "You don't put yourself out for anybody. You make gestures, but somebody else has to do the dirty work."

"That's not how it was, and you know it," he said

curtly. "You were fourteen years old. How would it have looked, to have you living with me? Especially with my lifestyle."

She wanted to argue that, but she couldn't. "I suppose you have a point."

He didn't reply. He just watched her.

She moved to the sofa and perched on one of its broad, floral-patterned arms. "I'm very grateful for what your family has done for me," she said gently. "But nobody can say that I haven't pulled my weight. I've cleaned and cooked for Marge and the girls, been a live-in babysitter, helped keep her books—I haven't just parked myself here and taken advantage of the situation."

"I never said you did," he replied.

"You're implying it," she shot back. "I can't remember when I've ever dated anybody around here…!"

"Of course not, you were too busy mooning over me!"

Her face went white. Then it slowly blossomed into red rage. She stood up, eyes blazing. "Yes," she said. "I was, wasn't I? Mooning over you while you indulged yourself with starlet after debutante after Miss Beauty Contest winner! Oh, excuse me, Miss Runner-up Beauty Contest winner," she drawled insolently.

He glared at her. "My love life is none of your business."

"Don't be absurd," she retorted. "It's everybody's business. You were in a tabloid story just last week, something about you and the living fashion doll being involved in some sleazy love triangle in Hollywood…"

"Lies," he shot back, "and I'm suing!"

"Good luck," she said. "My point is, I date a nice man who hasn't hurt anybody…"

He let out a vicious curse, interrupting her, and moved

closer, towering over her. "He was Special Forces in Iraq," he told her coldly, "and he was brought up on charges for excessive force during an incursion! He actually slugged his commanding officer and stuffed him in the trunk of a civilian car!"

Her eyes widened. "Did he, really?" she mused, fascinated.

"It isn't funny," he snapped. "The man is a walking time bomb, waiting for the spark to set him off. I don't want him around you when it happens. He was forced out of the army, Tellie, he didn't go willingly! He had the choice of a court-martial or an honorable discharge."

She wondered how he knew so much about the other man, but she didn't pursue it. "It was an honorable discharge, then?" she emphasized.

He took off his white Stetson and ran an irritated hand through his black hair. "I can't make you see it, can I? The man's dangerous."

"He's in good company in Jacobsville, then, isn't he?" she replied. "I mean, we're like a resort for ex-mercs and ex-military, not to mention the number of ex-federal law enforcement people..."

"Grange has enemies," he interrupted.

"So do you, J.B.," she pointed out. "Remember that guy who broke into your house with a .45 automatic and tried to shoot you over a horse deal?"

"He was a lunatic."

"If the bullet hadn't been a dud, you'd be dead," she reminded him.

"Ancient history," he said. "You're avoiding the subject."

"I am not likely to be shot by one of Grange's mythical old enemies while watching a science-fiction film at the local theater!" Her small hands balled at her hips. "The only thing you're mad about is that you can't make me do what you want me to do anymore," she challenged.

A deep, dark sensuality came into his green eyes and one corner of his chiseled mouth turned up. "Can't I, now?" he drawled, moving forward.

She backed up. "Oh, no, you don't," she warded him off. "Go home and thrill your beauty queen, J.B., I'm not on the market."

He lifted an eyebrow at her flush and the faint rustle of her heartbeat against her tank top. "Aren't you?"

She backed up one more step, just in case. "What happened to you was…was tragic, but it was a long time ago, J.B., and Grange wasn't responsible for it," she argued. "He was surely as much a victim as you were, especially when he found out the truth. Can't you imagine how he must have felt, when he knew that his own actions cost him his sister's life?"

He seemed to tauten all over. "He told you all of it?"

She hadn't meant to let that slip. He made her nervous when he came close like this. She couldn't think. "You'd never have told me. Neither would Marge. Okay, it's not my business," she added when he looked threatening, "but I can have an opinion."

"Grange was responsible," he returned coldly. "His own delinquency made it impossible for her to get past my father."

"That's not true," Tellie said, her voice quiet and firm. "If I wanted to marry someone, and his father tried to blackmail me, I'd have gone like a shot to the man and told him…!"

The effect the remark had on him was scary. He

seemed to grow taller, and his eyes were terrible. His deep, harsh voice interrupted her. "Stop it."

She did. She didn't have the maturity, or the confidence, to argue the point with him. But she wouldn't have killed herself, she was sure of it. She'd have embarrassed J.B.'s father, shamed him, defied him. She wasn't the sort of person to take blackmail lying down.

"You don't know what you're talking about," he said, his eyes furious. "You'd never sacrifice another human being's life or freedom to save yourself."

"Maybe not," she conceded. "But I wouldn't kill myself, either." She was going to add that it was a cowardly thing to do, but the way J.B. was looking at her kept her quiet.

"She loved me. She was going to have to give me up, and she couldn't bear to go on living that way. In her own mind, she didn't have a choice," he said harshly. He searched her quiet face. "You can't comprehend an emotion that powerful, can you, Tellie? After all, what the hell would you know about love? You're still wrapped up in dreams of happily-ever-after, cotton-candy kisses and hand-holding! You don't know what it is to want someone so badly that it's physically painful to be separated from them. You don't understand the violence of desire." He laughed coldly. "Maybe that's just as well. You couldn't handle an affair!"

"Good, because I don't want one!" she replied angrily. He made her feel small, inadequate. It hurt. "I'm not going to pass myself around like a cigarette to any man who wants me, just to prove how liberated I am! And when I marry, I won't want some oversexed libertine who jumps into bed with any woman who wants him!"

He went very still and quiet. His face was like a drawn cord, his eyes green flames as he glared down at her.

"Sorry," she said uneasily. "That didn't come out the way I meant it. I just don't think that a man, or a woman, who lives that permissively can ever settle down and be faithful. I want a stable marriage that children will fit into, not an endless round of new partners."

"Children," he scoffed.

"Yes, children." Her eyes softened as she thought of them. "A whole house full of them, one day, when I'm through school."

"With Grange as their father?"

She gaped at him. "I just went to a movie with him, J.B.!"

"If you get involved with him, I'll never forgive you," he said in a voice as cold as the grave.

"Well, golly gee whiz, that would be a tragedy, wouldn't it? Just think, I'd never get another present that you sent Jarrett to buy for me!"

His breath was coming quickly through his nose. His lips were flattened. He didn't have a comeback. That seemed to make him angrier. He took another step toward her.

She backed up a step. "You should be happy to have me out of your life," she pointed out uneasily. "I was never more than an afterthought anyway, J.B. Just a pest. All I did was get in your way."

He stopped just in front of her. He looked oddly frustrated. "You're still getting in my way," he said enigmatically. "I know that no matter what Marge may have said, she and the girls were disappointed that you missed the barbecue. It's the first time in seven years that you've done that, and for a man who represents as much hurt to Marge herself as he does to me."

She frowned. "But why? She never knew Grange!"

"You told her what my father did," he said deliberately.

She grimaced. "I didn't mean to!" she confessed. "I didn't want to. But she said it wouldn't matter."

"And you don't know her any better than that, after so long in her house? She was devastated."

She felt worse than ever. "I guess it was rough on you, too, when you found out what he'd done," she said unexpectedly.

His expression was odd. Reserved. Uneasy. "I've never hated a human being so much in all my life," he said huskily. "And he was dead. There was nothing I could do to him, no way I could pay him back for ruining my life and taking hers. You can't imagine how I felt."

"I'm sure he was sorry about it," she said, having gleaned that from what Marge had said about the way he'd treated J.B. "You know he'd have taken it back if he could have. He must have loved you, very much. Marge said that he would have been afraid of losing you if he'd told the truth. You were his only son."

"Forgiveness comes hard to me," he said.

She knew that. He'd never held any grudges against her, but she knew people in town who'd crossed him years ago, and he still went out of his way to snub them. He didn't forgive, and he never forgot.

"Are you so perfect that you never make mistakes?" she wondered out loud.

"None to date," he replied, and he didn't smile.

"Your day is coming."

His eyes narrowed as he stared down at her. "You won't leave Grange alone. Is that final?"

She swallowed. "Yes. It's final."

He gave her a look as cold as death. His head jerked. "Your choice."

He turned on his heel and stalked out of the room. She watched him go with nervous curiosity. What in the world did he mean?

Marge was very quiet at breakfast the next day. Dawn and Brandi kept giving Tellie odd looks, too. They went off to church with friends. Marge wasn't feeling well, so she stayed home and Tellie stayed with her. Something was going on. She wondered what it was.

"Is there something I've done that I need to apologize for?" she asked Marge while they were making lunch in the kitchen.

Marge drew in a slow breath. "No, of course not," she denied gently. "It's just J.B., wanting his own way and making everybody miserable because he can't get it."

"If you want me to stop dating Grange, just say so," Tellie told her. "I won't do it for J.B., but I will do it for you."

Marge smiled at her gently. She reached over and patted Tellie's hand. "You don't have to make any such sacrifices. Let J.B. stew."

"Maybe the man does bring back some terrible memories," she murmured. "J.B. looked upset when he talked about it. He must…he must have loved her very much."

"He was twenty-one," Marge recalled. "Love is more intense at that age, I think. Certainly it was for me. She was J.B.'s first real affair. He wasn't himself the whole time he knew her. I thought she was too old for him, too, but he wouldn't hear a word we said about her. He turned against me, against Dad, against the whole world. He ran off to get married and said he'd never come back. But she argued with him. We never knew exactly why, but when she took her own life, he blamed himself. And then when he learned the truth...well, he was never the same."

"I'm sorry it was like that for him," she said, understanding how he would have felt. She felt like that about J.B. At least, she thought, she wasn't losing him to death—just to legions of other women.

Marge put down the spoon she was using to stir beef stew and turned to Tellie. "I would have told you about her, eventually, even if Grange hadn't shown up," she said quietly. "I knew it would hurt, to know he felt like that about another woman. But at least you'd understand why you couldn't get close to him. You can't fight a ghost, Tellie. She's perfect in his mind, like a living, breathing photograph that never ages, never has faults, never creates problems. No living woman will ever top her in J.B.'s mind. Loving him, while he feels like that about a ghost, would kill your very soul."

"Yes, I understand that now," Tellie said heavily. She stared out the window, seeing nothing. "How little we really know people."

"You can live with someone for years and not know them," Marge agreed. "I just don't want you to waste your life on my brother. You deserve better."

Tellie winced, but she didn't let Marge see. "I'll get married one of these days and have six kids."

"You will," Marge agreed, smiling gently. "And I'll spoil your kids the way you've spoiled mine."

"The girls didn't look too happy this morning," Tellie remarked.

Marge grimaced. "J.B. had them in the kitchen help-ing prepare canapés," she said. "They didn't even get to dance."

"But, why?"

"They're just kids," Marge said ruefully. "They aren't old enough to notice eligible bachelors. To hear J.B. tell it, at least."

"But that's outrageous! They're sixteen and seventeen years old. They're not kids!"

"To J.B., you all are, Tellie."

She glowered. "Maybe Brandi and Dawn would like to go halves with me on a really mean singing telegram."

"J.B. would slug the singer, and we'd get sued," Marge said blithely. "Let it go, honey. I know things look dark at the moment, but they'll get better. We have to look to the future."

"I guess."

"The girls should be home any minute. I'll start dish-ing up while you set the table."

Tellie went to do it, her heart around her ankles.

If she'd wondered what J.B. meant with his cryptic remark, it became crystal clear in the days that followed. He came to the house to see Marge and pretended that Tellie wasn't there. If he passed her on the street at lunch-time, he didn't see her. For all intents and purposes, she had become the invisible woman. He was paying her back for dating Grange.

Which made her more determined, of course, to go out with the man. She didn't care if J.B. snubbed her for-ever; he wasn't dictating her life!

Grange discovered J.B.'s new attitude the following Saturday, when he took Tellie to a local community theater presentation of *Arsenic and Old Lace*. J.B. came in with his gorgeous blonde and sat down in the row across from Tellie and Grange. He didn't look their way all night, and when he passed them on the way out, he didn't speak.

"What the hell is wrong with him?" Grange asked her on the way home.

"He's paying me back for dating you," she said simply.

"That's low."

"That's J.B.," she replied.

"Do you want me to stop asking you out, Tellie?" he asked quietly.

"I do not. J.B. isn't telling me what to do," she replied. "He can ignore me all he likes. I'll ignore him back."

Grange was quiet. "I shouldn't have come here."

"You just wanted to know what happened," she defended him. "Nobody could blame you for that. She was your sister."

He pulled up in front of Marge's house and cut off the engine. "Yes, she was. She and Dad were the only family I had, but I was rotten to them. I ran wild when I hit thirteen. I got in with a bad crowd, joined a gang, used drugs—you name it, I did it. I still don't understand why I didn't end up in jail."

"Her death saved you, didn't it?" she asked.

He nodded, his face averted. "I didn't admit it at the time, though. She was such a sweet woman. She always thought of other people before she thought of herself. She was all heart. It must have been a walk in the park for Hammock's father to convince her that she was ruining J.B.'s life."

"Can you imagine how the old man felt," she began slowly, "because he was always afraid that J.B. would find out the truth and know what he'd done. He had to know that he'd have lost J.B.'s respect, maybe even his love, and he had to live with that until he died. I don't imagine he was a very happy person, even if he did what he felt was the right thing."

"He didn't even know my sister, my dad said," Grange replied. "He wouldn't talk to her. He was sure she was a gold digger, just after J.B.'s money."

"How horrible, to think like that," she murmured thoughtfully. "I guess I wouldn't want to be rich. You'd never be sure if people liked you for what you were or what you had."

"The old man seemed to have an overworked sense of his own worth."

"It sounds like it, from what Marge says."

"Did you ever know him?"

"Only by reputation," she replied. "He was in the nursing home when I came to live with Marge."

"What is she like?"

She smiled. "The exact opposite of J.B. She's sweet and kind, and she never knows a stranger. She isn't suspicious or crafty, and she never hurts people deliberately."

"But her brother does?"

"J.B. never pulls his punches," she replied. "I suppose you know where you stand with him. But he's uncomfortable to be around sometimes, when he's in a bad mood."

He studied her curiously. "How long have you been in love with him?"

She laughed nervously. "I don't love J.B.! I hate him!"

"How long," he persisted, softening the question with a smile.

She shrugged. "Since I was fourteen, I suppose. I

hero-worshipped him at first, followed him everywhere, baked him cookies, waylaid him when he went riding and tagged along. He was amazingly tolerant, when I was younger. Then I graduated from high school and we became enemies. He likes to rub it in that I'm vulnerable when he's around. I don't understand why."

"Maybe he doesn't understand why, either," he ventured.

"You think?" She smiled across the seat at him. "I'm surprised that J.B. hasn't tried to run you out of town."

"He has."

"What?"

He smiled faintly. "He went to see Justin Ballenger yesterday."

"About you?" she wondered.

He nodded. "He said that I was a bad influence on you, and he wondered if I wouldn't be happier working somewhere else."

"What did Justin say?" she asked.

He chuckled. "That he could run his own feedlot without Hammock's help, and that he wasn't firing a good worker because of Hammock's personal issues."

"Well!"

"I understand that Hammock is pulling his cattle out of the feedlot and having them trucked to Kansas, to a feedlot there for finishing."

"But that's horrible!" Tellie exclaimed.

"Justin said something similar, with a few more curse words attached," Grange replied. "I felt bad to cause such problems for him, but he only laughed. He said Hammock would lose money on the deal, and he didn't care. He wasn't being ordered around by a man ten years his junior."

"That sounds like Justin," she agreed, smiling. "Good for him."

He shrugged. "It doesn't solve the problem, though," he told her. "It's only the first salvo. Hammock won't quit. He wants me out of your life, whatever it takes."

"No, it's not about me," she said sadly. "He doesn't like being reminded of what he lost. Marge said so."

Grange's dark eyes studied her quietly. "He didn't want you to know about my sister," he said after a minute. "I ticked him off that first day we went to lunch, by telling you the family secret."

"Marge said that she would have told me herself eventually."

"Why?"

She smiled. "She thinks I'd wear my heart out on J.B., and she's right. I would have. He'll never get past his lovely ghost to any sort of relationship with a real woman. I'm not going to waste my life aching for a man I can't have."

"That's sensible," he agreed. "But he's been part of your life for a long time. He's become a habit."

She nodded, her eyes downcast. "That's just what he is. A habit."

He drew in a long breath. "If you want to stop seeing me…"

"I do not," she said at once. "I really enjoy going out with you, Grange."

He smiled, because it was obvious that she meant it. "I like your company, too." He hesitated. "Just friends," he added slowly.

She smiled back. "Just friends."

His eyes were distant. "I'm at a turning point in my

life," he confessed. "I'm not sure where I'm headed. But I know I'm not ready for anything serious."

"Neither am I." She leaned her head against the back of the seat and studied him. "Do you think you might stay here, in Jacobsville?"

"I don't know. I've got some problems to work out."

"Join the club," she said, and grinned at him.

He laughed. "I like the way I feel with you. J.B. can go hang. We'll present a united front."

"Just as long as J.B. doesn't go and hang us!" she exclaimed.

Five

Grange liked to bowl. Tellie had never tried the sport, but he taught her. She persuaded Marge to let the girls come with them one night. Marge tagged along, but she didn't bowl. She sat at the table sipping coffee and watching her brood fling the big balls down the alley.

"It's fun!" Tellie laughed. She'd left the field to the three experts who were making her look sick with her less-than-perfect bowling.

"That's why you're sitting here with me, is it?" Marge teased.

She shrugged. "I'm a lemon," she confessed. "Nothing I do ever looks good."

"That's not true," Marge disputed. "You cook like an angel and you're great in history. You always make As."

"Two successes out of a hundred false starts," Tellie sighed.

"You're just depressed because J.B.'s ignoring you," Marge said, cutting to the heart of the matter.

"Guilty," Tellie had to admit. "Maybe I should have listened."

"Bull. If you give J.B. the upper hand, he'll walk all over you. The way you used to be, when you were fourteen, I despaired of what would happen if he ever really noticed you. He'd have destroyed your life, Tellie. You'd have become his doormat. He'd have hated that as much as you would."

"Think so? He seems pretty uncomfortable with me when I stand up to him."

"But he respects you for it."

Tellie propped her elbows on the table and rested her chin in her hands. "Does the beauty queen runner-up stand up to him?" she wondered.

"Are you kidding? She won't go to the bathroom without asking J.B. if he thinks it's a good idea!" came the dry response. "She's not giving up all those perks. He gave her a diamond dinner ring last week for her birthday."

That hurt. "I suppose he picked it out himself?"

Marge sighed. "I think she did."

"I can't believe I've wasted four years of my life mooning over that man," Tellie said, wondering aloud at her own stupidity. "I turned down dates with really nice men in college because I was hung up on J.B. Well, never again."

"What sort of nice men?" Marge queried, trying to change the subject.

Tellie grinned. "One was an anthropology major, working on his PhD. He's going to devote his life to a dig in Montana, looking for Paleo-Indian sites."

"Just imagine, Tellie, you could work beside him with a toothbrush..."

"Stop that," Tellie chuckled. "I don't think I'm cut out for dust and dirt and bones."

"What other nice men?"

"There was a friend of one of my professors," she recalled. "He raises purebred Appaloosa stallions when he isn't hunting for meteorites all over the world. He was a character!"

"Why would you hunt meteorites?" Marge wondered.

"Well, he sold one for over a hundred thousand dollars to a collector," the younger woman replied, tongue in cheek.

Marge whistled. "Wow! Maybe I'll get a metal detector and go out searching for them myself!"

That was a real joke, because Marge had inherited half of her father's estate. She lived in a simple house and she never lived high. But she could have, if she'd wanted to. She felt that the girls shouldn't have too much luxury in their formative years. Maybe she was right. Certainly, Brandi and Dawn had turned out very well. They were responsible and kindhearted, and they never felt apart from fellow students.

Tellie glanced at the lanes, where Grange was throwing a ball down the aisle with force and grace. He had a rodeo rider's physique, lean in the hips and wide in the shoulders. Odd, the way he moved, Tellie mused, like a hunter.

"He really is a dish," she murmured, deep in thought.

Marge nodded. "He is unusual," she said. "Imagine a boy on a path that deadly turning his life around."

"J.B. said he was forced out of the military."

Marge gaped at her. "He told you that? How did he know?"

Tellie glowered. "I expect he's had a firm of private detectives on overtime, finding out everything they could about him. J.B. loves to have leverage if he has to go against people."

"He won't bother Grange," Marge said. "He just wants to make sure that the man isn't a threat to you."

"He wants to decide who I marry and how many kids I have," she returned coolly. "But he's not going to."

"That's the spirit, Tellie," Marge chuckled.

"All the same," Tellie replied, "I wish he wouldn't snub me. I'm beginning to feel like a ghost."

"He'll get over it."

"You think so? I wonder."

Saturday came, and Grange had something to do for Justin, so Tellie stayed home and helped Marge clean house.

A car drove up out front and two car doors slammed. Tellie was on her hands and knees in the kitchen, scrubbing the tile with a brush while Marge cleaned upstairs. J.B. walked in with a ravishing young blonde woman on his arm. She was tall and beautifully made, with a model-perfect face and teeth, and hair to her waist in back.

"I thought they abolished indentured servitude," J.B. drawled, looking pointedly at Tellie.

She looked up at him with cold eyes, pushing sweaty hair out of her eyes with the back of a dirty hand. "It's called housecleaning, J.B. I'm sure you have no idea what it consists of."

"Nell takes care of all that," he said. "This is Bella

Dean," he introduced the blonde, wrapping a long arm around her and smiling at her warmly.

"Nice to meet you," Tellie said, forcing a smile. "I'd shake hands, but I'm sure you'd rather not." She indicated her dirty hands.

Bella didn't answer her. She beamed up at J.B. "Didn't we come to take your sister and your nieces out to eat?" she asked brightly. "I'm sure the kitchen help doesn't need an audience."

Tellie got to her feet, slammed the brush down on the floor and walked right up to the blonde, who actually backed away.

"What would you know about honest work, lady, unless you call lying on your back, work…!"

"Tellie!" J.B. bit off.

The blonde gasped. "Well, I never!"

"I'll bet there's not much you've never," Tellie said coldly. "For your information, I don't work here. Marge gave me a home when my mother died, and I earn my keep. When I'm not scrubbing floors, I go to college to earn a degree, so that I can make a living for myself," she added pointedly. "I'm sure you won't ever have a similar problem, as long as your looks last."

"Tellie!" J.B. repeated.

"I'd rather be pretty than smart," the blonde said carelessly. "Who'd want to give you diamonds?" she scoffed.

Tellie balled a fist.

"Go tell Marge we're here," he demanded, his eyes making cold threats.

"Tell her yourself, J.B.," Tellie replied, eyes flashing. "I'm not anybody's servant."

She turned and left the room, so furious that she was shaking all over.

J.B. followed her right into her bedroom and closed the door behind them.

"What the hell was that all about?" he asked furiously.

"I am not going to be looked down on by any smarmy blonde tart!" she exclaimed.

"You behaved like a child!" he returned.

"She started it," she reminded him.

"She thought you were the housekeeper," he replied. "She didn't know you from a button."

"She'll know me next time, won't she?"

He moved closer, glaring at her. "You're so jealous you're vibrating with it," he accused, his green eyes narrowing. "You want me."

She drew in a sharp breath and her hands tightened into fists. "I do not," she retorted.

He moved a step closer, so that he was right up against her. His big hand went to her cheek, smoothing over it. His thumb rubbed maddeningly at her lower lip. "You want me," he whispered deeply, bending. "I can feel your heart beating. You ache for me to touch you."

"J.B., if...if you don't...stop," she faltered, fighting his arrogance and her own weakness.

"You don't want me to stop, baby," he murmured, his chiseled mouth poised just over her parted lips. "That's the last thing you want." His thumb tugged her lower lip down and he nibbled softly at the upper one. He heard her breath catch, felt her body shiver. His eyes began to glitter with something like triumph. "I can feel your heart beating. You're waking up. I could do anything I liked to you, whenever I pleased, and we both know it, Tellie."

A husky little moan escaped her tight throat and she moved involuntarily, her body brushing against his, her mouth lifting, pleading, her hands going to his hard upper arms to hold him there. She hated him for doing this to her, but she couldn't resist him.

He knew it. He laughed. He pulled away from her, arrogance in his whole bearing. He smiled, and it wasn't a nice smile at all. "She likes to kiss me, too, Tellie," he said deliberately. "But she's no prude. She likes to take her clothes off, and I don't even have to coax her…"

She slapped him. She was humiliated, hurt, furious. She put the whole weight of her arm behind it, sobbing.

He didn't even react, except to lift an eyebrow and smile even more arrogantly. "Next time I bring her over to see Marge, you'd better be more polite, Tellie," he warned softly, and the deep edge of anger glittered in his green eyes. "Or I'll do this in front of her."

Tellie was horrified at even the thought. Her face went pale. Tears brightened her eyes, but she would have died rather than shed them. "There aren't enough bad words in the English language to describe what you are, J.B.," she said brokenly.

"Oh, you'll think of some eventually, I'm sure. And if you can't, you can always give me another one of those god-awful dragon ties, can't you?"

"I bought boxes of them!" she slung at him.

He only laughed. He gave her a last probing look and went out of the room, leaving the door open behind him.

"Where have you been?" the blonde demanded in a honeyed tone.

"Just having a little overdue discussion. We'd better go. See you, Marge."

There were muffled voices. A door closed. Two car doors slammed. An engine roared.

Marge knocked gently and came into Tellie's room, her whole look apprehensive. She grimaced.

Tellie was as white as a sheet, shaking with rage and humiliation.

"I'll tell him not to bring her here again," Marge said firmly. She put her arms around Tellie and gathered her close. "It's all right."

"He's the devil in a suit," Tellie whispered huskily. "The very devil, Marge. I never, never want to see him again."

The thin arms closed around her and rocked her while she cried. Marge wondered why J.B. had to be so cruel to a woman who loved him this much. She had a good idea of what he'd done. It was unfair of him. He didn't want Tellie. Why couldn't he leave her alone? He'd brought his latest lover here deliberately. Tellie had refused to go to the barbecue, avoiding being around the woman, so J.B. had brought her over to Marge's to rub it in. He wanted Tellie to see how beautiful the woman was, how devoted she was to J.B. He was angry that he couldn't stop her from seeing Grange, not even by snubbing her. This was low, even for J.B.

"I don't know what's gotten into my brother," Marge said aloud. "But I'm very sorry, Tellie."

"It's not your fault. We don't get to choose our relatives, more's the pity."

"I wouldn't choose J.B. for a brother, after today." She drew away, her dark eyes twinkling, mischievous. "Tellie, the girls wouldn't let J.B. introduce them to his girlfriend. They gave her vicious looks, glared at J.B. and went to Dawn's room and locked themselves in. He's mad at them now, too."

"Good. Maybe he'll stay at his own house."

I wouldn't bet on that, Marge thought, but she didn't say it aloud. Tellie had stood enough for one day.

Grange took Tellie with him around the feedlot the next week, explaining how they monitored statistics and mixed the feed for the various lots of cattle. He'd asked Justin for permission. The older man was glad to give it. He liked the strange young man who'd come to work for him. It was a compliment, because Justin didn't like many people at all.

Grange propped one big booted foot on the bottom rail of one of the enclosures, with his arms folded on the top one. His dark eyes had a faraway look. "This is good country," he said. "I grew up in West Texas. Mostly we've got desert and cactus and mountains over around El Paso. This is green heaven."

"Yes, it is. I love it here," she confessed. "I go to school in Houston. It's green there, too, but the trees are nestled in concrete."

He chuckled. "Do you like college?"

"I do."

"I went myself, in the army."

"What did you study?"

He grinned at her. "Besides weapons and tactics, you mean?" He chuckled. "I studied political science."

She was surprised, and showed it. "That was your major?"

"Part of it. I did a double major, in political science and Arab dialects."

"You mean, you can speak Arabic?"

He nodded. "Farsi, Bedouin, several regional dialects. Well, and the Romance languages."

"All three of them?" she asked, surprised.

"All three." He glanced at her and smiled at her expression. "Languages will get you far in government service and the military. I mustered out as a major."

She tried not to let on that she'd heard about his release from the service. "Did you like the military?" she asked with deliberate carelessness.

He gave her a slow appraisal from dark, narrowed eyes. "Gossip travels fast in small towns, doesn't it?" he wondered aloud. "I expect Hammock had something to do with it."

She sighed. "Probably did," she had to admit. "He did everything he could to keep me from going out with you."

"So he holds grudges," he remarked. "Lucky for him that I don't, or he'd be sleeping with guards at every door and a gun under his pillow. If it hadn't been for him, I'd still have my sister."

"Maybe he thinks that, except for you, and his father, he'd be happily married with kids now."

He shrugged. "Nobody came out of it laughing," he said. He looked down at her, puzzled. "If he wanted you to stop going out with me, why haven't you?"

She smiled sadly. "I got tired of being a carpet," she said.

He cocked his head. "Walked all over you, did he?"

She nodded. "Since I was fourteen. And I let him. I never disagreed with anything he said, even when I didn't think he was right." She traced a pattern on the metal fence. "I saw what I could have become last Saturday. He brought his newest girlfriend over to show me. She thought I was the hired help and treated me accordingly. We had words. Lots of words. Now I'm not speaking to J.B."

He leaned back against the gate. "You may not believe it, but standing up to people is the only way to get through life with your mind intact. Nothing was ever gained by giving in."

"So that's how you left the army, is it?" she mused.

He laughed curtly. "Our commanding officer sent us against an enemy company, understrength, without proper body armor, with weapons that were misfiring. I took exception and he called me a name I didn't like. I decked him, wrapped him up in his blanket and gagged him, and led the attack myself. Tactics brought us all back alive. His way would have wiped us out to the last man. The brass didn't approve of my methods, so I had the choice of being honorably discharged or court-martialed. It was a close decision," he added with cold humor.

She just stared at him. "How could they do that? Send you into battle without proper equipment... That's outrageous!"

"Talk to Congress," he said coolly. "But don't expect them to do anything, unless it's an election year. Improvements cost money. We don't have enough."

She stared out over the distant pasture. "What happened to your commanding officer?"

"Oh, they promoted him," he said. "Called his tactics brilliant, in fact."

"But he didn't go, and they were your tactics!" she exclaimed.

He raised an eyebrow. "That's not what he told the brass."

She glowered. "Somebody should have told them!"

"In fact, just last week one of his execs got drunk enough to spill the beans to a reporter for one of the larger newspaper chains. A court-martial board is convening in the near future, or so I hear."

"Will they call you to testify?" she wondered.

He smiled. "God, I hope so," he replied.

She laughed at his expression. "Revenge is sweet?"

"So they tell me. Being of a naturally sweet and retiring disposition, I rarely ever cause problems...why are you laughing?"

She was almost doubled over. He was the last man she could picture that way.

"Maybe I caused a little trouble, once in a while," he had to admit. He glanced at his watch. "Lunch break's over. Better get back to work, so that Justin doesn't start looking for replacements."

"It was a nice lunch break, even if we didn't eat anything."

"I wasn't hungry. Sorry, I didn't think about food."

She smiled up at him. "Neither did I. We had a big breakfast this morning, and I was stuffed. Wouldn't you like to come over for pizza tonight?"

He hesitated. "I would, but I'm not going to."

"Why?"

"I'm not going to provide any more reasons for Hammock to take out old injuries on you."

"I'm not afraid of J.B."

"Neither am I," he agreed. "But let's give him time to calm down before we start any more trouble."

"I suppose we could," she agreed, but reluctantly. She didn't want J.B. to think she was bowing down to him.

The weekend went smoothly. J.B. and his blonde appendage were nowhere in sight, and neither was Grange. Tellie played Monopoly with Marge and the girls on

Saturday night, and went to church with them on Sunday morning.

Monday morning, Marge didn't get up for breakfast. Tellie took her a tray, worried because she seemed unusually pale and languorous.

"Just a little dizziness and nausea, Tellie," Marge protested with a wan smile. "I'll stay in bed and feel better. Really. The girls are here if I need help."

"You'd better call me if you do," she said firmly.

Marge smiled and nodded. Tellie noticed an odd rhythm in her heartbeat—it was so strong that it was shaking her nightgown. Nausea and an erratic heartbeat were worrisome symptoms. Tellie's grandfather had died of heart trouble, and she remembered the same symptoms in him.

She didn't make a big deal out of it, but she did put aside her hurt pride long enough to drive by J.B.'s office on the way to the feedlot.

He was talking to a visiting cattleman, but when he saw Tellie, he broke off the conversation politely and joined her in the outer office. He looked good in jeans and a chambray shirt and chaps, she thought, even if they were designer clothing. He was working today, not squiring around women.

"Couldn't stand it anymore, I gather?" he asked curtly. "You just had to come and see me and apologize?"

She frowned. "Excuse me?"

"It's about time," he told her. "But I'm busy today. You should have picked a better time."

"J.B., I need to talk to you," she began.

He gave her slender figure in the green pantsuit a curiously intent scrutiny, winding his way back up the modest neckline to her face, with only the lightest touch of makeup, and her wavy hair like a dark cap around her head. "On your way to work?"

"Yes," she said. "J.B., I have to tell you something…"

He took her arm and led her back outside to her car. "Later. I've got a full day. Besides," he added as he opened her car door, "you know I don't like to be chased. I like to do the chasing."

She let out an exasperated breath. "J.B., I'm not chasing you! If you'd just give me a chance to speak…!"

His eyes narrowed. "I don't like treating you like the enemy, but I also don't like the way you spoke to Bella. When you apologize, to her, we'll go from there."

"Apologize?"

His face hardened. "You took too much for granted. You aren't part of my family, and you aren't a lover. You can't treat my women like trespassers in my own sister's house. Maybe we were close, when you were younger, but that's over."

"She started it," she began, riled.

"She belongs with me. You don't." His eyes were hard. "I need more from a woman than a handshake at the end of the evening. That's as much as you're able to give, Tellie. You're completely unawakened."

She wondered what he was talking about. But she didn't have time to ponder enigmas. "Listen, Bella's not what I came here to talk about!"

"I'm not giving up Bella," he continued, as if she hadn't spoken. "And chasing after me like this isn't going to get you anything except the wrong side of my temper. Don't do it again."

"J.B.!"

He closed the door. "Go to work," he said shortly, and turned away.

Of all the arrogant, assuming, overbearing conceited jackasses, she thought as she reversed out of the parking space and took off toward town, he took the cake. She wasn't chasing him, she was trying to tell him about Marge! Well, she could try again later. Next time, she promised herself, she'd make him listen.

She walked in the front door after work, tired and dispirited. Maybe Marge was better, she hoped.

"Tellie, is that you?" Dawn exclaimed from the top of the staircase. "Come on up. Hurry, please!"

Tellie took the steps two at a time. Marge was lying on her back, gasping for breath, wincing with pain. Her face was a grayish tone, her skin cold and clammy.

"Heart attack," Tellie said at once. She'd seen this all before, with her grandfather. She grabbed the phone and dialed 911.

She tried to call J.B., but she couldn't get an answer on his cell phone, or on the phone at the office or his house. She waited until the ambulance loaded up Marge, and the girls went with her, to get into her car and drive to J.B.'s house. If she couldn't find him, she could at least get Nell to relay a message.

She leaped out of the car and ran to the front door. She tried the knob and found it unlocked. This was no time for formality. She opened it and ran down the hall to J.B.'s study. She threw open the door and stopped dead in the doorway.

J.B. looked up, over Bella's bare white shoulders, his face flushed, his mouth swollen, his shirt off.

"What the hell are you doing here?" he demanded furiously.

Six

Tellie could barely get her breath. Worried about Marge, half-sick with fear, she couldn't even manage words. No wonder J.B. couldn't be bothered to answer the phone. He and his beautiful girlfriend were half-naked. Apparently J.B. wasn't much on beds for his sensual adventures. She remembered with heartache that he'd wrestled her down on that very sofa when she was eighteen and kissed her until her mouth hurt. It had been the most heavenly few minutes of her entire life, despite the fact that he'd been furious when he started kissing her. It hadn't ended that way, though…

"Get out!" J.B. threw at her.

She managed to get her wits back. Marge. She had to think about Marge, not about how much her pride was hurting. "J.B., you have to listen…"

"Get out, damn you!" he raged. "I've had it up to here

with you chasing after me, pawing me, trying to get close to me! I don't want you, Tellie, how many times do I have to tell you before you realize that I mean it? You're a stray that Marge and I took in, nothing more! I don't want you, and I never will!"

Her heart was bursting with raw pain. She hoped she wouldn't pass out. She knew her face was white. She wanted to move, to leave, but her feet felt frozen to the carpet.

Her tormented expression and lack of response seemed to make him worse. "You skinny, ugly little tomboy," he raged, white hot with fury. "Who'd want something like you for keeps? Get out, I said!"

She gave up. She turned away, slowly, aware of the gloating smile on Bella's face, and closed the door behind her. Her knees barely gave her support as she walked back toward the front door.

Nell was standing by the staircase, drying her hands on her apron, looking shocked. "What in the world is all the yelling about?" she exclaimed. She hesitated when she saw the younger woman's drawn, white face. "Tellie, what's wrong?" she asked gently.

Tellie fought for composure. "Marge…is on her way to the hospital in an ambulance, with the girls. I think it's a heart attack. I couldn't make J.B. listen. He's…I walked in on him and that woman… He yelled at me and said I was chasing him, and called me horrible names…!" She swallowed hard and drew herself erect. "Please tell him we'll all be at the hospital, if he can tear himself loose long enough!"

She turned toward the door.

"Don't you drive that car unless you're all right, Tellie," Nell said firmly. "It's pouring down rain."

"I'm fine," she said in a ghostly tone. She even forced a smile. "Tell him, okay?"

"I'll tell him," Nell said angrily. Her voice softened. "Don't worry, honey. Marge is one tough cookie. She'll be all right. You just drive carefully. You ought to wait and go with him," she added slowly.

"If I got in a car with him right now, I'd kill him," Tellie said through her teeth. Helpless tears were rolling down her pale cheeks. "See you later, Nell."

"Tellie…"

It was too late. Tellie closed the door behind her and went to her car. She was getting soaked and she didn't care. J.B. had said terrible things to her. She knew that she'd never get over them. He wanted her to stop chasing him. She hadn't been, but it must have looked like it. She'd gone to his office this morning, and to the house this afternoon. It was about Marge. He wouldn't believe it, though. He thought Tellie was desperate for him. That was a joke, now. She was sure that she never wanted to see him again as long as she lived.

She started the car and turned it. The tires were slick. She hadn't realized how slick until she almost spun out going down the driveway. She needed to keep her speed down, but she wasn't thinking rationally. She was hearing J.B. yell at her that she was an ugly stray he'd taken in, that he didn't want her. Tears misted her eyes as she tried to concentrate on the road.

There was a hairpin curve just before the ranch road met the highway. It was usually easy to maneuver, but the rain was coming so hard and fast that the little car suddenly hydroplaned. She saw the ditch coming toward her and jerked the wheel as hard as she could. In a daze, she felt the car go over and over and over. Her seat belt broke and something hit her head. Everything went black.

J.B. stormed out of the study just seconds after he heard Tellie's little car scatter gravel as it sped away. His hair was mussed, like his shirt, and he was in a vicious humor. It had been a bad day altogether. He shouldn't have yelled at Tellie. But he wondered why she'd come barging in. He should have asked. It was just that it had shamed him to be seen in such a position with Bella, knowing painfully how Tellie felt about him. He'd hurt her with just the sight of him and Bella, without adding his scathing comments afterward. Tellie wouldn't even realize that shame had put him on the offensive. She had feelings of glass, and he'd shattered them.

Nell was waiting for him at the foot of the staircase. She was visibly seething, and her white hair almost stood on end with bridled rage. "So you finally came out, did you?"

"Tellie was tearing up the driveway as she left," he bit off. "What the hell got into her? Why was she here?" he added reluctantly, because he'd realized, belatedly, that she hadn't looked as if she were pursuing him with amorous intent.

Nell gave him a cold smile. "She couldn't get you on the phone, so she drove over to tell you that Marge has had a heart attack." She nodded curtly when she saw him turn pale. "That's right. She wasn't here chasing you. She wanted you to know about your sister."

"Oh, God," he bit off.

"*He* won't help you," Nell ground out. "Yelling at

poor Tellie like that, when she was only trying to do you a good turn…!"

"Shut up," he snapped angrily. "Call the hospital and see…"

"You call them." She took off her apron. "You've got my two weeks' notice, as of right now. I'm sick of watching you torture Tellie. I quit! See if your harpy girlfriend in there can cook your meals and clean your house while she spends you into the poorhouse!"

"Nell," he began furiously.

She held up a hand. "I won't reconsider."

The living room door opened, and Bella slinked into the hallway, smiling contentedly. "Aren't we going out to eat?" she asked J.B. as she moved to catch him by one arm.

"I'm going to the hospital," he said. "My sister's had a heart attack."

"Oh, that's too bad," Bella said. "Do you want me to go with you and hold your hand?"

"The girls will love that," Nell said sarcastically. "You'll be such a comfort to them!"

"Nell!" J.B. fumed.

"She's right, I'd be a comfort, like she said," Bella agreed, missing the sarcasm altogether. "You need me, J.B."

"I hope he gets what he really needs one day," Nell said, turning on her heel.

"You're fired!" he yelled after her.

"Too late, I already quit," Nell said pleasantly. "I'm sure Bella can cook you some supper and wash your clothes." She closed the kitchen door behind her with a snap.

"Now, you know I can't cook, J.B.," Bella said irritably. "And I've never washed clothes—I send mine to the laundry. What's the matter with her? It's that silly girl who was here, isn't it? I don't like her at all…"

J.B. reached into his pocket and pulled out two large bills. "Call a cab and go home," he said shortly. "I have to get to the hospital."

"But I should go with you," she argued.

He looked down at her with bridled fury. "Go home."

She shifted restlessly. "Well, all right, J.B., you don't need to yell. Honestly, you're in such a bad mood!"

"My sister has had a heart attack," he repeated.

"Yes, I know, but those things happen, don't they? You can't do anything about it," she added blankly.

It was like talking to a wall, he thought with exasperation. He tucked in his shirt, checked to make sure his car keys were in his pocket, jerked his raincoat and hat from the hall coatrack and went out the door without a backward glance.

Dawn and Brandi were pacing the waiting room in the emergency room at Jacobsville General Hospital while Dr. Coltrain examined their mother. They were quiet, somber, with tears pouring down their cheeks in silent misery when J.B. walked in.

They ran to him the instant they saw him, visibly shaken. He gathered them close, feeling like an animal because he hadn't even let Tellie talk when she'd walked in on him. She'd come to tell him that Marge was in the hospital with a heart attack, and he'd sent her running with insults. Probably she'd come to his office that morning because something about Marge had worried her. He'd been no help at all. Now Tellie was hurt and Nell was quitting. He'd never felt so helpless.

"Mama won't die, will she, Uncle J.B.?" Brandi asked tearfully.

"Of course she won't," he assured her in the deep, soft tone he used with little things or hurt children. "She'll be fine."

"Tellie said she was going to tell you about Mama. Why didn't Tellie come with you?" Dawn asked, wiping her eyes.

He stiffened. "Tellie's not here?"

"No. She had to go over to your house, because you didn't answer your phone," Brandi replied. "I guess the lines were down or something."

"Or something," he said huskily. He'd taken the phone off the hook.

"She may have gone home to get Mama a gown," Dawn suggested. "She always thinks of things like that, when everybody else goes to pieces."

"She'll be here as soon as she can...I know she will," Brandi agreed. "I don't know what we'd do without Tellie."

Which made J.B. feel even smaller than he already did. Tellie must be scared to death. She'd been with her grandfather when he died of a heart attack. She'd loved him more than any other member of her small family, including the mother she'd lost more recently. Marge's heart attack would bring back terrible memories. Worse, when she showed up at the hospital, she'd have to deal with what J.B. had said to her. It wasn't going to be a pleasant reunion.

Dr. Coltrain came out, smiling. "Marge is going to be all right," he told them. "We got to her just in time. But she'll have to see a heart specialist, and she's going to be on medication from now on. Did you know that her blood pressure was high?"

"No!" J.B. said at once. "It's always been low!"

Coltrain shook his head. "Not anymore. She's very lucky that it happened like this. It may have saved her life."

"It was a heart attack, then?" J.B. persisted, with the girls standing close at his side.

"Yes. But a mild one. You can see her when we've got her in a room. You'll need to sign her in at the office."

"I'll do that right now."

"But, where's Tellie?" Dawn asked when they were alone.

J.B. wished he knew.

He was on his way back from the office when he passed the emergency room, just in time to see a worried Grange stalking in beside a gurney that two paramedics were rushing through the door. On the stretcher was Tellie, unconscious and bleeding.

"Tellie!" he exclaimed, rushing to the gurney. She was white as a sheet, and he was more frightened now than he was when he learned about Marge. "What happened?" he shot at Grange.

"I don't know," Grange said curtly. "Her car was off the road in a ditch. She was unconscious, in a couple of inches of water, facedown. If I hadn't come along when I did, she'd have drowned."

J.B. felt sick all the way to his soul. It was his fault. All his fault. "Where was the car?" he asked.

"On the farm road that leads to your house," Grange replied, his eyes narrowed, suspiciously. "Why are you here?"

"My sister just had a heart attack," he said solemnly. "The girls and I have been in the emergency waiting room. She's going to be all right. Tellie came to tell me about it," he added reluctantly.

"Then why in hell didn't she ride in with you?" Grange asked, brown eyes flashing. "She must have been upset—she loves Marge. She shouldn't even have been driving in weather this dangerous."

That was a question J.B. didn't want to touch. He ignored it, following the gurney into one of the examination rooms with Grange right on his heels.

He got one of Tellie's small hands in both of his and held on tight. "Tellie," he said huskily, feeling the pain all the way to his boots. "Tellie, hold on!"

"She shouldn't have been driving," Grange repeated, leaning against the wall nearby. He was obviously upset as well, and the look he gave J.B. would have started a fight under better circumstances.

The entrance of Copper Coltrain interrupted him.

Copper gave J.B. an odd look. "It isn't your day, is it?" he asked, moving to Tellie's side. "What happened?"

"Her car hydroplaned, apparently," Grange said tautly. "I found it overturned. She was lying facedown in a ditch full of water. If I'd been just a little later, she'd have drowned."

"Damn the luck!" Coltrain muttered, checking her pupil reaction with a small penlight. "She's concussed as well as bruised," he murmured. "I'm going to need X-rays and a battery of tests to see how badly she's hurt. But the concussion is the main thing."

J.B. felt sick. One of his men had been kicked in the head by a mean steer and dropped dead of a massive concussion. "Can't you do something now?" he raged at Coltrain.

The physician gave him an odd look. It was notorious gossip locally that Tellie was crazy about J. B. Hammock, and that J.B. paid her as little attention as possible. The white-faced man with blazing green eyes facing him didn't seem disinterested.

"What would you suggest?" he asked J.B. curtly.

"Wake her up!"

Grange made a rough sound in his throat.

"You can shut up," J.B. told him icily. "You're not a doctor."

"Neither are you," Grange returned with the same lack of warmth. "And if you'd given her a lift to the hospital, she wouldn't need one, would she?"

J.B. had already worked that out for himself. His lips compressed furiously.

Tellie groaned.

Both men moved to the examination table at the same time. Coltrain gave them angry looks and bent to examine Tellie.

"Can you hear me?" he asked her softly. "Tellie?"

Her eyes opened, green and dazed. She blinked and winced. "My head hurts."

"I'm not surprised," Coltrain murmured, busy with a stethoscope. "Take a deep breath. Let it out. Again."

She groaned. "My head hurts," she repeated.

"Okay, I'll give you something for it. But we need X-rays and an MRI," Coltrain said quietly. "Anything hurt besides your head?"

"Everything," she replied. "What happened?"

"You wrecked your car," Grange said quietly.

She looked up at him. "You found me?"

He nodded, dark eyes concerned.

She managed a smile. "Thanks." She shivered. "I'm wet!"

"It was pouring rain," Grange said, his voice soft, like his eyes. He brushed back the blood-matted hair from her forehead, disclosing a growing dark bruise. He winced.

"You're concussed, Tellie," Dr. Coltrain said. "We're going to have to keep you for a day or two. Okay?"

"But I'll miss graduation!" she exclaimed, trying to sit up.

He gently pushed her back down. "No, you won't," he said with a quizzical smile.

She blinked, glancing at J.B., who looked very worried. "But it's May. I'm a senior. I have a white gown and cap." She hesitated. "Was I driving Marge's car?"

"No. Your own," J.B. said slowly, apprehensively.

"But I don't have a car, don't you remember, J.B.?" she asked pleasantly. "I have to drive Marge's. She's going to help me buy a car this summer, because I'm going to work at the Sav-A-Lot Grocery Store, remember?"

J.B.'s indrawn breath was audible. Before the other two men could react, he pressed Tellie's small hand closer in his own. "Tellie, how old are you?" he asked.

"I'm seventeen, you know that," she scoffed.

Coltrain whistled. J.B. turned to him, his lips parted in the preliminary to a question.

"We're going to step outside and discuss how to break it to Marge," Coltrain told her gently. "You just rest. I'll send a nurse in with something for your headache, okay?"

"Okay," she agreed. "J.B., you aren't leaving, are you?" she added worriedly.

Coals of fire, he was thinking, as he assured her that

he'd be nearby. She relaxed and smiled as she lay back on the examination table.

Coltrain motioned the other two men outside into the hall. "Amnesia," he told J.B. at once. "I'm sure it's temporary," he added quickly. "It isn't uncommon with head injuries. She's very confused, and in some pain. I'll run tests. We'll do an MRI to make sure."

"The head injury would cause it?" Grange asked worriedly.

J.B. had a flush along his high cheekbones. He didn't speak.

Coltrain gave him a curious look. "The brain tends to try to protect itself from trauma, and not only physical trauma. Has she had a shock of some kind?" he asked J.B. pointedly.

J.B. replied with a curt jerk of his head. "We had a… misunderstanding at the house," he admitted.

Grange's dark eyes flashed. "Well, that explains why she wrecked the car!" he accused.

J.B. glared at him. "Like hell it does…!"

Coltrain held up a hand. "Arguing isn't going to do her any good. She's had the wreck, now we have to deal with the consequences. I'm going to admit her and start running tests."

J.B. drew a quick breath. "How are we going to explain this to Tellie?"

Coltrain sighed. "Tell her as little as possible, right now. Once she's stabilized, we'll tell her what we have to. But if she thinks she's seventeen, sending her to Marge's house is going to be traumatic—she'll expect the girls to be four years younger than they are, won't she?"

J.B. was thinking, hard. He saw immediately a way to solve that problem and prevent Nell from escaping at once. "She can stay at the house with Nell and me," he said. "She and Marge and the girls did stay there when she was seventeen for a couple of weeks while Marge's house was being remodeled. We can tell her that Marge and the girls are having a vacation while workmen tend to her house. I'll make it right with Dawn and Brandi."

"You and Tellie were close when she was in her teens, I recall," Coltrain recalled.

"Yes," J.B. said tautly.

Coltrain chuckled, glancing at Grange. "She followed him around like a puppy when she first went to live with Marge," he told the other man. "You couldn't talk to J.B. without tripping over Tellie. J.B. was her security blanket after she lost her mother."

"She was the same way with Marge," J.B. muttered.

"Not to that extent, she wasn't," Coltrain argued. "She thought the sun rose and set on you…"

"I need to go back and check on Marge," J.B. interrupted, visibly uncomfortable.

"I'll stay with Tellie for a while," Grange said, moving back into the examination room before the other two men could object.

J.B. stared after him with bridled fury, his hands deep in his pockets, his eyes smoldering. "He's got no business in there," he told Coltrain. "He isn't even family!"

"Neither are you," the doctor reminded him.

J.B. glared at him. "Are you sure she'll be all right?"

"As sure as I can be." He studied the other man intently. "You said something to her, something that hurt, didn't you?" he asked, nodding when J.B.'s high cheekbones took on a ruddy color. "She's hiding in the past, when you were less resentful of her. She'll get her memory back, but it's going to be dangerous to rush it. You have to let her move ahead at her own pace."

"I'll do that," J.B. assured him. He drew in a long breath. "Damn. I feel as if my whole life crashed and burned today. First Marge, now Tellie. And Nell quit," he added angrily.

"Nell?" Coltrain exclaimed. "She's been there since you were a boy."

"Well, she wants to leave," J.B. muttered. "But she'll stay if she knows Tellie's coming to the house. I'd better phone her. Then I'll go back to Marge's room." He met Coltrain's eyes. "If she needs anything, *anything*, I'll take care of it. I don't think she's got any health insurance at all."

"You might stop by the admissions office and set things up," Coltrain suggested. "But I'll do what needs doing, finances notwithstanding. You know that."

"I do. Thanks, Copper."

Coltrain shrugged. "I'm glad she's rallying," he said. "And Marge, too."

"Same here."

J.B. left him to go back to the admissions office and sign Tellie in. He felt guilty. Her wreck was certainly his fault. The least he could do was provide for her treatment. He hated knowing that he'd upset her that much, and for nothing. She was only trying to help. Frustration had taken its toll on him and driven him into Bella's willing arms. The last thing he'd expected was for Tellie to walk in on them. He'd never been quite so ashamed of himself. Which was, of course, no excuse to take his temper out on her. He wished he could take back all the things he'd said. While her memory was gone, at least he had a chance to regain her trust and make up, a little, for what he'd done.

Tellie felt drained by the time Coltrain had all the tests he wanted. She was curious about the man who'd told her that he found her in the wrecked car and called the ambulance. He was handsome and friendly and seemed to like her very much, but she didn't know him.

"It was very kind of you to rescue me," she told Grange when she was in a private room.

He shrugged. "My pleasure." He smiled at her, his dark eyes twinkling. "You can save me, next time."

She laughed. Her head cocked to one side as she studied him. "I'm sorry, but I don't remember your name."

"Grange," he said pleasantly.

"Just Grange?" she queried.

He nodded.

"Have I known you a long time?"

He shook his head. "But I've taken you out a few times."

Her eyebrows lifted. "And J.B. let me go with you?" she exclaimed. "That's very strange. I wanted to go hiking with a college boy I knew and he threw a fit. You're older than any college boy."

He chuckled. "I'm twenty-seven," he told her.

"Wow," she mused.

"You're old for your age," he said, evading her eyes. "J.B. and I know each other."

"I see." She didn't, but he was obviously reluctant to talk about it. "Marge hasn't been to see me," she added suddenly. "That's not like her."

Grange recalled what J.B. and Coltrain had discussed.

"Her house is being remodeled," he said. "She and the girls are on a vacation trip."

"While school's in session?" she exclaimed.

He thought fast. "It's Spring Break, remember?"

She was confused. Hadn't someone said it was May? Wasn't Spring Break in March? "But graduation is coming up very soon."

"You got your cap and gown early, didn't you?" he improvised.

She was frowning. "That must be what happened. I'm so confused," she murmured, holding her head. "And my head absolutely throbs."

"They'll give you something for that." He checked his watch. "I have to go. Visiting hours are over."

"Will you come back tomorrow?" she asked, feeling deserted.

He smiled. "Of course I will." He hesitated. "It will have to be during my lunch hour, or after work, though."

"Where do you work?"

"At the Ballenger feedlot."

That set off bells in her head, but she couldn't think why. "They're nice, Justin and Calhoun."

"Yes, they are." He stood up, moving the chair back from her bed. "Take care. I'll see you tomorrow."

"Okay. Thanks again."

He looked at her for a long time. "I'm glad it wasn't more serious than it is," he told her. "You were unconscious when I found you."

"It was raining," she recalled hesitantly. "I don't understand why I was driving in the rain. I'm afraid of it, you know."

"Are you?"

She shook her head. "I must have had a reason."

"I'm sure you did." He looked thunderous, but he quickly erased the expression, smiled and left her.

She settled back into the pillow, feeling bruised and broken. It was such an odd experience, what had happened to her. Everyone seemed to be holding things back from her. She wondered how badly she was damaged. Tomorrow, she promised herself, she'd dig it out of J.B.

Seven

Tellie woke up early, expecting to find herself alone. But J.B. was sprawled in the chair next to the bed, snoring faintly, and he looked as if he'd been there for some time. A nurse was tiptoeing around to get Tellie's vitals, sending amused and interested glances at the long, lean cowboy beside the bed.

"Has he been there long?" Tellie wanted to know.

"Since daybreak," the nurse replied with a smile. She put the electronic thermometer in Tellie's ear, let it beep, checked it and wrote down a figure. She checked her pulse and recorded that, as well. "I understand the nurse on the last shift tried to evict him and the hospital administrator actually came down here in person to tell her to cease and desist." She gave Tellie a speaking glance. "I gather that your visitor is somebody very important."

"He paid for that MRI machine they used on me yesterday."

The nurse pursed her lips. "Well! Aren't you nicely connected?" she mused. "Is he your fiancé?"

Tellie chuckled. "I'm only seventeen," she said.

The nurse looked puzzled. She checked Tellie's chart, made a face and then forced a smile. "Of course. Sorry."

Tellie wondered why she looked so confused. "Can I go home today?" she wondered.

"That depends on what Dr. Coltrain thinks," she replied. "He'll be in to see you when he makes rounds. Breakfast will be up shortly."

"Thanks," Tellie told her.

The nurse smiled, cast another curious and appreciative glance at J.B. and left.

Tellie stared at him with mixed emotions. He was a handsome man, she thought, but at least she was safe from all that masculine charm that he used to such good effect on women he liked. She was far too young to be threatened by J.B.'s sex appeal.

It was easy to see why he had women flocking around him. He had a dynamite physique, hard and lean and sexy, with long, powerful legs and big hands. His face was rugged, but he had fine green eyes under a jutting brow and a mouth that was as hard and sensuous as any movie star's. But it wasn't just his looks that made him attractive. It was his voice, deep and faintly raspy, and the way he had of making a woman feel special. He had beautiful manners when he cared to display them, and a temper that made grown men look for cover. Tellie had rarely seen him fighting mad. Most of the time he had excellent self-control.

She frowned. Why did it sting to think of him losing his temper? He'd rarely lost it at Tellie, and even then it was for her own good. But something about her thoughts made her uneasy.

Just as she was focusing on that, J.B. opened his eyes and looked at her, and she stopped thinking. Her heart jumped. She couldn't imagine why. She was possessive of J.B., she idolized him, but she'd never really considered anything physical between them. Now, her body seemed to know things her mind didn't.

"How do you feel?" he asked quietly.

She blinked. "My head doesn't hurt as much," she said. She searched his eyes. "Why are you here? I'm all right."

He shrugged. "I was worried." He didn't add that he was also guilt ridden about the reason for the wreck and her injury. His conscience had him on the rack. He couldn't sleep for worrying about her. That was new. It was disconcerting. He'd never let a woman get under his skin since his ill-fated romance of years past. Even an unexpected interlude with Tellie on the sofa in his office hadn't made a lot of difference in their turbulent relationship, especially when he realized that Tellie was sexually unawakened. He'd deliberately pushed her out of his life and kept her at arm's length—well, mostly, except for unavoidable lapses when he gave in to the passion riding him. That passion had drawn him to Bella in a moment of weakness.

Then Tellie had walked in on him with Bella, and his whole life had changed. He'd never felt such pain as when Grange had walked into the emergency room with an unconscious Tellie on a gurney. Nothing was ever going to be the same again. The only thing worse than seeing her in such a condition was dreading the day when her memory returned, because she was going to hate J.B.

"I'm going to be fine," she promised, smiling. "Do you think Dr. Coltrain will let me go home today?"

"I'll ask him," he said, sitting up straighter. "Nell's getting a room ready for you. While Marge and the girls are away, you'll stay with Nell and me."

"I wish Marge was here," she said involuntarily.

He sighed. Marge was improving, too, but she was worried about Tellie. Dawn had let it slip that she'd been in a wreck, but J.B. had assured her that Tellie was going to be fine. There was this little problem with her memory, of course, and she'd have to stay at the house with him until it came back.

Marge was reassured, but still concerned. He knew that she'd sensed something was wrong between her brother and Tellie, but she couldn't put it into words. He wasn't about to enlighten her. He had enough on his plate.

"I'll be in the way there," she protested.

"You won't," he replied. "Nell will be glad of the company."

She studied her hands on the sheet. "There's something that bothers me, J.B.," she said without looking at him.

"What?"

She hesitated. "What was I doing at your house, at night, in the rain?"

He sat very still. He hadn't considered that the question would arise so soon. He wasn't sure how to answer it, to protect her from painful memories.

She looked up and met his turbulent green eyes. "You were mad at me, weren't you?"

His heart seemed to stop, then start again. "We had an argument," he began slowly.

She nodded. "I thought so. But I can't remember what it was about."

"Time enough for that when you're back on your feet," he said, rising up from the chair. "Don't borrow trouble. Just get well."

So there was something! She wished she could grasp what it was. J.B. was acting very oddly.

She looked up at him. "You leaving?" she asked.

He nodded. "I've got to get the boys started moving the bulls to summer pasture."

"Not on roundup?"

"Roundup's in March," he said easily.

"Oh." She frowned. It wasn't March. She knew it wasn't. "Is it March?"

He ignored that. "I'll talk to Coltrain on my way out," he said.

"But it's not time for rounds…"

"I met him coming in. He had an emergency surgery. I expect he's through by now," he replied.

"J.B., who is that man Grange?" she asked abruptly. "And why did you let me go out with him? He said he's twenty-seven, and I'm just seventeen. You had a hissy fit when I tried to go hiking with Billy Johns."

He looked indignant. "I don't have hissy fits," he said shortly.

"Well, you raged at me, anyway," she corrected. "Why are you letting me see Grange?"

His teeth set. "You're full of questions this morning."

"Answer a few of them," she invited.

"Later," he said, deliberately checking his watch. "I have to get to work. Want me to bring you anything?"

"A nail file and a ladder," she said with resignation. "Just get me out of here."

"The minute you're fit to leave," he promised. He smiled faintly. "Stay put until I get back."

"If I must," she sighed.

He was gone and she was left to eat breakfast and while away the next few hours until Dr. Coltrain showed up.

He examined Tellie and pronounced her fit to leave the hospital.

"But you still need to take it easy for a week or two," he told her. "Stay out of crowds, stick to J.B.'s house. No parties, no job, nothing."

She frowned. "I thought it was just a mild concussion," she argued.

"It is." He didn't quite meet her eyes. "We're just not taking chances. You need lots of rest."

She sighed. "Okay, if you say so. Can I go horseback riding, can I swim…?"

"Sure. Just don't leave J.B.'s ranch to do them."

She smiled. "What's going on, Dr. Coltrain?"

He leaned forward. "It's a secret," he told her. "Bear with me. Okay?"

She laughed. "Okay. When do I get to know the secret?"

"All in good time," he added, as inspiration struck him. "Keep an eye on J.B. for me."

Her eyebrows arched. "Is something wrong with him…?" she asked worriedly.

"Nothing specific. Just watch him."

She shook her head. "Okay. If you say so."

"Good girl." He patted her shoulder and left, congratulating himself on the inspiration. While she was focused on J.B., she wouldn't be preoccupied with her own health. Far better if she licked the amnesia all by herself. He didn't want her shocked with the truth of her condition.

J.B.'s house was bigger than Tellie remembered. Nell met them at the door, all smiles and welcome.

"It's so good to have you back," Nell said, hugging the younger woman. "I've got a nice room all ready for you."

"Don't think you're going to get to wait on me," Tellie informed her with a grin. "I'm not an invalid."

"You have a concussion," Nell corrected, and the smile faded. "It can be very dangerous. I remember a cowboy who worked here…"

"Remember us something to eat, instead," J.B. interrupted her, with a meaningful look.

"Oh. Of course." She glared at J.B. "You had a call while you were out. I wrote the information on the pad on your desk."

He read through the lines and assumed it was from Bella. "I'll take care of it."

"Who's bringing Tellie's suitcase?" Nell asked.

J.B. stood still. "What suitcase?"

"I'll have to go over to Marge's and get my things," Tellie began.

"I'll go—!"

"I can do that," J.B. interrupted Nell. "You look after Tellie."

"When haven't I?" Nell wanted to know belligerently.

"You two need to stop arguing, or I'm going to go sit on the front porch," Tellie told both of them.

They glared at each other. J.B. shrugged and went into his den. Tellie's eyes followed him past the big sofa. The sofa… She frowned. Something about that sofa made her uneasy.

"What's wrong?" Nell prompted.

Tellie put a hand to her forehead and laughed faintly. "I don't know. I looked at the sofa and felt funny."

"Let's go right up and get you settled," Nell said abruptly, taking Tellie by the arm. "Then I'll see about some lunch."

It was almost as if Nell knew something about the sofa, too, but that would be ridiculous, Tellie told herself. She was getting mental.

She'd wanted to watch television, but there wasn't one in the bedroom. Nell told her that there was a problem with the satellite dish and it wasn't working. Odd, Tellie thought, it was almost as if they were trying to keep her from watching the news.

She had to stay in bed, because Nell insisted. Just after she had supper on a tray, J.B. walked in, worn and dusty, still in his working clothes.

Tellie was propped up in bed in pink-striped pajamas that made her look oddly vulnerable.

"How's it going?" he asked.

"I'm okay. Why is the satellite not working?" she added. "I can't watch The Weather Channel."

His eyebrows arched. "Why do you want to?"

"You said it was March, but Nell says it's May," she said. "That's tornado season."

"So it is."

She glowered at him. "Grange said it was March and Marge and the girls were away on Spring Break."

He pursed his lips.

"I know better, so don't bother trying to lie," she told him firmly. "If it's May, where are they?"

He leaned against the doorjamb. "They're around, but you can't see them just yet. Nothing's wrong."

"That's not true, J.B.," she said flatly.

He laughed mirthlessly and twirled his hat through his fingers. "No use trying to fool you, is it? Okay, the concussion did something to your head. You're a little fuzzy about things. We're supposed to let your mind clear without any help."

She frowned. "What's fuzzy about it?"

He jerked away from the door. "Not tonight. I'm going to clean up, then I've got…someplace to go," he amended.

"A date," she translated, grinning.

There was faint jealousy in her expression, but she was hiding it very well. He felt uncomfortable. He was taking Bella out, and here was Tellie, badly injured on his account and hurting.

"I could postpone it," he began guiltily.

"Whatever for?" she exclaimed.

His eyebrows arched. "Excuse me?"

"I'm seventeen," she pointed out. "Even if I were crazy about you, it's obvious that you're far too old for me."

He felt odd inside. He studied her curiously. "Am I?"

"I still don't understand why you're letting Grange date me," she mused. "He's twenty-seven."

"Is he?" He considered that. Grange was seven years his junior, closer to Tellie's own age than he was. That stung.

"You're hedging, J.B.," she accused.

He checked his watch. "Maybe so. I've got to go. Nell will be here if you need anything."

"I won't."

He turned to go, hesitated, and looked back at her, brooding. If she tried the television sets, she'd discover that they all worked. "Don't wander around the house."

She gaped at him. "Why would I want to?"

"Just don't. I'll see you tomorrow."

She watched him go, curious about his odd behavior.

Later, she tried to pump Nell for information, but it was like talking to a wall. "You and J.B. are stonewalling me," she accused.

Nell smiled. "For a good cause. Just relax and enjoy being here, for the time that's left." She picked up the empty iced-tea glass on the bedside table, looking around the room. "Odd that J.B. would put you in here," she said, thinking aloud.

"Is it? Why?"

"It was his grandmother's room," she said with a smile. "She was a wonderful old lady. J.B. adored her. She'd been an actress in Hollywood in her youth. She could tell some stories!"

"Does he talk about her?" Tellie wondered.

"Almost never. She died in a tornado." She nodded, at Tellie's astonished look. "That's right, one of the worst in south Texas history hit here," she recalled. "It lifted the barn off its foundations and twisted it. His grandmother's favorite horse was trapped there, and old Mrs. Hammock put on a raincoat and rushed out to try to save it. Nobody saw her go. The tornado picked her up and put her in the top of an oak tree, dead. They had to get a truck with a cherry picker to get her down, afterward,"

Nell said softly. "J.B. was watching. He hates tornadoes to this day. It's why we have elaborate storm shelters here and in the bunkhouse, and even under the barn."

"That's why he looked funny, when I mentioned liking to watch The Weather Channel," she said slowly.

"He watches it religiously in the spring and summer," Nell confided. "And he has weather alert systems in the same places he has the shelters. All his men have cell phones with alert capability. He's something of a fanatic about safety."

"Have I ever been in a tornado?" she asked Nell.

Nell looked surprised. "Why do you ask?"

"J.B. said I'm fuzzy about the past," she replied. "I gather that I've lost some memories, is that it?"

Nell came and sat down in the chair beside the bed. "Yes. You have."

"And the doctor doesn't want me remembering too soon?"

"He thinks it's better if you remember all on your own," Nell said. "So we're conspiring to keep you in the dark, so to speak," she added with a gentle smile.

Tellie frowned. "I wish I could remember what I've forgotten."

Nell burst out laughing. "Don't rush it. When you remember, we'll leave together."

Tellie gaped at her. "You're quitting? But you've been here forever!"

"I've been here too long," Nell said curtly, rising. "There are other bosses who don't yell and threaten people."

"You yell and threaten back," Tellie reminded her.

"Remembered that, did you?" she teased.

"Yes. So why are you leaving him?"

"Let's just say that I don't like his methods," she replied. "And that's all you're getting out of me. I'll be in the kitchen. Just use the intercom if you need me, okay?"

"Okay. Thanks, Nell."

Nell smiled at her. "I like having you here."

"Who's he dating this week?" Tellie called after her.

"Another stacked blonde, of course," came the dry reply. "She has the IQ of a lettuce leaf."

Tellie chuckled. "Obviously he doesn't like competition from mere women."

"Someday he'll come a cropper," she said. "I hope I live to see the day."

Tellie watched her close the door with faint misgivings. J.B. did like variety, she seemed to know that. But there was something about the reference, about a blonde woman, that unsettled her. Why had she and J.B. argued? She wished she could remember.

Her light was still on when he came home. She was reading a particularly interesting book that she'd found in the bookcase, an autobiography by Libbie Custer, the woman who'd married General George Custer of Civil War and Little Bighorn fame. It was a tale of courage in the face of danger, unexpectedly riveting. Mrs. Custer, it seemed, had actually gone with her husband to the battlefield during the Civil War. Tellie had never read of women doing that. Mrs. Custer was something of a renegade for her oppressed generation, a daring and intelligent woman with a keen wit. She liked her.

J.B. opened the door to find her propped up in bed on her pillows with the book resting against her upraised knees under the covers.

"What are you doing up at this hour?" he asked sternly.

She glanced at him, still halfway in the book she was reading. He looked elegant in a dinner jacket and black tie, she thought, although the tie was in his hand and the shirt was open at the throat, over a pelt of dark hair. She frowned. Why did the sight of his bare chest make her heart race?

"I found this book on the shelf and couldn't put it down," she said.

He moved to the bed, stuck the tie in his pocket and sat down beside her. He took the book in a big, lean hand and checked the title. He gave it back, smiling. "Libbie Custer was one of my grandmother's heroines. She actually met her once, when she gave a speech in New York while my grandmother was visiting relatives there as a child. She said that Mrs. Custer was a wonderful speaker. She lived into her nineties."

"She wrote a very interesting book," Tellie said.

"There are three of them altogether," he told her. "I believe you'll find the other two on the shelf as well, along with several biographies of the Colonel and the one book that he wrote."

"General Custer," she corrected.

He grinned. "That was a brevet promotion, given during the Civil War for outstanding courage under fire. His actual military rank was Colonel, at the time he died."

"You read about him, too?" she asked.

He nodded. "These were some of the first books I was exposed to as a child. My mother was big on reading skills," he said coolly. "Her picks were nonfiction, mostly chemistry and physics. Grandmother's were more palatable."

She noted the play of emotions on his lean, hard face. "Your mother was a scientist," she said suddenly, and wondered where the memory came from.

"Yes." He stared at her intently. "A research chemist. She died when we were young."

"You didn't like her very much, did you?"

"I hated her," he said flatly. "She made my grandmother miserable, making fun of her reading tastes, the way she dressed, her skills as a homemaker. She demeaned her."

"Was your grandmother your mother's mother?"

He shook his head. "My father's mother. In her day, she was an elegant horsewoman. She won trophies. And she was an actress before she married. But that, to my mother's mind, was fluff. She only admired women with Mensa-level IQs and science degrees."

"What about your father, couldn't he stop her from tormenting the old lady?"

He scoffed. "He was never here. He was too involved with making money to pay much attention to what went on around the house."

Her eyes narrowed. "You must have had an interesting childhood."

He cocked an eyebrow. "There's a Chinese curse—'may you live in interesting times.' That would have been appropriate for it."

She didn't quite know what to say. He looked so alone. "Nell said she died in a tornado. Your grandmother, I mean."

He nodded. "She was trying to save her horse. She'd had him for twenty-five years, ridden him in competition. She loved him more than any other thing here, except maybe me." He grimaced. "I'll never forget watching them bring her down from the treetop. She looked like a broken doll." His eyes closed briefly. "I don't have much luck with women, when it comes to love."

That was a curious thing to say. She felt odd as he said it, as if she knew something more about that, but couldn't quite call it up.

"I guess life is a connected series of hard knocks," she mused.

He glanced at her. "Your own life hasn't been any bed of roses," he commented. "You lost your father when you were born, and your grandfather and your mother only six months apart."

"Did I?" she wondered.

He cursed under his breath. "I shouldn't have said that."

"It didn't trigger any memories," she assured him, managing a smile. "I'm pretty blank about recent events. Well, I remember I'm graduating," she amended, "and that I borrowed Marge's car to drive to your house…" She hesitated. "Marge's car…"

"Stop trying to force it," he said, tapping her knee with a hard finger. "Your memory will come back when it's ready to."

"Nell said she was quitting. Did you have a row with her?"

"Did she say that I had?" he asked warily.

"She didn't say much of anything, J.B.," she muttered. "I can't get a straight answer out of anybody, even that nice man who was in the emergency room with me." She hesitated. "Has he come by to see me?"

He shifted restlessly. "Why ask me?" he wondered, but he wouldn't meet her eyes.

"He did come to see me!" she exclaimed, seeing the truth in the ruddy color that ran along his high cheekbones. "He came, and you wouldn't let him in!"

Eight

J.B. not only looked angry, he looked frustrated. "Coltrain said you didn't need visitors for two or three days, at least," he said firmly.

She was still staring at him, with wide pale green eyes. "But why not? Grange won't tell me anything. Every time I asked a question, he pretended to be deaf." Her eyes narrowed. "Just like you, J.B.," she added.

He patted her knee. "We're all trying to spare you any unnecessary pain," he said.

"So you're admitting that it would be painful if I remembered why you and I argued," she said.

He glared. "Life is mostly painful," he pointed out. "You and I have had disagreements before."

"Have we? And you seem like a man with such a sunny, even disposition," she said innocently.

"Ha!" came an unexpected comment from the hall.

They both turned to the doorway, and there stood Nell, in a housecoat with her hair in curlers, glaring at both of them.

"I have an even disposition," he argued.

"Evenly bad," Nell agreed. "She should be asleep," she said, nodding at Tellie.

He got to his feet. "So she should." He took the book away from Tellie and put it on the bedside table. "Go to sleep."

"Can I get you anything before I go to bed, Tellie?" Nell asked.

"No, but thanks."

J.B. pulled the pillows out from under her back and eased her down on the bed. He pulled up the covers, studied her amusedly and suddenly bent and brushed his hard mouth over her forehead. "Sleep tight, little bit." He turned off the lamp.

"I don't need tucking in," she said.

"It never hurts," he mused. He passed Nell. "You going to stand there all night? She needs her sleep."

"You're the one who was keeping her awake!" Nell muttered.

"I was not…!"

Their voices, harsh and curt, came through the closed door after he'd pulled it shut. Tellie sighed and closed her eyes. What an odd pair.

The next morning, there was heavy rain and lightning. Thunder shook the house. Alarmed, Tellie turned on the weather alert console next to her bed and listened to the forecast. There was a tornado watch for Jacobs County, among others in south Texas.

She grimaced, remembering tornadoes in the past.

She'd seen one go through when she was a little girl. It hadn't touched down near their house, but she could never forget the color of the clouds that contained it. They were a neon green, like slimy pond algae, enclosed in thick gray swirls. She got to her feet, a little shakily, and went to the window to look out. The clouds were dark and thick, and lightning struck down out of them so unexpectedly and violently, that she jumped.

"Get away from that window!" J.B. snapped from the doorway.

She turned, her heart racing from the double impact of the storm and his temper. "I was just looking," she protested.

He closed the door behind him, striding toward her with single-minded determination. He swung her up in his powerful arms and carried her back to bed.

"Lightning strikes the highest point. There are no trees taller than the house. Get the point?" he asked.

She clung to his strong neck, savoring his strength. "I get it."

He eased her down on the pillow, his green eyes staring straight into hers as he rested his hands beside her head on the bed. "How's your head?"

"Still there," she mused. "It does throb a bit."

"No wonder," he said. He searched her eyes for so long that her heart raced. He looked down at her pajama jacket and his teeth clenched. She looked down, too, but she didn't see anything that would make him frown.

"What's wrong?" she asked.

He drew in a long breath. "You're still a child, Tellie," he said, more for his own benefit than for hers. He stood up. "Ready for breakfast?"

She frowned. "Why did you say that?"

He stuck his hands in his pockets and went to the window to look out.

"You'll get struck by lightning," she chided, throwing his own accusation back at him.

"I won't."

His back was arrow straight. She stared at it longingly. It had been sweet to lie in his arms while he carried her. She felt an odd stirring deep in her belly.

"You really hate storms, don't you?" she said.

"Most people do, if they've ever lived through one."

She remembered what he'd told her about the grandmother he loved so much, and how she'd died in a tornado. "I've only seen one up close."

He turned toward her, his eyes watchful and quiet.

"What are you thinking?" she asked.

"I don't remember you going out on more than two dates the whole time you were in high school."

The reference to the past, luckily, went right over her head. She blinked. "I was always shy around boys," she confessed. "And none of them really appealed to me. Especially not the jocks. I hate sports."

He laughed softly. "Was that why?"

She twisted the hem of the sheet between her fingers and stared at them. "You must have noticed at some point that I'm not overly brainy or especially beautiful."

He frowned. "What does that have to do with dating?"

"Everything, in high school," she reminded him curtly. "Besides all that, most boys these days want girls who don't mind giving out. I did. It got around after I poured a cup of hot chocolate all over Barry Cramer when he slid his hand under my skirt at a party."

"He did what?" he exclaimed, eyes flaming.

The rush to anger surprised her. He'd never shown any particular emotion about her infrequent dates.

"I told him that a hamburger and a movie didn't entitle him to that sort of perk."

"You should have told me," he said curtly. "I'd have decked him!"

Her cheeks colored faintly. "That would have got around, too, and I'd never have had another date."

He moved close to the bed and studied her like an insect on a pin. "I don't suppose you'd have encouraged a boy to touch you like that."

"Whatever for?" she asked curiously.

His jaw clenched, hard. "Tellie, don't you…feel anything…with boys?"

She cocked her head. "Like what?"

"Like an urge to kiss them, to let them touch you."

The color in her cheeks mushroomed. She could barely meet his eyes. "I don't…I don't feel that way."

"Ever?"

She shifted, frowning. "What's gotten into you, J.B.? I'm only seventeen. There's plenty of time for that kind of thing when I'm old enough to think about marriage."

His fist clenched in his pocket. Even at her real age, he'd never seen her get flustered around anything male, not even himself. The one time he'd kissed her with intent, on his own sofa, she'd given in at once, but she'd been reticent and shocked more than aroused. He was beginning to think that she'd never been aroused in her life; not even with him. It stung his pride, in one way, and made him hungry in another. It disturbed him that he couldn't make Tellie want him. God knew, most other women did.

"Is that what you meant, when you called me a kid earlier?" she asked seriously.

He moved to the foot of the bed, with his hands still shoved deep in his pockets, and stared at her. "Yes. That's what I meant. You're completely unawakened. In this modern day and age, it's almost unthinkable for a woman your age to know so little about men."

"Well, gee whiz, I guess I'd better rush right out there and get myself a prescription for the pill and get busy, huh?" she asked rakishly. "Heaven forbid that I should be a throwback to a more conservative age, especially in this house! Didn't you write the book on sexual liberation?"

He felt uncomfortable. "Running with the crowd is the coward's way out. You have to have the courage of your convictions."

"You've just told me to forget them and follow the example of the Romans."

He glowered. "I did not!"

She threw up her hands. "Then why are you complaining?"

"I wasn't complaining!"

"You don't have to yell at me," she muttered. "I'm sick."

"I think I'm going to be," he said under his breath.

"You sure have changed since I was in the wreck," she murmured, staring at him curiously. "I never thought I'd see the day when you'd advise me to go out and get experienced with men. I don't even know any men." She frowned. "Well, that's not completely true. I know Grange." Her eyes brightened. "Maybe I can ask him to give me some pointers. He looks like he's been around!"

J.B. looked more and more like the storm outside. He moved toward the bed and sat down beside her, leaning down with his hands on either side of her face on the pillow. "You don't need lessons from Grange," he said through his teeth. "When you're ready to learn," he added on a deep, husky breath, "I'll teach you."

Ripples of pleasure ran up and down her nerves, leaving chill bumps of excitement all over her arms. Her breath caught at the thought of J.B.'s hard, beautiful mouth on her lips.

His eyes went down to her pajama jacket, and this time they lingered. For an instant, he looked shocked. Then his eyes began to glitter and he smiled, very slowly.

She looked down again, too, but she couldn't see anything unusual. Well, her nipples were tight and hard, and a little uncomfortable. That was because of her sudden chill. Wasn't it?

Her eyes met his again, with a faint question in them.

"You don't even understand this, do you?" he asked, and suddenly, without warning, he drew the tip of his forefinger right over one distended nipple with the faintest soft brushing motion.

She gasped out loud and her body arched. She looked, and was, shocked out of her mind.

J.B.'s green eyes darkened with sudden hunger. His gaze fell to her parted, full lips, to the pulse throbbing in the hollow of her throat. He ached to open her pajama top and put his mouth right on her breast. Unthinkable pleasures were burning in the back of his mind.

Tellie was frightened, both of what was happening to her body, and of letting him know how vulnerable she was. There was something vaguely unsettling about the way he was looking at her. It brought back a twinge of memory, of J.B. mocking her because she was weak toward him...

She brought up her arms and crossed them over her breasts.

"Spoilsport," he murmured, meeting her shocked eyes.

She fought to breathe normally. "J. B. Hammock, I'm seventeen years old!" she burst out.

He started to contradict her and realized at once that he didn't dare. He scowled and got to his feet abruptly. What the hell was he thinking?

He ran a hand over his hair and turned away. "I've got to go to town and see a Realtor about a parcel of land that's just come up for sale," he said in a strangely thick tone. "It adjoins my north pasture. I'll send Nell up with breakfast."

"Yes, that would be…that would be nice."

He glanced back at her from the door. He felt frustrated and guilty. But behind all that, he was elated. Tellie was vulnerable to him, and not just in the girlish way she had been for the past few years. She was vulnerable as a woman. It was the first time her body had reacted to his touch in that particular way.

He should have been ashamed of himself. He wasn't. His eyes slid over her body in the pajamas as if she belonged to him already. He couldn't hide the pride of possession that he felt.

It made Tellie shake inside. Surely he wasn't thinking…?

"Don't beat yourself to death over it," he said. "We're all human, Tellie. Even me. See you later."

He went out quickly and closed the door behind him, before his aching body could provoke him into even worse indiscretions than he'd already committed.

* * *

Nell brought breakfast and stared worriedly at Tellie's high color. "You're not having a relapse, are you?" she asked, worried.

Tellie wished she could confide in the housekeeper, or in someone. But she had no close friends, and she couldn't even have told Marge. She couldn't talk to Marge about her brother!

"Nothing's wrong, honest," Tellie said. "I went to look out the window, and a big flash of lightning almost made me jump out of my skin. I'm still reeling."

Nell's face relaxed. "Is that all?" She smiled. "I don't mind storms, but J.B. is always uneasy. Don't forget his grandmother died in a tornado outbreak."

"He told me," she said.

"Did he, now?" Nell exclaimed. "He doesn't talk about the old lady much."

Tellie nodded. "He doesn't talk about much of anything personal," she agreed. She frowned. "I wonder if he confides in his fashion dolls?"

Nell didn't get the point at first, but when she did, she burst out laughing. "That was mean, Tellie."

Tellie just grinned. She was going to forget what J.B. had done in those few tempestuous seconds. She was certain that he'd regretted it.

Sure enough, he didn't come in to see her at all the rest of the day. Next morning, he went out without a word.

About lunchtime, Grange showed up. Since J.B. wasn't there to keep him out, Nell escorted him up to Tellie's room with a conspiratorial grin.

"Company," Nell announced. "He can stay for lunch. I'll bring up a double tray." She went out, but left the door open.

Grange moved toward the bed with his wide-brimmed hat in his hand. He'd had a haircut and a close shave. He smelled nice, very masculine. His dark eyes twinkled as he studied Tellie in her pink pajamas.

She felt self-conscious and pulled the sheet up higher.

He laughed. "Sorry."

She shrugged. "I'm not used to men seeing me in my nightclothes," she told him. It wasn't totally true. He didn't know, and J.B. seemed to constantly forget, that she'd been almost assaulted by a boy in her early teens. It hadn't left immense scars, but she still felt uneasy about her body. She wasn't comfortable with men. She wondered if she should admit that to J.B. It might soften his provocative attitude toward her.

"I'll try not to stare," Grange promised, smiling as he sat down in the chair beside her bed. "How are you feeling?"

"Much better," she said. "I wanted to get up, but Nell won't let me."

"Concussion is tricky," he replied, and he didn't smile. "The first few days are chancy. Better you stay put in bed, just for the time being."

She smiled at him. "I'll bet you've seen your share of injuries, being in the military."

He nodded. "Concussion isn't all that uncommon in war. I've seen some nasty head injuries that looked pretty innocent at first. Better safe than sorry."

"I hate being confined," she confessed. "I want to get out and do things, but Dr. Coltrain said I couldn't. Nell and J.B. are worse than jailers," she added.

He chuckled. "Nell's a character." He hesitated. "Did you know there's a chef in the kitchen, complete with tall white hat and French accent?"

She nodded. "That's Albert," she replied. "He's been here for the past ten years. J.B. likes continental cuisine."

"He seems to be intimidated by Nell," he observed.

"He probably is. Gossip is that when Albert came here, Nell was in possession of the kitchen and unwilling to turn it over to a foreigner. They say," she added in a soft, conspiratorial tone, "that she chased him into the living room with a rolling pin when he refused to make dumplings her way. It took a pay raise and a big-screen TV for his room to keep him here. J.B. and Nell had a real falling out about that, and she threatened to quit. She got a raise, too." She laughed shortly. She'd remembered something from the past! Surely the rest couldn't be far behind now.

Grange chuckled at what she'd told him about Nell. "She seems formidable enough."

"She is. She and J.B. argue most of the time, but it's usually in a good-natured way."

He put his hat on the floor beside his chair and raked a hand through his neatly trimmed straight dark hair. "When they let you out of here, we'll go take in a new science-fiction movie. How about that?"

She smiled. "Sounds like fun." She was curious about him. He didn't seem the sort of man to be vulnerable to women, but it was apparent that he liked Tellie. "Do you have family here in Jacobsville?" she asked in all innocence.

His face hardened. His dark eyes narrowed. "No."

She frowned. She'd struck a nerve. "I'm sorry, is there something else I don't remember—?"

"There's a lot," he cut her off, but gently. "You're bound to wander into a few thickets before you find the right path. Don't worry about it."

She drew in a long breath. "I feel like I'm walking around in a fog. Everybody's hiding things from me."

"It's necessary. Just for a week or so," he promised.

"You know about me, don't you? Can't you tell me?"

He held up a hand and laughed. "I'd just as soon not get on the wrong side of Hammock while you're living under his roof. I'd lose visiting privileges. I may lose them anyway, if Nell spills the beans that I've been here while he was out."

"Doesn't he like you?"

"He doesn't like most people," he agreed. "Especially me, at the moment."

"What did you do to him?"

"It's a long story, and it doesn't concern you right now," he said quietly.

She flushed. His voice had been very curt.

"Don't look like that," he said, feeling guilty "I don't want to hurt you. J.B. and I have an unfortunate history, that's all."

She blinked. "It sounds unpleasant."

"It was," he confessed. "But it happened a long time ago. Right now, our only concern is to get you well again."

Footsteps sounded on the staircase and a minute later, Nell walked in with a tray holding two plates, two glasses of iced tea and a vase full of yellow roses.

"Never thought I'd get up the stairs with everything intact," she laughed as Grange got up and took the tray from her, setting it down gently on the mahogany side table by the bed.

"The roses," Tellie exclaimed. "They're beautiful!"

"Glad you like them," Grange said easily, and with a smile. "We do live in Texas, after all."

"'The Yellow Rose of Texas,'" she recalled the song. She reached over and plucked one of the stems out of the vase to smell it. There was a delicate, sweet scent. "I don't think I've ever had a bouquet of flowers in my life," she added, confused.

"You haven't," Nell replied for her. She sounded irritated. "Nice of Grange to remember that sick people usually like flowers."

She smiled at him. "Wasn't it?" she laughed. "I'll enjoy them. Thank you."

"My pleasure," he replied, and his voice was soft.

Nell stuck a plate in his hands and then put Tellie's on her lap. "Eat, before the bread molds," she told them. "That's homemade chicken salad, and I put up those dill pickles myself last summer."

"Looks delicious," Grange said. "You didn't have to do this, Nell."

"I enjoy making a few things on my own," she said. She grimaced. "I had to lock Albert in the closet, of course. His idea of a sandwich involves shrimp and sauce and a lettuce leaf on a single piece of toasted rye bread." She looked disgusted.

"That's not my idea of one," Grange had to admit.

"This is really good," Tellie exclaimed after she bit into her sandwich.

"Yes, it is," Grange seconded. "I didn't have time for breakfast this morning."

"Enjoy," Nell said, smiling. "I'll be back up for the tray later."

They both nodded, too involved with chewing to answer.

Grange entertained her with stories from his childhood. She loved the one about the cowboy, notorious for his incredible nicotine habit, who drove his employer's Land Rover out into the desert on a drunken joyride, forgetting to take along a shovel or bottled water or even a flashlight. He ran out of gas halfway back and when they found him the next morning, almost dead of dehydration, the first thing he asked for was a cigarette.

"What happened to him?" she asked, laughing.

"After he got over the experience, the boss put him on permanent barn duty, cleaning out the horse stalls. The cowboy couldn't get a job anywhere else locally because of that smoking habit, so he was pretty much stuck."

"He couldn't quit?"

"He wouldn't quit," he elaborated. "Then he met this waitress and fell head over heels for her. He quit smoking, stopped drinking and married her. He owns a ranch of his own now and they've got two kids." His dark eyes twinkled. "Just goes to show that the love of a good woman can save a bad man."

She pursed her lips. "I'll keep that in mind."

He laughed. "I'm not a bad man," he pointed out. "I just have a few rough edges and a problem with authority figures."

"Is that why you don't get along with J.B.?"

He shook his head. "That's because we're too much alike in temperament," he said. He checked his watch. "I've got to run," he said, swooping up his hat as he got to his feet. "Can't afford to tick off my boss!"

"Will you come again?" she asked.

"The minute the coast is clear," he promised, laughing. "If Nell doesn't sell us out."

"She won't. She's furious at J.B. I don't know why, nobody tells me anything, but I overheard her say that she'd quit and had to come back to take care of me. Apparently she and J.B. had a major blowup before I got hurt. I wish I knew why."

"One of these days, I'm sure you'll find out. Keep getting better."

"I'll do my best. Thanks again. For the roses, and for coming to see me."

"I enjoyed it. Thanks for lunch."

She grinned. "I'll cook next time."

"Something to look forward to," he teased, winking at her.

J.B. came in late. Apparently he'd been out with whichever girlfriend he was dating, because he was dressed up and a faint hint of perfume clung to his shirt as he sat down in the chair beside Tellie's bed. But he looked more worried than weary, and he wasn't smiling.

She eyed him warily. "Is something wrong?" she asked.

He leaned back in the chair, one long leg crossed over the other. She noted how shiny his hand-tooled black boots were, how well his slacks fit those powerful legs. She shook herself mentally. She didn't need to notice such things about him.

"Nothing much," he said. Actually he was worried about Marge. She was in the early stages of treatment for high blood pressure, and she'd had a bad dizzy spell this afternoon. The girls had called him at work, and he'd gone right over. He'd phoned Coltrain, only to be reassured that some dizziness was most likely a side effect of the drug. She was having a hard time coping, and she missed Tellie, as well as being worried about her health. J.B. had assured Marge that Tellie was going to be fine, but his sister wanted to see Tellie. He couldn't manage that. Not yet.

He drew in a long breath, wondering how to avoid the subject. That was when he looked at her bedside table carelessly and saw the huge bouquet of yellow roses. His green eyes began to glitter as he stared at her.

"And just where," he asked with soft fury, "did you get a bouquet of roses?"

Nine

"They were a present," Tellie said quickly.

"Were they?" he asked curtly. "From whom?"

She didn't want to say it. There was going to be a terrible explosion when she admitted that she'd had a visitor. It didn't take mind-reading skills to realize that J.B. didn't like Grange.

She swallowed. "Grange brought them to me."

The green eyes were really glittering now. "When?"

"He stopped by on his lunch hour," she said. She glared up at him. "Listen, there's nothing wrong with having company when you're sick!"

"You're in your damned pajamas!" he shot back.

"So?" she asked belligerently. "You're looking at me in them, aren't you?"

"I don't count."

"Oh. I see." She didn't, but it was best not to argue with a madman, which is how he looked at the moment.

His lips made a thin line. "I'm family."

She might have believed that before yesterday, she thought, when he'd touched her so intimately.

The memory colored her cheeks. He saw it, and a slow, possessive smile tugged up his firm, chiseled lips. That made the blush worse.

"You don't think of me as family?" he asked softly.

She wanted to dive under the covers. It wasn't fair that he could reduce her to this sort of mindless hunger.

He leaned over her, the anger gone, replaced by open curiosity and something else, less definable.

His fingers speared through her dark hair, holding her head inches from the pillow behind her. His chest rose and fell quickly, like her own. His free hand went to her soft mouth and traced lazily around the upper lip, and then the lower one, with a sensuality that made her feel extremely odd.

"I'm...seventeen," she choked, grasping for a way to save herself.

His dark green gaze fell to her parted lips. "You're not," he said huskily, and the hand in her hair contracted. "It can't hurt for you to know your real age. You're almost twenty-two. Fair game," he added under his breath, and all at once his hard, sensuous mouth came down on her lips with firm purpose.

She gasped in surprise, and her hand went to his chest. That was a mistake, because it was unbuttoned in front and her fingers were enmeshed in thick, curling dark hair that covered the powerful muscles.

His head lifted, as if the contact affected him. His eyes narrowed. His heart, under her fingertips, beat strongly and a little fast.

"You shouldn't…" she began, frightened of what was happening to her.

"I've waited a long time for this," he said enigmatically. He bent to her mouth again. "There's nothing to be afraid of, Tellie," he whispered into her lips. "Nothing at all…"

The pressure increased little by little. Her fingers dug into his chest as odd sensations worked themselves down her body, and she shivered.

He smiled against her parted lips. "It's about time," he murmured, and his mouth grew insistent.

She felt his body slowly move closer, so that they were lying breast to breast on the soft mattress. One lean hand slid under the pajama top, against her rib cage, warm and teasing. She should grab his wrist and stop him, her mind was saying, because this wasn't right. He was a notorious womanizer and she was like his ward. She was far too young to be exposed to such experienced ardor. She was…but he'd said she was almost twenty-two years old. Why hadn't she remembered her age?

His hand contracted in her soft hair. "Stop thinking," he bit off against her mouth. "Kiss me, Tellie," he breathed, and his hand suddenly moved up and cupped her soft, firm breast. His head lifted, to watch her stunned, delighted reaction.

For an instant, she stiffened. But then his thumb rubbed tenderly over the swollen nipple, and a ripple of ardent desire raged in her veins. She drew in a shivery, shaking breath. The pressure increased, just enough to be arousing. She arched involuntarily, and moaned.

"Yes," he said, as though she'd spoken.

His hand swallowed her whole, and his mouth moved gently onto her parted lips, teasing, exploring, demanding. All her defenses were down. There was no tomorrow. She had J.B. in her arms, wanting her. Whether it was wrong or not, she couldn't resist him. She'd never known that her body could experience anything so passionately satisfying. She felt swollen. She wanted to pull him closer. She wanted to touch him, as he was touching her. She wanted…everything!

Her arms slid up around his neck and she arched into the warm pressure of his hand on her body.

His mouth increased its pressure, until he broke open her mouth and his tongue moved inside, in slow, insistent thrusts that made her moan loudly. She'd never been kissed in such an intimate way. She'd never wanted to be. But this was delicious. It was the most delicious taste of a man she'd ever had. She wanted more.

He hadn't meant to let things get so far out of control, but he went under just as quickly as she did. His hand left her breast to flick open the buttons of her pajama jacket. She whispered something, but he didn't hear it. He was blind, deaf, dumb to anything except the taste and feel of her innocence.

He kissed her again, ardently, and while she followed his mouth, he stripped her out of the pajama top and opened the rest of the buttons over his broad chest. He gathered her hungrily to him, dragging his chest against hers so that the rasp of hair only accentuated the pleasure she was feeling.

When his lean, hard body moved over hers, she was beyond any sort of protest. Her long legs parted eagerly to admit the intimacy of his body. She shivered when she felt him against her. She hadn't realized how it would feel, when a man was aroused, although she'd read enough about it in her life. Other women were vocal about their own affairs, and Tellie had learned from listening to them talk. She'd been sure that she would never be vulnerable to a man like this, that she'd never be tempted to give in with no thought beyond satisfaction. What she was feeling now put the lie to her overconfidence. She was as helpless as any woman in love.

Even knowing that J.B. was involved more with his body than his mind didn't help her resist him. Whatever he wanted, he could have. She just didn't want him to stop. She was drowning in sensation, pulsating with the sweetest, sharpest hunger she'd ever known.

"I've waited so long, Tellie," he groaned into her mouth. His hand went under her hips and lifted her closer into a much more intimate position that made her shudder all over. "God, baby, I'm on fire!"

So was she, but she couldn't manage words. She arched up toward him, barely aware that he was looking down at her bare breasts. He bent and put his mouth on them, savoring their firm softness, their eager response to his ardor.

Her nails bit into his shoulders. She rocked with him, feeling the slow spiral of satisfaction that was just beginning, like a flash of light that obliterated reason, thought, hope. She only wanted him never to stop.

His lean hand went to the snap that held her pajama bottoms in place, just as loud footsteps sounded on the staircase, accompanied by muttering that was all too familiar.

J.B. lifted his head. He looked as shocked as Tellie felt. He looked down at her breasts and ruddy color flamed over his high cheekbones. Then he looked toward the hall and realized belatedly that the door was standing wide open.

With a furious curse, he moved away from her and got

to his feet, slinging the cover over her only a minute before Nell walked in with a tray. Luckily for both of them, she was too concerned over not dumping milk and cookies all over the floor to notice how flushed they were.

J.B. had time to fasten his shirt. Tellie had the sheet up to her neck, covering the open pajama jacket she'd pulled on.

"Thought you might like a snack," Nell said, smiling as she put the tray down next to the vase of roses.

"I would. Thanks, Nell," Tellie said in an oddly husky tone.

J.B. kept his back to Nell as he went toward the door. "I've got a phone call to make. Sleep tight, Tellie."

"You, too, J.B.," she said, amazed at her acting ability, and his.

When he was gone, Nell moved the roses a little farther onto the table. "Aren't they beautiful, though?" she asked Tellie as she sniffed them. "Grange has good taste."

"Yes, he does," Tellie said, forcing a smile.

Nell glanced at her curiously. "You look very flushed. You're not running a fever, are you?" she asked worriedly.

Tellie bit her lower lip and tasted J.B. there. She looked at Nell innocently. "J.B. and I had words," she lied.

Nell frowned. "Over what?"

"The roses," Tellie replied. "He didn't like the idea that Grange was here."

Nell sighed, falling for the ruse. "I was afraid he wouldn't."

"Do you know why he dislikes him so much?" Tellie asked. "I mean, he agreed that I could go out with

Grange, apparently. It seems odd that he wouldn't have stopped me."

"He couldn't," Nell said. "After all, you're of age…" She stopped and put her hand over her mouth, looking guilty.

"I'm almost twenty-two," Tellie said, avoiding Nell's gaze. "I…remembered."

"Well, that's progress!"

It wasn't, but Tellie wasn't about to admit to Nell that she'd had a heavy petting session with J.B. in her own bed and learned about her age that way. She could still hardly believe what had happened. If Nell hadn't walked up the staircase just at that moment… It didn't bear thinking about. What had she done? She knew J.B. was a womanizer. He didn't love women; she knew that even though she couldn't remember why. She'd given him liberties that he wasn't entitled to. Why?

"You look tired," Nell said. "Drink up that milk and eat those cookies. Leave the tray. I'll get it in the morning. Can I bring you anything else?"

A good psychiatrist, Tellie thought, but didn't dare say. She smiled. "No. Thanks a lot, Nell."

"You're very welcome. Sleep well."

She'd never sleep again, she imagined. "You, too."

The door closed behind her. Tellie sat up and started to rebutton her jacket. Her breasts had faint marks on them from J.B.'s insistent mouth. She looked at them and got aroused all over again. What was happening? She knew, she just knew, that J.B. had never touched her like that before. Why had he done it?

She lay awake long into the night, worrying the question.

* * *

The next morning, Nell told her that J.B. had suddenly had to fly to a meeting in Las Vegas, a cattlemen's seminar of some sort.

Tellie wasn't really surprised. Perhaps J.B. was a little embarrassed, as she was, about what they'd done together.

"He didn't take his girlfriend with him, either," Nell said. "That's so strange. He takes her everywhere else."

Tellie felt her heart stop beating. "His girlfriend?" she prompted.

"Sorry. I keep forgetting that your memory's limping. Bella," she added. "She's a beauty contestant. J.B.'s been dating her for several weeks."

Tellie stared at her hands. "Is he serious about her?"

"He's never serious about women," Nell replied. "But that doesn't mean he won't have them around. Bella travels with him, mostly, and she spends the occasional weekend in the guest room."

"This room?" Tellie asked, horrified, looking around her.

"No, of course not," Nell said, not noticing Tellie's look of horror. "She stays in that frilly pink room that we usually put women guests in. Looks like a fashion-doll box inside," she added with a chuckle. "You'd be as out of place there as I would."

The implication made her uneasy. J.B. was intimate with the beauty contestant, if she was spending weekends with him. The pain rippled down her spine as she considered how easily she'd given in to him the night before. He was used to women falling all over him, wasn't he? And Tellie wasn't immune. She wasn't even respected, or he'd never have touched her when she was a guest in his house. The more she thought about it, the angrier she got. He was involved with another woman, and making passes at Tellie. What was wrong with him?

On the other hand, what was wrong with her? She only wished she knew.

She got out of bed and started helping Nell around the house, despite her protests.

"I can't stay in bed my whole life, Nell," Tellie argued. "I'll never get better that way."

"I suppose not," the older woman admitted. "But you do have to take it easy."

"I will." She pushed the lightweight electric broom into the living room. The sofa caught her attention again, as it had when she'd come home from the hospital. She moved to its back and ran her hand over the smooth cloth fabric, frowning. Why did this sofa make her uneasy? What had happened in this room in the past that upset her?

She turned to Nell. "What did J.B. and I argue about?" she asked.

Nell stopped dead and stared. She was obviously hesitating while she tried to find an answer that would be safe.

"Was it over a woman?" Tellie persisted.

Nell didn't reply, but she flushed.

So that was it, Tellie thought. She must have been jealous of the mysterious Bella and said something to J.B. that hit him wrong. But, why would she have been jealous? She was almost certain that J.B. had never touched her intimately in their past.

"Honey, don't try so hard to remember," Nell cautioned. "Enjoy these few days and don't try to think about the past."

"Was it bad?" she wondered aloud.

Nell grimaced. "In a way, yes, it was," she replied. "But I can't tell you any more. I'll get in trouble. It might damage you, to know too much too soon. Dr. Coltrain was very specific."

Tellie gnawed her lower lip. "I've already graduated from high school, haven't I?" she asked.

Nell nodded, reluctantly.

"Do I have a job?"

"You had a summer job, at the Ballenger Brothers feedlot. That's where you met Grange."

She felt a twinge of memory trying to come back. There was something between J.B. and Grange, something about a woman. Not the beauty contestant, but some other woman. There was a painful secret...

She caught her head and held it, feeling it throb.

Nell moved forward and took her by the shoulders. "Stop trying to force the memories," she cautioned. "Take it one day at a time. Right now, let's do some vacuuming. Then we'll make a cake. You can invite Grange over to supper, if you like," she added, inspired. "J.B. won't be around to protest."

Tellie smiled. "I'd enjoy that."

"So would I. We'll call him at the feedlot, when we're through cleaning."

"Okay."

They did the necessary housekeeping and then made a huge chocolate pound cake. Grange was enthusiastic about coming for a meal, and Tellie was surprised at the warm feeling he evoked in her. It was friendly, though, not the tempestuous surging of her heart that she felt when she remembered the touch of J.B.'s hard lips on her mouth.

She had a suitcase that she didn't remember packing. Inside was a pretty pink striped dress. She wore that, and light makeup, for the meal. Grange showed up on time, wearing a sports jacket with dress slacks, a white shirt and a tie. He paid for dressing. He was very good-looking.

"You look nice," Tellie told him warmly as he followed her into the dining room, where the table was already set.

"So do you," he replied, producing another bouquet of flowers from behind his back, and presenting them with a grin.

"Thanks!" she exclaimed. "You shouldn't have!"

"You love flowers," he said. "I didn't think you had enough."

She gave him a wary look. "Is that the whole truth?" she asked suspiciously and with a mischievous grin, "or did you think you'd irritate J.B. if I had more flowers in my room?"

He chuckled. "Can't put anything past you, can I?" he asked.

"Thanks anyway," she told him. "I'll just put them in water. Sit down! Nell and I chased Albert out of the kitchen and did everything ourselves. I understand he's down at the goldfish pond slitting his wrists..."

"He is not!" Nell exclaimed. "You stop that!"

Tellie grinned. "Sorry. Couldn't resist it. He seems to think he owns the kitchen."

"Well, he doesn't," Nell said. "Not until I leave for good."

Leave. Leave. Tellie frowned, staring into space. Nell had quit. Tellie had been crying. Nell was shouting. J.B. was shouting back. It was raining…

Grange caught her as she fell and carried her into the living room. He put her down on the sofa. Nell ran for a wet cloth.

Tellie groaned as she opened her eyes. "I remembered an argument," she said huskily. "You and J.B. were yelling at each other…"

Nell frowned. "You couldn't have heard us," she said. "You'd already run out the door, into the rain."

Tellie could see the road, blinded by rain, feel the tires giving way, feel the car going into the ditch…!

She gasped. "I wrecked the car. I saw it!"

Nell sat down beside her and put an arm around her. "Grange saved you," she told the younger woman. "He came along in time to stop you from drowning. The ditch the car went into was full of water."

Tellie held the cloth to her forehead. She swallowed, and then swallowed again. There were odd, disturbing flashes. J.B.'s furious face. A blonde woman, staring at her. There were harsh words, but she couldn't remember what they were. She didn't want to remember!

"Did I thank you for saving me?" she asked Grange, trying to ward off the memories.

He smiled worriedly. "Of course you did. How do you feel now?"

"Silly," she said sheepishly as she sat up. "I'm sorry. There were some really odd flashbacks. I don't understand them at all."

"Don't try to," Nell said firmly. "Come on in here and eat. Let time take care of the rest."

She got up, holding on to Grange's arm for support.

She drew in a long, slow breath. "One way and another, it's been a rough few days," she said.

"You don't know the half," Nell said under her breath, but she didn't let Tellie hear her.

The next day was Saturday. Tellie went out to the barn to see the sick calf that was being kept there while it was being treated. In another stall was a huge, black stallion. He didn't like company. He pawed and snorted as Tellie walked past him. He was J.B.'s. She knew, without remembering or being told. She moved to another stall, where a beautiful palomino mare was eating from a feed trough. The horse perked up when she saw Tellie, and left her food to come to the front of the stall and nose Tellie's outstretched hand.

"Sand," Tellie murmured. She laughed. "That's your name. Sand! J.B. lets me ride you!"

The horse nudged her hand again. She smoothed the white blaze between the mare's eyes lazily. She was beginning to recover some memories. The rest, she was sure, would come in time.

She wandered past the goldfish pond on the patio and stared down at the pretty red and gold and white fish swimming around water lilies and lotus plants. The facade was stacked yellow bricks, and there were huge flat limestone slabs all around it, making an endless seat for people to watch the fish. There were small trees nearby and a white wrought-iron furniture set with a patio umbrella. In fair weather, it must be heavenly to sit there. She heard a car drive up and wondered who it was. Not J.B., she was sure. It was too soon for him to be back. Monday, Nell said, was the earliest they could expect him. Perhaps it was one of the cowboys.

It was a dreary day, not good exploring weather. She wondered how Marge and the girls were, and wanted to see them. She dreaded seeing J.B. again. Things had changed between them. She was uneasy when she considered that J.B. had left town so quickly afterward, as if his conscience bothered him. Or was it that he was afraid Tellie would start thinking about something serious? She knew so little about relationships…

She walked back through the side door into the living room and stopped suddenly. There was a beautiful blonde woman standing in the doorway to J.B.'s office. She was wearing a yellow dress that fit her like a second skin. She had long, wavy, beautiful hair and a perfectly made-up face. She was svelte and sophisticated, and she was giving Tellie a look that could have boiled water.

"So you're the reason I've had to be kept away from the house," the woman said haughtily.

That blonde was familiar, Tellie thought suddenly, and she wanted to run. She didn't want to talk to this person, to be around her. She was a threat.

The woman sensed Tellie's discomfort and smiled coldly. "Don't tell me you've forgotten me?" she drawled. "Not after you walked right in and interrupted me and J.B. on that very sofa?"

Sofa. J.B. Two people on the sofa, both half-naked. J.B. furious and yelling. Nell rushing to see why Tellie was crying.

Tellie put her hands to her mouth as the memories began to rush at her, like daggers. It was all coming back. J.B. had called her ugly. A stray. He could never love her. He didn't want her. He'd said that!

There was more. He'd missed her graduation from college and lied about it. He'd had his secretary buy Tellie a graduation present—he hadn't even cared enough to do it himself. He'd accused Tellie of panting after him like a pet dog. He'd said he was sick of her...pawing him... trying to touch him.

She felt the rise of nausea in her throat like a living thing. She brushed past the blonde and ran for the hall bathroom, slamming the door behind her. She barely made it to the sink before she lost her breakfast.

"Tellie?"

The door opened. Nell came in, worried. "Are you all right? Oh, for goodness sake...!"

She grabbed a washcloth from the linen closet and wet it, bathing Tellie's white face. "Come on. Let's get you back to bed."

"That woman..." Tellie choked.

"I showed her the door," Nell said coldly. "She won't come back in a hurry, I guarantee!"

"But I recognized her," Tellie said unsteadily. "She and J.B. were on the sofa together, half-naked. He yelled at me. He accused me of trying to paw him. He said he was sick of the way I followed him around. He said..." She swallowed the pain. "He said I was nothing but an ugly stray that he'd taken in, and that he could never want me." Tears rolled down her cheek. "He said he never... wanted to see me again!"

"Tellie," Nell began miserably, not knowing what to say.

"Why did he bring me here, after that?" she asked tearfully.

"He felt guilty," Nell said gently. "It was his fault that you wrecked the car. You would have died, if Grange hadn't found you."

Tellie wiped her eyes with the wet washcloth. "I knew there was something," she choked. "Some reason that he wasn't giving me. Guilt. Just guilt." Was that why he'd kissed her so hungrily, too? Was he trying to make amends for what he'd said? But it was only the truth. He didn't want her. He found her repulsive…

The tears poured down her face. She wanted to climb into a hole. That beautiful blonde was J.B.'s woman. She'd come to Marge's house with J.B., and she'd insulted Tellie. They'd argued, and J.B. had shown Tellie what a hold he had over her, using her weakness for him as a punishment. She closed her eyes. How could he have treated her so horribly?

"I want to go back to Marge's house," Tellie said shakily. "Before he comes home." She looked into Nell's eyes. "And then I never want to see him again, as long as I live!"

Ten

Nell couldn't talk Tellie into staying at the house, not even when she assured her that J.B. wouldn't be back until Monday. Tellie had remembered that Marge had a heart attack, and she was frantic until Nell assured her that Marge was going to be all right. It was even lucky that they'd found the high blood pressure before it killed her.

Now that Tellie remembered everything, there were no more barriers to her going to Marge. She remembered her job at the feedlot, as well, and hoped she still had it. But she phoned Justin at home and he assured her that her job would be waiting when she was recovered. That was a load off her mind.

She didn't dare think about J.B. It was too terrible, remembering the hurtful things he'd said to her. She knew she'd never forgive him for the way he'd reacted when she'd tried to tell him about Marge, much less for his ardor when he knew there was no future in it. He'd taunted her with her feelings one time too many. She wondered what sort of cruel game he'd been playing in her bedroom at his house.

Marge and the girls met her at the door, hugging her warmly. Nell had driven her there, and she was carrying two suitcases.

"Are you sure about this?" Nell asked worriedly.

Marge nodded, smiling warmly. "You know you're welcome here. None of us will yell at you, and we'll all be grateful that we don't have to depend on Dawn's cooking for…"

"Mother!" Dawn exclaimed.

"Sorry," Marge said, hugging her daughter. "I love you, baby, but you know you're terrible in the kitchen, even if you can sing like an angel. Nobody's perfect."

"J.B. thinks he is," Nell muttered.

Marge laughed. "Not anymore, I'll bet. I hope you left him a note, at least."

"I did," Nell confessed. "Brief, and to the point. I hope that blonde fashion doll of his can cook and clean."

"That isn't likely," Tellie said coolly. "But they can always get takeout."

"Are you sure you're okay?" Marge asked Tellie, moving to hug her, too. "Your color's bad."

"So is yours, worrywart," Tellie said with warm affection, returning the hug. "But I reckon the two of us will manage somehow, with a little help."

"Between us," Marge sighed, "we barely make one well person."

"I'll fatten you both up with healthy, nonsalty fare,"

Nell promised. "Dawn and Brandi can see me to my room and help me unpack. Right?"

The girls grinned. "You bet!" they chorused, delighted to see the end of meal preparation and housework. Nell was the best in town at housekeeping.

They marched up the staircase together, the girls helping with the luggage.

Marge studied Tellie closely, her sharp eyes missing nothing. "You wouldn't be here unless something major had happened. What was it?"

"My memory came back," Tellie said, perching on the arm of the sofa.

"Did it have any help?" the older woman asked shrewdly.

Tellie grimaced, her eyes lowering to the sea-blue carpet. "Bella kindly filled me in on a few things."

Marge cursed under her breath as forcefully as J.B. ever had. "That woman is a menace!" she raged. "Copper Coltrain said it would be dangerous for us to force-feed you facts about the past until you remembered them naturally!"

"I'm sure she only wanted J.B. to herself again, and thought she was helping him get me out of the way. I don't mind," Tellie added at once. "J.B. raised hell when Grange came and brought me roses. At least you're not likely to mind that."

Marge smiled. "No, I'm not. I like your friend Grange."

Tellie's eyes were sad and wise. "He's been a wonderful friend. Who'd have thought he'd turn out to be pleasant company, with his background?"

"Not anyone locally, that's for sure." Marge sat down on the sofa, too. She was still pale. "Nothing wrong," she assured Tellie, who was watching her closely. "The medicine still makes me a little dizzy, but it's perfectly natural. Otherwise, I'm seeing an improvement all around. I think it's going to work."

"Goodness, I hope so," Tellie said gently. She smiled. "We can't lose you."

"You aren't going to. Nice of you to bring Nell with you," she added wryly. "Housework and cooking was really getting to us, without you here. Did she come willingly?"

"She met me at the front door with her suitcase," she replied. "She was furious at what Bella had done. She thinks maybe J.B. put her up to it."

Marge scowled. "That isn't likely. Whatever his faults, J.B. has a big heart. He was really concerned about you."

"He felt guilty," Tellie translated, "because he felt responsible for the wreck. He yelled at me and said some terrible things," she added, without elaborating. Her sad eyes were evidence enough of the pain he'd caused Tellie. "I couldn't stay under his roof, when I remembered them."

Marge picked at a fingernail. "That bad?"

Tellie nodded, averting her eyes.

"Then I suppose it's just as well for you to stay here."

"I don't want to see him," she told Marge. "Not ever again. He's had one too many free shots at me. I'll finish out the week at Ballenger's when I get back on my feet, and then I'm going to ask my alma mater for an adjunct position teaching history for night students. I can teach at night and go to classes during the day. The semester starts very soon."

"Is it wise, to run away from a problem?" the other woman queried.

"In this case, it's the better part of valor," she replied grimly. "J.B. didn't just say unpleasant things to me, Marge, he actually taunted me with the way I felt about him. That's hitting below the belt, even for J.B."

"He did that?" Marge exclaimed.

"Yes. And that's why I'm leaving." She got up. She smiled at Marge. "Not to worry, you'll have Nell to take over here for me, and pamper all three of you. I won't have to be nervous about leaving you. Nell will make sure you do what the doctor says, and she'll cook healthy meals for you."

"J.B. is going to be furious when he gets home and finds you both gone," Marge predicted. She was glad she wasn't going to have to be the one to tell him.

It was dark and raining when J.B. climbed out of the limo he'd hired to take him to and from the airport. He signed the charge slip, tipped the driver with two big bills and carried his flight bag and attaché case up the driveway to the house.

It was oddly quiet when he used his key to open the front door. Usually there was a television going in Nell's room, which could be heard faintly coming down the staircase. There were no lights on upstairs, and no smells of cooking.

He frowned. Odd, that. He put down his suitcase and attaché case, and opened the living room door.

Bella was stretched out on the sofa wearing a pink gown and negligee and a come-hither smile.

"Welcome home, darling," she purred. "I knew you wouldn't mind if I moved into my old room."

He was worn-out and half out of humor. Bella's mood

didn't help. What in the world must Tellie be thinking of this new development, despite her lack of memory.

"What did you tell Tellie?" he asked.

Her eyebrows arched. "I only reminded her of how she found us together the night your sister had to go to the hospital," she drawled. "She remembered everything else just fine, after that, and she went to your sister's." She smiled seductively. "We've got the whole night to ourselves! I'm cooking TV dinners. They'll be ready in about ten minutes. Then we can have champagne and go to bed..."

"You told her that?" he burst out, horrified.

She glowered, moving to sit up. "Now, J.B., you know she was getting on your nerves. You never go to those stupid seminars, you just wanted to get away from her."

"That isn't true," he shot back. And it wasn't. He'd gone to give Tellie, and himself, breathing space. Her ardent response had left his head spinning. For the first time in their relationship, Tellie had responded to him as a woman would, with passion and hunger. He hadn't slept an entire night since, reliving the delicious inter-lude time after time. He'd had to leave, to make sure he didn't press Tellie too hard when she was fragile, make sure he didn't force memories she wasn't ready for. He'd hoped to have time to show her how tender he could be, before she remembered how cruel he'd been. Now the chance was gone forever, and the source of his failure was sprawled on his sofa in a negligee planning to replace Tellie. He felt a surge of pure revulsion as he looked at Bella.

"Nell!" he called loudly.

"Oh, she went with the girl to your sister's," Bella said, yawning. "She left a note on your desk."

He went to his study to retrieve it, feeling cold and dead inside. The note was scribbled on a memo pad. It just said that Nell was going to work for Marge, and that she hoped Bella was domesticated.

He threw it down on the desk, overwhelmed with frustration. Bella came up behind him and slid her arms around him.

"I'll check on the TV dinners," she whispered. "Then we can have some fun…"

He jerked away from her, his green eyes blazing. "Get dressed and go home," he said shortly. He took out his wallet and stuffed some bills into her hand.

"Where are you going?" she exclaimed when he walked toward the front door.

"To get Nell and Tellie back," he said shortly, and kept walking.

Bella actually screamed. But it didn't do any good. He didn't even turn his head.

Marge met him at the door. She didn't invite him in.

"I'm sorry," she said, stepping onto the porch with him. "But Tellie's been through enough today. She doesn't want to see you."

He shoved his hands into his pockets, staring at her. "I leave town for two days and the world caves in on me," he bit off.

"You can thank yourself for that," his sister replied. Her dark eyes narrowed. "Was it necessary to use Tellie's weakness for you against her like a weapon?"

He paled a little. "She told you?" he asked slowly.

"The bare bones, nothing more. It was low, J.B., even for you. Just lately, you're someone I don't know."

His broad shoulders lifted and fell. "Grange brought back some painful memories."

"Tellie wasn't responsible for them," she reminded him bluntly.

He drew in a sharp breath. "She won't give up Grange. It's disloyal."

"They're friends. Not that you'd recognize the reference. You don't have friends, J.B., you have hot dates," she pointed out. "Albert phoned and said your current heartthrob was preparing dinner for you. Frozen dinners, I believe…?"

"I didn't ask Bella to move in while I was away!" he shot back. "And I sure as hell didn't authorize her to fill Tellie in on the past!"

"I'm sure she thought she was doing you a favor, and removing the opposition at the same time," Marge said, folding her arms across her chest. "I love you, J.B., but I'm your sister and I can afford to. You're hard on women, especially on Tellie. Lately it's like you're punishing her for having feelings for you."

His high cheekbones went ruddy. He looked away from Marge. "I didn't want anything permanent, at first."

"Then you should never have encouraged Tellie, in any way."

He sighed roughly. He couldn't explain. It flattered him, softened him, that Tellie thought the world revolved around him. She made him feel special, just by caring for him. But she hadn't been able to give him passion, and he was afraid to take a chance on her without it. For years, he'd given up passionate love, he was afraid of it. When Tellie left for college he didn't want her to be hurt, but he didn't want to be hurt himself. He loved too deeply, too intensely. He couldn't live with losing another woman, the way he'd lost his late fiancée. But now Tellie was a woman, and he felt differently. How was he going to explain that to Tellie if he couldn't get near her?

"Tellie's changed in the past few weeks. So have I." He shifted. "It's hard to put it into words."

Marge knew that he had a difficult time talking about feelings. She and J.B. weren't twins, but they'd always been close. She moved toward him and put a gentle hand on his arm. "Tellie's going back to Houston in a week," she said quietly. "Do her a favor, and leave her alone while she finishes out her notice at the feedlot. Let her get used to being herself. Then maybe you can talk to her, and she'll listen. She's just hurt, J.B."

"She wasn't going back to school until fall semester," he said shortly. "She's been through a lot. She shouldn't start putting pressure on herself this soon."

"She doesn't see it that way. She's going to teach adult education at her college at night and attend classes during the day during summer semester." She lowered her eyes to his chest. "I want her to be happy. She's never going to be able to cope with the future until you're out of her life. I know you're fond of her, J.B., but it would be kinder to let her go."

He knew that. But he couldn't let her go, now that he knew what he wanted. He couldn't! His face reflected his inner struggle.

Her hand closed hard on his forearm. "Listen to me," she said firmly, "you of all people should know how painful it is to love someone you can't have. Everyone knows you don't want marriage or children, you just want a good time. Bella's your sort of woman. You couldn't hurt her if you hit her in the head with a brickbat, she's so thick. Just enjoy what you've got, J.B., and let Tellie heal."

He met her eyes. His were turbulent with frustrated need and worry. "I wanted to try to make it up to her," he bit off.

"Make what up to her?"

He looked away. "So much," he said absently. "I've never given her anything except pain, but I want to make her happy."

"You can't do that," his sister said quietly. "Not unless you want her for keeps."

His eyes narrowed in pain. He *did* want her for keeps. But he was afraid.

"Don't try to make her into a casual lover," Marge cautioned. "You'd destroy her."

"Don't you think I know?" he asked curtly. He turned away. "Maybe you're right, Marge," he said finally, defeated. "It would be kinder to let go for the time being. It's just that she cared for me, and I gave her nothing but mockery and indifference."

"You can't help that. You can't love people just because they want you to," Marge said wisely. "Tellie's going to make some lucky man a wonderful wife," she added gently. "She'll be the best mother a child could want. Don't rob her of that potential by giving her false hope."

Tellie, with a child. The anguish he felt was shocking. Tellie, married to another man, having children with another man, growing old with another man. He'd never considered the possibility that Tellie could turn her affections to someone else. He'd assumed that she'd always worship him. He'd given her the best reason on earth to hate him, by mocking her love for him.

"I've been taking a long look at myself," he said quietly. "I didn't like what I saw. I've been so busy protecting myself from pain that I've inflicted it on Tellie continuously. I didn't mean to. It was self-defense."

"It was cruel," Marge agreed. "Throwing Bella up to her, parading the woman here in Tellie's home, taunting her for wanting to take care of you." She shook her head. "I'm amazed that she was strong enough to take it all these years. I couldn't have."

"What about Grange?" he asked bitterly.

"What about him?" she replied. "She's very fond of him, and vice versa. But he isn't really in the running right now. He's a man with a past, a rebel who isn't comfortable in domestic surroundings. He likes having someone to take to the movies, but he's years away from being comfortable with even the idea of marriage."

That made J.B. feel somewhat better. Not a lot. He was thinking how miserable Tellie must be, having been force-fed the most horrible memories of her recent life. Coltrain said that her mind had been hiding from the trauma of the past. He didn't know that J.B. was responsible for it. He kept seeing Tellie on the gurney as she came into the emergency room, bruised and bleeding, and unconscious. If Grange hadn't shown up, Tellie would have drowned. He'd have had two dead women on his conscience, when one had always been too many.

The thought of Tellie, dead, was nauseating. She'd looked up to him since her early teens, followed him around, ached to just have him look at her. He'd denigrated those tender feelings and made her look like a lovesick fool. That, too, had been frustration, because he wanted a woman's passion from Tellie and she hadn't been able to give it to him. Not until now. He was sorry he'd been cruel to her in his anguish. But he couldn't go back and do it over again. He had to find some way back to Tellie. Some way to make up for what he'd done to her. Some way to convince her that he wanted a future with her.

"Tell her that I'm sorry," he said through his teeth. "She won't believe it, I know, but tell her anyway."

"Sorry for what?"

He met her eyes. "For everything."

"She'll be all right," Marge told him. "Really she will. She's stronger than I ever imagined."

"She's had so little love in her life," he recalled bitterly. "Her mother didn't really care much for her. She lost her grandfather at the time she needed him most. I shoved her off onto you and took it for granted that she'd spend her life looking up to me like some sort of hero." He drew in a long breath. "She was assaulted, you know, when she was fourteen. I've pushed that to the back of my mind and neither of us insisted that she go on with therapy after a few short sessions. Maybe those memories had her on the rack, and she couldn't even talk about them."

Marge chuckled. "Think so? Tellie beat the stuffing out of the little creep and testified against him, as well. He never even got to touch her inappropriately. No, she's over that, honestly."

"Even if she is, I made her suffer for having the gall to develop a crush on me."

He sounded disgusted with himself. Marge could have told him that it was no crush that lasted for years and years and took all sorts of punishment for the privilege of idolizing him. But he probably knew already.

He looked up at the darkening sky. "I know how it

must look, that I've had Bella staying at the house, and taken her on trips with me. But I've never slept with her," he added with brutal honesty.

Marge's eyebrows arched. That was an odd admission, from a rounder like her brother. "It can't be from lack of encouragement," she pointed out.

"No," he agreed. "It couldn't."

She felt inadequate to the task at hand. She wondered if she was doing the right thing by asking him not to approach Tellie. But she didn't really know what else there was to do. She felt sorry for both of them, especially for her brother who'd apparently discovered feelings for Tellie too late.

"I don't want a wife right now," he said, but without the old conviction. "She knows that, anyway."

"Sure she does," his sister agreed.

He turned and looked down at her with soft affection. "You doing okay?"

She nodded, smiling. "Nell's going to be a treasure. I can't do a lot of the stuff I used to, and the girls hate cooking and housework. With Tellie gone, it's up to us to manage. Nell will make my life so much easier. I can probably even go back to work when the medicine takes hold."

"Do you want to?" he asked curiously.

"Yes," she said. "I'm not the sort of person who enjoys staying at home with nothing intellectually challenging to do. I'd at least like to work on committees or help with community projects. Money isn't enough. Happiness takes more than a padded bank account."

"I'm finding that out," J.B. agreed, smiling. "You take care of yourself. If you need me, I'm just at the other end of the phone."

"I know that. I love you," she said, hugging him warmly.

He cleared his throat. "Yeah. Me, too." Expressing emotion was hard for him. She knew it.

She pulled away. "Go home and eat your frozen dinner."

He grimaced. "I sent Bella home in a cab. It's probably carbon by now."

"Albert will fix you something."

"When he finds out why Tellie's gone, I wouldn't bet on having anything edible in the near future."

"There are good restaurants all over Jacobsville," she pointed out.

He laughed good-naturedly. "I suppose I'll find one. Take care."

"You, too. Good night."

She closed the door and went back inside. Tellie's light was off when she went upstairs. The younger woman was probably worn completely out from the day's turmoil. She wished Tellie had never spent any time with J.B. at all. Maybe then she'd have been spared so much heartache.

Tellie was hard at work on her last day at the feedlot. It was a sweltering hot Friday, and storm clouds were gathering on the horizon. The wind was moving at a clip fast enough to stand the state flag out from its flagpole. When she went to lunch, sand blew right into her face as she climbed into Marge's car to drive home and eat.

The wind pushed the little car all over the road. It wasn't raining yet, but it looked as if it might rain buckets full.

She turned on the radio. There was a weather bulletin,

noting that a tornado watch was in effect for Jacobsville and surrounding counties until late that afternoon. Tellie was afraid of tornadoes. She hoped she never had to contend with one as long as she lived.

She ate a quick lunch, surrounded by Marge and Nell and the girls, since it was a teacher workday and they weren't in school. But when she was ready to leave, the skies were suddenly jet-black and the wind was roaring like a lion outside.

"Don't you dare get in that car," Marge threatened.

"Look at the color of those clouds," Nell added, looking past them out the door.

The clouds were a neon green, and there was a strange shape growing in them, emphasized by the increasing volume and force of the wind.

While they stood on the porch with the doors open, the sound of a siren broke into the dull rumble of thunder.

"Is that an ambulance?" Dawn asked curiously.

"No," Nell said at once. "It's the tornado alert, it's the siren on top of the courthouse." She ran for the weather radio, and found it ringing its batteries off. There was a steady red light on the console. Even before it blared out the words *tornado warning*, Nell knew what was coming.

"We have to get into the basement, right now!" Nell said, rushing to the hall staircase. "Come on!"

They piled after her, down the carpeted stairs and into the basement, into the room that had been especially built in case of tornadoes. It was steel-reinforced, with battery-powered lights and radio, water, provisions and spare batteries. The wind was audible even down there, now.

They closed themselves into the sheltered room and sat down on the carpeted floor to wait it out. Nell turned on the battery-powered scanner and instead of the weather, she turned to the fire and police frequencies.

Sharp orders in deep voices heralded the first of the damage. One fire and rescue unit was already on its way out to Caldwell Road from a report of a trailer being demolished. There came other reports, one after another. A roof was off this building, a barn collapsed, there were trees down in the road, trees down on power lines, trees falling on cars. It was the worst damage Tellie had heard about in her young life.

She thought about J.B., alone in his house with memories of his grandmother dying in such a storm. She wished she could stop caring about what happened to him. She couldn't. He was too much a part of her life, regardless of the treatment he'd handed out to her.

"I hope J.B.'s all right," Tellie murmured as the overhead light flickered and went out on the heels of a violent burst of thunder.

"So do I," Marge replied. "But he's got a shelter of his own. I'm sure he's in it."

The violence outside escalated. Tellie hid her head in her crossed arms and prayed that nobody would be killed.

Several minutes later, Nell eased the door open and listened for a minute before she went up the staircase. She was back shortly.

"It's over," she called to the others. "There's a little thunder, but it's far away, and you can see some blue sky. There are two big oak trees down in the front yard, though."

"I hope nobody got hurt," Marge mumbled as they went up the staircase.

"Call the house," Tellie pleaded with Nell. "Make sure J.B.'s all right."

Nell grimaced, but she did it. Argue they might, but she was fond of her old boss. The others stared at Nell while she listened. She winced and put down the receiver with a sad face.

"The lines are down," she said worriedly.

"We could drive over there and see," Dawn suggested.

Tellie recalled painfully the last time she'd driven over to J.B.'s place to tell him about a disaster. She couldn't bear to do it again.

"We can't get out of the driveway," Marge said uneasily. "One of the oaks is blocking the whole driveway."

"Give me your cell phone," Nell told Marge. "I'll call my cousin at the police department and get him to have someone check."

The joy of small-town life, Tellie was thinking. Surely the police could find out for them if J.B. was safe. Tellie prayed silently while Nell waited for her cousin to come to the phone.

She listened, spoke into the phone, and then listened again, grimacing. She thanked her cousin and put down the phone, facing the others with obvious reluctance.

"The tornado hit J.B.'s house and took off the corner where his office was. He's been taken to the hospital. My cousin doesn't know how bad he's hurt. There were some fatalities," she added, wincing when she saw their faces go white. Arguments and disagreements aside, J.B. was precious to everyone in the room.

Tellie spoke for all of them. "I'm going to the hospital," she said, "if I have to walk the whole five miles!"

Eleven

As it happened, they managed to get around the tree in their raincoats and walk out to the main highway. It was still raining, but the storm was over. Marge got on her cell phone and called her friend Barbara, who phoned one of the local firemen, an off-duty officer who agreed to pick them up and take them to the hospital.

When they got there, J.B. was in the emergency room sitting on an examination table, grinning. He had a cut across his forehead and a bruise on his bare shoulder, but his spirit seemed perfectly unstoppable.

Tellie almost ran to him. Almost. But just as she tensed to do it, a blond head came into view under J.B.'s other arm. Bella, in tears, sobbing, as she clung to J.B.'s bare chest mumbling how happy she was that he wasn't badly hurt.

She drew back and Marge and Nell and the girls joined her, out of sight of J.B. and Bella.

"You go ahead," she told them. "But…don't tell him I was here. Okay?"

Marge nodded, the others agreed. They understood without a word of explanation. "Go on out front, honey," Marge said gently. "We'll find you there when we're through."

"Okay. Thanks," Tellie said huskily, with a forced smile. Her heart was breaking all over again.

As Marge and the girls moved into the cubicle, Tellie walked back to the front entrance where there were chairs and a sofa around the information desk. She couldn't bring herself to walk into that room. J.B. hadn't looked as if he disliked Bella, despite what Marge had told her about his anger that Bella had spilled the beans about Tellie's past. He looked amazingly content, and his arm had been firm and close around Bella's shoulders.

Why, Tellie asked herself, did she continually bash her stupid head against brick walls? Love was such a painful emotion. Someday, she promised herself, she was going to learn how to turn it off. At least, as far as J. B. Hammock was concerned!

She didn't see Bella walk past the waiting room. She hardly looked up until Marge and the girls came back.

"He's going to be all right," Marge told her, hugging her gently. "Just a few cuts and bruises, nothing else. Let's go home."

Tellie smiled back, but only with her eyes.

J.B. buttoned his shirt while Bella stood waiting with his tie. He felt empty. Tellie hadn't even bothered to come and see about him. Nothing in recent years had hurt so much. She'd finally given up on him for good.

"We can get Albert to fix you something nice for breakfast," Bella said brightly.

"I'm not hungry." He took the tie and put it in place. "At least Marge and the girls cared enough to brave the storm to see me. Tellie couldn't be bothered, I guess," he said bitterly.

"She was in the waiting room," Bella said blankly.

He scowled. "Doing what?"

Bella shrugged one thin shoulder. "Crying."

Crying. She'd come to see about him after all, but she hadn't come into the room? Then he remembered that when Marge and the girls came in, he had Bella in his arms. He winced mentally. No wonder Tellie had taken off like that. She thought...

He looked down at Bella shrewdly. "I'm going to have to let Albert go," he said with calculated sadness. "With all the damage the storm did to the house and barn, I'm going to go in the hole for sure. It's been a bad year for cattle ranchers anyway."

Bella was very still. "You mean, you might lose everything?"

He nodded. "Well, I don't mind hard work. It's a challenge to start from scratch. You can move in with me, Bella, and take over the housekeeping and cooking..."

"I, uh, I have an invitation from my aunt in the Bahamas to come stay the summer with her," Bella said at once. "I'm really sorry, J.B., but I'm not the pioneering type, and I hate housework." She smiled. "It was fun while it lasted."

"Yes," he said, hiding a smile. "It was."

The next day was taken up finding insurance adjusters and contractors to repair the damage at the ranch.

He'd lost several head of livestock to injuries from falling trees and flying debris. The barn would have to be rebuilt, and the front part of the house would need some repair, as well. He wasn't worried, though. He could well afford what needed doing. He smiled at his subterfuge with Bella. As he'd suspected, she'd only wanted him for as long as she thought he was rich and could take her to five-star restaurants and buy her expensive presents.

When he had the repairs in hand, he put on a gray vested business suit, polished boots and his best creamy Stetson, and went over to Marge's to have a showdown with Tellie.

Nell opened the door, her eyes guilty and welcoming all at once. "Glad you're okay, boss," she said stiffly.

"Me, too," he agreed. "Where is everybody?"

"In the kitchen. We're just having lunch. There's plenty," she added.

He slipped an arm around her shoulders and kissed her wrinkled forehead with genuine affection. "I've missed you," he said simply, and walked her into the kitchen.

Marge and the girls looked up, smiling happily. They all rushed to hug him and fuss over him.

"Nell made minestrone," Marge said. "Sit down and have a bowl with us."

"It smells delicious," he remarked, putting his hat on the counter. He sat down, looking around curiously. "Where's Tellie?"

There was a long silence. Marge put down her spoon. "She's gone."

"Gone?" he exclaimed. "Where?"

"To Houston," Marge replied sadly. "She phoned some classmates and found an apartment she could share, then she phoned the dean at home and arranged to teach as an adjunct for night classes. Orientation was today, so she was able to sign up for her master's classes."

J.B. looked at his bowl with blind eyes. Tellie had gone away. She'd seen him with Bella, decided that he didn't want her, cut her losses and run for the border. Added to what she'd remembered, the painful things he'd said to her the day of the wreck, he couldn't blame her for that. She didn't know how drastically he'd changed toward her. Now he'd have to find a way back into her life. It wasn't going to be easy. She'd never fully trust him again.

But he wasn't giving up before he'd started, he told himself firmly. He'd never really tried to court Tellie. If she still cared at all, she wouldn't be able to resist him—any more than he could resist her.

Tellie was finding her new routine wearing. She taught a night class in history for four hours, two nights a week, and she went to classes three other days during the week. She was young and strong, and she knew she could cope. But she didn't sleep well, remembering Bella curled close in J.B.'s arm the night of the tornado. He wouldn't marry the beautiful woman, she knew that. He wouldn't marry anyone. But he had nothing to offer Tellie, and she knew, and suffered for it.

One of her classmates, John, who'd helped her find a room the night before she came back to Houston, paused by her table in the college coffeehouse.

"Tellie, can you cover for me in anthropology?" he asked. "I've got to work tomorrow morning."

She grinned up at him. John, like her, was doing master's work, although his was in anthropology. Tellie was taking the course as an elective. "I'll make sure I take good notes. How about covering for me in literature? I'll have a test to grade in my night-school course."

"No problem," he said. He grinned down at her, with a hand on the back of her chair. "Sure you don't want to go out to dinner with me Friday night?"

He was good-looking, and sweet, but he liked to drink and Tellie didn't. She was searching for a reply when she turned her gaze to the door.

Her heart jumped up into her throat. J.B. was standing just inside the door of the crowded café, searching. He spotted her and came right on, his eyes never leaving her as he wound through the crowd.

He stopped at her table. He spared John a brief glance that made veiled threats.

"I'd better run," John said abruptly. "See you later, Tellie."

"Sure thing."

J.B. pulled out a chair and sat down, tossing his hat idly onto the chair beside hers. He didn't smile. His eyes were intent, curiously warm.

"You ran, Tellie."

She couldn't pretend not to know what he was talking about. She pushed back her wavy hair and picked up her coffee cup. "It seemed sensible."

"Did it?"

She sipped coffee. "Did the tornado do much damage at the ranch?"

He shrugged. "Enough to keep me busy for several days, or I'd have been here sooner," he told her. He paused as the waitress came by, to order himself a cup of cappuccino. He glanced at Tellie and grinned. "Make that two cups," he told the waitress. She smiled and went to fill the order, while J.B. watched Tellie's face. "You can't afford it on your budget," he said knowingly. "My treat."

"Thanks," she murmured.

He leaned back in his chair and looked at her, intently, unsmiling. "Heard from Grange?"

She shook her head. "He phoned before I left Jacobsville to say he was going back to Washington, DC. Apparently he was subpoenaed to testify against his former commanding officer, who's being court-martialed."

He nodded. "Cag Hart told me. He and Blake Kemp and Grange served in the same division in Iraq. He said Grange's commanding officer had him thrown out of the army and took credit for a successful incursion that was Grange's idea."

"He told me," she replied.

The waitress came back with steaming cappuccinos for both of them. J.B. picked his up and sipped it. Tellie sniffed hers with her eyes closed, smiling. She loved the rich brew.

After a minute J.B. met her eyes again. "Tellie, is this what you really want?" he asked, indicating the coffee-house and the college campus.

The question startled her. She toyed with the handle of her cup. "Of course it is," she lied. "When I get my doctorate, I can teach at college level."

"And that's all you want from life?" he asked. "A career?"

She couldn't look at him. "We both know I'll never get very far any other way. I have plenty of friends who cry on my shoulder about their girlfriends or ask me to take notes for them in class, or keep their cats when they go on holiday." She shrugged. "I'm not the sort of woman that men want for keeps."

He closed his eyes on a wave of guilt. He'd said such horrible things to her. She already had a low self-image. He'd lowered it more, in a fit of bad temper.

"Beauty alone isn't worth much," he said after a minute. "Neither is wealth. After I got out of the emergency room, I went home to an empty house, Tellie," he said sadly. "I stood there in the vestibule, with crystal chandeliers and Italian marble all around me, mahogany staircases, Persian rugs...and suddenly it felt like being alone in a tomb. You know what, Tellie? Wealth isn't enough. In fact, it's nothing, unless you have someone to share it with."

"You've got Bella," she said with more bitterness than she knew.

He laughed. "I told her I was in the hole and likely to lose everything," he commented amusedly. "She suddenly remembered an invitation to spend the summer in the sun with her aunt."

Tellie's eyes lifted to his. She was afraid to hope.

He reached across the table and curled her fingers into his. "Finish your cappuccino," he said gently. "I want to talk to you."

She was hardly aware of what she was doing. This must be a dream, J.B. sitting here with her, holding her hand. She was going to wake up any minute. Meanwhile, she might as well enjoy the fantasy. She smiled at him and sipped her cappuccino.

He took her out to his car and put her in the passenger side. When he was seated behind the wheel, he reached back and brought out a shopping bag with colored paper tastefully arranged in it. "Open it," he said.

She reached in and pulled out a beautiful lacy black mantilla with red roses embroidered across it. She caught her breath. She collected the beautiful things. This was the prettiest one she'd ever seen. She looked at him with a question in her eyes.

"I picked it out myself," he told her quietly. "I didn't send Jarrett shopping this time. Don't stop. There's more, in the bottom of the bag."

Puzzled, she reached down and her fingers closed around a velvety box with a bow on it. She pulled it out and stared at it curiously. Another watch? she wondered.

"Go on. Open it."

She took off the bow and opened the box. Inside was…another box. Frowning, she opened that one, too, and found a very small square box. She opened that one, too, and caught her breath. It was a diamond. Not too big, not too small, but of perfect quality in what looked like expensive yellow gold. Next to it was an equally elegant band studded with diamonds that matched the solitaire.

J.B. was holding his breath, although it didn't show.

She met his searching gaze. "I…don't understand."

He took the box from her, lifted out the solitaire and slid it gently onto her ring finger. "Now, do you understand?"

She was afraid to try. Surely it was still part of the dream. If not, it was a cruel joke.

"You don't want me," she said bitterly. "I'm ugly, and you can't bear me to touch you…!"

He pulled her across into his arms and kissed her with unabashed passion, cradling her against his broad chest while his mouth proceeded to wear down all her protests. When she was clinging to him, breathless, he folded her in his arms and rocked her hungrily.

"I was ashamed that you found me like that with Bella," he said through his teeth. "It was like getting caught red-handed in an adulterous relationship. For God's sake, don't you have any idea how I feel about you, Tellie?" he groaned. "I was frustrated and impatient, and Bella was handy. But I've never slept with her," he added firmly. "And I never would have. You have to believe that."

She was reeling mentally. She let her head slide back on his shoulder so that she could see his face. "But... why were you so cruel...?"

His lean hand pressed against her cheek caressingly. "Do you remember when you were eighteen?" he asked huskily. "And I made love to you on the couch in the study?"

She flushed. "Yes."

"You loved being kissed. But when I started touching you, I felt you draw back. You liked kissing me, but you weren't comfortable with anything more intimate than that. You didn't feel anything approaching passion, Tellie. You were like a child." He sucked in a harsh breath. "And I was burning, aching, to have you. I knew you were too young. It was unfair of me to push you into a relationship you weren't nearly ready for." He studied her shocked face. "So I drew back and waited. And waited. I grew bitter from the waiting. It made me cruel."

Her eyes were wide, shocked, delighted, as she realized what had been going on. She hadn't dreamed that he might feel something this powerful for her, and for so long.

"Yes, now you see it, don't you?" he breathed, lowering his mouth to hers again, savoring its shy response. "I was at the end of my rope, and you seemed just the same. Desperation made me cruel. Then," he whispered, "you lost your memory and I had you in my house. I touched you…and you wanted me." He kissed her hungrily, roughly. "I was over the moon, Tellie. You'd forgotten, temporarily, all the terrible things I said to you when you caught me with Bella. But it ended, all too soon. Your memory came back." He buried his face in her neck, rocking her. "You hated me. I didn't know what to do. So I waited some more. And hoped. I might still be waiting, except that Bella told me she saw you crying in the emergency room when I thought you hadn't even come to see about me after the tornado hit." He kissed her again, hungrily, and felt with a sense of wonder her arms clinging to him, her mouth answering the passion of his own.

"You brought that awful woman to Marge's house and let her insult me," she complained hotly.

He kissed her, laughing. "You were jealous," he replied, unashamedly happy. "It gave me hope. I dangled Bella to make you jealous. It worked almost too well."

"You vicious man," she accused, but she was smiling.

"Look who's talking," he chided. "Grange gave me some bad moments."

"I like him very much, but I didn't love him," she replied quietly.

"No. You love me," he whispered. His eyes ate her face. "And I love you, Tellie," he whispered as he bent again to her mouth. "I love you with all my heart!"

She closed her eyes and gave in to his ardor, blind to the fact that they were sitting in a parked car on a college campus.

She felt some disturbance around her and looked up. In front of the car were three students with quickly printed squares of poster paper. One said "9," and two said "10." They were grading J.B. on his technique. He followed her amused gaze and burst out laughing.

He drew her up closer. "Don't protest," he murmured as his head bent. "I'm going for a perfect score…"

He took her back to his hotel. His intentions were honorable, of course, but it was inevitable that once they were alone, he'd kiss her. He did, and all at once the raging fever he'd contained for so many years broke its bonds with glorious abandon.

"J.B.," she protested weakly as he picked her up and carried her into one of the bedrooms in his suite, closing the door firmly behind them.

"You can't stop an avalanche, honey," he ground out against her mouth. "I'm sorry. I love you. I can't wait any longer…!"

She was flat on her back, her jeans on the floor, swiftly joined by her blouse and everything underneath. He looked down at her with a harsh, heartfelt groan. "I knew you'd be perfect, Tellie," he whispered as he bent to touch his mouth reverently to her breasts.

There was hardly any sane answer to that sort of rapt delight. She felt faintly apprehensive, but she was wearing an engagement ring and it was apparent that it wasn't a sham, or a dream. She came straight up off the bed as his mouth increased its warm pressure on her breast and began to taste it with his tongue.

"Like that, do you?" he whispered huskily. "It's only the beginning."

As he spoke, he sat up and quickly removed every bit of fabric that would have separated them.

Shyly she looked at his hard, muscular body with eyes that showed equal parts of awe and apprehension.

"People have been doing this for millennia," he whispered as he lowered his body against hers. "If it didn't feel good, nobody would indulge."

"Well, yes, but..." she began.

His lean hand smoothed over her belly. "You have to trust me," he said softly. "I won't hurt you. I swear it."

Her body relaxed a little. "I've heard stories," she began.

"I'm not in them," he replied easily, smiling. "If I were less modest, I'd tell you that women used to write my telephone number on bathroom walls."

That tickled her and she laughed. "Don't you dare brag about your conquests," she muttered.

He laughed. "Practice," he said against her mouth. "I was practicing, while I waited for you. And this is what I learned, Tellie," he added as his body slid against hers.

She felt his hands and his mouth all over her. The lights were on and she couldn't have cared less. Sensation upon sensation rippled through her untried body. She saw J.B.'s face harden, his dark green eyes glitter as he increased the pressure of his powerful legs to part hers, as his mouth swallowed one small, firm breast and drew his tongue against it in a sweet, harsh rhythm.

He was touching her in ways she'd only read about. She gasped and moaned and, finally, begged. She hadn't dreamed that her body could feel such things, could react in this headlong, demanding, insistent way to a man's slow, insistent ardor.

The slow thrust of his body widened her eyes alarmingly and she tensed, but he whispered to her, kissed her eyes closed and never stopped for an instant. He found the place, and the pressure, that made her begin to sob and dig her nails into his hips. Then he smiled as he increased the rhythm and heard her cry out again and again with helpless delight.

It seemed hours before he finally gave in to his own need and shuddered against her in a culmination that exceeded his wildest dreams of fulfillment. He held her close, intimately joined to him, and fought to get enough air to breathe.

"Cataclysmic," he whispered into her throat. "That's what it was."

She was shivering, too, having experienced what the self-help articles referred to as "multiple culminations of pleasure."

"I never dreamed…!" she exclaimed breathlessly.

"Neither did I, sweetheart," he said heavily. "Neither did I."

He moved and rolled over, drawing her close against his side. They were both damp with sweat and pulsating in the aftermath of explosive satisfaction.

"Marge would kill us both," she began.

He chuckled. "Not likely. She's been busy on our behalf."

"Doing what?" she asked.

He ruffled her dark hair. "Sending out emailed invitations, calling caterers, ordering stuff. Which reminds me, I hope you're free Saturday. We're getting married at the ranch."

She sat up, gasping. "We're what?"

"Getting married," he replied slowly. "Why do you think I bought two rings?"

"But you've been swearing for years that you'd never get married!" Then she remembered why and her eyes went sad. "Because of that woman, the one you were going to marry," she said worriedly.

He drew her down beside him and looked at her solemnly. "When I was twenty-one, I fell in love. She was my exact opposite, and because my father opposed the marriage, I rebelled and ran headlong into it. She took the easy way out, rather than fighting him. You were right about that, although it hurt me to acknowledge it," he said quietly. "You'd have marched right up to my father and told him to do his worst." He smiled. "It's one of the things I love about you, that stubborn determination. She wasn't strong enough to stand up to him. So she killed herself. It would have been a disaster, if she hadn't," he added. "I'd have walked all over her, and she'd have been miserable. As things worked out, she saved her brother from prison and both of us from a bitter life together. I'm sorry it happened that way. I think she was mentally unstable. She was unhappy and she couldn't see a future without me. If she'd been able to talk to anyone about it, I don't think she'd have done it. I'll always regret what my father did, but he paid for it, in his way. So did I, unfortunately. Until you came along, and shook up my life, I didn't have much interest in living."

She felt happier, knowing that. She was sad for his fiancée, but she couldn't be sad that she'd ended up with J.B.

He traced her eyebrows, exploring her face, her soft body, with slow, tender tracings. "I never knew what love was, until you were eighteen. It was too soon, but I'd have married you then, if you'd been able to return what I felt for you."

Her arms closed around him. "It was too soon. I have a degree and I've had independence."

"And now?" he asked. "What about college?"

She drew in a slow, lazy breath. "You can always go

back to college," she murmured. "I'd like to be with you for a few years. We might have a baby together and I'll be needed at home for a while. I can teach adult education at our community college if I get the urge. I only need a BA for that, and I've got it."

"We might have a baby together?" he teased, smiling. "How would that happen?"

She drew up one long leg and slid it gently over one of his. "We could do a lot more of what we've just done," she suggested, moving closer to him. "If we do it enough, who knows what might happen?"

He pursed his lips and moved between her legs. "More of this, you mean?" he drawled, easing down.

"Definitely…more of this," she whispered unsteadily. She closed her eyes and tugged his mouth down over hers. Then she didn't speak again for a long, long time.

Twelve

Nell was overcome with delight when Tellie walked into Marge's house with J.B.'s arm around her. "You're back," she exclaimed to Tellie. "But what…how…why?"

J.B. lifted Tellie's left hand and extended it, with the diamond solitaire winking on her ring finger.

"Oh, my goodness!" Nell exclaimed, and hugged both of them with tearful enthusiasm. "Have you told Marge and the girls?" she asked.

"Marge is making all the arrangements for us," J.B. said with an ear-to-ear grin. "I'm sure she's told the girls. But it looks as if she was saving it as a surprise for you!"

"I can't believe it," Nell repeated, dabbing at her wet eyes. "I've never been so happy for anyone in my life! Have you had lunch?"

"Not yet," J.B. replied. "I thought we might have it with you, if that's all right?" he added with unexpected courtesy.

Nell's eyebrows went up. "Well! That's the first time you've ever treated me with any sort of courtesy."

"She's been working on me," he said, nodding toward Tellie.

"To good effect, apparently, too," Nell agreed. "I'm just floored!"

"Cook while you're getting adjusted," J.B. suggested. "I'm going to get Tellie's bag from her room and put it in the car. Marge packed it for her."

"Thanks," she said shyly, and not without a smile.

"How did you do it?" Nell asked when he was out of sight.

Tellie shook her head. "I have no idea. He showed up at the café where I was having coffee, and the next thing I knew, I was engaged. I thought he was involved with Bella."

"So did I," Nell agreed.

"But he wasn't," she replied, with a happy smile. "I went away thinking my life was over. Now look at me."

"I couldn't be happier for you," Nell said. "For both of you."

"So am I," Tellie told her. "In fact, I'm over the moon!"

Later, Marge and the girls came home, and all of them spent the evening going over wedding plans, because there wasn't much time.

J.B. drove Tellie to his house and installed her in the same guest bedroom he'd given her when she stayed with him during her bout of amnesia. They'd already decided that they'd abstain from any more sensual adventures until after the wedding, however old-fashioned it sounded.

The next day, J.B. bounced Tellie out of bed early. "Get up, get up," he teased, lifting her free of the covers to kiss her with pure delight. "We're going shopping."

"You and me?" she asked, breathless.

He nodded, smiling. "You look pretty first thing in the morning."

"But I'm all rumpled and my hair isn't brushed."

He kissed her again, tenderly. "You're the most beautiful thing in my house, and in my heart," he whispered against her lips.

She kissed him back, sighing contentedly. She had the world in her arms, she thought. The whole world!

Albert fixed them croissants and strong coffee for breakfast, and J.B. privately lamented the lack of bacon and eggs and biscuits that Nell had always provided. Albert considered such a breakfast too heavy for normal people.

After breakfast, J.B. drove Tellie to a boutique in San Antonio to shop for a wedding gown.

"But you can't see it!" she insisted.

He glowered at her. "That's an old superstition!"

"Whether it is or not, you aren't looking," she said firmly. "Go get a cup of coffee and come back in an hour. Okay?"

He sighed irritably. "All right."

She reached up and kissed him sweetly. "I love you. Humor me."

He stopped glowering and smiled. "Headache," he accused.

"I'll make it all up to you. I promise."

He bent and brushed his mouth over her closed eyelids. "You already have. Everything!"

She hugged him close. "Go away."

He laughed, winking as he left her to go down the street toward a nearby Starbucks.

The owner of the boutique gave her a wicked grin. "You manage him very well."

"I do, don't I? But he doesn't know I'm doing it, and we're not going to tell him. Deal?"

"Deal! Now let me show you what I've got in your size…"

Tellie ended up with a gloriously embroidered gown with cap sleeves, a tight waist, a vee neckline and an exquisite long train, also embroidered. The veil was held in place by jeweled combs and fell to the waist in front. It was the most beautiful gown she'd ever seen, and it suited her nice tan.

"I love it," Tellie told the owner. "It's a dream of a wedding gown."

"It looks lovely on you," came the satisfied reply. "Now for the accessories!"

By the time J.B. came back, the gown and accessories were all neatly boxed and ready to carry out.

"Did you get something pretty?" he asked.

"Something beautiful," Tellie told him, smiling.

"I wish you'd let me pay for it," he said as they drove home. "I'd have taken you to Neiman Marcus."

"What I got is lovely," she said, "and one of a kind. The owner of the boutique is a designer in her own right. You'll see. It's going to make a stir."

He clasped her hand tight in his own. "You'll make the stir, sweetheart. You're lovely."

She gave him an odd look, and his jaw tautened.

"I didn't mean it, Tellie," he said quietly. "I was ashamed and frustrated and I took it all out on you. I wanted you so much. I thought you'd never be able to feel desire for me. It made me cruel."

"Maybe if you'd tried a little harder," she pointed out, "it wouldn't have taken me so long."

He sighed. "Leave it to you to put your finger on a nerve and push," he said philosophically. "Yes, I should have. But I was still living in the past, afraid of being devastated again by love. It wasn't until Grange came along, and cauterized the wound, that I realized I was using the past as an excuse. Maybe I sensed that it was going to be different with you."

"I can see why you were reluctant," she said. Her hand tightened in his. "But I'd never hurt you, J.B. I love you too much."

"Thank God for that," he said, sighing contentedly. He smiled. "You'll never get away from me, Tellie."

"I'll never want to." She meant it, too.

The wedding was a small, private one, but two reporters with cameramen showed up, and so did Grange, resplendent in a blue vested suit. He looked very different from the cowboy Tellie had dated. The Ballengers were there, also, with their wives, and of course Marge and Dawn and Brandi and Nell. Even Albert put on a suit and gave Tellie away.

Tellie couldn't see much of J.B. as she walked down the aisle with her veil neatly in place. But when she got to the altar, she was shocked, delighted and amused to see what he was wearing with his suit. It was one of the ties—the gaudy, green-and-gold dragon tie that she'd given him for every single birthday and Christmas for years. She had to force herself not to laugh. But she didn't miss his wink.

When the minister pronounced them man and wife, he turned and lifted her veil, and the look on his face was the most profound she'd ever seen. He smiled, tenderly, and bent and kissed her with soft, sweet reverence.

Nell and Marge cried. The girls sighed. Tellie pressed close into J.B.'s arms and just hugged him, feeling radiant and happier than she'd ever been in her life. He hugged her back, sighing contentedly.

"I suppose the best man won," Grange mused at the reception Albert and the caterers had prepared in the ballroom at the ranch.

"I guess he did," J.B. replied, with a forced smile.

"She's very special," the other man said quietly. "But it was always you, and I always knew it. I'm a bad marriage risk."

"I thought I was, too," J.B. replied. He looked toward Tellie with his heart in his eyes. "But maybe I'm not."

Grange just laughed, and lifted his champagne glass in a toast.

"How'd you come out at the court-martial?" J.B. asked.

Grange grinned. "He got five years. I got a commendation and the offer of reinstatement."

"Are you going to take them up on it?"

Grange shrugged. "I don't know yet. I'll have to think about it. I've had another offer. I'm thinking it over."

"One that involves staying here?" J.B. asked shrewdly.

"Yes." He met the other man's gaze. "Is that going to be a problem?"

J.B. smiled wryly. "Not now that Tellie's married to me," he drawled.

Grange laughed. "Just checking."

J.B. sipped champagne. "The past is over," he said. "We can't change it. All we can do is live with it. I loved your sister. I'm sorry things worked out the way they did."

"She was a sad person," the other man replied solemnly. "It wasn't the first time she'd thought about taking her own life. There were two other times, both connected with men she thought didn't want her."

J.B. looked shocked.

Grange grimaced. "Sorry. Maybe I shouldn't have said anything. But in the long run, you're better off with the truth. She was emotionally shattered, since childhood. She went to a psychiatrist when she was in high school for counseling, because she slashed her wrists."

"I didn't know," J.B. ground out.

"Neither did I until my father was dying, and told me everything. He said my mother had always worried that suicide would end my sister's life. She couldn't handle stress at all. It's nothing against her. Some people are born not being able to cope with life."

"I suppose they are," J.B. said, and he was remembering Tellie, and how she would have handled the same opposition from his father.

Grange clapped J.B. on the shoulder. "Go dance with your wife. Let the past bury itself. Life goes on. I hope both of you will be very happy. And I mean that."

J.B. shook his hand. "Thanks. You can come to dinner sometimes. As long as you don't bring roses," he added dryly.

Grange burst out laughing.

* * *

That night, Albert went to see his brother for the weekend, and Tellie and J.B. spent lazy, delicious hours trying out new ways to express their love for each other in his big king-size bed.

She was shivering and pouring sweat and gasping when they finally stopped long enough to sip cold champagne.

"I just didn't read enough books," she said breathlessly.

He grinned. "Good thing I did."

She laughed, curling close to his hairy chest. "Don't brag."

"I don't need to. Will you be able to walk tomorrow?"

"Hobble, maybe," she murmured sleepily. "I'm so tired…!"

He bent and kissed her eyelids shut. "You're magnificent."

"So are you," she said, kissing his chest.

He took the champagne glass away, put it on the table along with his own and stroked her hair. "Tellie?"

"Hmm?"

"I hope you want kids right away."

"Hmm."

He drew in a lazy breath and closed his eyes. "That had better be a yes, because we forgot to think about precautions."

She didn't answer. He didn't worry. She'd already made her stand on children very clear. He figured he'd get used to fatherhood. It would be as natural as making love to Tellie. And *that* he seemed to do to perfection, he thought, as he glanced down at her satisfied, dreamy expression.

* * *

"It's just indecent, that's what it is," Marge groaned as she and Tellie went shopping at the mall outside Jacobsville. She glowered at the younger woman. "I mean, honestly, J.B. didn't have to be so impatient!"

"It was a mutual impatience," Tellie pointed out with a grin, "and I'm happier than I ever dreamed I could be."

"Yes, but Tellie, you've just been married two weeks!"

"I noticed."

Marge shook her head. "J.B.'s strutting already. You shouldn't let him send you on errands like this. I mean, things do go wrong, sometimes…"

"They won't this time," Tellie said dreamily. "I'm as sure of it as I've ever been of anything. Besides," she added with a grin, "tell me you aren't excited."

Marge grimaced. "Well, I am, but…"

"No buts," Tellie said firmly. "We just take one day at a time and enjoy it. Hi, Chief!" she broke off to greet their police chief. "How's it going?"

"Life is beautiful," Cash Grier said with a grin.

"We heard that Tippy laid a frying pan across the skull of her would-be assassin," Marge said, digging gently.

"She did. And have you seen the tabloid story about it, by any chance?" he asked them, and his dark eyes twinkled.

"The one that says you're getting married soon?" Tellie teased.

"That's the one. In fact, we're getting married tomorrow." He chuckled. "I'm not going to let her get away now!"

"Congratulations," Tellie told him. "I hope you'll both be as happy as J.B. and I are."

"We're going to be," he said with assurance. "I expect to grow old fighting what little crime I can dig up here in Jacobsville. In between, Tippy may make a movie or two before we start our family."

Tellie put a hand on her belly. "J.B. and I already have started," she said, smiling from ear to ear. "The blood test came back positive just yesterday."

He whistled. "You two don't waste time, do you? You've only been married two weeks!"

"We were sort of in a hurry," Tellie chuckled.

"A flaming rush," Marge added. "And now we're out prematurely buying maternity clothes, do you believe it?"

"That's the spirit," Cash said. "If you've got it, flaunt it, I always say."

He went on toward his squad car, and Tellie dragged Marge into the maternity shop.

Three months later, J.B. came in looking like two miles of rough road. He was wet and muddy and his chaps were as caked as his shirt. But when he saw Tellie in her maternity pants and blouse, all the weariness went out of his face.

He chuckled, catching her by the waist. "I love the way that looks," he said, and bent to kiss her. "I'm all muddy," he murmured when she tried to move closer. "We don't want to mess up that pretty outfit. Tell you what, I'll clean up and we'll call Marge and the girls and go out for a nice supper. How about that?"

She hesitated, looking guilty. "Well..."

His eyebrows arched. "Is something wrong?" he asked, suddenly worried.

"It's not that."

"Then, what?"

"So you're finally home!" came a stringent voice from the direction of the kitchen. Nell came out, wearing a dirty apron and carrying a big spoon. "I made you chicken and dumplings, homemade rolls and a congealed fruit salad," she announced with a smile.

J.B. drew in a sharp breath. "You're back? For good?" he asked hopefully.

"For good," she said. "I have to take care of Tellie and make sure she eats right. Marge is getting some help of her own, so it isn't as if I'm leaving her in the lurch. And I gave her Albert. Is that okay?" she added worriedly.

"Thank God!" he exclaimed. "I didn't have the heart to let him go, but I'm damned tired of French cooking! All I want is meat and potatoes. And apple pie," he added.

"I made one," Nell said. "Albert likes Marge, and the girls love his cooking. They're of an age to like parties. So, all our problems are solved. Right?"

He grinned. "Most of them, anyway. I'll get cleaned up and we'll have a romantic dinner for…"

"Six," Nell informed him.

"Six?" he exclaimed.

Tellie moved close to him and reached up to kiss his dirt-smudged cheek. "I invited Marge and the girls over for chicken and dumplings. It will be romantic, though, I promise. We'll have lots of candles."

He laughed, shaking his head. "Okay. An intimate little romantic dinner for six." He kissed her back. "I love you," he said.

She smiled. "I love you back."

He went upstairs and Nell sighed. "I never thought

I'd see the boss look like that," she told Tellie. "What a change!"

"I inspire him," Tellie mused. "And while I'm inspiring, I'd really like to remodel that frilly pink bedroom and make a nursery out of it."

Nell wriggled her eyebrows. "Count on me as a co-conspirator. I'll be in the kitchen."

Tellie watched her go. She looked toward the staircase, where J.B. had disappeared. So much pain, she thought, had led to so much pleasure. Perhaps life did balance the two after all. She knew that she'd been so happy. J.B. and a baby, too. Only a few months before, she'd been agonizing over a lonely, cold future. Now she was married, and pregnant, and her husband loved her obsessively. It was a dream come true.

She turned and followed Nell into the kitchen. Life, she thought dreamily, was sweet.

Later, she spared a thought for that poor young woman who'd died so tragically years ago, and for Grange, who'd paid a high price for his illegal activities. She hoped Grange would find his own happiness one day. He'd gone to DC, but was planning to come back and do something a little more adventurous than working for the Ballengers, but he didn't mention what it was. He'd sent her a postcard telling her that, with his new address. J.B. had seen the card, and murmured that he hoped Tellie wasn't planning any future contact with Grange. She assured him that she hadn't any such plans, and kissed him so enthusiastically that very soon he forgot Grange altogether.

Marge and the girls were happy about the baby, and Marge was finally in the best of health on her new medicines. Tellie was relieved that she continued to improve.

That night, while J.B. slept, Tellie sat and watched his lean, hard face, wiped clean of expression, and thought how very lucky she was. He wasn't perfect, but he was certainly Tellie's dream of perfection. She bent and very softly kissed his chiseled mouth.

His dark eyes slid open and twinkled. "Don't waste kisses, sweetheart," he whispered, and reached up to draw her down into his warm, strong arms. "They're precious."

"Yours certainly are," she whispered back, and she smiled contentedly against his mouth.

"Yours, too," he murmured.

She closed her eyes and thought of a happy future, where they'd be surrounded by children and, later, grand-children. They'd grow old together, safe in the cocoon of their love for each other, with a lifetime of memo-ries to share. And this, Tellie thought with delight, was only the beginning of it all! Her arms tightened around J.B. Life was sweeter than her dreams had ever been. Sweeter than them all.

* * * * *

IN BED WITH
THE WRANGLER

Barbara Dunlop

For my husband.

One

Strains from the jazz band followed Royce Ryder as he strode across the carpeted promenade between the ballroom and the lobby lounge of the Chicago Ritz-Carlton Hotel. He tugged his bow tie loose, popping the top button on his white tuxedo shirt while inhaling a breath of relief. His brother, Jared, and his new sister-in-law, Melissa, were still dancing up a storm in the ballroom, goofy smiles beaming on their faces as they savored every single moment of their wedding reception.

But it had been a long night for Royce. He'd stood up for his brother, joked his way through an endless receiving line, then toasted the bride and the bridesmaids. He'd socialized, danced, eaten cake and even caught the garter—a reflexive action that had everything to do with his years as a first baseman in high school and college, and nothing whatsoever to do with his future matrimony prospects.

Now his duty was done, and it was time for a final night in the civilized surroundings of downtown Chicago before his sentence began in Montana. Okay, so managing the family ranch wasn't exactly hard labor in Alcatraz, but for a man who'd been piloting a jet plane around the world for the past three years, it was going to be a very long month.

It wasn't that he begrudged Jared his honeymoon. Quite the contrary, he was thrilled that his brother had fallen in love and married. And the better he got to know Melissa, the more he liked her. She was smart and sassy, and clearly devoted to both Jared and their younger sister, Stephanie. Royce wished the couple a fantastic, well-deserved trip to the South Pacific.

It was just bad luck that McQuestin, the family's Montana cattle ranch manager, had broken his leg in three places last week. McQuestin was down for the count. Stephanie was busy training her students for an important horse jumping competition. So Royce was it.

He slipped onto a padded bar stool, the majority of his focus on the selection of single malts on the mirrored backlit shelf as he gave the woman next to him a passing glance. But he quickly did a double take, disregarding the liquor bottles and focusing on her. She was stunningly gorgeous: blond hair, dark-fringed blue eyes, flushed cheeks, wearing a shimmering, skintight, red-trimmed, gold dress that clung to every delectable curve. Her lips were bold red, and her perfectly manicured fingers were wrapped around a sculpted martini glass.

"What can I get for you?" asked the bartender, dropping a coaster on the polished mahogany bar in front of Royce.

"Whatever she's having," said Royce without taking his gaze from the woman.

She turned to paste him with a back-off stare, her look of disdain making him wish he'd at least kept his tie done up. But a split second later, her expression mellowed.

"Vodka martini?" the waiter confirmed.

"Sure," said Royce.

"You were the best man," the woman stated, her voice husky-sexy in the quiet of the lounge.

"That I was," Royce agreed easily, more than willing to use tonight's official position to his advantage. "Royce Ryder. Brother of the groom. And you are?"

"Amber Hutton." She held out a feminine hand.

He took it in his. It was small, smooth, with delicate fingers and soft skin. His mind immediately turned to the things she could do to him with a hand like that.

"Tired of dancing?" he asked as the waiter set the martini in front of him. He assumed she would have had plenty of partners in the crowded ballroom.

"Not in the mood." Her fingers moved to the small plastic spear that held a trio of olives in her glass. She shot a brief glance behind her toward the promenade that led to the sparkling ballroom. Then she leaned closer to Royce. He met her halfway.

"Hiding out," she confided.

"From?" he prompted.

She hesitated. Then she shook her head. "Nothing important."

Royce didn't press. "Any way I can be of assistance?"

She arched a perfectly sculpted brow. "Don't hit on me."

"Ouch," he said, feigning a wounded ego.

That prompted a smile. "You did ask."

"I was expecting a different answer."

"I'll understand if you want to take off."

Royce gazed into her eyes for a long moment. Past her smile, he could see trouble lurking. Though women with trouble usually sent him running for the hills, he gave a mental shrug, breaking one of his own rules. "I don't want to take off."

"You one of those nice guys, Royce Ryder?"

"I am," he lied. "Good friend. Confidant. A regular boy next door."

"Funny, I wouldn't have guessed that about you."

"Ouch, again," he said softly, even though she was dead right. He'd never been any woman's good friend or confidant.

"You strike me as more of a playboy."

"Shows you how wrong you can be." He glanced away, taking a sip of the martini. Not a lot of taste to it.

"And you left the party because…"

"I wasn't in the mood for dancing, either," he admitted.

"Oh…" She let her tone turn the word into a question.

He swiveled on the stool so he was facing her. "I'm a jet pilot," he told her instead of explaining his mood. Time had proven it one of his more successful pickup lines. Sure, she'd asked him not to hit on her, but if, in the course of their conversation, she decided she was interested, well, he had no control over that, did he?

"For an airline?" she asked.

"For Ryder International. A corporate jet."

Her glass was empty, so he drained his own and signaled the bartender for another round.

"Getting me drunk won't work," she told him.

"Who says I'm getting you drunk? I'm drowning my own sorrows. I'm only including you to be polite."

She smiled again and seemed to relax. "You don't strike me as a man with sorrows, Mr. 'I'm a Jet Pilot' Best Man."

"Shows you how wrong you can be," he repeated. "I'm here celebrating my last night of freedom." He raised his skewer of olives to his mouth, sliding one off the end.

"Are you getting married, too?"

He nearly choked on the olive. "No."

"Going to jail?" she tried.

He resisted the temptation to nod. "Going to Montana."

She smiled at his answer. "There's something wrong with Montana?"

"There is when you were planning to be in Dubai and Monaco."

Her voice turned melodic, and she shook her head in mock sympathy. "You poor, poor man."

He grunted his agreement. "I'll be babysitting the family ranch. Our manager broke his leg, and Jared's off on his honeymoon."

Her smile stayed in place, but something in her eyes softened. "So, you really are a nice guy?"

"A regular knight in shining armor."

"I like that," she said. Then she was silent for a moment, tracing a swirl in the condensation on the full glass in front of her. "There are definitely times when a girl could use a knight in shining armor."

Royce heard the catch in her voice and saw the tightness in her profile. The trouble was back in her expression.

"This one of those times?" he found himself asking, even though he knew better.

She propped an elbow on the polished bar and leaned her head against her hand, facing him. "Have you ever been in love, Royce Ryder?"

"I have not," he stated without hesitation. And he didn't ever intend to go there. Love guaranteed nothing and complicated everything.

"Don't you think Melissa looked happy today?"

"I'm guessing most brides are happy."

"They are," Amber agreed. Then she lifted her head and moved her left hand, and he realized he'd missed the three carats sparkling on the third finger.

Rookie mistake. What the hell was the matter with him tonight?

Amber should have had more sense than to attend a wedding in her current mood. She should have made up an obligation or faked a headache. Her mother was in New York for the weekend, but it wasn't as if her father needed moral support at a social function.

"You're engaged." Royce Ryder's voice pierced her thoughts, his gaze focused on her ring.

"I am," she admitted, reflexively twisting the diamond in a circle around her finger.

"Don't I feel stupid," Royce muttered.

She cocked her head, and their gazes met and held. "Why?" she asked.

He gave a dry chuckle and raised his martini glass to his lips. "Because I may be subtle, but I *am* hitting on you."

She fought a grin at his bald honesty. "Sorry to disappoint you."

"Not your fault."

True. She had been up-front with him. Still, she couldn't help wondering if there was something in her expression, her tone of voice, or maybe her body language that had transmitted more than a passing interest. Not that she'd cheat on Hargrove. Even if…

She shut those thoughts down.

She'd never cheat on Hargrove. But there was no denying that Royce was an incredibly attractive man. He seemed smart. He had a good sense of humor. If she was the type to get picked up, and if he was the one doing the picking, and if she wasn't engaged, she might just be interested.

"What?" he prompted, scanning her expression.

"Nothing." She turned back to her drink. "I'll understand if you leave."

He shifted, and his tone went low. "I'll understand if you ask me to go."

Her brain told her mouth to form the words, but somehow they didn't come out. A few beats went by while the bartender served another couple at the end of the bar, a smoky tune vibrated from the ballroom and a group of young women laughed and chatted as they pulled two tables together in the center of the lounge.

"He here?" asked Royce, cutting a glance to the ballroom. "Did you have a fight?"

Amber shook her head. "He's in Switzerland."

Royce straightened. "Ahh."

"What ahh?"

His deep, blue-eyed gaze turned cocky and speculative. "You're lonely."

Amber's mouth worked in silence for an outraged

second. "I am *not* lonely. At least not that way. I'm here with my father."

"What way, then?"

"What way what?" She stabbed the row of olives up and down in her drink.

"In what way are you lonely?"

Why on earth had she put it that way? What was wrong with her? "I am not lonely at all."

"Okay."

"I'm…" She struggled to sort out her feelings.

In a very real way, she *was* lonely. She couldn't talk to her parents. She sure as heck couldn't talk to Hargrove. She couldn't even talk to her best friend, Katie.

Katie was going to be the maid of honor at Amber's wedding next month. They'd bought the bridesmaid dress in Paris. Oriental silk. Flaming orange, which sounded ridiculous, but was interspersed with gold and midnight plum, and looked fabulous on Katie's delicate frame.

Hargrove Alston was the catch of the city. And it wasn't as if there was anything wrong with him. At thirty-three, he was already a partner in one of Chicago's most prestigious law firms. He had a venerated family, impeccable community and political connections. If everything went according to plan, he'd be running for the US Senate next year.

She really had no cause for complaint.

It wasn't as if the sex was bad. It was perfectly, well, pleasant. So was Hargrove. He was a decent and pleasant man. Not every woman could say that about her future husband.

She downed the rest of her martini, hoping it would ease the knot of tension that had stubbornly cramped her stomach for the past month.

Royce signaled the bartender for another round, and she let him.

He polished off his own drink while the bartender shook a mixture of ice and Gray Goose that clattered against the frosted silver shaker. Then the man produced two fresh glasses and strained the martinis.

"His name is Hargrove Alston," she found herself telling Royce.

Royce gave a nod of thanks to the man and lifted both glasses. "Shall we find a table?"

The suggestion startled Amber. She gave a guilty glance around the lounge, feeling like an unfaithful barfly. But nobody was paying the slightest bit of attention to them.

She'd started dating Hargrove when she was eighteen, so she'd never taken up with a stranger in a bar. Not that Royce was a stranger. He was the best man, brother of her father's business associate. It was a completely different thing than encouraging a stranger.

She slipped off the bar stool. "Sure."

At a quiet corner table, Royce set their drinks down. He pulled one of the padded armchairs out for her, and she eased into the smooth, burgundy leather, crossing her legs and tugging her gold dress to midthigh.

"Hargrove Alston?" he asked as he took the seat opposite, moving the tiny table lamp to one side so their view of each other was unobstructed.

"He's going to run for the US Senate."

"You're marrying a politician?"

"Not necessarily—" She cut herself short. Wow. How had *that* turned into real words? "I mean, he hasn't been elected yet," she quickly qualified.

"And what do you do?" asked Royce.

Amber pursed her lips and lifted the fresh drink. "Nothing."

"Nothing?"

She shook her head. It was, sadly, the truth. "I graduated University of Chicago," she offered.

"Fine Arts?" he asked.

"Public Administration. An honors degree." It had seemed like a good idea, given Hargrove's political aspirations. At least she'd be in a position to understand the complexities of his work.

"You've got my attention," said Royce, with a look of admiration.

"Only just now?" she joked. But the moment the words were out, she realized what she'd done. She was flirting with Royce.

His blue eyes twinkled with awareness. Then they darkened and simmered. He eased forward. "Amber, you had my attention the second I laid eyes on you."

She stilled, savoring the sound of her name, wrapping her mind around his words as a dangerous warmth sizzled up inside her. The rest of the room disappeared as seconds ticked by, while he waited for her response.

Then his smiled softened, and the predatory gleam went out of his eyes. "I take it that was an accident?"

"I'm not sure," she admitted.

"Well, let me know when you decide."

If flirting with him wasn't an accident, it was definitely a mistake. She needed to get herself back under control. "Tell me about Montana," she tried. "I've never been there."

He drew back, tilting his head to one side for a second, then obviously deciding to let her off the hook. "What do you want to know?"

"Your ranch," she rushed on. "Tell me about your ranch."

"We have cattle."

A cocktail waitress set a small bowl of mixed nuts on the table and took note of their drink levels as Royce thanked her.

"How many?" asked Amber as the woman strode away.

"Around fifty thousand head."

"That's a lot of cows to babysit."

"Tell me about it."

"Horses?" she prompted, determined to keep the conversation innocuous.

"Hundreds."

She plucked an almond from the clear bowl. "I took dressage lessons when I was eleven."

His wide smile revealed straight, white teeth. "In Chicago?"

"Birmingham Stables." She nibbled on the end of the nut. "I didn't last long. I wasn't crazy about sweat and manure."

"You'd hate Montana."

"Maybe not. Tell me something else about it."

"My sister has a horse ranch up in the hills. It has huge meadows with millions of wildflowers."

"Wildflowers are nice." Amber was pretty sure she'd like fields of wildflowers. "What else?"

"She jumps Hanoverians."

"Really? Is she good?"

"We expect her to make the next Olympic team."

"I bet she loves it." Amber tried to imagine what it would be like to be so passionate about something that you were one of the best in the world.

Royce nodded. "Ever since she was five." The glow in his eyes showed his pride in his sister.

Amber sighed and took a second almond. "I wish I loved something."

He considered her words for a few seconds. "Everybody loves something."

She dared to meet his eyes and rest there. "What do you love?"

He didn't hesitate. "Going Mach 1 in a gulf stream. On a clear night. Over the Nevada desert."

"Get to do it often?"

"Not often enough."

Amber couldn't help but smile. "Are you good?"

His gaze flicked to the low neckline of her dress as his voice turned to a rumble. "I am very, very good."

"You are very, very bad," she countered, with a waggle of her finger.

He grinned unrepentantly, and the warmth sizzled up inside her all over again.

"Your turn," he told her.

She didn't understand.

"What do you love?"

Now, there was a question.

She bought herself some time by taking a sip of her drink.

"Designer shoes," she decided, setting the long-stemmed glass back down on the table.

He leaned sideways to peer under the table. "Liar."

"What do you mean?" She stretched out a leg to show off her black stiletto sandals.

"I've dated women with a shoe fetish."

"I never said I had a fetish."

"Yours are unpretentious." Before she knew it, he'd

scooped her foot onto his knee. "And there's a frayed spot on the strap." His thumb brushed her ankle as he gestured. "You've worn them more than twice."

"I didn't say I was extravagant about it." She desperately tried to ignore the warmth of his hand, but her pulse had jumped, and she could feel moisture forming at her hairline.

"Try again," he told her.

"Birthday cake." She was more honest this time. "Three layers with sickly, sugary buttercream icing and bright pink rosebuds."

He laughed and set her foot back on the floor.

Thank goodness.

"How old are you?" he asked, scooping a handful of nuts.

"Twenty-two. You?"

"Thirty-three."

"Seriously?"

"Yeah. Why?"

She shrugged, hesitated, then plunged in. "Hargrove is thirty-three, and he seems a lot older than you."

"That's because I'm a pilot—daring and carefree. He's a politician—staid and uptight. No comparison, really."

"You've never even met him." Yet the analysis was frighteningly accurate.

Royce's expression turned serious. "Why are you hiding out?"

"What?"

"When I first saw you over at the bar, you said you were hiding out. From what?"

What, indeed.

Amber took a deep breath, smoothing both palms in

parallel over her hair. She scrunched her eyes shut for a long moment.

She was hiding out from the glowing bride, the happy guests and the pervasive joy of happily-ever-after.

But even as she rolled the explanation around, she knew it wasn't right. She didn't begrudge Melissa her happiness.

Truth was, she was hiding out from herself, from the notion that she was living a lie, from the realization that she'd wrapped her life around a man she didn't love.

The truth was both frightening and exhausting, and she needed time to figure it all out. More than an evening. More than a day. Even more than a weekend.

She needed to come to terms with the colossal mess she'd made of her life and decide where to go next. Ironic, really. Where Royce dreaded his ranch in Montana, she'd give anything—

Her eyes popped open, and she blinked him into focus. "Take me with you."

His brow furrowed. "What?"

"Take me with you to Montana." Nobody would look for her in Montana. She'd be free of dress fittings and florists and calligraphers. No more gift registries or parties or travel agents.

No more Hargrove.

The thought took a weight off her shoulders, and the knot in her stomach broke free. Not good.

"Are you joking?" asked Royce.

"No."

"Are you crazy?"

"Maybe." Was she crazy? This certainly felt insane. Unfortunately, it also felt frighteningly right.

"I'm not taking an engaged woman with me to Montana."

"Why not?"

He held out his palms, gesturing in the general vicinity of her neckline and the rest of her dress. "Because... Because... Well, because your fiancé would kill me, for one."

"I won't tell him."

"Right. That plan always ends well."

"I'm serious. He'll never know."

"Forget it."

No. She wouldn't forget it. This was the first idea in weeks that had felt right to her.

She pulled off her diamond ring, setting it on the table between them. "There. No more fiancé. No more problem."

"It doesn't have to be on your finger to count."

"Yeah?" she challenged.

"Yeah," he confirmed.

"What if I wasn't engaged?" Her words cut to absolute silence between them. The other sounds in the room muted, and time slowed down.

His gaze took a methodical trip from her cleavage to her waist, then backtracked to her eyes. "Sweetheart, if you weren't engaged, I'd say fasten your seat belt."

She snapped open her handbag. "Then how about this?" Retrieving her slim, silver cell phone, she typed a quick message and handed it over to Royce.

He squinted in the dim light, brows going up as he read the typed words.

I'm so sorry. I can't marry you. I need some time to think.

"Press Send," she told him. "Press Send, and take me to Montana."

"*There you are*, pumpkin." Amber's father stepped up behind her, and his broad hand came down on her shoulder.

Shock rushed straight from her brain all the way to her toes. She whipped her head around to look up. "Daddy?"

"The limo's at the curb." Her father's glance went to Royce.

Royce placed the cell phone facedown on the table and stood up to hold out his hand. "Royce Ryder. Jared's brother."

Her father shook. "David Hutton. We met briefly in the receiving line."

"Good to see you again, sir."

"You've been entertaining my daughter?"

"The other way around," said Royce, his gaze going to Amber. "She's an interesting woman. You must be proud."

Her father gave her shoulder a squeeze. "We certainly are. But it's getting late, honey. We need to get home."

No, Amber wanted to yell. She didn't want to go home. She wanted to stay here with Royce and completely change her life. She wanted to break it off with Hargrove and escape to Montana. She truly did.

Royce picked up the phone and slipped it back into her purse, clicking the purse shut with finality then handing it to her. "It was fun meeting you."

Amber opened her mouth, but no words came out.

Her father scooped a hand under her elbow and gently urged her to her feet.

She stared at Royce, trying to convey her desperation, hoping he'd understand the look in her eyes and do something to help her. But he didn't. And her father took a step, and she took a step. And another, and another.

"Amber?" Royce called, and relief shot though her. He knew. He understood. He was coming to her rescue.

But when she turned, he was holding out her engagement ring.

"Amber," her father admonished, shock clear in his tone.

"My hands were swelling," she answered lamely.

Royce didn't bother making eye contact as he dropped the diamond into the palm of her hand.

Two

"Who was that?" Stephanie's voice startled Royce as he watched Amber exit the lounge on her father's arm.

Tearing his eyes from the supple figure beneath the gold-and-red dress, he turned to face his sister. Stephanie looked young and unusually feminine in her ice-pink strapless satin bridesmaid dress. It had a full, flowing, knee-length skirt and a wide, white sash that matched her dangling, satin-bead earrings.

"Are all women crazy?" he asked, trying to recall the last time he'd seen Stephanie in anything other than riding clothes.

"Yes, we are," she answered without hesitation, linking her arm with his. "So you probably don't want to upset us. Like, for example, turning down our perfectly reasonable requests."

Royce sighed, steering her back to the table as he

pushed the bizarre conversation with Amber out of his mind. "What do you want, Steph?"

"A million dollars."

"No."

"Hey," she said, sliding into Amber's vacated seat as the cocktail waitress removed the empty martini glass. She kicked off one sandal and tucked her ankle under the opposite thigh on the roomy chair. "I'm a woman on the edge here."

"On the edge of what?" He pushed his half-full drink away. Had Amber's text message been an elaborate joke? If so, how warped was her sense of humor?

"Sanity," said Stephanie. "There's this stallion in London."

"Talk to Jared." Royce wasn't getting caught up in his sister's insatiable demands for her jumping stable.

"It's Jared's wedding night. He already went upstairs. You're in charge now."

Royce glanced at his watch. "And you think I'm a soft touch?"

"You always have been in the past."

"Forget it."

"His name's Blanchard's Run."

"I said forget it." He had time for maybe four hours of sleep before he had to get to the airport and preflight the jet.

"But—" Stephanie suddenly stopped, blinking in surprise as she glanced above his head.

"I sent it," came a breathless voice that Royce already easily recognized.

He jerked his head around to confirm it was Amber.

"Sent what?" asked Stephanie.

Amber's jewel-blue eyes were shining with a mixture of trepidation and excitement.

She hadn't.

She wouldn't.

"Where's your father?" asked Royce. Was this another warped joke?

"He left. I told him to send the limo back for me later."

Royce shook his head, refusing to believe any woman would do something that impulsive. "You did not send it."

But Amber nodded, then she glanced furtively around the lounge. "I figure I have about ten minutes to get out of here."

"What did you send?" Stephanie demanded. "To *who*?"

Amber slipped into the vacant third seat between them and leaned forward, lowering her voice. "I broke off my engagement."

Stephanie looked both shocked and excited. She reached for Amber's hand and squeezed it. "With *who*?"

"Hargrove Alston."

"The guy who's going to run for the Senate?"

Royce stared at his sister in astonishment.

"I read it in *People*," she told him with a dismissive wave of her hand. Then she turned her attention back to Amber. "Is he mad? Is he after you now?"

"He's in Switzerland."

"Then you're safe."

"Not for long. As soon as Hargrove reads my text, he'll call my dad, and my dad will turn the limo around."

Stephanie's lips pursed into an O of concern, and her breath whooshed out.

Amber nodded her agreement, and both women turned expectantly to Royce.

"What?"

"We have to go," said Stephanie, her expression hinting that he was a little slow on the uptake.

"To Montana," Amber elaborated.

"Now," said Stephanie with a nod of urgency.

"They'll never think to look for me in Montana," Amber elaborated.

"I'm not taking you to—"

But Stephanie jumped up from her chair. "To the airport," she declared in a ridiculously dramatic tone.

"Right." Amber nodded, rising, as well, smoothing her sexy dress over her hips as she stood on her high heels.

"Stop," Royce demanded, and even the laughing women at the table next to them stopped talking and glanced over.

"Shh," Stephanie hissed.

Royce lowered his voice. "We are *not* rushing off to the airport like a bunch of criminals."

Stephanie planted both hands on the tabletop. "And why not?"

"Six minutes," Amber helpfully informed them.

He shot her a look of frustration. "Don't be such a wimp. If he yells at you, he yells at you."

Amber's brows rose. "I'm not afraid he'll yell at me."

"Then, what's the problem?"

"I'm afraid he'll talk me out of it."

"That's ridiculous. You're a grown woman. It's your life."

"It is," Amber agreed. "And I want to come to Montana."

The look she gave him was frank and very adult. Perhaps his first instinct had been right. Maybe there was something between them. Maybe he was the reason she'd made the decision to finally dump the loser fiancé and move on.

He felt a rush of pride, a hit of testosterone and, quite frankly, the throb of arousal. Having Amber around would definitely make Montana more palatable. Only a fool would put barriers in her way.

He stood and tossed a couple of twenties on the table. "The airport, then."

Since he'd had the martinis, it would be a few hours before he could fly. But there was plenty to do in preparation.

By the time they arrived at the Ryder Ranch, Amber had had second, third, even fourth thoughts. Both her father and Hargrove were powerful men. Neither of them took kindly to opposition, and she'd never done anything remotely rebellious in her life.

Hargrove was probably on a plane right now, heading back to Chicago, intending to find her and demand to know what she was *thinking.* And her father was likely out interrogating her friends this morning, determined to find out what had happened and where she'd gone.

Katie would be flabbergasted.

Amber had been questioning her feelings for Hargrove for a couple of months now, but she hadn't shared those fears with Katie. Because, although Katie was a logical and grounded lawyer, she was saddled with an emotional case of hero worship when it came to Hargrove. She thought the sun rose and set on the man. She'd never understand.

Amber had sent her father a final text last night from the airport, assuring him that he didn't need to worry, that she needed some time alone and that she'd be in contact soon. Then she'd turned off her cell phone. She'd seen enough crime dramas to know there were ways to trace the signal. And Hargrove had friends in both high and low places. Where the police couldn't accommodate him, private investigators on the South Side would be happy to wade in.

The sun was emerging from behind the eastern mountains as Amber, Royce and Stephanie crossed the wide porch of the Ryder ranch house. She was dead tired but determined to keep anyone from seeing her mounting worry.

In the rising light of day, she admitted to herself that this had been a colossally stupid plan. Her father and Hargrove weren't going to sit quietly and wait while she worked through her emotions. Plus, she had nothing with her but a pair of high heels, her cocktail dress and a ruby-and-diamond drop necklace with a set of matching earrings.

And of all the nights to go with a tiny pair of high-cut, sheer panties—sure, they smoothed the line of her dress, but that was their only virtue.

"You heading home?" Royce asked his sister as he tossed a small duffel bag onto the polished hardwood floor, against the wall of a spacious foyer.

"Home," Stephanie echoed, clicking the wide double doors shut behind her. "I can grab a couple hours' sleep before class starts."

Amber turned to glance quizzically at Stephanie. "Home?" She'd assumed they were already there. The sign on the gate two miles back had clearly stated Ryder Ranch.

"Up to my place." Stephanie pointed. "I've got students arriving this afternoon."

"You don't live here?" Amber kept her voice even, but the thought was unsettling. Sure, Royce was the brother of her father's business associate, but he was still a stranger, and there was safety in numbers.

Stephanie was shaking her head. "They kicked me out years ago."

"When your horses took over the entire yard." Royce loosened his tie and moved out of the foyer. He'd changed out of his tux at the airport in favor of a short-sleeved, white uniform shirt and a pair of navy slacks.

Stephanie made to follow him into a massive, rectangular living room with a two-story, open, timber-beamed ceiling and a bank of glass doors at the far end, flanking a stone fireplace. Amber moved with her, taking in a large patterned red rug; cream and gold, overstuffed furniture groupings; and a huge, round, Western-style chandelier suspended in the center of the room.

"You want me to show Amber a bedroom?" asked Stephanie. She was still wearing her bridesmaid dress.

"She's probably hungry," Royce pointed out, and both looked expectantly at Amber.

"I'm...uh..." The magnitude of her actions suddenly hit Amber. She was standing in a stranger's house, completely dependent on him for food, shelter, even clothes. She was many miles from the nearest town, and every normal support system—her cell phone, credit card and chauffeur—were unavailable to her, since they could be traced.

"Exhausted," Stephanie finished for her, linking an

arm with Amber's. "Let's get you upstairs." She gently propelled Amber toward a wide, wooden staircase.

"Good night, then," Royce called from behind them.

"You look shell-shocked," Stephanie whispered in her ear as they mounted the staircase.

"I'm questioning my sanity," Amber admitted as the stairs turned right and walls closed in around them.

Stephanie hit a light switch, revealing a half-octagonal landing, with four doors leading off in separate directions.

"You're not insane," said Stephanie, opening one of the middle doors.

"I just abandoned my fiancé and flew off in the middle of the night with strangers."

"We're not that strange." Stephanie led the way into an airy room that fanned out to a slightly triangular shape.

It had a queen-size, four-poster brass bed, with a blue-and-white-checked comforter that looked decadently soft. Two royal blue armchairs were arranged next to a paned-glass balcony door. White doors led to a walk-in closet and an en suite bath, while a ceiling fan spun lazily overhead and a cream-colored carpet cushioned Amber's feet.

Stephanie clicked on one of two ceramic bedside lamps. "Or do you think you're insane to leave the fiancé?"

"He's not going to be happy," Amber admitted.

"Does he, like, turn all purple and yell and stuff?" Stephanie looked intrigued and rather excited by the prospect.

Amber couldn't help but smile. "No. He gets all stuffy and logical and superior."

Hargrove would never yell. He'd make Amber feel as

though she was a fool, as though her opinions and emotions weren't valid, as though she was behaving like a spoiled child. And maybe she was. But at least she was out of his reach for a little while.

"I hear you." Stephanie opened the double doors of a tall cherrywood armoire, revealing a set of shelves. "My brothers are like that."

"Royce?" Amber found herself asking. In their admittedly short conversation, Royce hadn't seemed at all like Hargrove.

"And Jared," said Stephanie. "They think I'm still ten years old. I'm a full partner in Ryder International, but I have to come to them for every little decision."

"That must be frustrating." Amber sympathized. She had some autonomy with her own credit cards and signing authority on her trust fund. She'd never really thought about independence beyond that.

Well, until now.

"There's this stallion," said Stephanie, selecting something in white cotton from the shelves. "Blanchard's Run, out of Westmont Stables in London. He's perfect for my breeding program. His dam was Ogilvie and his sire Danny Day." She shook her head. "All I need is a million dollars." She handed Amber what turned out to be a cotton nightgown.

"For one horse?" The price sounded pretty high.

"That's mine," said Stephanie, nodding to the gown. "You should help yourself to anything else in the dresser. There's jeans, shirts, a bunch of stuff that should fit you."

"If it's any consolation," said Amber, putting her hand on Stephanie's arm, "I can't see Hargrove ever letting me spend a million dollars, either."

"And *that's* why you should leave him."

"I'm leaving him—" Amber paused a beat, debating saying the words out loud for the first time "—because I don't love him."

Stephanie's lips formed another silent O. She nodded slowly for a long moment. "Good reason."

Amber agreed.

But she knew her parents would never accept it. And it wasn't because they had some old-fashioned idea about the value of arranged marriages or about love being less important than a person's pedigree. It was because they didn't trust Amber to recognize love one way or the other.

And that was why Amber couldn't go home yet. Nobody would listen to her. They'd all gang up, and she'd find herself railroaded down the aisle.

As usual, it was frighteningly easy for Royce to slip back into the cowboy life. He'd stretched out on his bed for a couple of hours, then dressed in blue jeans, a cotton shirt and his favorite worn cowboy boots. Sasha had quick-fried him a steak and produced a big stack of hotcakes with maple syrup. After drinking about a gallon of coffee, he'd hunted down the three foremen who reported directly to McQuestin.

He'd learned the vet had recommended moving the Bowler Valley herd because seasonal flies were impacting the calves. A well had broken down at the north camp and the ponds were drying up. And a lumber shipment was stuck at the railhead in Idaho because of a snafu with the letter of credit. But before he'd had a chance to wade in on any of the issues, an SOS had come over his cell phone from Barry Brewster, Ryder International's vice president of finance, for a letter from China's Ministry of Trade Development. The original had gone missing in the Chicago office, but they thought Jared might have left a copy at the ranch.

So Royce was wading through the jumble of papers on the messy desk in the front office of the ranch house, looking for a letter from Foreign Investment Director Cheng Li. Without Cheng Li's approval, a deal between Ryder International and Shanxi Electrical would be canceled, costing a fortune, and putting several Ryder construction projects at risk.

Giving up on the desk, and cursing out his older brother for falling in love and getting married at such an inconvenient time, Royce moved to the file cabinet, pulling open the top drawer. His blunt fingers were awkward against the flimsy paper, and the complex numbering system made no sense to him. What the hell was wrong with using the alphabet?

"The outfit seems at odds with the job duties," a female voice ventured from the office doorway.

He turned to see Amber in a pair of snug jeans and a maroon, sleeveless blouse. Her feet were bare, and her blond hair was damp, framing her face in lush waves. There was an amused smile on her fresh, pretty face.

"You think this is funny?" he asked in exasperation.

"Unexpected," she clarified.

"Well, don't just stand there."

"Should I be doing something?"

He directed her to the desktop. "We're looking for a letter from the Chinese Ministry of Trade and Development."

She immediately moved forward.

"Do you know what it looks like?" she asked, picking up the closest pile of papers.

He grunted. "It's on paper."

"Long letter? Short letter? In an envelope? Attached to a report?"

"I don't know. It's from Cheng Li, Foreign Investment Director. I need his phone number."

She moved on to the next pile, while Royce went back to the filing cabinet.

"Have you tried Google?" she asked.

"This isn't the kind of number you find on the internet."

She continued sorting. "I take it this is important?"

"If I don't get hold of him today, we're going to blow a deal."

"What time is it in China?"

"Sometime Monday morning. Barry says if the approval's not filed in Beijing by the end of business today, we're toast."

"Their time?" Amber asked.

"Their time," Royce confirmed. "What the hell happened to the alphabet?"

She moved closer, brushing against him. "You want me to—"

"No," he snapped, and she quickly halted.

He clamped his jaw and forced himself to take a breath. It wasn't her fault the letter was lost. And it wasn't her fault that his body had a hair-trigger reaction to her touch. "Sorry. Can you keep looking over there? On the desk?"

"Sure." Her features were schooled, and he couldn't tell if she was upset.

"I didn't mean to shout."

"Not a problem." She turned back.

He opened his mouth again, but then decided the conversation could wait. If she was upset, he'd deal with it later. For now, he had three more drawers to search.

"Something to do with Shanxi Electrical?" she asked.

Royce's head jerked up. "You found it?"

She handed him a single sheet of paper.

He scanned his way down to the signature line and found the number for Cheng Li's office. "This is it." He heaved a sigh, resisting the urge to hug her in gratitude.

Then he took in her rosy cheeks, her jewel-blue eyes, her soft hair and smooth skin. The deep-colored blouse molded to her feminine curves, while the skintight blue jeans highlighted a killer figure. There was something completely sexy about her bare feet, and he had to fight hard against the urge to hug her.

"Thanks," he offered gruffly, reaching for the phone.

He punched in the international and area codes, then made his way through the rest of the numbers.

After several rings, a voice answered in Chinese at the other end.

"May I speak with Mr. Cheng Li?" he tried.

The voice spoke Chinese again.

"Cheng Li? Is there someone there who speaks English?"

The next words were incomprehensible. He might have heard the name Cheng Li, but he wasn't sure.

"English?" he asked again.

Amber held out her hand and motioned for him to give her the phone.

He gave her a look of incomprehension while the woman on the other end tried once more to communicate with him.

"I'm sorry," he said into the phone, but then it was summarily whisked from his hand.

"Hey!" But before he could protest further, Amber spoke. The words were distinctly non-English.

Royce drew back in astonishment. "No way."

She spoke again. Then she waited. Then she covered the receiver. "Your phone number?" she whispered.

He quickly flipped open his cell to the display, and she rattled something into the phone. Then she finished the call and hung up. "Cheng Li will call you in an hour with an interpreter."

"You speak *Chinese*?" was all Royce could manage.

She gave a self-deprecating eye roll. "I can make myself understood. But for them, it's kind of like talking to a two-year-old."

"You speak Chinese?" he repeated.

"Mandarin, actually." She paused. "I have a knack." When he didn't say anything, she bridged the silence. "My mother taught me Swedish. And I learned Spanish in school." She shrugged. "So, well, considering the potential political impact of the rising Asian economies, I decided Mandarin and Punjabi were the two I should study at college. I'm really not that good at either of them."

He peered at her. "You're like a politician's dream wife, aren't you?"

Her lips pursed for a moment, and discomfort flickered in her eyes. "Are you saying I have no life?"

"I'm saying he's going to come after you." Royce put a warning in his tone. "I sure as hell wouldn't let you get away."

She blinked, and humor came back into her blue eyes. "I doubt I'd make it very far from here. After all, there is only one road out of the ranch."

Royce wasn't in the mood to joke. "He *is* going to come after you, isn't he?"

She sobered. "I don't think he'll find me."

"And if he does?"

She didn't answer.

"What's the guy got on you?"

From what Royce could see, Amber was an intelligent, capable woman. There was no reason in the world for her to let herself get saddled with a man she didn't want.

"Same thing Jared has on you," she answered softly. "Duty, obligation, guilt."

"Jared needs me for a month," said Royce, not buying into the parallel. "What's-his-name—"

"Hargrove."

"Hargrove wants you forever." Royce felt a sudden spurt of anger. "And where the hell are your parents in all this? Have you told them?"

"They think he's perfect for me."

"He's not."

Amber smiled. "You've never even met him."

"I don't have to. You're here. He's there." Royce ran his brain through the circumstances one more time. "Your cell's turned off, right?"

She nodded.

"Don't use your credit cards."

"I didn't bring them."

"Good."

"Not really." She hesitated. "Royce, I have no money whatsoever."

"You don't need money."

"And I have no clothes, not even underwear."

Okay, that gave him an unwanted visual. "We have everything you need right here."

"I can't live off your charity."

"You're our guest."

"I forced you to bring me here."

Royce set the letter back down on the desktop and tucked his phone back into his shirt pocket. "Ask anybody, Amber. I don't do anything I don't want to do." He let his gaze shade the meaning of the words. He'd brought her home with him because she was a beautiful and interesting woman. It was absolutely no hardship having her around.

"I need to earn my keep."

Royce resisted the temptation to make a joke about paying her way by sleeping with him. It was in poor taste, and the last thing he wanted to do was insult her. Besides, the two were completely unrelated.

He hoped she was attracted to him. What red-blooded man wouldn't? And last night he had been fairly certain she was attracted to him. But whatever was between them would take its own course.

Her gaze strayed to the messy desk. "I could…"

He followed the look.

"…maybe straighten things up a little? I've taken business management courses, some accounting—"

"No argument from me." Royce held up his palms in surrender. "McQuestin's niece, Maddy, usually helps out in the office, but she's gone back to Texas with him while he recovers." He spread his arms in welcome. "Make yourself at home."

Three

Several hours later, eyes grainy from reading ranch paperwork, Amber wandered out of the office. The office door opened into a short hallway that connected to the front foyer and then to the rest of the ranch house. It had grown dark while she worked, and soft lamplight greeted her in the empty living room. The August night was cool, with pale curtains billowing in the side windows, while screen doors separated the room from the veranda beyond.

Muted noise came from the direction of the kitchen, and she caught a movement on the veranda. Moving closer, she realized it was a plump puff ball of a black-and-white puppy. Amber smiled in reaction as another pup appeared, and then a third and a fourth.

They hadn't seen her yet, and the screen door kept them locked outside. Just as well. They were cute, but

Amber was a little intimidated by animals. She'd never had a pet before. Her mother didn't like the noise, the mess or the smell.

Truth was, she dropped out of dressage riding lessons because one of the horses had bit her on the shoulder. She hadn't told the grooms, or her parents, or anybody else about the incident. She was embarrassed, convinced that she'd done something to annoy the horse but not sure of what it might have been. When a creature couldn't talk or communicate, how did you know what they wanted or needed?

The pups disappeared from view, and she moved closer to the door, peeking at an angle to see them milling in a small herd around Royce's feet while he sat in a deep, wooden Adirondack chair, reading some kind of report under the half-dozen outdoor lamps that shone around the veranda.

Then the pups spotted her and made a roly-poly bee-line for the door, sixteen paws thumping awkwardly on the wooden slats of the deck. She took an automatic step back as they piled up against the screen.

Royce glanced up from the papers. "Hey, Amber." Then his attention went to the puppies. He gave a low whistle, and they scampered back to him.

"It's safe to come out now," he said with a warm smile.

"I'm not…" She eased the door open. "I'm not scared to come out."

Royce laughed. "Didn't think you were. Shut the screen behind you, though, or these guys will be in the kitchen in a heartbeat."

She closed the screen door behind her. "Your puppies?"

He reached down to scratch between the ears of the

full-grown border collie sprawled between the chair and the railing. "They belong to Molly. Care to take one home when you leave?"

"My mother won't have pets in the house." The puppies rushed back to Amber again.

Royce gestured for her to take the chair across from his. "Is she allergic?"

"Not exactly." Warm, fuzzy bodies pressed against her leg; cool, wet noses investigated her bare feet and she felt a mushy tongue across the top of her toes. She struggled not to cringe at the slimy sensation. "She doesn't want any accidents on the Persian rug."

"The price you pay," said Royce.

Amber settled into the chair. One of the pups put its paws on her knee, lifting up to sniff along her jeans.

"Most people pet them." Royce's tone was wry.

"I'm a little…" She gingerly scratched the puppy between its floppy, little ears. Its fur was soft, skin warm, and its dark eyes were adorable.

"It's okay," he said. "Not everybody likes animals."

"I don't dislike them."

"I can tell."

"They make me a little nervous, okay?"

"They're puppies, not mountain lions."

"They—" Another warm tongue swiped across her bare toes, and she jerked her feet under the chair. "Tickle," she finished.

"Princess," he mocked her.

"I was once bitten by a horse," she defended. Her interactions with animals hadn't been particularly positive so far.

"I was once gored by a bull," he countered with a challenging look.

"Is this going to be a contest?"

"Kicked in the head." He leaned forward and parted his short, dark hair.

She couldn't see a scar, but she trusted it was there.

"By a bronc," he finished. "In a local rodeo at fourteen."

Amber lifted her elbow to show a small scar. "Fell off a top bunk. At camp. I was *thirteen*."

"Did you break it?"

"Sprained."

"What kind of camp?"

"Violin."

His grin went wide. "Oh, my. Such a dangerous life. Did you ever break a nail? Get a bad wax job?"

"Hey, buddy." She jabbed her finger in the direction of his chest. "*After* your first wax job, we can talk."

Devilment glowed in his deep blue eyes. "You can wax anything I've got," he drawled. "Any ol' time you want."

Her stomach contracted, and a wave of unexpected heat prickled her skin. How had the conversation taken that particular turn? She sat up straight and folded her hands primly in her lap. "That's not what I meant."

He paused, gaze going soft. "That's too bad."

The puppies had grown bored with her feet, and one by one, they'd wandered back to Royce. They were now curled in a sleeping heap around his chair. The dog, Molly, yawned while insects made dancing shadows in the veranda lights.

"You hungry?" asked Royce.

Amber nodded. She was starving, and she was more than happy to let their discussion die.

He flipped the report closed, and she was reminded of their earlier office work.

"Did you talk to Cheng Li?"

"I did," said Royce. "He promised to fax the paper-work to the Ryder financial office."

"In Chicago."

"Yes." He rose cautiously to his feet, stepping around the sleeping puppies. "Disaster averted. Sasha'll have soup on the stove."

"Soup sounds great." It was nearly nine, and Amber hadn't eaten anything since their light snack on the plane around 5:00 a.m. Any kind of food sounded terrific to her right now.

They left the border collies asleep on the deck and filed through the living room, down a hallway to the kitchen on the south side of the house.

"Have you talked to your parents?" asked Royce as he set a pair of blue-glazed, stoneware bowls out on the breakfast bar.

The counters were granite, the cabinets dark cherry. There were stainless-steel appliances with cheery, yellow walls and ceiling reflecting off the polished beams and natural wood floor. A trio of spotlights was suspended above the bar, complementing the glow of the pot lights around the perimeter of the ceiling.

"I texted them both before I got on the plane."

"Nothing since then?" He set a basket of grainy buns on the breakfast bar, and she slipped onto one of the high, padded, hunter-green leather chairs.

She shook her head. "I don't know how this GPS and triangulating-the-cell-towers thing works."

Royce's brows went up, and he paused in his work.

"Crime dramas," she explained. "I don't know how

much of all that is fiction. My dad, and Hargrove for sure, will pull out all the stops."

Royce held out his hand. "Let me see your phone."

She pulled back on the stool and dug the little phone out of the pocket of her blue jeans.

He slid it open and pressed the on button.

"Are you sure—"

"I won't leave it on long." He peered at the tiny screen. "Nope. No GPS function." He shut it off and tossed it back to her. "Though they could, theoretically, triangulate while you're talking, but you're probably safe to text."

"Really?" That was good news. She'd like to send another message to her mother. And Katie deserved an explanation.

He set out two small plates and spoons while she tucked the phone back into her pocket. She'd have to think about how to phrase her explanation.

Royce ladled the steaming soup into the bowls and set them back on the bar, taking the stool at the end.

"Thanks," she breathed, inhaling the delectable aroma.

Royce lifted his spoon. "So, how long have you known?"

She followed suit, dipping into the rich broth. "Known what?"

"That you didn't love him?"

Royce knew his question was blunt to the point of rudeness, but if he was going to make a play for Amber, he needed to know the lay of the land. He knew he'd be a temporary rebound fling, which was not even remotely a problem for him. In fact, he'd gone into the situation *planning* to be her temporary rebound fling. She wasn't going to stay the whole month. She probably wouldn't even last a week. But he was up for it, however long it lasted.

Last night, he'd known Amber was beautiful. Today, he'd learned she was positively fascinating. She was intelligent, poised and personable, and she could actually speak Chinese. Her reaction to the puppies was cute and endearing. While her fiancé's and family's ability to intimidate her made him curious.

Why would such an accomplished woman give a rat's hind end what anybody thought of her decisions?

She stirred her spoon thoughtfully through the bowl of soup. "It's not so much…" she began.

He waited.

She looked up. "It's not that I knew I didn't love him. It's more that I didn't know that I did. You know?"

Royce hadn't the slightest idea what she meant, and he shook his head.

"It seems to me," she said, cocking her head sideways, teeth raking momentarily over her full bottom lip, "if you're going to say 'till death do us part' you'd better be damn sure."

Royce couldn't disagree with that. His parents obviously hadn't been damn sure. At least his mother wasn't. His father, on the other hand, had to have been devastated by her betrayal.

Amber was right to break it off. She had absolutely no business marrying a man she didn't love unreservedly.

"You'd better be damn sure," Royce echoed, fighting a feeling of annoyance with her for even considering marrying a man she didn't love. This Hargrove person might be a jerk. So far, he sounded like a jerk. But no man deserved a disloyal wife.

Amber nodded as she swallowed a spoonful of the soup. "Melissa looked sure."

"Melissa *was* sure."

Amber blinked at the edge to Royce's tone. "What?"

"Nothing." He tore a bun in half.

"You annoyed?"

He shook his head.

"Melissa and Jared seem really good together."

"You do know it's kinder to break it off up front with a guy." Royce set down his spoon.

"I—"

"Because, if you don't, the next thing you know, you'll have two or three kids, the PTA and carpool duty. You'll get bored. You'll start looking around. And you'll end up at the No-Tell Motel on Route 55, in bed with some young drifter. And Hargrove, whoever-he-is, will be going for his gun."

"Whoa." Amber's eyes were wide in the stark kitchen light. "You just did my whole life in thirty seconds."

"I didn't necessarily mean you."

"What? Are we talking about Melissa?"

"No." Royce gave himself a mental shake. "We are absolutely not talking about Melissa."

"Then who—"

"Nobody. Forget it." He drew a breath. So much for making a play for her. It wouldn't be tonight. That was for sure. "I just don't understand why you're feeling guilty," he continued. "You are absolutely doing the right thing."

"I believe that," she agreed.

He held her gaze with a frank stare. "And anybody

who tries to talk you out of it is shortsighted and just plain stupid."

"You know you're talking about my father."

"I know."

"He's Chairman of the City Accountants Association, and he owns a multimillion-dollar financial consortium."

"Pure blind luck, obviously."

A small smile crept out, though she clearly fought against it. "The No-Tell Motel?"

"Metaphorically speaking. I'm sure you'd pick the Ritz."

"I've never been unfaithful."

Royce knew he should apologize.

"I've dated Hargrove since I was eighteen, and even though he's not the greatest—" She snapped her mouth shut, and a flush rose in her cheeks as she reached for one of the homemade buns.

Okay, this was interesting. "Not the greatest what?"

"Nothing."

"You're blushing."

"No, I'm not." She tore into the bun.

Royce grinned. "Were you going to say *lover*?"

"No." But everything in her body language told him she was lying.

He gazed at her profile for a long minute.

Eighteen. She was eighteen when she took up with Hargrove. Royce could be wrong, but he didn't think he was. Amber hadn't had any other lovers. She was dissatisfied with Hargrove, but she had no comparison.

Interesting. He chewed a hunk of his own bun.

A woman deserved at least one comparison.

* * *

"What did you find?" Royce's voice from the office doorway interrupted Amber's long day of office work.

The sun was descending toward the rugged mountains, while neat piles of bills and correspondence had slowly grown out of the chaos on the desktop in front of her.

Now she stretched her arm out to place a letter on the farthest pile. It was another advertisement for horse tack. She was fairly sure the junk mail could be tossed out, but she wasn't about to make that decision on her own.

"You've got some overdue bills," she answered Royce, twisting her head to see him lounging in the doorway, one broad shoulder propped against the doorjamb, his hair mussed and sweaty across his forehead and a streak of dirt marring his roughened chin. She met his deep blue gaze, and a surge of longing clenched her chest.

"Pay them," he suggested in a sexy rumble, crossing his arms over his chest.

"You going to hand over your platinum card?"

His lips parted in a grin. "Sure."

"Then you better have a high limit. Some of them are six figures." Feed, lumber, vet bills. The list went on and on.

He eased away from the door frame and ambled toward her. "There must be a checkbook around here somewhere."

"I didn't see one." Not that she'd combed through the desk drawers. There was plenty to do sorting through what was piled on top. "How long did you say McQuestin had been off?"

"Three weeks. Why?"

"Some of these bills are two months old. That's hell on your credit rating, you know."

He moved closer, and she forced herself to drag her gaze from his rangy body.

To distract herself, she lifted the closest unopened envelope and sliced through the seam with the ivory-handled opener, extracting another folded invoice. The distraction didn't help. Her nostrils picked up his fresh, outdoorsy scent, and his arm brushed her shoulder, sending an electric current over her skin as he slid open a top desk drawer.

Lifting several items out of the way, he quickly produced a narrow leather-bound booklet and tossed it on the desk. "Here you go. Start protecting my credit rating."

"Like the bank would honor my signature." She knew she should shift away, but something magnetic kept her sitting right where she was, next to his narrow hip and strong thigh. She didn't even care that his jeans were dusty.

Not that it would matter if anything rubbed off. She was dressed in a plain, khaki T-shirt and a pair of faded jeans she'd borrowed from Stephanie's cache in the upstairs bedroom. She could press herself against Royce from head to toe, and simply clean up later with soap and water.

The idea was far too appealing. She felt heat flare in the pit of her stomach as an image bloomed in her mind.

"I'll sign a bunch for you." His voice interrupted her burgeoning fantasy as he flipped open the checkbook.

She blinked herself back to reality. "I assume you're joking."

"Why would I be joking?" He leaned over, hunting

through the drawer again, bringing himself into even closer contact with her.

She shifted imperceptibly in his direction, and his cotton-clad arm brushed her bare one. She sucked in a tight breath.

He retrieved a pen.

She suddenly realized he was serious, and placed her hand over the top check. "You can't do that."

He turned, pen poised, bringing their faces into close proximity. "Why not?"

"Because I could write myself a check, a *very big* check, and then cash it."

He rolled his eyes

"Don't give me that 'shucks ma'am' expression—"

"'Shucks, ma'am'?"

"You didn't just wander in off the back forty. You know I could drain your account."

"Would you?"

"I *could*," she stressed. Theoretically, of course.

He twirled the pen over two fingers until it settled into his palm. "And then what?"

"And then I disappear. Tahiti, Grand Cayman."

"I'd find you."

"So what?" She shrugged. "What could you do? The money would already be in a Swiss bank account."

He braced one hand against the desk and moved the other to the back of her chair, bending slightly over. "Then I'd ask you, politely, for the number."

She was blocked by the V of his arms. It was unnerving, but also exciting. He emanated strength, power and raw virility.

"And if I refuse to tell you?" she challenged, voice growing breathy.

"I'd stop being polite."

"What? You'd threaten to break my legs?"

He smiled and leaned closer. Self-preservation told her to shrink away, but the chair back kept her in place. His sweet breath puffed against her skin. "Violence? I don't think so. But there are other ways to be persuasive."

She struggled for a tone of disbelief. "What? You kiss me and I swoon?"

His grin widened. "Maybe. Let's try it."

And before she could react, he'd swooped in toward her. She gasped as his smooth lips settled on hers. They were warm and firm, and incredibly hot, as the contact instantly escalated to a serious kiss.

It took her only seconds to realize how much she'd longed for his taste. His scent filled her, and his hands settled on her sides, surrounding her rib cage as he deepened the kiss. Her head tipped back, and her mouth responded to his pressure by opening, allowing him access, drinking in the sensation of his intimate touch.

She clutched his upper arms, steadying herself against his hard, taut muscles. He flexed under her touch, and she imagined she could feel the blood coursing through his body. She could definitely feel the blood coursing through her own. It heated her core, flushed her skin and made her tingle from the roots of her hair to the tips of her toes.

His hands convulsed against her body, thumbs tightening beneath her breasts. Her nipples hardened almost painfully as arousal thumped its way to the apex of her thighs. She gave him her tongue, answering his own erotic invitation. A river of sound roared in her ears as he drew her to her feet, engulfing her, pressing her against his hard body.

His touch was unique, yet achingly familiar, as if she'd been waiting for this moment her entire life. Her palms slid across his shoulders, around his neck, stroking the slick sweat of his hairline as their kiss pulsed endlessly between them.

His hands slipped to her buttocks, pulling her against the cradle of his thighs, demonstrating the depth of his arousal and shocking her back to her senses.

She jerked away, hands pressing against his chest, putting a barrier between them. He leaned in, trying to capture her mouth.

"I can't," she gasped.

He froze.

"I'm…uh…" She wasn't exactly sorry. That had definitely been the best kiss of her life. But she couldn't take things any further. They barely knew each other. She'd only just left Hargrove. And she hadn't come to Montana for casual sex.

"Something wrong?" he asked.

She tried to take a step back, but the damn chair still blocked her way. "This is too fast," she explained, struggling to bring both her breathing and her pulse rate back under control.

He heaved an exasperated sigh. "It was a kiss, Amber."

But they both knew it was more than a kiss. Then, to her mortification, her gaze reflexively flicked below his waistline.

He gave a knowing chuckle, and she wished the floor would swallow her whole.

"Are you blushing?" he asked.

"No." But she couldn't look him in the eyes.

"You seemed a whole lot more sophisticated when we met in the lounge," he ventured.

She couldn't interpret his flat tone, so she braved a glance at his expression. Was he annoyed?

He looked annoyed.

She hadn't intended to lead him on. Nor had she meant for the kiss to spiral out of control.

Surely he could understand that.

Or was he always so quick to leap to expectations?

Then, an unsettling thought hit her. What if Royce hadn't leaped to expectations in the past two minutes? What if his expectations had been there since their meeting in the lounge?

Had she been hopelessly naive? Did he consider her a one- or two-night stand?

"Is *that* why you brought me here?" she asked, watching closely, giving him the chance to deny it.

"Depends," he said, cocking his head and giving her a considering look. "On what you mean by *that*."

"Because you thought I'd sleep with you?"

"It had crossed my mind," he admitted.

Her embarrassment turned to anger. "Seriously?"

He sighed. "Amber—"

"You are the most egotistical, opportunistic—"

"Hey, you were the one who was dressed to kill and insisted on 'taking a ride in my jet plane.'"

"That *wasn't* a euphemism for sex."

"Really?" He looked genuinely surprised. "It usually is."

Amber compressed her lips. How had she been so naive? How could she have been so incredibly foolish? Royce wasn't some knight in shining armor. He was a charming, wealthy, well-groomed pickup artist.

Her distaste was replaced again by embarrassment.

She'd proposed paying her way here by doing office work. He'd had a completely different line of work in mind.

She pushed the wheeled chair aside and moved to go around him. "I think I'd better leave."

She'd have to call her parents to rescue her, head back to Chicago with her tail between her legs, maybe even reconsider her relationship with Hargrove, since, as the three of them so often told her, she was naive in the ways of the real world.

At least with Hargrove, she knew where she stood.

"Why?" Royce asked, putting a hand on her arm to stop her.

She glanced at his hand, and he immediately let go.

"There's obviously been a misunderstanding." She'd hang out in the upstairs bedroom until a car could come for her. Then she'd head back to the airport, home to her parents' mansion and back to her real life.

This had been a crazy idea from beginning to end.

"Clearly," said Royce, his jaw tight.

She moved toward the door.

Royce's voice followed her. "Running back to Mommy and Daddy?"

Her spine straightened. "None of your business."

"What's changed?" he challenged.

She reached for the doorknob.

"What's changed, Amber?" he repeated.

She paused. Then she turned to confront him. No point in beating around the bush. "I thought I was a houseguest. You thought I was a call girl."

A grin quirked one corner of his mouth, and her anger flared anew.

"Are you always this melodramatic?" he asked.

"Shut up."

He shook his head and took a couple of steps toward her. "I meant what's changed on your home front?"

"Nothing," she admitted, except it had occurred to her that her parents might be right. She had been protected from the real world for most of her life. Maybe she wasn't in a position to judge human nature. They'd always insisted Hargrove was the perfect man for her, and they could very well be right.

"So, why go back?" Royce pressed.

"Where else would I go?" She could sneak off to some other part of the country, but her father would track her down as soon as she accessed her bank account. Besides, the longer she stayed away, the more awkward the reunion.

Royce took another step forward. "You don't have to leave."

She scoffed out a dry laugh.

"I never thought you were a call girl."

"You thought I was a barroom pickup."

"True enough," he agreed. "But only because it's happened so many times before."

"You're *bragging*?"

"Just stating the facts."

She scoffed at his colossal ego.

"You're welcome to stay as a houseguest." He sounded sincere.

"Are you kidding?" She couldn't imagine anything more uncomfortable. He'd been planning to sleep with her. And for a few seconds there, well, sleeping with Royce hadn't seemed like such a bad idea. And he must have known it. She was sure he'd known it.

Their gazes held.

"I can control myself if you can," he told her.

"There's nothing for me to control," she insisted.

He let her lie slide. "Good. Then it's settled."

"Nothing is—"

He nodded toward the desk. "You organize my office and pay my bills, and I'll keep my hands to myself." He paused. "Unless, of course, you change your mind about my hands."

"I'm not going to—"

He held up a hand to silence her. "Let's not make any promises we're going to regret."

She let her glare do the talking, but a little voice inside her acknowledged he was right. She didn't plan to change her mind. But for a few minutes there, it had been easy enough to imagine his hands all over her body.

Four

Royce felt the burn in his shoulder muscles as he hefted another stack of two-by-fours from the flatbed to a waiting pickup truck. The two ranch hands assigned to the task had greeted him with obvious curiosity when he joined the work crew. Hauling lumber in the dark, with the smell of rain in the air, was hardly a choice assignment.

But Royce needed to work the frustration out of his system somehow. How had he so completely misjudged Amber's signals? He could have sworn she was as into him as he was her.

He slid the heavy stack across the dropped tailgate and shifted it to the front of the box, admitting that he'd deluded himself the past few months in the hotel fitness rooms. High-tech exercise equipment was no match for the sweat of real work.

"Something wrong?" came Stephanie's voice as she appeared beside him in the pool of the yard light. She tugged a pair of leather work gloves from the back pocket of her jeans. "You looked ticked off."

"Nothing's wrong," Royce denied, turning on the dirt track to retrace his steps to the flatbed, passing the two hands who were on the opposite cycle. "Where'd you come from?"

Stephanie slipped her hands into the gloves, lifting two boards to Royce's five, balancing them on her right shoulder. "I drove down to join you for dinner. I wanted to see how Amber was doing."

"She's fine.

"She inside?"

He shrugged. "I assume so."

"You have a fight?"

"No. We didn't have a fight." An argument, maybe. In fact, it was more of a misunderstanding. And it was none of his sister's damn business.

"Something wrong with Bar—"

"No!" Royce practically shouted. Wait a minute. His sister might have changed topics. He forced himself to calm down. "What?"

"With Barry Brewster," she enunciated. "Our VP of finance? I talked to him earlier, and he sounded weird."

Royce slid his load into the pickup then lifted the boards from Stephanie's shoulder and placed them in the box. "Weird how?"

It was Stephanie's turn to shrug. "He yelled at me."

Royce's brow went up. "He *what*?"

They stepped out of the way of the two hands each carrying a load of lumber.

Stephanie lowered her voice. "With Jared gone. Well,

Blanchard's Sun, an offspring of Blanchard's Run, took silver at Dannyville Downs, and—"

"*S-o-n* son?" Royce asked.

"*S-u-n.* It's a mare."

"You don't think that will get confusing?"

Stephanie frowned at him. "I didn't name her."

"Still—"

"Try to stay on topic."

"Right."

The temperature dropped a few degrees. The wind picked up, and ozone snapped in the air. Royce went back to work, knowing the rain wasn't far off.

Stephanie followed. "Blanchard's Run is proving to be an incredible sire. With every week that passes, his price will go up. So I called Barry to talk about moving some funds to the stable account."

"Did you really expect him to hand over a million?"

"Sure." She paused, sucking in a breath as she hefted some more lumber. "Maybe. Okay, it was a long shot. But that's not my point."

"What is your point?"

The first fat raindrops clanked on the truck's roof, and one of the hands retrieved an orange tarp from the shed. Royce increased his pace to settle the last of the lumber on the pickup, then accepted the large square of plastic.

"You two get the flatbed," he instructed, motioning for Stephanie to move to the other side of the pickup box.

"My point," Stephanie called over the clatter from the tarp under the increasing rain, "is Barry's reaction. He went off on me about cash flow and interest rates."

"Over a million dollars?" Royce threaded a nylon rope through the corner grommet of the tarp and looped it around the tie-down on the running board. It was a lot to pay for a horse, sure. But there weren't enough zeros in the equation to raise Barry's blood pressure.

"I felt like a ten-year-old asking for her allowance."

"That's because you behave like a ten-year-old." Royce tossed the rope over the load to his sister.

"It's a great deal," she insisted as lightning cracked the sky above them. "If we don't move now, it'll be gone forever."

"Isn't that what you said about Nare-Do-Elle?"

"That was three years ago."

"He cost us a bundle."

"This is a completely different circumstance. I'm right this time." She tossed the rope back. "You don't think I've learned anything in three years?"

Royce cinched down the tarp. He wasn't touching that question with a ten-foot cattle prod. "What exactly do you want me to do?" he asked instead.

"Talk to Barry."

"And say what?"

"Tell him to give me the money."

Royce grinned.

"I'm serious." The rain had soaked into her curly auburn hair, dampening her cheeks, streaking down her freckled nose.

"You're always serious. You always need money. And half the time you're wrong."

She waggled her leather gloved finger at him. "And half the time I'm *right*."

"So I'll get you half a million."

"And you'll lose out on generations of champion jumpers."

Royce walked the rope around the back of the pickup, tying it off on the fourth corner. "Sorry, Steph."

Her hands went to her hips. "I own a third of this company."

"And I have Jared's power of attorney."

"You two have *always* ganged up on me."

"Now you're sounding like a child."

"I'm—"

"I'm not giving a million dollars to a child."

Her chin tipped up. "You weren't giving it to me anyway."

"True," Royce admitted. He couldn't resist chucking her under that defiant chin. "You've got a perfectly adequate operating budget. Live within your means."

"This is an extraordinary opportunity. I can't begin to tell you—"

"There'll be another one tomorrow. Or next week. Or next month." He'd known his sister far too long to fall for her impassioned plea.

"That's not fair."

"Life never is."

Thunder clapped above them, and the heavens opened up, the deluge soaking everything in sight. The ranch hands ran for the cook shed, and Royce grabbed Stephanie's hand, tugging her over the muddy ground toward the lights of the house.

Amber stood in the vast Ryder living room, rain pounding on the ceiling and clattering against the windows in the waning daylight as she stared at the cell phone in her hand. Royce had been a gentleman about it, but that didn't change the fact that she'd put herself in a predicament and behaved less responsibly than she'd admitted to herself.

She really needed to let someone know where she was staying. She also needed to make sure her parents weren't worrying about her. Her father tended to blow things out of proportion, and there was a real chance he was freeing up cash, waiting for a ransom note.

She pressed the on button with her thumb, deciding she'd keep it short and simple.

"Calling in the cavalry?" came Royce's dry voice.

Amber glanced up to see him and Stephanie in the archway leading from the front foyer.

"Did you hear the thunder?" Stephanie grinned as she stepped forward, stripping off a pair of leather gloves and running spread fingers through her unruly, wet hair.

Amber nodded. The storm had heightened her sense of isolation and disquiet.

"I love storms," Stephanie continued, dropping the gloves on an end table. "As long as I'm inside." She frowned, glancing down at her wet clothes. "I'm going upstairs to find something dry. Is that lasagna I smell?" Her pert nose wrinkled.

Amber inhaled the aromas wafting from the kitchen. "I think so."

"My fave." Stephanie smiled. "See you in a few." She skipped up the stairs.

As he stood there in the doorway, the planes and angles of Royce's face were emphasized by the yellow lamplight reflecting off the wood grain walls.

An hour ago, she'd come to the conclusion that she couldn't really blame him for thinking she was attracted to him. She imagined most women who requested a ride in his plane were coming on to him. Not that she blamed them. His shoulders were broad in his work clothes. His dark, wet hair glimmered and those deep blue eyes seemed to stare right down into a woman's soul.

"Did you decide to leave after all?" he asked, his deep

voice reverberating through her body, igniting a fresh wave of desire.

She shook her head. "I'm just reassuring my parents."

Royce moved into the room with an easy, rolling gait. He struck her as different than the man in the hotel lobby lounge. In just a couple of days, the wilds of Montana had somehow seeped into him.

"Not worried they'll track you down?" His steps slowed as he stopped in front of her, slightly closer than socially acceptable, just a few inches into her personal space, and she felt her heartbeat deepen.

"I'm worried they might be raising the ransom."

Royce quirked a brow. "Seriously?"

"I've never done anything like this before."

"No kidding."

"Royce." She wasn't sure what she was going to say to him, or how she should say it.

But before she could formulate the words, his voice and expression went soft. "I'm sorry."

She shook her head. "No. I'm the one who's sorry. I gave you the wrong impression. It wasn't on purpose, but I realize now that—"

"It was wishful thinking on my part."

"You flat out told me you were hitting on me."

"I was."

She fought a reflexive smile. "And I'm honored." She found herself joking.

"I don't want you to be honored." His expression said the rest.

"I know exactly what you want."

He eased almost imperceptibly closer. "Yes, you do."

They both went silent, sobering. Thunder rumbled

overhead, and the moisture-laden air hung heavily in the room.

Stephanie's light footsteps sounded on the landing above.

"You should make that call," said Royce, stepping back.

Amber nodded, struggling to get her hormones under control. She'd never been pursued by such a rawly masculine man. Come to think of it, she'd never been pursued by any man.

Oh, she received her fair share of flirtatious overtures on a girls' night at the clubs, but a flash of her engagement ring easily shut the guys down. Plus, usually she was out with Hargrove. And they generally attended functions where he was known. Nobody was about to hit on Hargrove Alston's fiancée.

While Stephanie skipped down the stairs, Amber pressed the speed-dial button for her mother. It rang only once.

"Sweetheart!" came her mother's voice. "What happened? Are you okay? Are you having a breakdown?"

Amber turned away from Royce, crossing the few steps to an alcove where she'd have a little privacy.

"I'm fine," she answered, ignoring the part about a breakdown.

"Your father is beside himself."

Royce's and Stephanie's footfalls faded toward the kitchen.

"And Hargrove," her mother continued. "He came home a day early. Then he nearly missed the Chamber dinner tonight worrying about you. He was the keynote, you know."

"He *nearly* missed it?" asked Amber, finding a hard

tone in her voice. Hargrove hadn't, in fact, missed his big speech while his beloved fiancée was missing, perhaps kidnapped, maybe dead.

As soon as the thoughts formed in her mind, she realized she was being unfair. She'd sent a text saying she was fine, and she had expected them to believe her. She wanted Hargrove to carry on with his life.

"The Governor was there," her mother defended.

"I'm glad he went to the dinner," said Amber.

"Where are you? I'll send a car."

"I'm not coming back yet."

"Why not?"

"Didn't Dad tell you?"

"That nonsense about not marrying Hargrove? That's crazy talk, darling. He wowed them last night."

"He didn't wow me." As soon as the words slipped out, Amber clamped her lips shut.

"You weren't there." Her mother either missed or ignored the double entendre.

"I wanted to let you know I'm fine." Amber got back on point.

"Where are you?"

"It doesn't matter."

"Of *course* it matters. We need to get you—"

"Not yet."

"Amber—"

"I'll call again soon." Amber didn't know how long it took to trace a cell phone call, but she suspected she should hurry and hang up.

"What do you expect me to tell your father?"

"Tell him not to worry. I love you both, and I'll call again. Bye, Mom." She quickly disconnected.

* * *

A slightly plump, fiftyish woman, who Amber had earlier learned was Sasha, was pulling a large pan of lasagna from the stainless-steel oven when Amber entered the kitchen. Stephanie was tossing a salad in a carved wooden bowl on the breakfast bar, while Royce transferred warm rolls into a linen-napkin-lined basket.

For the second time, she was struck by his domesticity. The men she knew didn't help out in the kitchen. Come to think of it, the women she knew didn't, either. And though Amber herself had taken French cooking lessons at her private school, the lessons had centered more on choosing a caterer than hands-on cooking.

"There's a wine cooler around the corner." Stephanie was looking to Amber as she indicated the direction with a toss of her auburn head. "Italian wines are on the third tier, left-hand side."

Royce didn't turn as Amber made her way to a small alcove between the kitchen and the back entryway. The cooler was set in a stone wall, reds in one glass-fronted compartment, whites in the other.

"See if there's a Redigaffi." Royce's voice was so close behind her that it gave her a start.

She took a bracing breath and opened the glass door, turning a couple of bottles on the third shelf so that she could see their labels.

"How'd the call go?" he asked.

"Fine."

There was a silence.

"That's it?" he asked. "Fine?"

"I talked to my mother. She wants me to come home." Amber found the right bottle of wine and slid it out of the holder, straightening and turning to discover Royce was closer than she'd expected. She pushed the glass door closed behind her.

"And?" he asked.

"And what?" She reflexively clutched the bottle.

"Are you going home?"

Though they'd agreed she'd merely be a houseguest, the question seemed loaded with meaning as his eyes thoroughly searched her expression.

"Not yet," she answered.

"Good."

She felt the need to clarify. "It doesn't mean—"

"I meant it's good because you don't love Hargrove, so it would be stupid to go back."

She gave him a short nod.

"Not that the other's gone away," he clarified.

Amber didn't know how to respond to that.

His gaze moved to the bottle. "Did you find one?"

She raised it, and he lifted it from her hands.

"Perfect," he said.

"Move your butts," called Stephanie from the kitchen, and Amber suddenly realized that her world had contracted to the tiny alcove, Royce and her wayward longings.

She gave herself a mental shake, while he took a step back and gestured for her to lead the way into the kitchen.

Stephanie was setting wineglasses at three places at the breakfast bar, while Sasha had disappeared. The Ryder family was a curious mix of informality and luxury. The glasses were fine blown crystal. The wine was from an exquisite vineyard that Amber recognized. But they were hopping up on high chairs at the breakfast bar to a plain white casserole pan of simple beef lasagna.

"Did you talk to your mom?" asked Stephanie as she took the end seat.

Amber took the one around the corner, and Royce settled next to her. He was both too close and too far away. She could almost detect the heat of his body, felt the change in air currents while he moved, and she was overcome with a potent desire to touch him. Of course, touching him was out of the question.

"I talked to her," she told Stephanie.

"What did she say?"

"She wants me to come home and, well, reconcile with Hargrove, of course."

"And?" Stephanie pressed. "What did you tell her?"

"That I wasn't ready." Amber found herself deliberately not looking in Royce's direction as she spoke.

"Good for you," said Stephanie with a vigorous nod. "We girls, we have to stick to our guns. There are too many people in our lives trying to interfere with our decisions." She cast a pointed gaze at her brother.

"Give it a rest," Royce growled at his sister, twisting the corkscrew into the top of the wine. "You're not getting a million dollars."

"You're such a hard-ass."

"And you're a spoiled brat."

"You *are* spending an awful lot for vet supplies and lumber," Amber put in. "Those are the bills I found stacked up on the office desk."

Stephanie blinked at her. "Oh."

Royce popped the cork and reached for Amber's wineglass. "Amber has some questions about the accounts. Who does McQuestin deal with at head office?"

"I think he talks to Norma Braddock sometimes."

Royce handed the wine bottle to his sister then

whisked his cell phone from his pocket. "I'll go straight to Barry."

"I'd watch out for him," Stephanie advised, forehead wrinkling.

Royce rolled his eyes at the warning.

Amber decided to stay quiet.

"Barry?" said Royce, while Stephanie handed the salad bowl to Amber.

Amber served herself some of the freshest-looking lettuce and tomatoes she'd ever seen.

"Royce, here."

Then she leaned toward Stephanie and whispered, "From your garden?"

Stephanie nodded, whispering in return. "You'll want to get out of here before canning season."

Amber grinned at the dire intonation.

"Sorry to bother you this late," Royce continued. "We've hired someone on to take care of the office while Jared and McQuestin are away." He gave Amber a wink, and something fluttered in her chest. She quickly picked up her wineglass to cover.

"She has some questions about the bank account. There have been a number of unpaid bills lately." He paused for a moment. "Why don't I let you talk to her directly?"

Amber hadn't expected that. She quickly swallowed and set down the glass. Good thing her questions were straightforward. She tucked her hair out of the way behind her ears, accepting the phone from Royce, ignoring the tingle when his fingers brushed hers.

"Hello?" she opened.

"Who am I speaking to?" asked Barry from the other end of the line.

"This is Amber, I'm—"

"And you're an employee at Ryder Ranch?" he asked directly.

She paused. "Uh, yes. That's right."

"Administrator? Bookkeeper?" There was an unexpected edge to the man's tone.

"Something like that." She gave Royce a confused look, and his eyes narrowed, crinkling slightly at the corners.

"Do you have a pen?" Barry asked, voice going even sharper.

"I—"

"Because you'd better write this down."

Amber glanced around at the countertops. "Just—"

"Sally Nettleton."

"Excuse me?"

"Sally Nettleton is the accounts supervisor. You can speak to her in the morning."

"Sure. Do you happen to have her—"

"And a warning, young lady. Don't you *ever* go above my head to Royce Ryder again."

Amber froze, voice going hollow. "What?"

"Share this conversation with him at your own peril. I don't tolerate insubordination, and he won't always be there to protect you."

Amber's mouth worked but sounds weren't coming out. Nobody had dared speak to her that way in her life.

"You're not the first, and you won't be the last. Don't fool yourself into thinking anything different." He stopped speaking, and the line fairly vibrated with tension.

She didn't know what to say. She had absolutely no idea what to tell this obnoxious man. Imagine if she really was an employee, dependent on her job. It would be horrible.

She heard a click and knew he'd signed off.

"Goodbye," she said weakly for the benefit of Royce and Stephanie.

"Told you he was feeling snarky today," said Stephanie.

"What did he say?" asked Royce. "You okay?"

"She looks a little pale," Stephanie put in.

"I'm fine," said Amber, debating with herself about what to tell Royce as she shut down the phone and handed it back.

"You didn't ask many questions," Royce ventured.

"He gave me a name. Sally Nettleton." She took a breath, framing her words carefully. "He was, well, annoyed that you'd put me in direct touch with him."

Royce frowned.

"He seems to think I broke the chain of command."

"So what?"

"I tell you, something's wrong with that man," Stephanie put in, dishing some of the crisp salad onto her plate.

Amber made up her mind, seeing little point in protecting Barry. In fact, she probably owed it to the rest of his staff to tell Royce the truth. "He seems to think I'm your lover."

It was Royce's turn to freeze. "He *said* that?"

"He said he didn't tolerate insubordination, and you won't always be around to protect me. That you'd lose interest."

A ruddy flush crept up Royce's neck, and he reached for his phone.

Amber put her hand over his. "Don't," she advised.

"Why the hell not?"

"Because he'll think you *are* protecting your lover."

"I don't give a rat's ass what—"

"Did I miss something?" asked Stephanie, glancing from one to the other, her tone laced with obvious anticipation and excitement. "Lovers?"

"No," they both shouted simultaneously.

"Too bad." She went back to her salad. "That would be cool."

Amber turned to Stephanie. "That would be tacky. You can't sleep with a man you've barely met." She silently commanded herself to pay close attention to those words.

"Sure you can," Stephanie chirped with a grin.

"No," Royce boomed at her. "You can't."

Stephanie giggled. "Good grief, you're an easy mark. There's nobody around here for me to sleep with anyway."

Some of the fight went out of Royce's posture, but his hand still gripped his phone.

Amber rubbed the tense hand. "Let it go."

"It's a firing offense."

"No, it's not."

"Yes, it is."

"At least give it some thought first." Barry had been a jerk, but she didn't want anyone getting fired on her account. "Maybe ask around. See if this was an isolated incident."

"He was rude to me this morning," said Stephanie.

"You're not helping," Amber warned.

Royce folded his arms across his chest. "It was *my* decision to call him directly. He doesn't get to second-guess me."

"Did you explain the circumstances?"

"I don't have to."

"So, he made an assumption. You can't fire a man for making an assumption."

He pasted her with a sharp look. "You like being spoken to that way."

"Of course not." But she'd like being Royce's lover. Heaven help her, she was pretty sure she'd like being Royce's lover.

Their gazes locked and held for a long moment, and she could have sworn he was reading her mind.

"The lasagna's getting cold," Stephanie pointed out conversationally.

Royce ended the moment with a sharp nod. "We'll talk about it later."

"Sure," Amber agreed, wondering if they were going to talk about Barry or about the energy that crackled between them like lightning.

Five

In Royce's mind, the issue was far from settled.

The storm had passed, leaving a bright moon behind. He closed the office door behind him for privacy, leaving Amber and Stephanie chatting out on the veranda, puppies scampering around them. He, on the other hand, flipped on the bright overhead light and crossed to the leather desk chair, snagging the desk phone and punching in Barry's home number.

It was nearly midnight in Chicago, but he didn't give a damn. Let the man wake up.

"Hello?" came a groggy, masculine voice.

"Barry?"

"Yes."

"It's Royce Ryder."

"Yes?" A shot of energy snapped into Barry's voice. "Anything wrong, Royce?"

There was plenty wrong. "Were you able to give Amber the information she needed?"

A pause. "I believe I did. Sally can cover anything else in the morning."

Royce waited a beat. "When I called you earlier, it wasn't because I wanted her to talk to Sally in the morning." Full stop. More silence.

"Oh. Well... I assumed—"

"Did you or did you not answer Amber's questions?" Royce repeated. And he could almost hear the wheels spinning inside Barry's head.

"I don't think you did," Royce said into the silence. "And the reason I don't think you did is because I was sitting right next to her during the call, and she didn't get a chance to ask you any questions." Once again, he stopped, giving Barry an opportunity to either contribute or sweat.

Hesitation was evident in the man's voice. "Did she... Mmm. Is she there?"

"No. She's not *here*. It's eleven o'clock. The woman's not working at eleven o'clock."

Silence.

"Here's my suggestion," said Royce. "To solve the problem. You hop on a plane in the morning. The corporate jet is unavailable, so you'll have to fly commercial. I'm thinking coach." He picked up an unopened envelope from the desktop and tapped it against the polished oak surface, dropping all pretence of geniality. "You get your ass to the ranch, and you apologize to Ms. Hutton. Then you answer any and all of her questions."

"I... But... Did you say Hutton?"

"David Hutton's daughter. But that couldn't matter less."

"Royce. I'm sorry. I didn't realize—"

"Apologize to *her*."

"Of course."

"You'll be here tomorrow?"

"As soon as I can get there."

Satisfied, Royce disconnected. Amber only needed to be sure funds would be available in the account. But that wasn't the point anymore.

He gazed at the envelope in his hand. It was windowed. From North Pass Feed. Typical bill.

Curious after Amber's concern about his credit rating, he slit it open. Then he glanced through the other piles she'd made, arming himself with some basic information on the ranch expenses.

Half an hour later, he thought he had a picture of the accounts-payable situation, so he headed back down the hallway to find Amber and Stephanie in the front foyer.

Stephanie was on her way out the door, and she gave him a quick kiss and a wave before piling into a pickup truck to head for home. As he closed the door behind her, the empty house seemed to hold its breath with anticipation.

Amber looked about as twitchy as he felt.

"You want to talk about Barry?" she asked, moving from the foyer into the great room.

"Taken care of," he answered, following a few paces behind her, letting his gaze trickle from her shoulders to her narrow waist, to her sexy rear end and the shapely thighs that were emphasized by her snug-fitting blue jeans.

She twisted her head. "What do you mean?"

"He'll be here in the morning."

She turned fully then. "I don't understand."

"He's coming by to apologize. And to answer your questions in person."

Her eyes widened in shock, red lips coming open in a way that was past sexy. "You didn't."

"He insisted."

"He did not."

Royce moved closer. "I suspect he understood the stakes."

She tipped her chin. "I don't need somebody to travel a thousand miles to offer me an insincere apology."

"But I do."

She didn't appear to have a comeback for that, and it was all he could do not to lean in for a kiss. She looked as if she wanted one. Her lips were full, eyes wide, body tipped slightly forward. If this was any other woman, at any other time...

But she'd made her position clear.

And he'd respect that.

Unless and until she told him otherwise.

Midday sun streaming through the ranch office window, Amber clicked through the headlines of a national news station on the office computer, reflecting with curiosity that she didn't feel out of touch with the rest of the world. She'd become a bit of a news junkie while finishing her degree, always on the lookout for emerging issues that might impact on her research. Having gone cold turkey in Montana, she should have missed watching world events unfold.

Of course, she had been a little distracted—okay, a lot distracted by a sexy cowboy who was quickly making her forget there was a world outside the Ryder Ranch.

She'd half expected him to kiss her last night.

He'd stared down at her with those intense blue eyes, nostrils slightly flared, hands bunched into fists, and the muscles in his neck bulging in relief against his skin. She'd imagined him leaning down, planting his lips against hers, wrapping his arms around her and pulling her into paradise all over again.

But then he'd backed off, and she hadn't been brave enough to protest.

Now she sighed with regret as she clicked the mouse, bringing up a live news broadcast from a Chicago network. The buffer loaded, and the announcer carried on with a story about a local bridge repair.

She turned back to the desk, lifting the stack that was the day's mail. Barry Brewster hadn't arrived to confirm the bank balance yet, so she couldn't make any progress paying the backlog of bills.

Truth was, she was dreading the man's arrival. No matter what he said or did, it was going to be embarrassing all around. Royce might think she needed an apology, but Amber had spent most of her life with people being polite to her because they either admired or were afraid of her father or Hargrove. She didn't need the same thing from Barry today.

"The Governor's Office can no longer get away with dodging the issue of Chicago's competitiveness." The familiar voice startled Amber. She whirled to stare at the computer screen, where a news clip showed Hargrove posed in front of the Greenwood Financial Tower with several microphones picking up his words.

"His performance at the conference was shameful," Hargrove continued. "If our own governor won't stand up for the citizens of Chicago, I'd like to know who will."

Guilt percolated through Amber, and she quickly shut

off the sound. She watched his face a few seconds longer, telling herself her actions had been defensible. If she'd stayed, she'd probably be standing right next him, holding his hand, the stalwart little fiancée struggling to come to terms with her role in his life.

He looked good on camera. Then, he'd always had a way with reporters, dodging their pointed questions without appearing rude, making a little information sound like a detailed dissertation. It was the reason the party was grooming him for the election.

A child shouted from outside the window, and Amber concentrated on the sound, forcing her mind from the worry about Hargrove to the seclusion of the ranch. Then another child shouted, and a chorus of cheers went up. Curious, she wandered to the window to look out.

Off to the left, on a flat expanse of lawn, a baseball game was underway. It was mostly kids of the ranch staff, but there were a few adults in the field. And there in the center, pitching the baseball, was Royce. She smiled when he took a few paces forward, lobbing a soft one to a girl who couldn't have been more than eight.

The girl swung and missed, but then she screwed her face up in defiance and positioned herself at the plate, tapping the bat on the white square in front of her. Royce took another step forward.

Amber smiled, then she glanced one more time at Hargrove on the computer screen—her old life.

As the days and hours had slipped by, she'd become more convinced that her decision was right. She had no intention of going back to her old life. And she owed it to Hargrove to make that clear.

She searched for her cell phone on the desktop, powered it up and dialed his number.

"Hargrove Alston," he answered.

"Hargrove? It's Amber."

Silence.

"I wanted to make sure you weren't worried about me," she began.

"I wasn't worried." His tone was crisp.

"Oh. Well, that's good. I'm glad."

"Your parents told me you were fine, and that you'd taken the trouble to contact them."

Amber clearly heard the "while you didn't bother to contact me" message underlying his words.

"Are you over your tantrum, then?" he asked.

She couldn't help but bristle. "Is that what you think I'm doing?"

"I think you're behaving like a child."

She gritted her teeth.

"You missed the Chamber of Commerce speech," he accused.

"I hear you didn't," she snarked in return.

Another silence. "And what is that supposed to mean?"

"Nothing."

"Honestly, Amber."

"Forget it. Of course you gave the speech. It was an important speech."

Her words seemed to mollify him. "Will you be ready in time for dinner, then? Flannigan's at eight with the Myers."

Amber blinked in amazement at the question. She'd been gone for three days. She'd broken off their engagement.

"I'm not coming to dinner," she told him carefully.

He gave a heavy sigh on the other end of the phone. "Is this about the Switzerland trip?"

"Of course not."

"I explained why I had to go alone."

"This is about a fundamental concern with our compatibility as a couple."

"You sound like a self-help book."

Amber closed her eyes and counted to three. "I'm breaking our engagement, Hargrove. I'm truly sorry if I hurt you."

A flare of anger crept into his tone. "I wish you'd get over this mood."

"This isn't something I'm going to get over."

"Do you have any idea how embarrassing this could get?"

"I'm sorry about that, too. But we can't get married to keep from being embarrassed." She flicked a gaze to the baseball game, watching two colorful young figures dash around the bases.

"Are you trying to punish me?" asked Hargrove, frustration mounting in his tone. "Do you want me to apologize for..." He paused. "I don't know. Tell me what you think I've done?"

"You haven't done anything."

"Then get ready for dinner," he practically shouted.

"I'm not in Chicago."

He paused. "Where are you?"

"It doesn't—"

"Seriously, Amber. This is getting out of hand. I don't have time to play—"

"Goodbye, Hargrove."

"Don't you dare—"

She quickly tapped the end button then shut down the

power on her phone. Talking around in circles wasn't going to get them anywhere.

She defiantly stuffed the phone into her pocket and drew a deep breath. After the tense conversation, the carefree baseball game was like a siren's call. Besides, it was nearly lunchtime, and she was tired of looking at numbers.

Determinedly shaking off her emotional reaction to the fight with Hargrove, she headed outside to watch.

Stephanie was standing at the sidelines.

"Looks like fun," said Amber, drawing alongside and opening the conversation. She inhaled the fresh air and let the cheerfulness of the crowd seep into her psyche.

"Usually it's just the kids," Stephanie told her. "But a lot of the hands are down from the range today, and Royce can't resist a game. And once he joined in, well..." She shrugged at the mixed-age crowd playing and watching.

A little girl made it to first, and a cocky teenage boy swaggered up to the plate, reversing his baseball cap and pointing far out to right field with the tip of his bat.

Royce gave the kid an amused shake of his head, walked back to the mound and smacked the ball into the pocket of his worn glove. Then he shook his head in response to the catcher's hand signals. Royce waited, then smiled, and nodded his agreement to the next signal.

He drew back, bent his leg and delivered a sizzling fastball waist high and over the plate. The batter swung hard but missed. Royce chuckled, and the kid stepped out of the batter's box, adjusting his cap then scuffing his runners over the dirt at home plate.

"That's Robbie Nome," Stephanie informed her. "He's at that age, constantly challenging the hands."

"How old?" asked Amber, guessing sixteen or seventeen.

"Seventeen," Stephanie confirmed. "They usually settle down around eighteen. But there's a hellish year there in between while their brain catches up to their size and their testosterone level." She shook her head as Robbie swung and missed a second time.

"Royce seems pretty good," Amber observed, watching him line up for another pitch. She knew she was staring way too intently at him, but she couldn't help herself.

He was dressed in faded jeans, a steel-gray T-shirt and worn running shoes. His bare arms were deeply tanned, and his straight, white teeth shone with an infectious grin.

"He played in the College World Series."

"Pitcher?" asked Amber, impressed.

"First base."

Royce rocketed in a third pitch, and the batter struck out.

The outfielders let out a whoop and ran for the sidelines. The shoulders of the girl on first base slumped in dejection. Royce obviously noticed. He cut to her path, whispered something in her ear and ruffled her short, brown hair. She smiled, and he gave her a playful high five.

Then he spotted Amber and Stephanie, and made a beeline for them. Amber's chest contracted, and her heart lifted at the thought that his long strides were meant to bring him closer to her.

His gaze flicked to Stephanie but then settled back on Amber.

"Impressive," she complimented as he drew near.

He shrugged. "They're kids."

Stephanie held out her hand, and Royce smacked the glove into her palm. "You want to play?" she asked Amber.

Amber shook her head. "I need to get back to work." Then, as Stephanie trotted toward the outfield, she confided in Royce. "I've never been much of an athlete."

His gaze traveled her body. "Could've fooled me."

"Pilates and a StairMaster."

"I bet you'd be a natural at sports."

"We're not about to find out." She'd never swung a bat in her life. There were eight-year-olds out there who would probably show her up.

"I'd lob you a soft one," Royce offered, beneath the cheers and calls from the teams.

"Think I'll stick to bookkeeping."

He sobered. "You worked all morning?"

She nodded.

"Anything interesting?"

She shook her head. Actually, she'd found a couple of strange-looking payments in the computerized accounting system. But they were probably nothing, so she didn't want to bother Royce with that. And she sure wasn't about to tell him about her conversation with Hargrove.

"You surprise me," he said in an intimate tone.

"How so?"

"I had you pegged for a party girl."

"No kidding," she scoffed, rolling her eyes at his understatement.

"I didn't mean it that way."

She looked him straight on. "Yeah, you did."

He raked a hand through his sweat-damp hair, giving a sheepish smile. "Okay, I did for a while. But I got over it."

She paused, debating for a few silent seconds, but then deciding she was going to quit censoring herself. "So," she dared, with a toss of her hair. "What do you think of me now?"

His eyes danced, reflecting the color of the endless summer sky. "It could go one of two ways."

"Which are?"

"Royce!" someone called. "You're on deck."

He twisted his head to shout over his shoulder. "Be right there." Then he turned back, slowly contemplating her.

"Well?" she prompted, ridiculously apprehensive.

His hand came up to cup her chin, his thumb and forefinger warm against her skin. "You're either shockingly ingenuous or frighteningly cunning." But his tone took the sting out of the labels.

"Neither of those are complimentary," she pointed out, absorbing the sparks from his touch.

His tone went low. "But both are very sexy."

Then his hand dropped away, and he turned to the game, trotting toward the batter's box as a player took a base hit.

Amber skipped down the staircase, recalling Royce smacking a three-base hit, bringing ten-year-old Colby Jones home to win the game by one run. She and Stephanie had decided to dress up for dinner, and she wore a white, spaghetti-strap cocktail dress and high-heeled sandals. She rounded the corner at the bottom of the stairs and caught sight of him in a pressed business suit. He was even sexier now than he'd been this afternoon in his T-shirt and jeans.

And he didn't look out of place in the rustic setting. She was glad she'd gone with the dress.

His gaze caught hers, dark and brooding, and she faltered on her high heels. This afternoon, he'd been almost playful. Had she done something to annoy him?

And then she caught sight of the second man, nearly as tall as Royce, somewhat thinner, his suit slightly wrinkled at the elbows and knees. The man turned at the sound of her footsteps, and she knew it had to be Barry Brewster. His jaw was tight, and beads of sweat had formed on his brow.

"Ms. Hutton," Royce intoned. "This is Barry Brewster. You spoke to him on the phone last night."

Amber fought an urge to laugh. The whole charade suddenly struck her as ridiculous. "Mr. Brewster," she said instead, keeping her face straight as she came to a stop and held out her hand.

"Barry, please."

"You can call me Amber."

"No, he can't."

"Royce, please."

But Royce didn't waver, shoulders square, expression stern.

"Ms. Hutton," Barry began, obviously not about to run afoul of his boss. "Please accept my apology. I was rude and insulting last night. I am, of course, available for anything you might need."

The irritation in his eyes belied the geniality of his tone. But then she hadn't expected him to be sincere about this.

"Thank you," she said simply. "I do have a couple of questions." She looked to Royce. "Should we sit down?"

"Unnecessary. Barry won't be staying."

286 In Bed with the Wrangler

"This is ridicul—"

Royce's hard expression shut her up, and she silently warned herself not to get on his bad side.

"I was hoping you could tell me the balance in the ranch bank account," she said to Barry. "There are a number of unpaid bills, so I wondered—"

"You don't need a reason to ask for the bank balance," Royce cut in.

"I'd need to look it up," said Barry, shifting from one black loafer to the other. He flexed his neck to one side and straightened the sleeves of his suit.

"So, look it up," said Royce.

"I don't have access to the server."

"Call someone who does."

Barry hesitated. "It's pretty late."

"Your point?"

"I guess I could try to catch Sally." With a final pause, Barry reached into his pocket for his phone.

While he dialed, Amber moved closer to Royce, turning her back on Barry.

"Is this completely necessary?" she hissed.

"I thought you wanted the bank balance."

"I do."

"Then it's completely necessary."

"You know that's not what I'm talking about."

"Let me handle this."

She took in the determined slant to Royce's chin while Barry's voice droned on in the background.

"Do I have a choice?" she asked.

"No."

"You can be a real hard-ass, you know that?"

"He insulted you."

"I'm a big girl. I'm over it."

"That's not the point."

She fought against a sudden grin at his need to get in the last word. "Do you ever give up?"

"No."

Barry cleared his throat, and Amber smoothly turned back to face him.

"Sally is looking into the overdraft and the line of credit to see where—"

"The balance," said Royce.

Barry's neck took on a ruddy hue, and he tugged at the white collar of his shirt. "It's, uh, complicated."

"I'm an intelligent man, and Amber has an honors degree."

Barry's gaze flicked to Amber, and she could have sworn she saw panic in its depths.

"I'd really rather discuss—"

"The balance," said Royce.

Barry drew a terse breath. "At the moment, the account is overdrawn."

There were ten full seconds of frozen silence.

Stephanie entered the room from the kitchen, stopping short as she took in the trio.

"Say again?" Royce widened his stance.

"There's been… That is…" This time when Barry glanced at Amber, he seemed to be pleading for help. There was no help she could give him. She didn't have a clue what was going on.

Royce's voice went dangerously low. "Why didn't you transfer something from corporate?"

Barry tugged at his collar again. "The China deal."

"What about the China deal?" Royce asked carefully. "Was the transfer held up?"

Barry swallowed, his Adam's apple bobbing, voice

turning to a raspy squeak. "The paperwork. From Cheng Li. It didn't make the deadline."

Stephanie's eyes went wide, while Royce cocked his head, brows creasing. "They assured me the fax would go through."

"It did. But...well...,"

Royce crossed his arms over his chest.

"Our acknowledgment," said Barry. "The time zone difference."

"You didn't send the acknowledgment?"

"End of day. Chicago time."

"You missed the deadline?" Royce's voice was harsh with disbelief.

"I've been trying to fix it for thirty-six hours."

Royce took a step forward. "You *missed* a fifty-million-dollar deadline?"

Barry's mouth opened, but nothing came out.

"And you didn't call me?" Royce's voice was incredulous now.

"I was trying to fix—"

"Yesterday," Royce all but shouted, index finger jabbing in Barry's direction. "*Yesterday*, I could have called Jared at his hotel. Today, he's on a sailboat somewhere in the South Pacific. You have..." Royce raked a hand through his hair. "I don't even know how much money you've lost."

"I—"

"What in the *hell* happened?"

"It was the time zones. Technology. The language barrier."

"You are *so* fired."

Amber's gaze caught Stephanie's. She felt desperate for an exit. She didn't want to witness Royce's anger,

Barry's humiliation. She wanted to be far, far away from this disturbing situation.

"You're done, Barry," Royce confirmed to the silent man.

Barry hesitated a beat longer. Then his shoulders dropped. The fight went out of him, and he turned for the door.

The room seemed to boom with silence as Barry's footsteps receded and the car pulled away outside.

Stephanie took a few hesitant steps toward her brother. "Royce?"

"Cancel his credit cards," Royce commanded. "Wake up someone from IT and change the computer passwords. And have security reset the codes on the building."

"What are we going to do?" Stephanie asked in a whisper.

Royce's hands curled into fists at his sides. He looked to Amber. "I have to call Beijing. If we don't fix this, the domino effect could be catastrophic."

Amber nodded. "Just tell me what you need."

"Can we talk to Jared?" asked Stephanie.

Royce shook his head. "Not a chance. Not for a week at least."

Six

Amber hung up the phone after their fifth call to China, her expression somber as Royce's mood.

"That's it." He voiced his defeat out loud.

"Are you sure?"

"Can you think of anything else?"

She shook her head.

He slipped the phone from her hands, setting it on the end table next to the sofa in the living room. The deadline was the deadline, and they hadn't been able to penetrate the Chinese bureaucracy to make their case to Cheng Li. The deal was canceled.

It was nearly 3:00 a.m. Only a few lights burned in the house, and Stephanie had headed to her own ranch an hour ago. Amber tipped her head back on the gold sofa cushion, closing her eyes. She'd struggled through

translations for hours on end, and the strain was showing in her pale complexion.

Royce gave in to the temptation to smooth a lock of
hair from her cheek. "You okay?"

"Just sorry I couldn't help."

He dropped his hand back down. "You did help."

She opened her eyes. "How so?"

"I understand now what is and isn't possible."

"Nothing's possible."

"Apparently not."

She blinked her dark lashes, and her hand covered
his. "How bad is it?"

He rested his own head against the sofa back. "It'll
play havoc with our cash flow. We may have to sell off
some of our companies. But, to start off, I'm going to
have to call the division heads to keep them from pan-
icking. Firing Barry was a significant move."

"Will they be angry?"

He shrugged. "That's the least of my worries."

Amber didn't answer, and Royce was content to sit in
silence. He turned his hand, palm up, wrapping it around
her smaller one. For some reason, it gave him comfort.
Simply sitting here quietly, with her by his side, made
the problems seem less daunting.

Her hand went limp in his, and he turned to gaze at
her closed eyes and even breathing. She was astonish-
ingly beautiful—smooth skin, delicate nose, high cheekbones and lustrous, golden hair that made a man want to
bury his face against it.

He felt a shot of pity for the hapless Hargrove. Imagine having Amber in your grasp then having her disappear? Not that the man wasn't better off. Royce glanced
at the portrait of his parents on their wedding day. He

usually put it away while he was at the ranch, unable to bear the look of unbridled adoration on his father's face.

And that's the way it would have been with Amber, too. Her husband would have gone completely stupid and helpless with longing, only to have her change her mind and move on. Poor, pathetic Hargrove. He wouldn't have known what hit him.

Royce extricated his hand from hers, shifting to the edge of the couch, positioning himself to lift her into his arms.

"Amber?" he whispered softly, sliding one arm around her back and the other beneath her knees.

She mumbled something unintelligible, but her head tipped to rest against his shoulder. He lifted her up, and she stayed sleeping, even as he adjusted her slight body in his arms.

She weighed less than nothing. She was also soft and her scent appealing. There was something completely right about the scent of a beautiful woman, particularly this beautiful woman, fresh, like wildflowers, he supposed, but sweeter, more compelling.

He moved his nose toward her hair, guessing it was her shampoo. Hard to tell, really. He mounted the staircase, taking his time, reluctant to arrive at her room where he'd have to put her down.

His imagination wandered to that moment. Should he help her undress? Slip her between the sheets in her underwear? Would a gentleman wake her up or leave her in her clothes? Never having been a gentleman, Royce wasn't sure.

This had to be the first time he'd put a woman to bed without immediate plans to join her. He couldn't help a self-deprecating smile. It figured. He also couldn't remember a moment in his life when he'd been more eager to join a woman in bed.

He pushed open her door, carefully easing her through the opening. Then he crossed to the queen-size brass bed and leaned down, laying her gently on top of the comforter.

She moaned her contentment, and his longing ratcheted up a notch. Their faces were only inches apart, his arm around her back, the other cradling her bare legs. He knew he had to leave her, but try as he might, he couldn't get his body to cooperate.

"Amber," he whispered again, knowing that if she woke he'd have no choice but to walk away.

"Mmm," she moaned. Then she sighed and wriggled in his arms.

His muscles tensed to iron. His gaze took in her pouty lips and, before he knew it, his head was dipping toward hers. Then he was kissing her sweet lips.

Just to say good-night, he promised himself. Just a chaste—

But then she was kissing back.

Her arms twined around his neck, and her head tipped sideways, lips parting, accommodating his ravenous kiss. Her back arched, and her fingertips curled into his short hair, even as her delicate tongue flicked into his mouth.

He leaned into her soft breasts, stroking the length of her bare legs, teasing the delicate skin behind her knees, tracing the outline of her shapely calves and daring the heat of her smooth thighs.

He wanted her, more than he'd ever wanted a woman in his life. Passion was quickly clouding reason, and his hormones warred with intelligence. Another minute, another second, and his logic would switch completely off.

He dragged his mouth from hers. "Amber?" he forced himself to ask. "Are you sure you're ready for this?"

Her eyes popped open, and she took a sudden jerk back against the pillow. She blinked in confusion at Royce's face, and in a split and horrible second, he realized what had happened.

The woman had been dreaming.

And Royce wasn't the man she'd been dreaming about.

In the morning, Amber was grateful to find Stephanie in the kitchen at breakfast. She needed a buffer between her and Royce while she got over her embarrassment.

She'd hesitated a moment too long last night. When she'd realized it wasn't a dream, she should have kept right on kissing him. She should have pressed her body tightly against his and sent the signal that she was completely attracted to him, nearly breathless with passion for him, and that making love was exactly what she wanted.

Instead, all he'd seen was her shock and hesitation. He'd been offended and abruptly left the room. She didn't blame him. And she wasn't brave enough to try to explain.

"Morning, Amber." Stephanie was her usual bright self as she bit into a strip of bacon, legs swinging from the high chair at the breakfast bar.

"Morning," Amber replied, daring a fleeting glance at Royce.

He gave her a cool nod then turned his attention back to Stephanie. "Two days at the most," he told Stephanie.

"I'll definitely get you something," she responded and blew out a sigh. "This is the worst possible time."

"I can't imagine there being a best possible time." Royce stood from the breakfast bar and carried his plate and coffee mug over to the sink. He downed the last of the coffee before setting everything on the counter.

Amber helped herself to a clean plate from the cupboard and took a slice of toast from the platter.

"Royce has to call a division heads meeting," Stephanie told her. "We need to ask for financial reports from everybody. But he's worried about panic."

"Who would panic?" Amber addressed her question first to Royce, but when he didn't meet her eyes, she turned back to Stephanie.

"I need a pretext for the meeting," said Royce. "Barry Brewster's firing is bad enough. Add to that a sudden meeting and financial reports, and the gossip will swirl.

"We have over two thousand employees," he continued. "Some very big contracts, and some very twitchy clients." His gaze finally went to Amber, but his face remained impassive, his tone flat. "If you don't mind, we'll start a rumor you were the cause."

"You mean the cause of Barry Brewster being fired, not the money problems?"

Royce didn't react to her joke. "Yes."

"Are you leaving today?" asked Stephanie.

At first Amber thought Stephanie meant her, and the idea made her clench her stomach in regret. But then she realized Stephanie was talking to her brother.

Royce nodded.

"Where—" Amber clamped her jaw to slow herself down. It was jarring to think of him leaving with this tension between them. "Where are you going?" she finished, feigning only a mild interest.

"Chicago."

"You don't think that will bring on the gossip?"

She assured herself her caution was sincere. It wasn't merely an attempt to keep Royce here at the ranch.

His eyes narrowed.

"If you come rolling into the office, people are sure to think something's up."

"She's right," Stephanie put in.

"I don't see an alternative. I have to talk to the division VPs."

"Bring them here," suggested Amber.

Both Royce and Stephanie stared at her.

"There's your pretext. Come up with a reason to bring them here. Something fun, something frivolous, then take them aside and have whatever discreet conversation you need to have." She paused, but neither of them jumped in.

"A barbecue." She offered the first thing that popped into her mind.

Royce's voice turned incredulous, but at least there was an emotion in it. "You want me to fly the Ryder senior managers to Montana for a barbecue?"

"They'd never suspect," she told him.

"A barn dance," Stephanie cried, coming erect on the seat. "We'll throw a dance to christen the new barn."

"You're both insane," Royce grumbled.

"Like a fox," said Stephanie. "Invite the spouses. Hire a band. Nobody throws a dance and barbecue when the company's in financial trouble."

Amber waited. So did Stephanie.

Royce's brows went up, and his mouth thinned out. "I find I can't disagree with that statement."

Finished with her own breakfast, Stephanie hopped up and transferred her dishes to the sink. She gave Royce a quick peck on the cheek. "See you guys in a while. I have to get the students started."

As she left the room, Amber screwed up her courage. She definitely needed to clear the air. "Royce—"

"If you have time today," he interrupted, "could you give me as much information as possible on the cattle ranch finances?" His voice was detached, professional, and his gaze seemed to focus on her hairline.

Amber hated the cold wall between them. "I…"

"Stephanie's going to pull something together for the horse operation, and I'll be busy—"

"Of course," Amber quickly put in, swallowing, telling herself she had no right to feel hurt. "Whatever you need."

He gave a sharp nod. "Thanks. Appreciate you helping out." Then he turned and strode out of the kitchen, boot heels echoing on the tile floor.

Amber was curled up on the webbed cushions of an outdoor love seat on the ranch house deck, clouds slipping over the distant mountains, making mottled shade on the nearby aspen groves. She flipped her way through a hundred-page printout from the ranch's financial system, highlighting entries along the way.

Gopher, one of Molly's young pups, had curled up against her bare feet. At first, she'd been wary of his wet nose and slurpy tongue. But then he'd fallen asleep, and she found his rhythmic breathing and steady heartbeat rather comforting.

She hadn't seen Royce since breakfast, and Stephanie was obviously busy getting her own financial records together. Amber's thoughts had vacillated from heading straight for home, to confronting Royce about last night, to seducing Royce, to helping him sort out his business problems and earning his gratitude.

She sighed and let her vision blur against the page. For the hundredth time, she contemplated her mistake. Why had she panicked last night? Why hadn't she kissed him harder, hugged him tighter and waited to see where it would all lead?

She was wildly attracted to him. She was truly free from Hargrove now, and there was no reason in the world she couldn't follow her desires. So what if she'd only known him a few days? They were both adults, and this was hardly the 1950s.

Gopher shifted his warm little body, reminding her of where she was and that, 1950s or not, she'd blown her chance with Royce. The choices left were to leave him, seduce him or impress him. Since she was completely intimidated by the thought of seducing a man she'd already rebuffed, she decided to go with impressing him.

She forced herself to focus on the column of numbers in her lap.

There it was again.

She stroked the highlighter across the page.

Yet another payment to Sagittarius Eclipse Incorporated. It was for one hundred thousand dollars, just like the last one, and the one before that.

She skipped back on the pages, counting the payments and pinpointing the dates of the transactions. They fell on the first day of every month. Where other payments in the financial report were for obvious things like feed, lumber, tools or veterinary services, the Sagittarius Eclipse payments were notated only as "services."

Amber's curiosity was piqued. She flipped to the back page. Scanning through the total columns, she discovered one-point-two million dollars had been paid out to Sagittarius Eclipse in the current year, the same amount the year before.

She pulled her feet from the love seat cushion. Gopher whimpered and quickly scooted up next to her thigh, flopping against her.

She smiled at the little puff ball, set the financial report aside and scooped him into her arms. He wiggled for a moment, but then settled in next to her like a fuzzy baby.

"I suppose if I hold on to you, you can't do any harm," she whispered to him, checking Molly and the other pups as she rose to her feet. They were curled together at the far end of the deck. Nobody seemed to notice as she carried Gopher through the doorway.

There was a computer close by in the living room, and she sat down in front of it, moving the mouse to bring the screen back to life. She hadn't graduated in Public Administration without knowing how to search a company. Using her free hand, she called up a favorite corporate registry search program.

An hour later, she knew nothing, absolutely nothing about Sagittarius Eclipse Incorporated. They had to be an offshore company, and a hard-to-trace one at that. She could hear her father's voice inside her head, warning her that when something didn't seem right, something definitely wasn't right. But since she wasn't nearly as suspicious as her father, she refused to jump to any conclusions.

Shifting the sleeping puppy, she dug into her pocket to retrieve her cell phone, dialing Stephanie's number.

"Yo!" came the young woman's voice.

"It's Amber."

"I know. What's going on?"

"You ever heard of a company called Sagittarius Eclipse?"

"Who?"

Amber repeated the name.

"What are they, astrologers or something?"

"I hope not." Amber nearly chuckled. If Ryder Ranch was paying for a hundred grand a month of astrology services, they'd better be accurately predicting the stock market.

"Never heard of them," said Stephanie. "How are things looking at your end?"

"Best I can come up with is to stop work on the new barn," said Amber. And maybe quit paying for unidentified "services." But something stopped her from mentioning the strange payments to Stephanie.

"I hate to say it," Stephanie returned, "but I'd better not buy Blanchard's Run."

"I thought that was a foregone conclusion."

"A girl can hope."

This time, Amber did laugh at the forlorn little sigh in Stephanie's voice. "Suck it up, princess."

"Easy for you to say. It's not your business being compromised."

Amber couldn't deny it. What's more, she couldn't ignore the fact that she didn't have a business to compromise. Nor did she have a career to compromise. The only thing she'd ever been able to call a vocation was her role as Hargrove's loyal fiancée and future wife. And she'd completely blown that job yesterday.

"What else have you got?" she asked, shoving the disagreeable thoughts to the back of her mind.

"Let me see." Stephanie shuffled some papers in the background. "I can delay a tack order, struggle through with our existing jumps. Man, I hate to do that. But the horses have to eat, the employees need paychecks and we don't dare cut back on the competition schedule."

Royce's deep voice broke in from behind Amber. "I see you've changed your mind."

She jerked around to face him in his Western shirt and faded jeans. A flush heated her face. Yes, she'd changed her mind. She'd changed her mind the second he left her bedroom last night.

But he was staring at the puppy in her lap, and she realized he was referring to a completely different subject.

"Royce is here," she said into the mouthpiece.

"Tell him I'll be down there before dinner."

"Sure." She signed off and hung up the phone, adjusting Gopher's little body when she realized her arm was beginning to tingle from lack of circulation. "He's very friendly," she told Royce.

"Are you taking him home?"

"Have you ever heard of a company called Sagittarius Eclipse?" she countered, not wanting to open the subject of her going home. She'd pretend she didn't notice he was anxious for her to leave.

"Never," he answered, watching her closely, the distance and detachment still there in his expression and stance.

She debated her next move, unable to shake the instinct that told her the payments were suspicious.

"Why do you ask?" he prompted.

"The ranch is making payments to them."

"For what?"

"That's just it. I can't tell."

"Tools? Supplies? Insurance?"

"Insurance, maybe." She hadn't thought of that. "The entries only say 'services.'" She reached behind her for the report, and Gopher wriggled in her lap.

"Better put him back outside," Royce suggested.

Amber moved to the screen door, deposited the puppy on the deck and returned to point out the entries to Royce.

"I searched for the company on the internet," she offered while he glanced through the pages she'd noted. "I can't find anything on them, not domestically, not offshore."

He raised a questioning brow.

"I learned corporate research at U of C."

Royce's jaw tightened, and she could feel the wheels turning inside his head.

She dared voice the suspicion that was planted inside her brain. "Do you think McQuestin could be—"

"No."

"His niece?"

"Not a chance. Not for these amounts."

"McQuestin had to know, right?" The man worked with the business accounts on a daily basis. Whatever was going on with Sagittarius Eclipse, McQuestin had to be aware.

"It's legit," Royce said out loud, but his spine was stiff, and he was frowning.

"What do you want to do?" she asked. Maybe this was the tip of the iceberg. Maybe Sagittarius Eclipse would help them solve some kind of embezzlement scheme. Maybe she could even help alleviate the company's cash flow problems.

He reached into the breast pocket of his blue-and-gray plaid shirt, retrieving his cell phone and searching for a number. His hair was damp with sweat, face streaked with dust, sleeves rolled up to reveal his tanned, muscular forearms. Amber's gaze went on a wayward tour down his body, her hormones reaching with predictability to his sex appeal.

He pressed a button on the phone, and the ringing tone became audible through the small speaker.

Amber pointed to the screen door. "Do you want me to—"

Royce shook his head. "You're the one that found it. Let's hear what McQuestin has to say."

A woman's voice bid them hello.

"Maddy? It's Royce."

"Oh, hey, Royce. He's doing okay today. They think they got the last of the bone fragments, and the infection's calming down."

"Good to hear," said Royce. "Can I talk to him for a minute?"

Maddy hesitated. "He's pretty doped up. Can I help with something?"

"It's important," said Royce, an apology in his voice.

"Well. Okay." The sounds went muffled for a few moments.

"Yeah?" came a gravelly voice.

"It's Royce, Mac. How're you feeling?"

"Like the bronc won," McQuestin grumbled.

Amber couldn't help but smile.

"You married yet?" McQuestin's voice was slightly slurred.

"That was Jared," Royce corrected.

"Mighty pretty girl," McQuestin mused. "Should have married her yourself."

"Jared might have had an objection to that."

"He's too busy... Hey! Did you wash the ears?"

Royce and Amber glanced at each other in amusement.

"Mac," Royce tried.

"What now?" MacQuestin grumbled.

"You know anything about Sagittarius Eclipse?"

There was a silence, during which their amusement turned to concern.

"I paid 'em," said McQuestin, obviously angry. "What else would a man do?"

"What exactly did you pay them for?"

McQuestin snorted. "You tell Benteen..." Then his voice turned to a growl. "Somebody should have shot the damn dog yesterday."

Maddy's voice came back. "Can this wait, Royce? You're really upsetting him."

"I'm sorry, Maddy. Of course it can wait. Keep me posted, okay?"

"Will do." McQuestin's voice still ebbed and flowed in the background. "Better go."

Royce signed off.

"Who's Benteen?" asked Amber.

Royce's voice was thoughtful, and he placed the phone back in his pocket. "My grandfather. He died earlier this year. You think you could dig a little deeper into this?"

Amber nodded. Her curiosity was piqued. She'd like nothing better than to sleuth around Sagittarius Eclipse and figure out its relationship to the Ryder Ranch.

Seven

"Royce?"

Royce's body reacted to the sound of Amber's voice. He hefted a hay bale onto the stack, positioning it correctly before acknowledging her presence.

"Yeah?" He didn't turn to look at her. It was easier for him to cope if only one of his senses was engaged with her at a time. He only hoped she'd keep her sweet scent on the far side of the barn.

Her footsteps echoed. So much for that plan.

"I didn't find any more information," she said. "I'm going to have to try again tomorrow."

He nodded, moving to the truckload of hay bales, keeping his gaze fixed on his objective.

"It's getting late," she ventured, and there was a vulnerability in her voice that made his predicament even worse. Though he didn't look at her now, an image of her this afternoon, in that short denim skirt, a peach tank top, her blond hair cascading softly around her bare shoulders, was stuck deep in the base of his brain. It was going to take dynamite to blast it out.

"I know." He gave the short answer.

"What are you doing?"

He grabbed the next bale, binder twine pressing against the reinforced palms of his leather work gloves. "Moving hay bales."

He retraced his steps. Extreme physical work was his only hope of getting any sleep tonight. If he wasn't dead-dog exhausted, he'd do nothing but lie awake and think about Amber sleeping across the hall.

"Is it that important?" she pressed.

"Horses have to eat."

"But do you—"

"Is there something you need?" he asked brusquely.

Her silence echoed between them, and he felt like a heel.

"No," she finally answered in a soft voice. "It's just…"

He didn't prompt her, hoping she'd take the hint and leave. He'd never found himself so intensely attracted to a woman, and it was physically painful to fight it.

"I'm surprised is all," she continued.

He mentally rolled his eyes. Couldn't the woman take a hint? Did she like that she was making him crazy? Was she one of those teases that got her jollies out of tempting a man then turning up her prissy little nose at his advances?

"When you said you had to babysit the ranch—"

How the hell long was she going to keep this up?

"—I thought you meant in a more managerial sense. I mean, can't somebody else move the hay?"

He turned to look at her then. Damn it, she was still wearing that sexy outfit. Only it was worse now, because the cool evening air had hardened her nipples, and they were highlighted against the soft cotton where she stood in the pool of overhead light.

The air whooshed right out of his lungs, and he almost dropped the bale.

"I'd rather do it myself," he finally ground out.

"I see." She held his gaze. There was something soft in the depths of her eyes, something warm and welcoming.

At this very second, he could swear she was attracted to him. But he'd been down that road before. Down that road was a long night in a very lonely bed.

He went back to work.

"Royce?" Her footsteps echoed again as she moved closer.

He heaved the bale into place, gritted his teeth and turned. "What?" he barked.

"I'm..." She glanced at the scuffed floor. "Uh... sorry."

He swiped his forearm across his sweaty brow. "Not as sorry as I am."

She glanced up in confusion. "For what? What did you do?"

"I didn't *do* anything."

"Then, what do you have to be sorry about?"

"You want to know why I'm sorry?" He'd reached the breaking point, and he was ready to give it to her with both barrels. "You really want to know why I'm sorry?"

She gave a tentative nod.

"I'm sorry I walked into the Ritz-Carlton lounge."

Her eyes widened as he stripped off his gloves.

"And I'm sorry I brought you home with me." He tossed the gloves on the nearest hay bale. "And I'm sorry you're so beautiful and desirable and sexy. But mostly, *mostly* I'm sorry my family's future is falling down around my ears, and all I can think of is how much I want you."

Their eyes locked.

For a split second, it looked as though she smiled.

"You think this is *funny*?"

She shook her head. Then she took a step forward. "I think it's ironic."

"You might not want to get too close," he warned, drinking in the sight, sound and scent of her all in one shot, wondering how many seconds he could hold out before he dragged her into his arms.

"Yeah?" She stepped closer still.

"Did you not hear me?"

She placed her flat palm against his chest. "I heard you just fine." Her defiant blue eyes held one of the most blatant invitations he'd ever seen.

He hoped she knew what she was doing.

Hell, who was he kidding? He couldn't care less if she knew or not. Just so long as she didn't back off this time.

His arms went around her and jerked her flush against him, all but daring her to protest.

Then he bent his head; his desire and frustration transmitted themselves into a powerful kiss. He all but devoured her mouth, reveling in the feel of her thighs, belly and breasts, all plastered against his aching flesh.

He encircled her waist, pulling in at the small of her back, bending her backward, kissing deeper as his free hand strummed from hip to waist over her rib cage to capture the soft mound of her breast.

She groaned against his mouth, lips parting farther, her tongue answering the impassioned thrusts of his own. Her nipple swelled under his caress, fueling his desire and obliterating everything else from his brain. He bent his knee, shifting his thigh between hers, pushing up on her short skirt, settling against the silk of her panties.

Her hands gripped his upper arms, nails scraping erotically against his thin shirt, transmitting her passion to the nerves of his skin. He lifted her, spreading her legs, hands cupping her bottom, shoving the skirt out of the way and pressing her heat against him.

Her arms went around his neck, legs tightening, her lips hot on his, her silky hair flowing out in all directions around her shoulders. She braced her arms on his shoulders, fingers delving into his short hair. Her kisses moved from his mouth to his cheek, his chin and his neck. She tugged at the buttons of his shirt, loosening them, before dipping her head and trailing her kisses across his chest.

He tipped back his head, drinking in the heat and moisture of her amazing lips. Then he took a few steps sideways, behind the bale stack, screening them from the rest of the cavernous room. He shrugged out of his loose shirt, dropping it on a bale before settling her on top. He braced his arms on either side of her and pulled back to look.

Her eyes were closed, lips swollen red. Her chest heaved with labored breaths, and his gaze settled on the outline of her breasts against the peach top.

"Royce?"

His name on her lips tightened his chest and sent a fresh wave of desire cascading through his veins. He swiftly stripped her top off over her head, revealing two perfect breasts peeking from a lacy, white bra that dipped low in the center and barely camouflaged her dusky nipples.

"Gorgeous," he breathed, popping the clasp and letting the wisp of fabric fall away. "Perfection."

Her lash-fringed lids came up, revealing blue eyes clouded with passion.

They stared at each other for a long suspended breath. Then he reached out, his tanned hand dark against her creamy breast. He stroked the pad of his thumb across her nipple.

She gasped, and he smiled in pure satisfaction.

He repeated the motion, and she grabbed for his waist, tugging him toward her. But he stood his ground, his gaze flicking to the shadow of her sheer, high-cut panties, the skirt pulled high to reveal her hips.

He traced the line of elastic, knuckle grazing the moist silk. She moaned, head tipping back against the golden hay, her arms falling to her sides, clenching her fists tightly.

He could feel his anticipation, his own blood singing insistently through his system, hormones revving up, his passion making demands on his brain. But he wasn't ready. He wasn't ready to let the roar toward completion hijack his senses.

While his fingertips roamed, he leaned forward, taking one plump nipple into his mouth, curling his tongue around the exquisite texture.

A deep sound burbled in Amber's throat, and her hands went for his belt buckle, the snap of his jeans, his zipper, his boxers, and then he was in her hand, and he knew time was running out.

He hooked his thumbs over the sides of her panties, stripping them down, letting them drop to the floor. Then his body moved unerringly to hers.

Her legs wrapped around his waist, and he raised his head, gazing into her eyes as he flexed his hips, easing slowly as he could to her center and into her core. Her eyes widened with every inch, she clenched her hands on his hips, and her sweet mouth fell open in a pout of awe.

Unable to resist, he bent his head, her features blurred as he grew close. Then her mouth opened against his, and his tongue thrust in, mimicking the motions of his hips as nature took over and he let the primal rhythm throb free between them.

He cupped her face, caressed her hair, kissed her neck, her temple, her eyelids. His hands roamed free, stroking her thighs, her bottom, her belly and breasts. Her panting breaths were music to his ears, her nails crescenting into his back transmitted her fervor.

Then she cried his name, urging him on, playing havoc with his self-control. But she was with him, and the small tremors contracting her body catapulted him over the edge into oblivion.

Amber blinked open her eyes.

She was vaguely aware of hay strands tickling her bare back. But she was much more aware of Royce's hard, hot body engulfing her own. Her lungs were struggling to get enough oxygen, and every fiber of her muscles danced with the aftershocks of lovemaking.

Royce's palm stroked over her hair, and he kissed her eyelids. Despite her exhaustion, her lips curled into a smile. But she was a long way from being able to speak.

Her skirt was in a bunch around her waist, her other

clothes scattered. Her hair was wild and disheveled, tangled with hay, while her lips tingled with the heat of his kisses.

"I don't know what to say," Royce whispered in her ear.

She struggled through a few more breaths. "Well, I'm definitely not sorry," she managed, and she heard him chuckle.

"Definitely not sorry," he echoed.

He eased back, taking in her appearance.

"Bad?" she asked.

He pulled some straw from her hair. "Telltale."

She raked spread fingers through her hair in an attempt to tame it while he refastened his jeans.

He bent and picked up her bra from the floor, frowned at the dirt streaks on it and tucked it into his back pocket. He located her tank top, gave her breasts one last, lingering look, then pulled her top back over her head. The peach color was blotted with dust. And Royce's attempts to brush it off made things worse.

"We'll probably want to sneak you in the back way," he joked as she tugged down her skirt. He watched her movements closely.

She slipped his wrinkled shirt from beneath her butt and held it out to him. "You're not looking so sharp yourself, cowboy."

"I've been working hard." As he shrugged into his shirt, his gaze strayed from the top of her head to the tips of her toes, and his tone went soft and intimate. "What's your excuse?"

"Someone stole my underwear."

He reached for the wisp of silk caught on the side of a bale and tucked it into his pocket with her bra.

"That's my only pair."

"Yeah?" He gave her body another long look. "Lucky me."

He fastened his buttons then helped her down, tucking her hand in his as they headed across the barn. "I hope you know you're sleeping in my bed tonight."

"Only if you give my underwear back."

"Maybe."

"Maybe?"

He turned to gaze at her. "Talk me into it."

Her footsteps slowed, and so did his. With their joined hands, he reeled her in, then he smoothed her hair back once more, moving closer still, voice intimate. "You know, you are stunningly gorgeous."

A smile tickled the corners of her mouth. "Is that why you're sneaking me in the back way?"

"I'm keeping you all to myself," he whispered, lips coming down on hers.

The kiss nearly exploded between them. For all that they'd just made love, Amber's arousal was strong as ever. She wrapped her arms around his neck, came up on her toes, welcomed his tongue and reveled in the feel of his warm hands as they stroked over her back, across her buttocks, down her thighs, then back up beneath her skirt.

She pressed her body against his as the kiss went on and on. A groan slipped from her lips.

"Again?" he asked, voice husky.

She nodded.

"Here or in bed."

"I don't care." She truly didn't. Royce could make her body sing, and propriety didn't appear to have a lot to do with it.

He backed off slightly on the kiss and smoothed her skirt back down. "In bed."

"Really?"

He grinned at the disappointment in her tone. "I want to make love to you for a very, very long time."

She cocked her head sideways. "And you need a bed for that?"

"I don't plan to be able to move afterward."

She breathed a mock, drawn-out sigh. "If you think I'll wear you out…"

"Is that a challenge?"

She gave a teasing half smile and rapidly blinked her lashes.

In return, he planted a playful swat on her buttocks. "You're on, sweetheart."

Amber stifled a yawn in the bright, midday sunshine, stretching her taut thigh muscles as she leaned on the railing of the ranch house deck. The puppies were below, chasing each other and rolling around on the meadow that sloped toward the river. Off the end of the deck, Amber could see the ranch hands putting up five giant tents in preparation for Saturday's barbecue and barn dance.

She was dividing her time between the Sagittarius Eclipse mystery and the barbecue. She'd never planned an event quite like this before. They'd hired a local band. Hamburgers and hot dogs were making up the main course, while salads, potato chips and condiments seemed to round out the rest. They had plans for a giant cake for dessert, with papers plates, soft drinks and canned beer all around.

Amber wasn't sure how the Ryder International ex-

ecutives would react to the dinner, though she was sure
their kids would love the wagon rides, horseshoes and
baseball game Stephanie had planned. When she'd
broached the possibility of steaks, wine and real china
with Sasha, the woman looked at her as though she'd
lost her mind.

Okay, so they did corporate entertaining a little differently here in Montana. Amber could conform. And
at least the event wasn't likely to damage the Ryder International bottom line.

Tucking her windblown hair behind one ear, she
pressed the on button of her cell phone, and dialed Katie's work number.

"Katie Merrick," came the familiar voice.

"It's Amber."

"What? Finally! Have you gone stark raving mad?"

"You've been talking to my mom, haven't you?"

"Of course I've been talking to your mom. And your
dad. And Hargrove. You've got him completely confused."

"I thought I cleared up the confusion yesterday."

"By breaking it off over the phone?" The accusation
was clear in Katie's tone.

"I'm a little ways away, Katie."

"Where?"

Amber scratched her fingernail over a dried flower
petal the rain had stuck to the painted railing, deciding
she couldn't keep it a secret forever. "Montana."

Silence.

"Katie?"

"Did you say Montana?"

"Yes. I'm staying with a...well, friend. I need your
help with something."

"I'd say you need a whole lot more than *my* help. The dress arrived yesterday."

"What dress?"

"Your *wedding* dress." Katie's voice was incredulous. "The one from Paris. The one with antique alençon lace and a thousand hand-sewn pearls."

"Oh." Right. That dress. Amber supposed they'd have to put it on consignment somewhere. "The thing I wanted to talk to you about at the moment, though, was business."

"What do you mean?"

"I have a problem."

"What problem?" Katie's voice immediately turned professional.

"It's a company called Sagittarius Eclipse. I haven't been able to trace it, but I think it's got to be offshore somewhere, maybe hiding behind a numbered company. It could be connected to embezzlement."

There was another moment's silence. "Where did you say you were?" asked Katie.

Amber drew a sigh. "You remember that thirty dollars I gave you last week?"

"To pay for the dry cleaning on my dress?"

"You're on retainer, Katie. I'm a client."

"*What* is going on?"

"Lawyer-client confidentiality. Say it."

"Lawyer-client confidentiality," Katie parroted with exasperation.

"I think Sagittarius Eclipse is involved in an embezzlement scheme against Ryder International."

"Montana." Katie drew out the word in a triumphant voice, obviously making the connection with Amber's father's business.

Fine by Amber, she'd rather have Katie connecting her to Jared Ryder than to Royce. Even thinking his name brought up an image of last night, and Amber was forced to shake it away in order to concentrate.

"You going into my line of work?" asked Katie.

Creighton Waverley Security was famous in Chicago for specializing in corporate espionage, and they'd investigated plenty of other corporate crimes along the way.

"Just for the week." Though Amber could already see the appeal of the profession. The harder she looked for information, the more involved she became in the hunt.

"You looking for anything specific?"

"A bank account. A name. A guy named McQuestin might be involved."

Although Royce was sure McQuestin was honest, Amber wasn't prepared to rule anything out. She'd looked back as far as she could in the financial records this morning, and Sagittarius Eclipse had received millions over the years. Maybe McQuestin hadn't even broken his leg. Maybe he was on his way to some offshore haven even now.

"I'll see what I can find. And, Amber?"

"Yes?"

"You serious about this breakup?"

Amber didn't hesitate. "Yes."

"Why?"

Good question. Hard to put into words. "He's just not the right guy for me."

Katie's accusing tone was back. "When did he become not the right guy for you?"

"Katie."

"When he made his first million? When he bought you a three-carat diamond? When he received the party nod for the nomination? Or when he planned the honeymoon to Tahiti?"

"Hargrove planned a honeymoon to Tahiti?" It was the first Amber had heard about it.

"Yes! Just last night he was showing me some—"

"You saw Hargrove last night?"

There was a small pause. "He was desperate, Amber. He needed a date for that hospital thing with the Myers."

"You went on a date with Hargrove?"

"Of *course* not." But there was something in Katie's tone. "He couldn't show up stag, and I've met Belinda Myers before, so…"

Amber rolled the image of Katie and Hargrove around in her head. No problem for her. She really didn't care. "Did you have a good time?" she asked.

"That's not the point."

Royce appeared in Amber's peripheral vision, on horseback, moving along the river trail between the staff cabins and the barbecue setup. Even at this distance, the sight of him took her breath away.

"Gotta go," she said to Katie. "Call me as soon as you find something."

"Uh… Okay, sure."

"Thanks, Katie. I miss you." Amber quickly signed off.

Royce spotted her, and the sizzle of his gaze shot right to her toes. He turned his horse toward the house, and she headed for the deck's staircase.

Glances and brief, public conversations were all Royce had managed to share with Amber throughout the day. So he was disappointed when he finally found her up at the jumping-horse outfit, and she was sitting on the front porch laughing with his sister and another man.

As he exited the pickup truck, Royce's first thought was that Hargrove had found her. The idea tightened his gut and sped up his stride. She certainly seemed happy to see this guy. She was listening to him with rapt attention, smiling, even laughing.

"Royce," Stephanie sang out as his boot hit the bottom stair. Amber glanced up, and the stranger twisted his head.

Royce immediately realized the man was too young to be Hargrove. Plus, he was wearing jumping clothes, not a business suit.

"Wesley, this is my brother, Royce. Wesley is our newest student. He was nationally ranked as a junior."

The young man stood up as Royce trotted up the remaining stairs.

"Good to meet you," Royce said with a hearty handshake, ignoring how relieved he felt that the guy wasn't Hargrove. Wesley looked to be about twenty-one. Not much younger than Stephanie and Amber, but no immediate competition.

"You, too." Wesley nodded. "I'm honored to be working with Stephanie."

Royce smirked at his sister. "Well, we'll see how honored you feel a month from now."

"Hey," she protested, reaching out to swat his arm.

"Can I grab you a beer?" Wesley offered, nodding to a cooler against the wall. "I picked up a dozen at a microbrewery in San Diego."

"Thanks," Royce agreed, and the younger man headed for the far side of the porch.

"I've got something for you," Amber stage-whispered, and Royce's attention shot immediately to her dancing eyes.

His chest tightened, and he wondered if she was going to proposition him right here in front of Stephanie. Not that it would be a bad thing. They'd seemed to come to a tacit agreement to keep their relationship secret. But there was no real reason to do that. They were both adults. She'd officially broken off her engagement. They were entitled to date each other if they wanted.

"Sagittarius Eclipse," she said, and he realized his brain had gone completely off on the wrong track. "I have a name."

"Yeah?" He pushed an empty deck chair into the circle.

"Norman Stanton."

Royce froze, brain scrambling while Amber kept talking.

"He's an American, originally from the Pacific North—"

"Later," Royce barked.

Amber drew back, squinting at his expression.

He moderated his voice, forcing a smile when he realized Stephanie was staring at him in confusion. "I want to hear how things are coming with the barbecue."

Then he nodded to Wesley as he returned with the beer. "Thanks," he told him. "So, are you training for any competition in particular?"

Out of the corner of his eye, he could see that Amber was confused, probably hurt, but there was nothing he could do about that at the moment. He pretended to listen to Wesley's answer, while his mind reeled.

Stanton. Damn it. A name out of his worst nightmare.

After all these years, they were being blackmailed by a Stanton?

How much did the bastard know? How long had he known it? And why the hell hadn't his grandfather or McQuestin told him before now?

Eight

Amber waited until they'd passed the lights of Stephanie's yard and were headed down the dark ranch driveway before turning to Royce in the pickup truck. "What did I do?"

"Nothing." But his answer was terse, and she could tell he was upset. Their speed was increasing on the bumpy road, and she gripped the armrest to stabilize herself.

"I don't understand. It's good information. I don't know if you realize how hard I had to dig—"

"Where did you get it? Where did you come up with the name Stanton?"

"Katie found a bank account in the Cayman Islands."

Royce hit her with a hard glance, staring a bit too long for safety. "Who's Katie?"

"Watch the road," she admonished as a curve rushed up at them in the headlights.

He glanced back, but only long enough to crank the wheel. "Who is Katie?"

"She's my best friend, my maid of honor."

"I thought you weren't getting married."

"I'm *not* getting married." Amber took a breath. "She would have been my maid of honor. She's a lawyer. Her firm specializes in corporate espionage, but they investigate all kinds of criminal activity."

Royce's voice went dark. "McQuestin is not a criminal."

"I never said he was."

"You had no right to disparage a man's name—"

"I didn't disparage anything. Katie's my friend. She works for Creighton Waverley Security, and she's our lawyer now. Everything she finds out is confidential."

Royce didn't answer, but she could almost hear his teeth gritting above the roar of the engine and the creak of the steel frame as the truck took pothole after pothole.

"Who is Stanton?" she dared.

His hands tightened on the steering wheel, face stony in the dim dashboard lights. "Nobody you need to worry about."

Something inside Amber shriveled tight. She'd felt so close to Royce last night. Between lovemaking, they'd shared whispered stories, opinions, worldviews. She'd thought they were becoming friends.

"I have more," she told him, not above bribery.

"What else?"

She crossed her arms over her chest. "Who's Stanton?"

Royce glared at her. It was the first time she'd had his true anger directed at her. But she stiffened her spine. "Who is Stanton?"

"Forget it."

"*Why?* Why won't you let me help you?"

He geared down for a hill. "There are things you don't understand."

"No kidding."

"No offense, Amber. But I barely know you."

"No offense, Royce. But you've seen me naked."

"And that's relevant how?"

"I'm just saying—"

"That it's not about to happen again unless I talk?"

"You think I'd use sex to bribe you?"

He let go of the steering wheel long enough for a jerking hand gesture of frustration. "Why do you jump to the absolute *worst* interpretation?"

"I'm trying to understand you."

"Well, I'm not having the slightest success understanding you." He sucked in a deep breath.

She let a few beats go by in silence, forcing herself to calm down. In her mind, this argument was completely separate from any future sexual relationship. She moderated her voice. "Maybe if you told me what was going on."

"Maybe if you let me keep my private business private."

Okay, now that crack would probably impact on their future sexual relationship.

"Fine," she huffed. "There's this numbered holding company." She pulled a note from her pocket and checked it in the dim light. "One-four-nine-five-eight, twelve-zero-ninety-three is registered in Liechtenstein with bank accounts in Liechtenstein, Switzerland and Grand Cayman. Its only asset is a company called Eastern Exploration Holdings. Eastern Exploration owns several parcels of property, mostly in the Bahamas. It also owns one company, Sagittarius Eclipse. One-four-nine-five-eight, twelve-zero-ninety-three is solely owned by Norman Stanton."

The truck rocked to a halt in front of the ranch house.

"His last known address was in Boston, Massachusetts," Amber finished.

Royce killed the lights and turned the key, shutting down the engine. "You don't know where he is now?"

"Not yet." She yanked up on the door handle, and the door creaked wide.

"But you're looking?" Royce followed suit.

"We're looking," said Amber, sliding off the high bench seat and onto the dirt driveway. She'd taken to wearing a pair of tattered, flat, canvas runners she'd found in a closet by the back door. They weren't as sturdy as the cowboy boots favored by everyone else, but they beat the heck out of the high heels she'd arrived in.

"How long will it take?" he asked as they headed for the porch.

"I don't know." Her voice was still testy.

Royce frowned at her.

"It'll take as long as it takes. He could be hiding. He might have left the country." She headed up the stairs. "Maybe someone warned him McQuestin was hurt, and he's worried he'll get caught."

"Who would warn him McQuestin was hurt?"

Amber paused at the front door. "Maybe McQuestin."

Royce turned the knob and shoved open the door. "McQuestin wouldn't do that."

She walked inside. "You're putting a lot of faith in a man who's been authorizing secret payments."

"He has his reasons." The door slammed shut, and Royce moved up close.

Amber turned, then drew back from the intensity in his eyes.

He moved closer.

She stepped back again, coming up against the wall in the foyer.

He braced a hand on either side of her, dipping his head.

"Royce?"

"Yeah?" He kissed her, and her protest was muffled against his mouth.

He kissed her again, softer, deeper, and a flame of desire curled to life in the pit of her belly.

His hands cupped her chin, deepening the kiss, pressing his strong body flush against hers, evoking near-blinding memories of the night before.

"What are you doing?" she finally gasped.

"It's not obvious?" There was a thread of laughter deep in his throat, his warm breath puffing against her skin.

"No."

"Makeup sex."

"But I'm still mad at you."

"You are?" He feigned surprise as he kissed her neck, her collarbone, her shoulder. He found the strip of bare skin at the top of her jeans, skimming his knuckles across her navel. "Then let's see what we can do to change that."

Royce feathered his fingertips across Amber's stomach, the narrowing at her waist, the indentation of her navel and the small curve of her belly. Her skin was pale and supple, a light tan line at bikini level, barely above where the sheet covered her legs.

She was by far the most beautiful woman he'd ever seen. Her blond hair, mussed at the moment, was thick and lustrous, reflecting the pink rays of the rising sun. Her eyes were deep blue, a midsummer sky right now, but they'd been jewel bright last night while they made love. Her lips were full, deep red and tempting.

Even her ears were gorgeous, delicate and small, while her neck was graceful, her shoulders smooth, and her breasts were something out of his deepest fantasy. Add to that her quick wit, her intelligence and her sense of fun, and she was somebody he could keep in his bed for days on end.

He'd had sex with plenty of women over the years, slept with only some of them, ate breakfast with fewer still. And in all that time, he'd never had an urge to bare his soul to a single one.

Now, he did.

Now, he wanted to tell her anything and everything.

He let his fingers trace the curve of her hip bone, made up his mind and took the plunge. "My father killed a man named Stanton."

Amber's head turned sharply on the stark white pillow. "He what?"

"Killed him," Royce repeated, hand stilling, cupping her hip.

"Was it an accident?"

"Nope."

"I don't understand."

"It was on purpose. Frank Stanton was having an affair with my mother."

Amber's eyes widened and she rolled sideways, propping her head on one elbow. "Did they get into a fight?"

"I guess you could say that. My father shot him."

Amber stilled. The sun broke free from the horizon, and the pink rays morphed to white.

"Did your father go to jail?" Her voice was hoarse.

Royce shook his head. "He died that same day."

Amber swallowed. "And your mother?"

"Died with my father. Their truck went off the ranch road in the rain. They both drowned in the river."

"After he shot Stanton."

"I always assumed he panicked." Though Royce had never delved too deeply into his father's possible motivations for speeding down the ranch road with his unfaithful mother. "There was no trial, of course. Everybody chalked the shooting up to a failed robbery, and the accident was ruled just that, an accident. For years, I thought I was the only one who knew the truth."

"How did you know?"

"I found my mother's confession letter."

Amber sighed, eyes going shiny with sympathy. "Oh, Royce."

"I burned the letter, and the secret was safe. But then, on his deathbed, my grandfather Benteen told Jared he'd heard the shot. When my father drove away, Benteen dumped the gun in the river because he didn't want his son tried for murder."

Royce had wished that Jared never found out. But now it was better that he had. "So, I know, and Gramps knew, and Jared knows." Royce blew out a breath.

"Plus McQuestin," Amber said softly, obviously putting the pieces together. "And somehow Norman Stanton."

"Allowing him to blackmail my family."

She lay back down. "To keep the secret?"

"Our reputation was important to Benteen."

"But, millions of dollars' worth of important?"

Royce had asked himself that same question, and he didn't have a good answer. What the hell were Benteen and McQuestin thinking? His father couldn't be tried. There wasn't a man in the state who'd fault Royce's father for retaliating against Stanton.

That left their mother's reputation. And, as far as Royce was concerned, she'd made her own bed. He couldn't imagine paying millions of dollars protecting a woman who'd betrayed her own family.

Well, from this point on, he and Jared were in charge, and not a single dime of Ryder money was getting into the hands of a Stanton.

"The payments stop now," he vowed to Amber. "And I want to know everything there is to know about Norman Stanton."

She put her hand on Royce's shoulder. "You're not going after revenge, are you?"

He turned his head to look her in the eyes. "I *am* going after my money."

"Royce."

He raised his eyebrows, all but daring her to argue.

She searched his expression. "I don't want you to get yourself in trouble."

His anger switched to resolve, and he couldn't help but smile. Her sentiment was admirable, but completely unnecessary.

"Darlin'," he told her. "If I was you, I'd be worried about Norman Stanton, not about me."

* * *

Six worried Ryder International division heads stared back at Royce around the ranch house dining room table. The doors were closed to the rest of the house, but the windows were open, the happy sounds of an ongoing barbecue and baseball game a jarring counterpoint to the uncomfortable conversation.

If the four men and two women were unsettled by Barry Brewster's firing, they were positively rattled by the potential fallout from the loss of the China deal. Ryder International was a strong company, but it wasn't invincible. They were going to have to take quick and decisive action if they wanted to recover.

Jared was still out of touch, but it didn't take a rocket scientist to figure out the answer. Some of the Ryder companies would need to be sold, perhaps entire divisions, which explained the ashen faces around the table. Nobody wanted to be the sacrificial lamb.

"Construction is the bread and butter of the company." Konrad Klaus opened the conversation. He was out-front and aggressive as always. As the head of the largest and longest-standing division of the corporation, he wielded considerable influence with his counterparts.

"It's pretty shortsighted to mess with high tech," Carmen Volle put in.

Mel Casper threw down his pen. "Oh, sure. Everybody look at sports and culture. It's not always the bottom line, you know. We're carrying the marketing load for everybody else."

Royce cut them all off. "This isn't divide and conquer," he warned. "Jared's not coming back to a war. I've got your reports—"

"We wrote those before we had the facts," said Konrad.

Konrad's respect factor for Royce had never been high. But it was rare that it mattered. It mattered today.

Royce gave him a level look. "Precisely why I asked for them up front. I wanted the facts, not half a dozen individual lobbying efforts."

"So you can pick us off like fattened ducks?" asked Mel.

"*That's* the attitude you want to project?" Royce needed loyalty and teamwork right now. He wasn't looking to get rid of anybody else, but he wasn't looking to babysit any prima donnas, either.

"I say we wait for Jared to get back," said Konrad.

Royce turned to stare the man down. "What part of fifty million dollars didn't you understand?

Konrad glowered but didn't answer.

"We start today," said Royce. He might not be as involved in the operations of Ryder International as Jared, but he was still an owner, and he'd had about enough of people assuming he could be marginalized.

Barry Brewster would never have treated Melissa the way he'd treated Amber. Just because Royce flew a jet didn't mean he was incapable of anything else. Starting here and now, he was taking a stand—both with Norman Stanton, and with the brass at Ryder International.

"I don't see how we do that." Konrad tossed out a direct challenge to Royce's leadership.

"Did this company turn into a democracy when I wasn't looking?" Royce asked softly.

"Our loyalty is to Jared."

"Your loyalty should be to Ryder International."

Konrad compressed his lips. The rest of the division

heads looked down at the table. Royce realized it was now or never. He had to firmly pick up the corporate reins.

"I'm hiring an expert to do a review," he announced, having made a split-second decision.

The group exchanged dubious glances, but nobody said anything.

"Creighton Waverley Security."

"You think we're criminals?" Konrad thundered across the table.

"I think they're one hell of a research firm," Royce countered calmly. "We're going to review every company we own, take stock and make our decisions. Anybody who's not on board with it is free to leave."

He looked to each of the people in turn around the table. Nobody was happy, but nobody was walking away, either.

Now that he'd taken the first step on the fly, he supposed the second step had better be to have Amber put him in touch with her best friend's firm.

Amber helped a waiting group of children into the back of the wooden wagon, while a Ryder cowboy double-checked the harnesses on the matched Clydesdale team out front. Sasha was handing out giant chocolate chip cookies while, off to one side, Wesley was teasing Stephanie with his lariat. Amber did a double take of the two. If she wasn't mistaken, Wesley had developed a crush on his riding instructor.

She smiled to herself. Wesley was a very attractive, fun-loving man. It wouldn't surprise her in the least if the crush was reciprocated.

"I have to talk to you." The mere sound of Royce's

voice behind her caused a little thrill to zip through Amber's body. But in contrast to Wesley, Royce sounded tense and serious.

"Something wrong?" She helped the last little boy into the wagon, dusting her hands off on the sides of her jeans.

Royce moved to the corner of the wagon and pushed up the tailgate, sliding the latch to keep everyone safely inside.

Stephanie planted a foot on the wagon wheel and jumped in with the kids. Wesley quickly followed suit, taking a seat next to her on one of the padded benches, and Amber was sure she'd guessed right.

Royce backed out of the way, towing Amber with him as a cowboy unhitched the lead horse and turned the team toward the road.

"I've been meeting with the division heads," said Royce.

"What did you find out?" Amber had realized Royce and the senior managers were missing, and she'd easily guessed they were talking business. She raised her hand to wave to the cheering children as the wagon creaked down the road.

Royce pulled her toward the shadow of the barn, speaking low into her ear, his voice bringing flash memories of their night together. "I was wondering if you could do something for me."

"I don't know, Royce." She glanced around at the crowds. "There's an awful lot of people in the barn right now."

"You have a one-track mind," he admonished.

She grinned at him. She did seem particularly obsessed with making love.

"Not that I'd say no to a more interesting offer," he

clarified. "But I was hoping to get in touch with your friend Katie. I need to know the who's who of Creighton Waverley."

The request brought Amber back to reality. "I thought you were going to let *me* investigate Norman Stanton."

"What?"

"I'm doing a good job," she informed him, pursing her lips.

Royce suddenly grinned.

"What?"

"You. Jumping to conclusions."

"Quit laughing at me."

"Then stop being so entertaining."

"Stop being condescending."

"Stop pouting."

"I like investigating. I want to see this through."

Royce's smile turned sly, and he cocked his head meaningfully toward the barn. "Yeah?" he drawled.

"Now who's got a one-track mind?"

"Guilty," he agreed with an easy smile, but at the same time, he backed off.

A cheer went up at the baseball game, while a freshening breeze brought the aroma of hamburgers from the cook tent.

Amber brushed at a lazy fly.

"I'm commissioning a review of all the Ryder companies," said Royce. "We're going to have to make some tough decisions, and I thought Creighton Waverley might be able to help."

"So, I'm keeping my job?"

He brushed the back of his hand along her upper arm and leaned closer again. "Now *that* remains to be seen."

"I'm not bribing you with sex."

He exaggerated an offended tone. "I'd bribe you with sex."

She extracted her cell phone from her jeans pocket. "I'm bribing you with Katie's phone number."

"Fair enough. I'll bribe you for something else later."

Amber couldn't help but smile as she punched in Katie's cell number.

"Amber," came the breathless answer. "I was just about to call you. Are you at a hoedown or something?"

Amber glanced around for the source of a noise that might have made it through the phone. "What makes you ask that?"

"Checked tablecloths, cowboy hats, horses."

Amber glanced down at her phone, then put it back to her ear. "Do you have some kind of monitor on me?"

"No, I have a white Lexus, over in front of the house. At least I think it's the house. The building with the porch and, yep, it's a hitching rail."

Amber whirled around.

Sure enough, Katie was emerging from a low-slung sports car, wearing a short blue clingy dress, high-heeled pumps, with her honey-blond hair in a jaunty updo. Her small bag was beaded, and she reminded Amber of how long it had been since she'd had a manicure or a facial.

Amber took a reflexive step away from Royce. "What are you *doing* here?"

"I have to talk to you."

"That's what telephones are for." A sudden fear gripped Amber. "There's nobody with you, is there?" Like Hargrove or her parents.

"Relax," said Katie as she picked her way along the edge of the baseball field. "Your secret is safe." She grinned and gave Amber a wave.

Several dozen cowboys followed her progress.

"That's Katie," Amber told Royce.

"She does know how to make an entrance," he muttered, watching as raptly as anyone else on the ranch.

Amber felt an unwelcome pinch of jealousy.

"Who's that with you?" asked Katie as she drew ever closer.

"Royce Ryder."

"Nice."

Okay, jealousy was silly. Katie was an attractive woman, and Royce was an attractive man. They'd noticed. So what?

"Do you have any idea how far away this place is?" Katie called across the grass, folding her phone closed now that she was in shouting range.

"It's Chicago that's far away," Royce countered. "Montana is right here."

Katie grinned as she stepped up, holding out her perfect, magenta-tipped hand. "Katie Merrick. Creighton Waverley Security." She shook, then opened her purse, dropped the phone inside and extracted a business card, handing it to Royce.

"I was about to call you," said Royce.

"Well, isn't that perfect," Katie returned, glancing around the ranch yard. "Any chance they're serving margaritas at this shindig?"

It was a slow walk back to the ranch house, where Sasha whipped up a blender of margaritas while Amber, Royce and Katie settled in on the deck. Gopher immediately jumped into Amber's lap.

"You'll want Alec Creighton's help," said Katie. She'd been all business while Royce had explained his plans for Ryder International.

"Your boss?" asked Royce as he poured the frozen green concoction into tall glasses.

"My boss's son. He's not with Creighton Waverley. He's sort of a lone-wolf troubleshooter. We subcontract to him on occasion. I can give you a list of a hundred satisfied clients if you like." Katie accepted the drink with a nod of thanks.

"How do I get hold of him?" Royce handed Amber a drink. She still couldn't believe Katie had come all the way to Montana. And since they'd done nothing but discuss Ryder International business since she'd arrived, Amber couldn't begin to guess *why* she'd come all the way to Montana.

"I'll get him to call you." Katie took a sip of her drink. "He won't take on a client without a referral."

"Appreciate that," said Royce with a salute of his drink.

Amber couldn't keep quiet any longer, and her voice came out more demanding than she'd intended. "What are you doing here, Katie?"

Katie shrugged. "I missed you."

It didn't ring true. There was something in Katie's eyes—guilt, maybe fear.

Amber was suspicious. "Did you tell my parents I was here?"

"I can't believe you'd even ask me that. Can't a girl visit her best friend?" Katie took another swig, smiling far too brightly. "Okay if I stay over tonight?"

Nine

Wrapped in a fluffy robe, Katie sat cross-legged on the end of Amber's bed while Amber washed her face at the sink inside the en suite bathroom door.

"Just how long are you planning to stay here?" Katie asked, her voice muffled by the gush of the running water.

"I haven't decided," Amber answered, dipping her face forward to rinse it, then blindly grabbing for a towel.

As the days went by, she thought less and less about going home. Oh, she knew she'd have to, and probably soon. But there simply wasn't anything tugging her in that direction.

"You know the wedding shower's coming up, right?"

Amber peeked out from behind the towel. "Nobody canceled it?"

"Nobody believed you were serious. There are people flying in from all over the country."

Amber tossed the towel over the rack and paced back into the room. "They're still putting on my wedding shower?"

Katie nodded, while Amber dropped down onto the bed.

"The shower cake's gorgeous," Katie offered.

"This is a disaster."

Katie reached out to rub Amber's arm. "You breaking it off with Hargrove was the disaster. The shower, the dress..." Her hand gripped on Amber's shoulder. Then she abruptly stood up and crossed the room.

"I tried on your dress," she blurted out, turning to brace her back against the bureau.

Amber blinked in surprise. "You did? How'd it look?"

"Gorgeous. Absolutely stunningly gorgeous."

"It's too bad we'll have to sell it," said Amber. "I can't see ever wearing it."

Katie nodded, her eyes staring blankly into space. "Gorgeous. Really gorgeous."

Amber pictured her friend twirling in front of the mirror. Katie always did have a romantic streak.

Suddenly, Katie clenched her fists, and her eyes scrunched shut. "Oooh, you have to promise me you won't get mad."

"Why would I get mad?" Truth was, Amber wondered if Katie had taken pictures while she modeled the dress. It might be interesting to see how it had turned out.

"I...did something," Katie confessed in a harsh whisper.

"To the dress?"

Katie didn't answer, but the color drained from her face.

"Did you spill something on it? Tear it?" Amber

waited for an emotional reaction to her wedding dress being ruined, but it didn't come.

Katie emphatically shook her head. "No. The dress is fine."

"Then what are you so worried about?"

Katie picked up a china horse figurine from the top of the bureau, stroking her fingertip across its glossy surface. She looked at Amber then drew a breath.

"Katie?"

"He saw me in it."

"Who saw you in what?"

"Hargrove. He saw me in the wedding dress."

Amber didn't exactly understand why that was a problem.

Katie set down the figurine, her words speeding up, hands clasping together. "After it was delivered, and I had it on and was prancing around my apartment, he knocked on the door. I didn't know it was him. And, well, when I opened it…" She stopped talking.

"That's when Hargrove saw you in the wedding dress?"

Katie nodded miserably.

Amber fought an urge to smile. "I don't think that's bad luck or anything."

"I'm not so sure."

"Seriously, Katie. I can imagine he was annoyed." Hargrove was nothing if not mired in propriety. "But we're selling the damn thing anyway."

Katie drew a deep breath and squared her shoulders. "Thing is, he really, uh, liked the dress."

"Well, at that price, he'd better have liked it."

"I mean, well…" Katie gazed down at her front, picking a dark speck from the terry-cloth pile of the robe. "He really liked *me* in it."

Amber blinked. "So?" It was probably a good fit. She and Katie were pretty close to the same size.

"And—" Katie buried her face in her hands "—turns out, he liked me out of it, too."

Amber was silent for a full ten seconds. "You're going to have to repeat that."

Katie spread her fingers, peeking out as if she was looking at a horror movie. "I am the *worst* friend *ever*."

Amber gave her head a little shake. "What are you saying?"

Katie just stared at her.

"Are you saying you *slept* with Hargrove?" It wasn't possible. Nothing made less sense than that.

But Katie nodded. "It happened so fast. One minute he was staring at me. Then he was kissing me. Then the dress came off, and well, yeah, there might have been a bit of a tear around the buttonholes—"

Amber shook her head. "You're not making any sense."

"I am *so* sorry," Katie wailed, pressing a fist against her mouth. "You must hate me."

"No. No, it's not that."

"I had to come and tell you in person."

"I'm confused, not mad." Amber tried to make her point. "Hargrove doesn't get overcome with passion and tear off dresses." Not the Hargrove she knew.

Katie blinked like an owl.

"He's staid, proper, *controlled*."

Katie blinked once more. A flush rose up from the base of her throat, coloring her face. "Actually…"

Amber rose from the bed. "Actually, what?"

"Sexually speaking, I wouldn't call him staid, and I definitely wouldn't call him proper."

"Are you telling me…?"

Katie gave a meaningful nod.

"You had wild, impulsive sex with Hargrove?"

Something deep and warm flared in Katie's eyes, and she nodded.

"And…it was…*good*?" Amber asked in disbelief.

"It was fantastic."

Amber tried to wrap her head around that. "But… What…" She gripped the bedpost to steady herself. "Sorry. We can't get technical about this." She paused. "Can we?"

Katie cocked her head. "I take it it wasn't always good for you?"

"It was, um…" How did she say this? "Kind of boring."

"No way. You mean he didn't—" Katie's blush deepened.

Amber was forced to stifle a laugh. "Whatever it is you're not saying, I'm pretty sure he didn't do it with me."

Katie fought a grin and lost. "So, you're not mad?"

Amber shook her head, sitting back down on the bed. "I broke up with him."

Katie crossed the room to sit beside her, relieved amusement coloring her tone. "You're probably not going to want the wedding dress back."

"Keep it. Maybe you should keep Hargrove, too. Think of them as a set."

"Maybe I will," Katie said softly.

Amber turned to gaze at her friend and saw the glow in

Katie's eyes. She raised her brows in a question, and Katie nodded, wiping a single tear with the back of her hand.

Surprised, but not the least bit unhappy, Amber wrapped her arm around Katie's shoulders. "You do realize what this means, don't you?"

"What?"

"I get to wear the maid of honor's dress." Amber paused. "You know, I always liked that one better anyway."

"Take it," said Katie. "It's yours."

Amber drew a deep sigh. "Wow. Does Hargrove know?"

"That I slept with him?" There was a strengthening thread of laughter in Katie's voice.

"That you came here to confess."

Katie shook her head. "He thinks… Wait. I almost forgot." She bounced off the bed to her small suitcase. "I found something for you."

Hunting through her things, she extracted a manila envelope. "Pictures of Norman Stanton. And his brother, Frank. Also a sister and parents—the three of them died quite a few years back."

Amber accepted the envelope, her thoughts going to Royce. Now it was her turn to feel guilty.

"What?" Katie asked, gauging Amber's expression.

"There's something you don't know."

"About the investigation?"

Amber shook her head. "About me." She shut her eyes for a second. "Oh, hell. I'm sleeping with Royce."

Katie drew back. "Whoa. You cheated on Hargrove?"

"No." Amber swatted Katie with the envelope. "I did not cheat on Hargrove. I broke up with Hargrove. Lucky for you."

"True," Katie agreed. Then she sobered. "This cowboy dude? He rocks your world?"

"And how."

"So." Katie cocked her head toward the bedroom door. "What are you waiting for?"

"I didn't want to be rude."

"Unlike me who slept with your fiancé."

"Ex."

"Whatever. Go see your cowboy. I'll catch you at breakfast."

"You sure?"

"Of course I'm sure. *I* don't want to sleep with you."

Amber grinned, came to her feet and headed out the door.

On the way across the hall, she slit the envelope open, sliding out some eight-by-ten photos.

First one was labeled Norman. He had receding hair, dark, beady eyes and a little goatee. Yeah, she could see him as a blackmailer.

The next was Frank, an older picture. This was the guy who'd broken up Royce's family. He wasn't bad-looking, but not fantastic, either. He seemed a little on the thin side. But maybe that was a generational thing.

She flipped to the next picture, raising her hand to rap on Royce's door. But she froze, hand in midair, the picture of Frank and Norman's sister stopping her cold.

The young girl had a trophy in her hand and a broad smile on her face. Amber stared for a long minute, then slowly turned to the next picture. It was the parents, and the next one was a thirty-year-old family portrait. The final picture was another headshot of Norman.

Amber paged back to the picture of the sister for a

final look. Then, stomach twisting around nothing, she rapped on Royce's bedroom door.

His voice was muffled and incomprehensible, but she opened the door anyway. He was lying in bed, a hardcover book in his hands, the bedside lamp glowing yellow against his natural wood walls.

"Hey." He smiled, letting the book fall to his lap.

"Hi." She clicked the door shut behind her.

"Something wrong?"

She nodded.

His smile immediately faded. "Katie?"

"Kind of." Amber moved across the room.

His eyes cooled. "News from…home?"

Amber sat down on the bed. "We have a problem."

He tossed the book aside. "You're reconciling with Hargrove."

"What? *No.* How could you say that?"

Royce didn't answer.

"This has nothing to do with Hargrove." She wanted to be annoyed with Royce for even thinking that it might have been Hargrove, but there wasn't time for that. Instead, she covered his hand, trying to prepare him. "I have pictures of the Stantons. And it's not what we think."

"What do we think?"

She slipped the pictures out of the envelope and spread them on the bed. "Look."

Royce clenched his jaw as he leafed through them. "I've seen Frank Stanton before. He lived on the ranch for a while. Worked with the horses. That's how they met."

"Look at the sister," Amber whispered.

Royce shifted his gaze. "She was into horses, too," he surmised. The trophy was obviously equestrian.

"Look at her chin," said Amber. "Her eyes, the hairline."

Royce glanced from the picture to Amber, brows furrowing.

"Stephanie, Royce."

"What about Stephanie?"

"Stephanie is the spitting image of…" Amber flipped the picture over to read the handwriting on the back. "Clara Stanton, Frank and Norman's sister."

"No." He glanced back down. "She doesn't look anything like…" Royce's breathing went deep.

"He's not blackmailing you over murder."

"Son of a bitch."

She didn't want to say it out loud.

"Son of a bitch!"

"Shh."

Royce turned to her with haunted eyes. "This can't be right."

There was nothing she could say to cushion the blow.

"It can't be real."

It was real all right. Stephanie was Frank Stanton's daughter.

"Who else knows?" he demanded.

"No one."

"Katie?"

Amber shook her head. "Not even Katie. I only figured it out in the hallway thirty seconds ago."

He glanced back down at the picture. "We can't tell Stephanie. It'll kill her. She was two years old when they died. She doesn't even know about the affair."

"I won't tell Stephanie." But Amber realized that meant paying off Norman again.

Royce rolled out of bed, pacing across the floor, photo still gripped in his hand. He was stark naked, but the fact didn't seem to register.

He strode past the bay window, raking a hand through his hair. "We..."

Then he turned at the wall, glanced at the picture and threw it down on a dresser. "I..."

He stopped dead, fisted both hands and glared at Amber. "There's got to be a way out."

"I'm sure there is," she agreed in the most soothing voice she could muster.

He crossed back over to the bed, sat down and uttered a crude cuss. "That bastard's got us by the balls."

Amber didn't know how to answer. It was true, but agreeing seemed counterproductive.

"We can't tell Stephanie," he reaffirmed.

Amber nodded.

Royce snagged his phone from the table. He punched a couple of numbers and put it to his ear.

"Who—" Amber stopped herself.

"Jared."

She knew Jared had been out of touch for several days now.

It appeared he still was.

Royce's voice was terse as he left the voice-mail message. "Jared. Royce. Call me now. Right now." He punched the off button then leaned back against the headboard.

She dared to reach out and touch his bare shoulder. It was hot, hard as a rock. "Anything I can do?"

"Short of fixing a deal with the Chinese, finding a

sailboat in the middle of the South Pacific or giving Norman Stanton a fatal disease? Not really."

"Right." She slipped across the bed to sit close beside him, curling her arm around his tense back. "Moral support doesn't really cut it at the moment, does it?"

He wrapped one of his arms around her and then the other. Then he bent to kiss the top of her head. "Moral support is better than nothing."

She struggled to find a smile. "That's always been a dream of mine. To be better than nothing."

He gave her a gentle squeeze and whispered above her head. "Will you stay?"

She nodded against his neck, knowing she was falling fast and hard. His troubles were her troubles, and she'd be by his side just as long as he needed her.

In the morning, when Katie asked for a tour of Stephanie's jumping ranch, Royce resisted the temptation to tag along. Much as he'd love to spend the time with Amber, he was afraid he'd end up studying his sister's expressions, movements and mannerisms for traces of the man he'd hated for twenty long years.

She was still his baby sister. He loved her, and he'd move heaven and earth to protect her. But he needed some time to come to terms with the knowledge she was also Frank Stanton's daughter.

What the hell had his mother been thinking?

Had she known which man fathered Stephanie? What was her plan? Was she going to take Stephanie with her and Stanton? Would she have destroyed that many lives for her own selfish happiness?

The knowledge crept like a cold snake into his belly. He smacked open the front door, marching onto the

porch to take a deep breath of fresh air. He didn't wish
anybody dead, not even Frank Stanton. But he wasn't
sorry his mother's plan had failed. He couldn't imagine
his life without Stephanie.

An engine roared in the distance, dust wafting up at
the crest of the drive. Royce squinted against the mid-
morning sunshine. He knew it was too early for Amber
and Katie to return, but he couldn't help hoping.

Amber had been amazing last night. First she'd let
him rail in anger. Then she'd offered practical advice.
She seemed to have an uncanny knack for knowing when
to stay quiet and when to talk. Finally, against all odds,
she helped him find a touch of humor in the face of ca-
tastrophe.

Afterward, he'd stayed awake for hours, simply holding her in his arms, letting the feel of her body make his
troubles seem less daunting.

It was a car that appeared over the rise. A dark sedan,
dusty from the long road in, but unmistakably new, and
undeniably expensive. The windows were tinted, and
the driver moved tentatively around the potholes dot-
ting dirt and sparse gravel.

Not a local, that was for sure.

Royce made his way down the front stairs, wondering
if this could be the mysterious Alec Creighton, or perhaps someone from the Ryder Chicago office.

The car eased to a halt. The engine went silent. And
the driver's door swung open wide.

Royce didn't recognize the tall man who emerged. He
looked to be in his late thirties. He was clean shaven,
his hair nearly black. He wore a Savile Row suit and an
expensive pair of loafers. His white shirt was pressed,
the patterned silk tie classic and understated.

To his credit, he didn't flinch at the dust, simply slammed the car door shut and gave Royce a genuine smile, stepping forward to offer his hand. "Hargrove Alston."

Royce faltered midreach but quickly recovered. "Royce Ryder."

He resisted the urge to grip too hard, though he squared his shoulders and straightened his spine, watching Hargrove's expression closely for signs that there was going to be a fight.

"Good to meet you," Hargrove offered. There wasn't a trace of anger or resentment in the man's eyes. Either he didn't know about Royce and Amber, or the man had one hell of a poker face.

"What brings you to Montana?" Royce opened.

A split second of annoyance narrowed the man's eyes. "For starters, I understand you're harboring my fiancée."

Royce resented the accusation. "It was at her request."

Hargrove's smile flattened. "I'm sure it was. I'd like to speak with her if you don't mind."

"She's not here." The statement was true enough. Amber might be close by, she wasn't specifically on the ranch this very moment.

Hargrove glanced to the house then back to Royce. "You have a reason to lie to me?"

"I have no reason to lie."

Hargrove regarded him with obvious impatience.

"I can try to pass along a message," Royce offered, folding his arms over his chest and planting his feet apart on the dusty drive.

"You do know who I am, right?"

"You said you were Hargrove Alston."

"I'm not accustomed to being stonewalled, Mr. Ryder."

"And I'm not accustomed to uninvited guests on my land, Mr. Alston."

Hargrove's expression went hard. "I know she's here."

"I told you she wasn't."

There was a pause while the entire ranch seemed to hold its breath.

"But you do know where she is."

Royce did. Since he preferred not to lie, he didn't answer.

Hargrove gave a cool, knowing smile. "She does bring out the protective instincts."

The assessment rang true. And it reminded Royce how well Hargrove knew Amber. She had been bringing out Royce's protective instincts from the moment they'd met.

He decided it was time to stop the pretense. "I assume you're here to drag her back to Chicago."

The shot of pain that flitted through Hargrove's eyes was quickly masked by anger. "I'm here to tell her she can't solve her problems by running away from them."

Guilt hit Royce square in the solar plexus. Amber had, in fact, run away from Hargrove. And Royce had helped her.

His thoughts went to his father, and an unwelcome chill rippled up his spine. His mother had written a letter. Amber had settled for a text.

Not that Royce was anything like Frank Stanton. Looking back to his teenage memories, Frank had deliberately and methodically lured a woman away from her husband and children.

"Do you have any idea why she left?" he found himself asking.

"Only Amber knows the answer to that." Hargrove shook his head in disgust. "Forget that the wedding dress arrived from Paris this week, that the caterer's put the Kobe beef on hold, that the florist has a Holland order in limbo and that the press has been commenting on Amber's absence. We have fifty people arriving for the wedding shower on Saturday. Her mother's frantic with worry."

Royce swallowed, considering for the first time the destruction Amber had left in her wake.

Hargrove's dark eyes glittered. "I can't wait to sit her down and ask a few questions."

"Did you think about canceling everything?" Royce ventured. If it was him, and the bride went AWOL, as Amber had, Royce couldn't see himself waiting around.

"Are you married, Mr. Ryder?"

Royce shook his head.

"Ever been in love?"

"Nope."

"Well, once you get there, you'll find yourself making allowances for the most inappropriate behavior."

"So, you'd take her back?"

"You don't throw this away over some prewedding jitters. Our plans have been in the works for four years. Our relationship is built on mutual goals and respect. And the foundation of my entire campaign has been built around the fresh faces of Mr. and Mrs. Hargrove Alston. If we're lucky, she'll be pregnant by the primaries."

It sounded a little cold-blooded to Royce. But it also sounded as though Amber was fundamentally entwined in Hargrove's life. And he hadn't considered the situation from Hargrove's perspective.

Amber herself had admitted he was a decent guy. He wasn't malicious or abusive. He simply wasn't as exciting as she'd hoped.

Well, hell, honey, it had been four years. When you were in it for the long haul, the thrill of romance eventually turned into the routine of everyday life.

"There's no way you end something like this on a whim," Hargrove finished, and Royce couldn't deny the man's point.

Relationships took work. They took patience and commitment. They didn't need third-party interference. An honorable man would have walked away the minute he saw her diamond ring.

And what the hell had Royce expected? Amber wouldn't stick with him any more than she'd stuck with Hargrove. In the end, he would have been left with nothing but a broken heart and the knowledge he'd destroyed another man's life.

Another engine sounded on the driveway. Before the blue pickup even crested the hill, Royce knew exactly who had arrived.

Ten

"You *didn't*," Amber rasped to Katie as the truck rocked to a stop behind Hargrove's car, and the dust cleared around them.

"I really didn't," Katie responded, her face pale.

"Did you talk to him last night?"

"Just about business."

"Did you tell him we were together?" Amber squinted at Hargrove, then at Royce, trying to interpret their posture.

Katie clutched the dashboard. "I hinted we were in Chicago."

"He knew I wasn't in Chicago. He must have tracked you here."

"Damn it," Katie cursed.

"You go talk to him," said Amber.

"No way."

"You're the one who slept with him. Maybe he's here for you."

Katie frantically shook her head. "Neither of us have even mentioned it. He's here for you."

"He doesn't want me."

But Hargrove's accusatory gaze was focused directly on Amber.

"I don't think he knows that," Katie offered.

This time Amber swore between clenched teeth. She grabbed the gearshift, setting up to pull it into Reverse. "I say we run for it."

"I don't think that's an option," Katie ventured, her gaze tracking Royce as he paced toward the truck.

He looked angry.

Had Hargrove been rude?

Royce reached for the handle and swung open her door. "There's somebody here to see you."

"I'm sorry, Royce. I didn't expect—"

"You knew he'd come," said Royce, hand gripping the top of the door frame. "*I* knew he'd come."

Amber had fervently hoped he wouldn't. She glanced at Katie, who sat completely still, eyes front. No help there. Finally, she took a breath and pulled the key from the ignition.

Royce stepped back out of the way, as Hargrove marched up.

"Montana?" Hargrove accused. "Honestly, Amber, could you make things any more difficult?"

Royce backed off farther, and she knew he was leaving.

"Royce, don't—"

But he shook his head, sliding his eyes meaningfully toward Hargrove.

And he was right. They might as well get this conversation over with.

"We need to talk," rasped Hargrove, moving in too close and pushing the truck door closed.

"There's not a lot left to say," she responded, pushing her windblown hair behind her ears and gathering her courage as Royce left.

It was hard for her to imagine what came after *you slept with the bridesmaid, and I fell for someone else.*

"Do you have any idea how much trouble you've caused?" Hargrove growled. "We've got a thousand people working on the wedding. Nobody knows whether to stop, go, or hold."

"I already told you. They can stop."

"You can't just shut this down on a dime, Amber. We had plans. There's the campaign, the press."

"I'm not marrying you to get good press, Hargrove."

He held up his hands in frustration. "This isn't a one-shot article, Amber. We're talking about my entire political career."

"Yours won't be the first high-profile wedding that was canceled."

"And do you *know* what happened to the others?"

"I don't care what happened to the others. I don't love you, Hargrove. And you don't love me."

"That's ridiculous."

"Then why did you sleep with Katie?"

His jaw went taut. "*That* was a mistake."

"Excuse me?" Katie squeaked from beyond the open window, reminding them both of her presence.

Hargrove's nostrils flared.

"A mistake?" Amber scoffed. "What? Did you trip and accidentally tear off the wedding dress?"

"I don't know what she told you."

"I'm right *here*," Katie pointed out, exiting the truck and slamming the passenger door for emphasis.

"She said you were wild with passion."

"That's ridiculous." But a flush rose up his neck.

"You never tore off *my* dress," said Amber.

"That was out of respect."

Amber shook her head at Hargrove. "It was out of disinterest. Admit it."

"I'm not here to fight with you."

"That's good," said Amber as she dared a glance to where Katie was glaring daggers at him. "Because I think I'd have to take a number."

Hargrove glanced at Katie. "Can you give us some privacy?"

"No." She stood her ground.

"This isn't about you."

"The hell it isn't."

"*I'm* going to give *you two* some privacy," said Amber.

Hargrove quickly reached for her arm. "Amber—"

"It's over, Hargrove." She backed out of his reach. "I'm truly sorry about the press and the campaign, but I can't marry you."

"Amber!" He looked genuinely fearful. "You don't know what you're doing to me."

She shook her head. "You don't know what you're doing to yourself. Talk to Katie."

"This isn't about Katie."

"It should be." Amber backed up a few more steps. "Don't screw this up, Hargrove," she warned.

Then she turned away, scanning the yard and finding Royce in a round pen, doing groundwork with a black horse.

Heart still pounding, stomach still cramped, she made her way to the rail and leaned over to watch.

Royce shifted his arms, and the horse sped up. Then he slowed it down, turned it and had it trotting in the opposite direction. It was near poetry, and the tension leached out of her body.

Several minutes later, he approached the animal. He stroked its neck, clipping a lead rope to its bridle then tying it to a rail. He walked through the soft dirt toward Amber.

He braced his hands on the opposite side of the fence. "You here to say goodbye?"

She drew back in surprise. "No."

He nodded toward Hargrove. "He came a long way."

"I told you, I'm not marrying him."

"Why not?"

Amber peered at Royce in confusion. "What do you mean why not?" She leaned forward. "I've just spent the last week with you."

He shrugged. "That doesn't mean anything."

She opened her mouth, struggling to form words.

"I'm new, Amber." He stripped off a pair of leather gloves. "I seem interesting and exciting. You're on vacation, having a fling."

Amber's fingertips went to her temple. "A fling?"

He calmly tucked the gloves under his arm and adjusted his Stetson. "Hargrove is willing to take you back. You should seriously consider his offer."

Her frustration was turning to anger. "You said anybody who told me that was short-sighted and stupid."

"Guess I was wrong."

She shook her head, but he stayed stubbornly silent.

She clenched her jaw, then enunciated her words slowly and carefully. "I do not love Hargrove."

"You don't know that for sure."

"I absolutely know that for sure. Because I love *you*, Royce."

The words went unanswered. But she wasn't sorry. This was no fling. He was falling for her, too. She'd bet her life on it.

No one had ever treated her the way Royce did. He was compassionate, attentive and so very sexy. And she was positive he didn't open up with many other people the way he'd opened up with her. He'd flat out told her nobody else knew about his father. And their lovemaking was off the charts.

He scoffed out a laugh. "You don't love me."

She smacked her hand on the rail in frustration. "What is the matter with you? Are you afraid of Hargrove?"

Royce's eyes glittered. "I'm not afraid of anybody."

"Well, I *know* you feel it, too."

He whipped off his hat, banging it on his thigh to release the dust. "If by *it*, you mean lust, then you're right."

"I don't mean lust."

"People don't fall in love in a week."

"People can fall in love in an hour."

"Not so it lasts." It was his turn to lean in. "It's lust, Amber. It's a fling. What you have with Hargrove is real, and you need to go back to him."

"Hargrove loves Katie."

Royce smacked his hat back on his head. "Then why's he here looking for you?"

"He doesn't know it yet." She realized that sounded lame, but it was completely true. Amber had very high hopes that Hargrove would wake up to the truth about Katie.

"Now you're grasping at straws. Go back to reality, Amber. Get married in that big cathedral and have beautiful babies for the campaign trail."

"Are you *listening* to yourself?" She gripped the rail. "You're willing to throw away everything that's between us?"

A part of her couldn't believe it. A part of her expected to wake up any second. But another brusque, insidious part of her realized she'd made a horrible mistake.

She might have fallen for Royce. But Royce hadn't fallen for her.

"You've spun a nice fantasy, here," he said. Then he nodded toward Hargrove's car. "But your reality is over there."

Her throat closed over, and she swallowed hard. "You're asking me to leave?"

His expression was unreadable. "I'm asking you to leave."

She gave a stiff nod, unable to speak. Royce didn't love her. He didn't want her. And she'd made a complete and total fool of herself.

Two days later, Amber alternated between misery and mortification. Royce might not have loved her, but her heart had fallen hard and fast for him.

It was easy to see what made him such a great pick-up artist. He must make every woman feel loved and cherished—at least temporarily. She wondered about the string of broken hearts he'd left behind.

Then she wondered who he'd be with next. But that

thought hurt so much she banished it, blinking back the familiar sting in her eyes as she focused on her mother far across her family's great room.

The replacement-for-the-shower party was in full swing. But Amber didn't feel remotely like celebrating.

Maybe if Royce had simply sweet-talked her into bed, if they'd had fantastic sex, if he'd put her in a cab in the morning, maybe then she could have handled it. But he hadn't simply made love to her. He'd joked and laughed with her, shared his secrets with her, made her feel valuable, important, a part of his world.

"Amber?" Her mother, Reena, approached, concern in her expression.

Amber tried to smile at her mother. Her family had been told that she was the one to break it off with Hargrove. But nobody but Katie knew anything about Royce. Amber planned to keep it that way.

Reena's floor-length chiffon dress rustled to a halt. "Why aren't you visiting, sweetheart?"

"I'm a little tired."

"Are you sure that's all it is?"

"I'm sure." She mustered up a smile.

"That's the best you can do? You look like you're headed for the gallows."

Amber signed. "I'm really not in the mood for a party, Mom."

Reena moved in closer. "But I thought this was what you wanted."

"I didn't want a party."

"Well, you didn't want a shower, either. And the guests were already on their way."

Amber drew a shuddering breath, fighting the tears that were never far from the surface. Emotions alone shouldn't hurt this much. Still, a single teardrop escaped, trailing coolly down her cheek.

"Sweetheart," her mother entreated, drawing Amber close to her side. "Do you miss him so much?"

Amber startled in surprise. How had her mother guessed?

Reena cupped Amber's chin with gentle fingertips, peering deeply into her eyes. "Shall I give Hargrove a call for you? We might be able to talk him into—"

"She's not missing Hargrove," came Katie's voice as she swooped in to join them.

"Of course she is," said Reena. "Just look at her."

"I'm not missing Hargrove," Amber confirmed.

Katie gave Amber a level, challenging look. "She's missing Royce Ryder."

Amber sucked in a gasp.

"Who?" asked her mother, glancing from Amber to Katie and back again.

Katie gave Amber a helpless shrug. "What's the point in hiding it? It's obvious to anyone that you've had your heart broken."

"Who is Royce Ryder?"

"The man she met in Montana."

"I met him at Jared Ryder's wedding," Amber corrected. Where he'd picked her up in the bar for a quick fling. At least that's the way *he* remembered it.

Reena's jaw dropped a notch, and her hand went to her chest. "You were unfaithful to Hargrove?"

"I *wasn't* unfaithful to Hargrove." Frustration finally gave Amber an emotion to replace despair. "In fact, Hargrove was unfaithful to me." She returned Katie's look. "With *Katie*."

Katie's face went pale, and Reena's jaw dropped another notch.

"They'd already split up," Katie hastened to assure Reena.

"That's true," Amber admitted. "Nobody was unfaithful to anybody."

Katie's voice went soft. "And she did fall in love with Royce."

Amber was too exhausted to deny it.

"Oh, sweetheart." Reena took Amber's hand. Her mother was a romantic to the core. "That terrible man broke your heart?"

"I broke my own heart." As she said the words out loud, Amber admitted to herself they were true. "We barely knew each other. And my expectations were... Well, he's just such an incredible man. You'd love him, Mom. You really would."

Reena's narrow arm curled around her shoulders. "I wouldn't like him at all. He broke my baby's heart."

Jared's familiar voice barked at Royce over the phone. "What the hell did you do?"

"Jared? Finally. Where are—"

"I need an explanation," Jared demanded.

Royce swiveled on the ranch house office chair, assuming Jared had been in contact with the Ryder office in Chicago. "I don't even know where to start."

"Start with how you broke Amber Hutton's heart and infuriated one of our most important clients."

Royce nearly dropped the phone. "Huh?"

"I've only been gone a week, and you screw up this badly."

"She *called* you?" Royce could hardly believe it. What was Amber doing running to Jared?

"David Hutton called me. He's threatening to cancel his lease. You are aware that he's our second-biggest client, right?"

"Don't patronize me."

"Then don't sleep with our clients' daughters."

What could Royce say to that? "It just…happened."

"Right. Well, un-happen it."

"I don't think that's physically possible."

"You know what I mean. Fix it."

"I can't fix it. She's engaged to someone else."

"What?" Jared's voice rose to a roar.

"Hargrove Alston."

"Then why did you sleep with her?"

Royce didn't have an answer for that. There wasn't an excuse in the world for what he'd done.

Jared was silent for a moment. "David thinks she's in love with *you*?"

"I'm not breaking up her engagement."

"Admirable," said Jared.

"Thank you."

"Could've thought of it *before* you slept with her."

Royce grunted.

"So, how're you going to fix it?"

"I'll talk to her."

"What are you going to say?"

"None of your business." Royce didn't have the first clue.

He'd been thinking about it for days, and had come to the conclusion that by bringing Amber to Montana, he'd turned a momentary hesitation into a life-altering event. Whatever crazy fantasy Amber had spun around

Royce wasn't real. She barely knew him. And he barely knew her. If relationships built on years didn't last, there was no hope at all for one that was built on a mere week.

"Make it my business."

"No."

Jared went silent on the other end of the line for a few beats. "You ever think…"

Royce drummed his fingers on the desktop.

"That maybe she's not…"

"Not what?" Did Jared have something intelligent to add here or not?

Jared drew a breath. "I mean, she might really be in love—"

"No!" Royce barked.

"Could happen."

"No, it could not."

"I'm a married man, Royce. And I'm telling you it could happen."

"You've been married a week. Talk to me in twenty years."

"You're going to make a woman wait twenty years?"

Royce felt his frustration level rise. "I'm going to make a woman wait until she's sure."

"How're you going to know that?"

"I'll just know."

"Like you do now?"

"What I know now is that she's taken, and she's confused, and she has obligations that have nothing to do with me."

"She's not Mom," Jared said softly.

"Don't even go there."

"And you're not Frank Stanton."

"I'm hanging up now."

"Mom and Dad's relationship was demanding and complex. He worked too hard and she had stars in her eyes."

"And you don't think all marriages are demanding and complex?" That was what the long haul was all about. It meant sticking together through the rough times, knowing better times would come again. It didn't mean bailing the second life got a little humdrum.

"Did it ever occur to you that Dad might have shared the blame?"

"He didn't screw around on her," Royce practically shouted.

"Yeah, but he wasn't perfect. He had a temper. Hell, he shot a guy."

"The son of a bitch deserved it. I'd have shot him, too."

"You mean, if he slept with Amber?"

"Hell, yes."

"Gotcha."

Royce went silent, his jaw clamping down.

What had just happened? He was the illicit lover in this triangle, not the betrayed husband.

Jared's voice turned jovial. "Okay, fixing this is going to be way easier than I thought."

"Shut up."

Jared chuckled, and Royce bit down harder on his outrage. His brother could be positively infuriating.

"Let's move on to other problems," he ground out. He wasn't wrong, and Jared wasn't right. And it was definitely time to end this discussion.

His brother's tone changed. "What problems?"

"The China deal fell apart."

"Yeah," Jared sighed. "I was afraid of that."

"We're in a cash crunch because of it. I've got a guy taking a thorough look at our operations. I think we're going to have to streamline."

"He any good?"

"He came highly recommended." Royce drew a breath. "And, Jared. I fired Barry Brewster over China."

"Seriously?"

"He missed the deadline, blew the deal." He'd also insulted Amber, but Royce wasn't going anywhere near that conversation.

"There are a thousand ways to blow a deal with China."

"Yeah, well, he's gone."

"Okay. Your call. You need me to come back early?"

"Let's give it a few more days. There's one more thing…" Royce stopped himself. "You know what? It can wait."

If Jared learned about Norman Stanton and Stephanie, he'd be on the next plane back to the States.

But Royce had already made this month's blackmail payment. Norman Stanton had no idea they were on to him, and there was nothing Jared could do in the short term but worry.

"You sure?" asked Jared.

"I'm sure."

"And fix it with Amber, bro. She's not Mom. You're not Stanton. And everything's a leap of faith."

Amber and Katie stood side by side, gazing into the three-way mirror in Amber's bedroom.

"You don't think it would be too weird?" asked Katie as they admired their reflections in the sleek, sleeveless, pearl-adorned wedding gown and the dramatic oriental silk bridesmaid dress.

"Like I said before," Amber replied. "Think of them as a set. You know I like this one better." She turned and watched the orange, gold and midnight plum shimmer in the sunlight that streamed through her big windows.

"Did I miss something?" came a masculine voice from the doorway.

Amber and Katie whirled simultaneously to see all six foot two of Royce standing in the bedroom doorway. He was wearing a steel-gray business suit, a blue silk tie and a crisp white shirt. His face was freshly shaven, and his blue gaze hungry as he stared at her.

She swallowed the tears that were never far from the surface. His appearance was her dream come true. But she couldn't let herself hope.

"Where did you come from?" asked Katie.

Instead of answering, he strolled into the bedroom, gaze fixed on Amber as he grew closer. "Someone named Rosa said you were trying on your wedding gown."

Amber glanced down at the silk bridesmaid dress. "Something got lost in the translation."

"I was going to rip it from your body." The hunger in his eyes grew more intense.

Amber tipped her head, not sure what to think.

"I flew here at Mach 1," he told her. "All the way over South Dakota, Iowa and Illinois, I told myself you belonged to Hargrove."

"I don't belong—"

"I told myself I'd reason with you, I'd make you understand you had an obligation to your fiancé, I'd explain again that nobody falls in love in a week, and what you thought you felt for me was an illusion."

He took her hands.

Katie took a few steps toward the door. "Uh, I'm… just going to…" She slipped outside and shut the door behind her.

"At least that's what I told myself," said Royce. "And then Rosa told me you were trying on your wedding dress. And I knew I had to stop you. I knew there was no way I could let you marry someone else."

"I'm not marrying—"

"I still find it impossible to believe a week is any kind of a foundation for a lifelong commitment. I looked up the mathematical odds on marital success. They're not good.

"But I do know I want you. And I know I'll shoot any guy who touches you. And I'm thinking maybe that's a sign that there's something to this."

Amber fought the smile that tightened her lips.

As declarations of love went, this left a whole lot to be desired. But this was Royce, and she knew his demons, and she knew just how difficult it was for him to even contemplate the possibility of happily-ever-after.

"I love you, Royce."

"You can't know—"

She put her fingertips over his lips. "I do know. And, guess what? I know you love me, too. And I know you're going to figure it out eventually. And if I have to wait a year, or ten or twenty, for you to decide we should stay together, that's fine with me."

His arm snaked around her waist, and he jerked her up tight against him. "I want to start staying together now."

"No problem." She smiled at him, trailing her palms over his chest, wrapping them loosely around his neck.

"We'll hang out together while you give this love thing some serious thought."

He settled his other arm around her. "And by hanging out, I hope you mean living together, working together and sleeping together."

"I do," she told him.

"Good." He gave a decisive nod. "Then I'm thinking we'd better be married while we're hanging out. I don't want anyone else to try to steal you. Your father's already a little ticked off at my brother. And there's the whole propriety thing."

"You think it's logical for us to be married while we figure out if we're in love?"

"Completely logical," he said. "Especially if we want a few kids. You're not getting any younger—"

"Hey!" She smacked him on the shoulder.

"And who knows how long it'll take for us to be sure."

"Maybe twenty years?" she asked.

"Maybe even fifty." His expression sobered. His gaze caressed her as he slowly dipped his head. Then his warm, soft lips came down ever so gently onto hers, sealing their bargain.

"What do you say, Amber?" he whispered against her mouth. "Will you spend the next fifty or so years married to me, just in case I love you?"

She nodded, coming up on her bare toes to kiss him again, longer this time, more soundly.

"Yes, I will," she whispered. "Just in case."

His arms engulfed her, and he lifted her completely off the floor. His mouth slanted and his kiss deepened, and she clung to him, heart bursting with joy.

When he finally set her down, slowly sliding her along his body, his grin widened. "Well, what do you know."

"What?"

"I think it might be happening already."

She couldn't help but smile in return. "Imagine that."

He nodded. "And it's really easy. You know, I think I'm going to be very good at this."

"There's not a doubt in my mind."

His blue eyes stared down into hers. "I love you, Amber."

"I know you do, Royce."

"Forever."

"Absolutely."

"Who knew."

"I did."

"You did at that." And he bent to kiss her one more time.

Eleven

Royce couldn't think of a single thing he liked better than the sight of Amber at Hargrove's wedding—wearing the bridesmaid's dress. Katie had been radiant on her walk down the aisle. She'd beamed at Hargrove during the first dance, then laughed with him when they cut the cake. Royce caught the garter again, and this time he knew it was fate.

"She looked spectacular," said Amber as they walked, hand in hand, beneath the lighted tress of the waterfront patio. The reception was in full swing inside the restaurant, notables from both the business and political worlds dancing it up at the black-tie event.

"Your life's not going to be anything like hers," Royce observed, thinking about the reporters hovering in the parking lot.

"No, it's not." Amber grinned, turning to the rail to

stare out across the sparkling water. She took a sip of the bubbly liquid in her champagne flute.

Royce moved up behind her, tracing a fingertip along her bare shoulder. "Any regrets?"

"Yes," she sighed, and he felt a moment's pause.

But she covered his hand with her own, holding his touch against her skin. "I regret saying no to you in the hotel room earlier."

A surge of masculine pride swelled within him, and he leaned down to kiss her shoulder. "I told you so."

"You did."

"Weddings have a way of making women feel all romantic and mushy."

"It's true." She nodded, taking another drink.

"And all those romantic and mushy feelings have a way of turning to—"

"Lust?"

"Which could have been pre-empted," he whispered in her ear. "If you'd only let—"

"There you are, pumpkin," came David Hutton's hearty voice.

Royce immediately stepped back from Amber.

"Seems like I'm always finding you off in a corner with this Ryder fellow at wedding receptions."

"He does have a way of finding me," Amber joked, turning to face her father.

Royce was still a bit jumpy around the man. The two-carat solitaire on Amber's finger had mitigated some of the antagonism, but Royce wasn't sure David had forgiven him for breaking things off with Amber. He also wasn't sure that a jet pilot was an acceptable substitute for a senator as a son-in-law.

"You look amazing," David told his daughter, kissing her gently on the forehead.

"And you look handsome as always," Amber returned.

Royce held out his hand to shake, refusing to let David see anything but confidence. "Good to see you again, sir."

"I trust you'll be making your own wedding plans soon?" David asked him.

"Daddy," Amber admonished.

"Don't want to give the man time to change his mind again."

Royce held the handshake a little longer. "I'm not going to change my mind."

David harrumphed.

"I love your daughter, Mr. Hutton." Royce wrapped an arm around Amber's shoulder and drew her close. "I'm going to marry her and make her happy for the rest of her life."

"I would hope so. What with all the turmoil you caused."

"Daddy, I stopped loving Hargrove before Royce got anywhere near me."

Royce nearly choked on her choice of words. "The wedding will be soon," he assured David.

Amber glanced up at him in surprise. "Royce, we haven't—"

"Very soon." He gave Amber a meaningful squeeze.

David cracked a smile. "You keep my baby girl happy, son. And we'll get along just fine."

"I will," Royce assured the man.

"Call me David."

"Okay."

David winked at Amber and started away. "Don't stay out too late."

"I'm not coming home tonight," she warned him.

David turned his attention to Royce again. "Soon." He waggled a warning finger before he turned away.

"You want to head for Vegas tonight?" Royce asked Amber.

"Vegas is a terrible idea," said Stephanie.

Royce had left the jet under the command of his copilot and dropped into one of the seats in the main passenger cabin.

"Thank you," Amber said to Stephanie from the seat next to him.

They'd picked Stephanie up from a junior jumping show in Denver, and Jared and Melissa were hitching a ride from Chicago to the ranch for the last few days of their honeymoon.

"Well, she'd better come up with something," Royce told his sister. "I don't want her father gunning for me for the next year."

"He likes you," said Amber.

"No, he likes you. He tolerates me because you love me."

"I do love you," she confirmed, giving him a quick kiss on the cheek.

"And I love you," he automatically returned.

"Oh, gag me," Stephanie groaned.

"I thought you were a romantic," Melissa put in, moving up from the back of the cabin where she'd been sitting with Jared.

"I am a romantic. But, yuck, she's kissing my brother."

"Well, I totally get it," said Melissa.

"That's because you kiss my other brother."

Melissa got a gleam in her eyes. "You know what else I do to your other brother?"

Stephanie clapped her hands over her ears. "Pink fuzzy bunnies. Pink fuzzy bunnies."

"What the hell?" asked Royce.

"She's obliterating the image from her brain," Amber informed him.

Royce shook his head at the nonsense. "You," he said to Amber. "Come up with a wedding plan, or we *are* heading for Vegas." Then he exited his seat and moved to the back with his brother.

"Hey." Jared nodded to him, looking up from a table full of reports.

Royce sat down, lowering his voice. "You met with Alec Creighton?"

"I did."

"What did you think?"

Jared glanced to the front of the plane where the three women were chatting. "Seems like a good guy. Smart. On the ball."

"Did you talk to the VPs?"

Jared nodded. "They were shocked about Barry Brewster. It's got them looking over their shoulders. But I think in a good way."

"What about Konrad?"

Jared grinned. "Oh, he really hates you."

"Yeah. I kinda got that."

"He's demanded to deal directly with me from now on. Threatened to quit if you're involved in the construction division."

Royce clamped his jaw, while a burning anger roiled up in his stomach.

"Told him no," Jared said mildly. "Told him you were

taking over the construction division, and if he didn't like it, he should have his letter of resignation on your desk Monday morning."

Royce gaped at his brother. Konrad might be a jerk, but he was an incredibly valuable employee.

"Family is family," said Jared. "It's your company, too, and you did one hell of a job while I was away. Well, except for ticking off David Hutton."

"I'm working on that," said Royce, glancing to Amber, struck as always by how much he adored her.

"That's what counts, bro. Everybody's working hard at head office, looking to streamline, reallocating cash flow. We've survived trouble before."

Royce's attention shifted to his sister, and he lowered his voice. "After that, there's Stephanie."

"Yeah," Jared agreed. "We need to talk about that one."

"Does Melissa know?" asked Royce.

"That Frank Stanton is Stephanie's father?" Jared shook his head. "I'm keeping the club as small as possible for now."

Royce nodded. He was glad Amber already knew; he wouldn't want to have to make the choice to keep a secret from her.

"It was hard enough on me," said Jared. "Finding out what I did the way I did."

Royce nodded his agreement with that, too.

"Stephanie can *never* find out," Jared vowed.

"She won't." Royce had had most of his life to come to terms with his parents' secret, and it had still colored him in ways he hadn't even realized. It had almost cost him the love of his life.

He caught Amber's gaze.

She sobered at the sight of his expression, eyes narrowing. Then she unobtrusively stood from her seat to move toward him.

He smiled and snagged her wrist, pulling her into his lap to wrap his arms around her.

"What's wrong?" she asked.

"Nothing."

She raised her brows to Jared.

Jared shook his head. "It's all good." His smile was back, and it was easy. "Except *you* can't seem to decide on a wedding."

Royce knew Amber wasn't buying their jovial mood, but she played along. "This is not a decision to take lightly. I'm only getting married once."

"In Vegas," said Royce.

Amber socked him in the arm.

"Tahiti, maybe." Melissa joined in. "On a beach, just family?"

"I vote for Tuscany," Stephanie called out. "Or Paris in the spring."

"She'll be pregnant by spring," said Royce, and Amber gave him a wide-eyed look of surprise.

"And we'd better damned well be married by then," he growled low.

"Babies?" she mused.

"I want babies," he confirmed.

"Good," she whispered and hugged him tightly, pressing her face into the crook of his neck, sighing in contentment, while the rest of his family joked about wedding plans.

* * * * *

We hope you enjoyed reading
HEARTBREAKER
by *New York Times* bestselling author
DIANA PALMER
and **IN BED WITH
THE WRANGLER**
by *USA TODAY* bestselling author
BARBARA DUNLOP.

Both were originally
Harlequin® Desire stories!

Harlequin Desire stories feature sexy, romantic
heroes who have it all: wealth, status, incredible
good looks…everything but the right woman.
Add some secrets, maybe a scandal,
and start turning pages!

◆ HARLEQUIN®

Desire

Powerful heroes…scandalous secrets…burning desires.

Look for six *new* romances every month
from **Harlequin Desire!**

Available wherever books are sold.

www.Harlequin.com

NYTHD0315

SPECIAL EXCERPT FROM

HARLEQUIN

Desire

*Disowned and pregnant after one passionate night in
Vegas, Cassidy Corelli shows up on the doorstep of the
only man who can help her...*

Read on for a sneak peek at
TWINS ON THE WAY,
the latest in USA TODAY *bestselling author*
Janice Maynard's
THE KAVANAGHS OF SILVER GLEN *series.*

Without warning, Gavin stood up. Suddenly the office
shrank in size. His personality and masculine presence
sucked up all the available oxygen. Pacing so near
Cassidy's chair that he almost brushed her knees, Gavin
shot her a look laden with frustration. "We need some
ground rules if you're going to stay with me while we sort
out this pregnancy, Cassidy. First of all, we're going to
forget that we've ever seen each other naked."

She gulped, fixating on the dusting of hair where the
shallow V-neck of his sweater revealed a peek of his
chest. "I'm pretty sure that's going to be the elephant in
the room. Our night in Vegas was amazing. Maybe not for
you, but for me. Telling me to forget it is next to impossible."

"Good Lord, woman. Don't you have any social
armor, at all?"

"I am not a liar. If you want me to pretend we haven't
been intimate, I'll try, but I make no promises."

He leaned over her, resting his hands on the arms of the chair. His beautifully sculpted lips were in kissing distance. Smoke-colored irises filled with turbulent emotions locked on hers like lasers. "I may be attracted to you, Cass, but I don't completely trust you. It's too soon. So, despite evidence to the contrary, I do have some self-control."

Maybe *he* did, but hers was melting like snow in the hot sun. His coffee-scented breath brushed her cheek. This close, she could see tiny crinkles at the corners of his eyes. She might have called them laugh lines if she could imagine her onetime lover being lighthearted enough and smiling long enough to create them.

"You're crowding my personal space," she said primly.

For several seconds, she was sure he was going to steal a kiss. Her breathing went shallow, her nipples tightened and a tumultuous feeling rose in her chest. Something volatile. For the first time, she understood that whatever madness had taken hold of them in Las Vegas was neither a fluke nor a solitary event.

Don't miss
TWINS ON THE WAY
by USA TODAY *bestselling author Janice Maynard.*

Available April 2015,
wherever Harlequin® Desire books and ebooks are sold.

www.Harlequin.com

HARLEQUIN®

Desire

Powerful heroes…scandalous secrets…burning desires.

Save $1.00

on the purchase of

TWINS ON THE WAY
by Janice Maynard, available
April 7, 2015, or on any other
Harlequin® Desire book.

Available wherever books are sold, including most
bookstores, supermarkets, drugstores and discount stores.

Save $1.00

on the purchase of any Harlequin Desire book.

Coupon valid until June 3, 2015. Redeemable at participating outlets in the
U.S. and Canada only. Not redeemable at Barnes and Nobles stores.
Limit one coupon per customer.

5 2 6 1 2 2 9 1

Canadian Retailers: Harlequin Enterprises Limited will pay the face value of this coupon plus 10.25¢ if submitted by customer for this product only. Any other use constitutes fraud. Coupon is nonassignable. Void if taxed, prohibited or restricted by law. Consumer must pay any government taxes. Void if copied. Millennium1 Promotional Services ("M1P") customers submit coupons and proof of sales to Harlequin Enterprises Limited, P.O. Box 3000, Saint John, NB E2L 4L3, Canada. Non-M1P retailer—for reimbursement submit coupons and proof of sales directly to Harlequin Enterprises Limited, Retail Marketing Department, 225 Duncan Mill Rd., Don Mills, Ontario M3B 3K9, Canada.

U.S. Retailers: Harlequin Enterprises Limited will pay the face value of this coupon plus 8¢ if submitted by customer for this product only. Any other use constitutes fraud. Coupon is nonassignable. Void if taxed, prohibited or restricted by law. Consumer must pay any government taxes. Void if copied. For reimbursement submit coupons and proof of sales directly to Harlequin Enterprises Limited, P.O. Box 880478, El Paso, TX 88588-0478, U.S.A. Cash value 1/100 cents.

5 65373 00076 **2** (8100)0 12014

® and TM are trademarks owned and used by the trademark owner and/or its licensee.

© 2015 Harlequin Enterprises Limited

NYTCOUP0315

Love the Harlequin book you just read?

Your opinion matters.

Review this book on your favorite book site, review site, blog or your own social media properties and share your opinion with other readers!